POST MORTAL SYNDROME

Borgo Press Books by DAMIEN BRODERICK

Chained to the Alien: The Best of ASFR: Australian SF Review (Second Series) [Editor]

Climbing Mount Implausible: The Evolution of a Science Fiction Writer

Embarrass My Dog: The Way We Were, the Things We Thought

Ferocious Minds: Polymathy and the New Enlightenment

Human's Burden: A Science Fiction Novel (with Rory Barnes)

I'm Dying Here: A Crime Novel (with Rory Barnes)

Post Mortal Syndrome: A Science Fiction Novel (with Barbara Lamar)

Skiffy and Mimesis: More Best of ASFR: Australian SF Review (Second Series) [Editor]

Unleashing the Strange: Twenty-First Century Science Fiction Literature

Warriors of the Tao: The Best of Science Fiction: A Review of Speculative Literature [Editor with Van Ikin]

x, y, z, t: Dimensions of Science Fiction

POST MORTAL SYNDROME

A SCIENCE FICTION NOVEL

DAMIEN BRODERICK &

BARBARA LAMAR

THE BORGO PRESS

MMXI

POST MORTAL SYNDROME

FIRST EDITION

Published by Wildside Press LLC

www.wildsidebooks.com

DEDICATION

For *Aubrey de Grey*,

Who's doing something about it.

POST MORTAL SYNDROME

Some have argued that even if we had the technological capability to change human personality in fundamental ways, we would never *want* to do so because human nature in some sense guarantees its own continuity. This argument, I believe, greatly underestimates human ambition and fails to appreciate the radical ways in which people in the past have sought to overcome their own natures.... We may be about to enter into a posthuman future, in which technology will give us the capacity gradually to alter that essence over time.

Francis Fukuyama,
Our Posthuman Future

Because an artificial chromosome provides a reproducible platform for adding genetic material to cells, it promises to transform gene therapy from the hit-and-miss methods of today.... It would be an inert scaffolding dotted with independent insertion sites where modules of genes and their control sequences could be placed using the various enzymes that splice and clip DNA.... By not altering a single one of the 3 billion bases on our existing chromosomes, geneticists would minimize the chance of inadvertently stepping on the many as yet unappreciated interactions within our genome.

Gregory Stock,
Redesigning Humans

PROLOGUE

Prickly with sweat, Payback carefully lowered the foot-long white cylinder and its attached transponder into the trash can. He'd gotten the instructions for building the bomb from a website called *A Practical Handbook for the New Social Engineer*. It contained only easily obtained materials, packed into a foot-long length of two-inch diameter PVC sewer pipe. He planned to set off the bomb himself, from a safe distance, with a small model airplane radio transmitter. No one would ever think to look in there. The whole laboratory would be long gone, blown to hell in the night, before anyone came to empty the trash. He breathed deeply, straightened his old stolen AT&T cap, and stepped from the closet into the hallway. Nobody noticed him leave the building, work bag in his gloved hand. Late afternoon Virginia winter air was crisp in his nostrils.

§

"Can't I go in with you, Mom?" Ashley liked the Research Center with its huge windows and stone walls. In the twilight, with the soft lights on its walls, it looked like an enchanted castle.

"Hon, I'm just ducking in to check my experiment, I won't be a moment."

"Do they *hate* children?"

"Don't give me a hard time, darling. And don't give me that awful face. Oh, come on, you can sit in the lobby while I nip upstairs." Her mom opened the car door, took Ashley's hand to help her out. The air was chilly. "Leave that, you don't need your bag."

"It's got my coloring book and my iPod and—"

"Okay, okay. Here, arms through the straps." Her mother walked them both briskly past the stone benches, carded them through the door, called a cheerful greeting to the security guard.

"Ash can sit here for a minute, okay, DeShaw? Here, honey, just stay put and listen to *Beauty and the Beast* on your iPod. I'll be back in two shakes of a lamb's tail."

Ashley sat kicking her legs. She'd heard the stupid story a hundred times. The DeShaw guy finished writing something on his computer, gave her a grin and a wink, said, "You just stay put there, little lady, like your Mom said," and headed off down a side corridor, swinging his flashlight. Ashley wriggled out of her backpack and put the iPod away. It won't hurt anything to just peek inside some of these rooms, she told herself. Mom always says she'll only be a few minutes, and it always takes *forever.* I'll have time to take a look around before she gets back.

With some difficulty, the little girl pulled open the heavy glass door leading from the lobby to the main part of the building, and found herself in a long hallway with a shiny green floor. The first four doors she tried were locked. The next one opened, but it was only a closet. Ashley started to close the door when she saw the white tube in the trash container, with the little machine taped to the top. Looked like a smart missile. Darrell could use it for playing war games with his friends. It wasn't stealing, the thing was in the trash. Nobody wanted it. Careful not to get her new pink tee shirt dirty, Ashley reached into the trash can and pulled out the white tube. She stowed it in her bag, pulled the pack on again, and went back to the lobby. The guard still hadn't returned. She sat innocently, excitedly plotting what she could win in exchange for it from her brother, until her mother returned.

§

Harriet Wilson finished drying the supper dishes, glanced at the clock. Eight forty, and the TV was still on in her daughter's room, a *Xena: Warrior Princess* re-run from the sound of it. She stepped into the living room of the small apartment she shared with her son and daughter, a mile from the Roanoke Center.

"Ashley," she called into the bedroom, "Time to brush your teeth and get ready for bed."

"Okay, Mom."

"Don't just say okay, young lady. I want to see you *in the bathroom*. Now." No response. Harriet started toward the closed bedroom door to switch the TV off and haul her daughter to the bathroom. The phone rang, and she returned to the kitchen to answer it. Probably Darrell calling from the Mall, saying he'd be home late and he'd already eaten at KFC. She sighed. Kids. Thought you were made of money.

§

Payback pressed the transmitter button.

Across the dark street, nothing happened. There was a distant rumble of thunder. He pushed it again, harder.

He had expected to hear a roar, see an eruption of molten light from the lab windows. Disappointingly, nothing.

What the fuck?

§

Something terrible happened.

Something incomprehensible.

Harriet reeled, deafened.

Had an *airplane* crashed into the roof?

She ran to her daughter's room. Inexplicably, the door hung off its hinges. Flames lapped at torn picture books on the floor. The bed was on its side. She started screaming. Ashley's face, the skull split down the front with blood and fragments of bone and brain spilling out, nose still whole but shoved far to one side, pigtails intact with their pink ribbons. This sickening thing from a horror movie wore Ashley's pink shirt, stained with blood but still recognizable.

§

Payback opened the morning paper. He was dreadfully tired. But if he slept, Wayne would be back.

On the second page of the first section the mysterious death of a six-year-old girl was reported. Police had determined that a bomb of some kind had exploded in the child's bedroom, probably home-made. The mother, a biologist at Roanoke Pharmaceuticals, was being questioned by the authorities.

Shit.

Payback felt the sick, dull draining of depression. He shook his head. Hey—this was a war. Okay, he'd fucked up; he hadn't intended to hurt a little kid. But hell, it wasn't his fault. Stupid child must have taken the bomb out of the trash can. Sometimes you had collateral damage in a war. Couldn't be helped. And anyways, the sons of bitch scientists were guilty of worse than killing one innocent bystander. Dr. Rutherford was right. The so-called scientists were trying to kill the whole planet. It was his sworn duty to stop the bastards. Even if he had to kill them one at a time, and their kids with them.

DEATH

1: THURSDAY, MAY 1

Two mice, one white, one brown, lay curled together like Yin and Yang. The rattle of pellets pouring into the metal feeder woke them, and they stretched and yawned. For the first two months of the experiment, Paul had kept them in separate cages. Yesterday, the protocol had paired them up, testing for effects on their social interaction. To his surprise, he found none of the usual jockeying for dominant position or fighting over food. Next time, he told himself, I should try putting larger groups together. More crowding, more stress. Put pressure on the treatment.

"Hey, guys. Hey." The brown mouse was sitting up on its hind legs, holding a food pellet in both front paws. Paul reached into the cage and gently ran a finger along its back. It stared up at him with beady black eyes and took a bite of the pellet.

"If I didn't know better, little fellow, I'd think you were curious about me." Latching the door, Paul moved to the next cage, where the two occupants were grooming each other. He blinked, still hardly believing it. Not mousy behavior, not at all. As he dumped in the food pellets, both animals ran eagerly to the feeder. Instead of fighting or jostling for the food, the first mouse to reach the feeder took a pellet, then moved back to give the other one access.

He'd seen the same pattern in all ten cages.

"Cool," he told the mice. "Peace and love for all mousekind."

He grinned, opened his laptop to record his observations. This completely unexpected result might finally disprove the old myth about unfeeling intellects. How many times had he been assured that a person could have brains or a heart, but not both? Bizarre prejudice, especially here in Austin, Texas. The locals boasted Austin was both the live music capital of the world *and* the home of advanced medical research.

He smiled, watching the small animals. These modified mice were smart as a whip, yet they surely loved each other.

Paul completed his journal entry, downloaded his email, then checked Trash to make sure his spam filter hadn't thrown away something important. The filter had automatically deleted a couple of "PAUL.GIBSON DONT IGNORE THIS NOTICE" spam messages, offers of cheap V1agr.a and Human Growth Hormone, and a worm-laden attachment. The bastards were always coming up with new ways to burst in. He paused at a news flash from the Organization of Biotechnology Development, retrieved it from Trash.

Subject: *Nature Forever lobbies for anti-tech law*

Really should read that, he told himself. But the next message was from his colleague in San Antonio, Drew Chang.

Subject: FWD: Viral Vectors in Pharmakinetics

Eagerly, Paul opened it, and instantly forgot about everything but tracking Drew's url links and reading his comments.

In their cages, the mice shared their dinner and chittered.

2: FRIDAY, MAY 2

On good days, Jill loved working for Allen-Hoffman. The nineteenth-century mansion, home of the Austin offices of the national law firm, had been painstakingly restored to its original beauty and then some. She especially loved her small second floor suite with its delicately carved moldings and French doors opening onto a balcony that stretched the length of the building, looking down into the rose garden.

This was not one of the good days.

Jill glanced at her computer clock again. Half past five. Her secretary Clothile had already left for the day. Feeling sick with guilt, Jill acknowledged that she'd broken her promise to Alex. But what choice did she have? Hired in a recession economy, Jill was expected to be so grateful for the job that she'd put her professional life ahead of all else, no questions or demurs. A little boy's eighth birthday dinner didn't count. Not compared with multinational business transactions affecting hundreds of people. Not when you were the lowest of the low, newest associate of the two partner office.

For most of the day she'd stared at the computer monitor, fingers tapping in a haze of concentrated competence. At five thirty she was in a final rush, organizing and summarizing case law on the issue of conversion of limited partnerships to LLCs. Fighting anxiety, she tried to focus on her work. Maybe I can plead with Will Flory just to let me take my kid for a quick dinner, she thought, then come back and finish the work later. The intercom buzzed.

"Jill?" Fran. Will's secretary. "Mr. Flory wants to know when you'll have the research on the Leon case. He needs it asap."

Damn it.

§

Alex looked pitiful, sitting on a swing in a deserted play yard, last kid to be picked up from after-school care. Dennis, the teacher on duty, gazed pointedly at his watch. "You owe us twenty-two dollars," he said sharply. A dollar "fine" for each minute past six-thirty. Well, couldn't blame him, he had his own dinner and evening plans to think about.

When Jill and Alex finally got home at seven-thirty they were greeted by a vile odor and a frantic cat.

"We forgot to put Miz Kitty out," Alex said, breaking a silence that had lasted since she got him from after school care. "Eeew, she has diarrhea."

"Never mind." Jill willed herself to smile. "I'll clean it up in no time, and then we eat and watch *X-Men*."

"I don't *wanna* eat. Just wanna watch the *video*."

"You have to eat, Alex." Lately he seemed like two different people. He could change almost instantaneously from her own sweet lovable son to an angry and sullen stranger. My fault, she told herself with renewed guilt. She'd been neglecting him terribly since she took the Allen-Hoffman position.

"Not hungry," Alex whined. "My head hurts."

"It's probably from not eating. I'm *sorry* I was so late, sweetie. Nothing I could do about it, honest."

He scowled. She couldn't blame him, but this mulishness was worse than a tantrum.

"Alex, c'mon, we have this delicious pizza and cake and a video to watch. And I've got a present for you too. Let's try to cheer up."

"Don't want your stupid present."

Exasperated, Jill told him, "I don't want you talking that way to me. If you don't straighten up, there'll be no video tonight."

"I don't care!" He stomped into his room, slammed the door.

Sighing, annoyed with herself and with her job's demands, Jill turned to the task of cleaning up the cat's mess. Through the door, she heard Alex sobbing in his room. She wanted desperately to go in and comfort him, but she knew he would push her away.

3: TUESDAY, MAY 6

Wayne woke early, screaming again. The roar of his terror jolted Fern awake. "Oh dear God! Somebody help me! Please! Dr. Ruther—"

Her heart thundered, hearing his raw-throated distress. "Wayne? Honey, it's okay. Listen to me, honey. You're safe at home in bed." Fern wanted to put her arms around him, but she'd learned not to touch him when he was like this, he got so crazy, lashing out at her.

He moaned, turned to her. She felt his warmth, smelled the familiar odor of his night-time breath. "Just another one of your dreams, honey."

Without a word, he rolled away from her, stumbled to the bathroom, slammed the door. Lately the nightmares had taken him nearly every night. Wayne would never admit it, but Fern knew he was afraid to go to sleep. He'd stay up till all hours watching TV, reading magazines. Wouldn't talk about what was happening to him. "It's nothing," he'd say. "Everybody has bad dreams."

Not like these. Not this bad.

The toilet flushed. Wayne came back in, giving Fern the adorable little boy look that could always soften her up, even in the middle of their worst arguments. Gotta be firm now, she reminded herself. "Sweetheart, we need to talk." When he opened his mouth to protest she shushed him. "I mean it, Wayne. Seen yourself in the mirror lately? You look like one of the walking dead. You haven't been sleeping more'n two or three hours a night for months." Me neither, she thought.

He stopped smiling. "I'd a thought you'd give me a little sympathy, 'stead of this whiny complaining shit."

"Wayne, your nightmares wake me up too. I can hardly keep my eyes open at work." Better be careful. Don't want this to turn into a fight before I even tell him—

"You think *you're* tired?" he said, "What do you think *I* feel like?"

"You're right, honey. It's you I'm worried about. We need to do something."

"Aw come on, Baby."

"No, Wayne." She put her hand firmly over his. "I want you to let me finish what I have to say. I *do* love you, Wayne. That's why I want you to talk to Dr. Pritchett." She held her breath, waiting for the explosion. "Dr. Nathan Pritchett. He's a psychologist."

"Fuck that!" Wayne was furious. "Fuckin' shrink started all

the trouble. Injections, knock-out drugs."

It took her aback. "What do you mean?"

"I don't—" Frowning, he shook his head. "Nothing."

Don't give him a chance to start yelling. "Listen, Wayne, Linda met Dr. Pritchett at a—"

"That dyke?" Wayne had never met Linda, but that didn't keep him from hating her. From the moment Fern quit her job as secretary for Clyde's Auto Repairs and started working at the Radisson, Wayne had accused her of trying to climb above her breeding. He seemed to prefer her as a mousy little country girl.

"We're talking about you, honey, not Linda. About us. If you don't get help, Wayne, I'm going to—" She swallowed. "I'm going to have to move out." There. She'd said it. Trembling a little, Fern waited for the yelling to start. Or maybe he'd just stalk out and slam the door. "I've made you an appointment," she added tentatively.

Wayne sat down heavily on the edge of the sofa, knees apart, arms hanging limply down. "Cost a damn fortune."

"No, listen." Eagerly, she said in a rush, "His clinic just opened up recently. They're offering a discount to attract customers. I already put it on my Mastercard, Wayne." She paused, took a deep breath. "Honey, I really want you to go."

4: FRIDAY, MAY 9

Senator Burcham Huber sat in the garden, an untouched drink on the glass topped table at his side. Bruce Blick felt sure Huber had no idea how rarely anyone from outside was allowed into the inner sanctum. Sedately, he approached the senator.

"Burcham."

Huber remained seated, lips stretched into a half smile. "We've missed you in D.C. and Manhattan. But this is certainly a most beautiful retreat."

"And I do appreciate your flying down here to see me. We seldom get such illustrious guests in San Miguel Regla."

Burcham Huber shifted uncomfortably and covered his mouth with one hand.

"Are you feeling all right?" Bruce studied Burcham's face intently.

"Actually, no. I think I ate too much rich food last night at the reception. And the plane trip down—"

"Martita." Bruce raised his voice slightly. "By the way, Burcham, the press coverage of your speech was gratifying."

A young woman of nineteen or twenty appeared, pushing aside a curtain of greenery.

"My friend has an upset stomach. Could you get him a glass of your mother's medicine?"

Martita bowed her head and walked briskly away.

"A herbal decoction. Works wonders. We'd patent it if we could. It'll fix you up in no time." Bruce leaned forward so that his knees and Burcham's were almost touching. "Now. About this genetic engineering bill that's with your committee—"

"Don't worry, Blick. I'll make sure we kill it."

Bruce sighed. "Read Tom's memos a bit more carefully from now on. I *support* that bill. It will—" Martita appeared, bearing a glass of thick white liquid. "Thank you, my dear."

The girl inclined her head, left silently.

Burcham took a small sip, showed his eye teeth.

"Drink it down. It's medicine," said Bruce. "That bill is necessary to protect not just consumers of drugs but possibly the human species itself."

"I was not aware—" Burcham's upper lip was coated with white foam.

"As chairman of the Science and Technology Committee, I believe it's your business to *be* aware."

"Be reasonable, Bruce. As a majority pharmaceutical share-holder, why the hell would you support a bill limiting what you'll be permitted to produce?"

"My concerns go far beyond my own selfish interests." Bruce pulled a clean linen handkerchief from his belt and passed it to Burcham. "Here. Wipe your face."

"What's your game, Blick? I don't get it."

"Certain scientists are tampering with technologies that threaten to end the human species as we know it. We have not encouraged this line of research at Blick Pharmaceuticals, and when we've tried to purchase the key patents we've been unsuccessful."

"Ah."

"I need you to do whatever it takes to get that bill recommended by the committee and passed by the Senate. Tom and his staff are there to help you in any way they can."

"Do you have any notion how embarrassing this is going to be for me? I've already publicly expressed my opposition to the bill. I can't see how it could be all that important to you."

"Let me put it this way, Senator Huber, maybe you'll understand more completely." Bruce's voice and eyes were now undisguisedly cold and threatening. "You and Patricia owe me. Getting this bill passed is very important to me. This bill is therefore very important to you."

Burcham Huber tried to give the handkerchief back to Bruce, who waved it away. "I see. Okay, Blick, it's clearly a crucial bill. Very necessary for the good of the economy and the people of America and the human species."

5: FRIDAY, MAY 9

A week ago, Jill had postponed Alex's promised birthday dinner until tonight, and her son had seethed in resentment ever since. At least she would keep faith with the boy tonight.

The intercom buzzed, making her heart sink.

"Mr. Flory wants the research on the Blick case. And the petition. Asap."

With an effort, Jill put her son out of her thoughts. This case was critical. Flory would go ballistic if she gave it less than her best. Or, more to the point, if that damned fool strutting rooster Preston Bowie screwed it up for her. Jill pulled together all her files on the latest Blick initiative.

Inspired by growing public sentiment against genetically modified foods, BlickPharm had agreed to fund a special project for Nature Forever, the international environmentalist organization. Nature Forever did not want to jeopardize their not-for-profit status with IRS, so they could not be directly involved in political activities. Starting with education and publicity, the project would culminate in an anti-genetic-engineering petition to be presented to Congress. That *did* verge on activism. So their star lawyer, Preston Bowie, had flown down from Washington D.C. to mastermind the first draft of the petition.

Before she met him, Jill had been in awe of this world-famous environmental advocate, darling of TV and radio shows. The reality was bleak. Preston was an alcoholic womanizer who did little of the real work himself.

I'm damned if I'll let them mess up my plans for Alex again, she told herself fiercely.

Really, though, drawbacks and all, she was lucky to be doing meaningful work. The salary wasn't all that terrific, considering the hours she put in, and she had less and less time to spend with her son. Still. Blick Enterprises Incorporated was, after all, the major Texas client of Allen, Hoffman and Flory—the reason the firm had an Austin office at all. BEI did much of its business through BlickPharm, a wholly owned subsidiary. It felt good to be working at last for an ethically upright firm, one that was doing well by doing good. When Bruce Blick had inherited his father's company, sales had been less than two million per year. Bruce had seen the Green movement coming and launched a line of all-natural healthcare products, increasing sales to more than six hundred million over a five year period. Although the company also produced conventional drugs, including a popular antidepressant, they stood vigorously against animal testing, bovine growth hormone, and human genetic engineering.

Garden scents drifted in through the open French doors, along with a whiff of tobacco. Clothile was talking to one of the paralegals on the balcony, taking a cigarette break. Their muted voices made a pleasant background music. One of the enjoyable features of working for Allen-Hoffman was this sense of belonging to an extended family, something she'd never known as an only child. Like Alex. Although he had his half-sisters.

Using the petition Preston had given her as a model, Jill keyed onto the screen:

PETITION SEEKING IMMEDIATE ACTION BY CONGRESS TO PROHIBIT EXPERIMENTAL MODIFICATION OF HUMAN DNA—

"...found out he was flat broke. Can you believe it?" Clothile shrieked with laughter.

Pursuant to the Right to Petition Government Clause contained in the First Amendment of the United States Constitution—

"...didn't get the loan and may have to move out of her house...."

...the legal, social, and ethical implications of human genetic modification must be considered....

A phone rang. After a long moment Clothile said, "Just a moment, I'll get her." She walked in carrying the cordless phone, paused. Jill tensed. "It's Cindy from Alex's school," Clothile said soberly. "Something's happened to Alex."

Oh God. Ohgodohgodohgod. She snatched at the phone. Please, not another broken bone. Last year her son had jumped exuberantly from a high playground swing. His fractured arm had taken forever to heal and the itching under the cast had almost driven Alex crazy.

Cindy seemed on the verge of hysteria. "Ms. Shannon, Alex had some kind of seizure."

"What?" Jill couldn't take it in. A *what*? "Is he okay? Can I talk to him?"

"He's unconscious, Ms. Shannon. He lost control of his bowels and bladder. Dennis is trying to clean him up. Can you come right away?"

No. No. Oh dear God, no. "Yes. Okay, thank you." Heart pounding, Jill barely saw the anxious faces of Clothile and the paralegal in the outer office. Dazed with terror, she grabbed her car keys and fled down the stairs.

6: FRIDAY, MAY 9

The automatic chime sounded to announce the arrival of Nathan Pritchett's client. He took a last look around his low-rent Houston office, moved the rug slightly so it completely covered the missing vinyl floor tiles, straightened one of his framed diplomas. The frame rattled faintly against the cigar smoke-stained wallpaper; his fingers were tremoring. Breathe, breathe.

The Serenity Holistic Health Clinic was in the Blue Bayou Shopping Center, which had not been noteworthy even when it was new and clean. Now, with several store fronts empty and papered over or boarded up, the suburban strip mall was a hair's breadth away from decrepit. Its star tenant was the B K Laundromat. Serenity Clinic was two doors down, between Kat's Kraft Korner and a vacant shop.

Okay, Nathan told himself. It's not great, but at least I can pay for it. Affordable rent had been at the top of the priority list when Nathan set about planning his new practice, his comeback from disgrace. He'd resigned himself to financing it with personal credit cards at obscene interest rates, plus a $1,000 loan from his brother. For the first couple of months, though, it'd be touch and go. Maybe too damned risky. What the hell. Here he was. Nathan checked his reflection in the mirror, smoothed his hair, touched his left wrist with his right hand to trigger his calming anchor, and glided into his eight-by-eight waiting room.

A brown haired man of medium height was examining an array of aroma therapy oils and self-help books in the display case by the front door.

"Mr. Elliot? How do you do?"

The man turned quickly, dropped the bottle of healing oil he'd been holding. It bounced on the uncovered floor but failed to break. Jesus, Nathan asked himself, what am I doing stuck in this asshole of a place? Doing penance, he answered. Paying for my fucking sins, literally.

Elliot's face was square, masculine, almost handsome. He did not smile as he bent down to retrieve the bottle. Nathan took it from him, slipped it back into the rack.

"Is it all right if I call you Wayne? I'm Dr. Pritchett."

Wayne nodded, audibly sniffing the air. Nathan held out his hand. He liked to shake hands with new clients. Friendly physical contact tended to create the first link in a bond of trust between psychologist and client. Especially the women. Wayne was hesitating. Nathan saw that the last two fingers on his right hand had been badly injured. The pinky was almost entirely gone. Nathan withdrew his hand. "Won't you come in?" He motioned Wayne toward the consultation room, locked the entrance door. Wayne eyed the locked outside door apprehensively.

"I like to keep the front door secured unless I'm expecting someone," said Nathan, ushering Wayne in. He squared up a copy of *Awakening the Genius Inside You: Eleven Steps to a More Powerful Mind* sitting ready on his desk. "Kind of a rough neighborhood. Please. Sit down."

Wayne guardedly took in the brown leather recliner and the straight-backed wooden chair. Nathan liked to give his clients a choice. The kind of chair a person chose said something about his personality. Wayne sat down uneasily on the wooden chair, rubbed his feet back and forth on the rug. Nathan decided on manly candor.

"Let's get right to the point, shall we, Wayne? You've come here to humor your wife, right? I know you'd much rather be doing just about anything but sitting here talking to me."

The man jerked his head up; mouth and eyes relaxed a bit. "Well, doc, I don't guess there's all that much you can do to help me. But Fern paid good money for me to come here, so...." He seemed to be casting about. Nathan watched, nerves trilling. The man looked like a bomb waiting to go off. He picked the book up from his desk, passed it across.

"I think this might interest you."

Wayne took *Awakening the Genius Inside You* with his good hand, flipped the pages too quickly to be reading anything. Clearly on the brink of bolting. Shitload of anxiety there. Fitted with what the wife had said about the nightmares. "Take it home with you if you like, run through some of the early exercises. I think you'll find them helpful. Give it a try, anyway." Nathan rose. "We're done for now."

"Uh...."

"It'll give us something to talk about next week. Don't worry. Since we're cutting this session short, I'll give you an extra half hour next time. Or whenever. You can decide."

"That's it?" Wayne looked vastly relieved.

"Unless there's something you'd like to talk about." With an effort, Nathan kept his voice casually unconcerned.

"Can't think of anything." Wayne edged toward the door.

"See you next week, then."

Wayne walked away, clutching the book protectively against his chest. Gritting his teeth, Nathan wondered if he'd be back.

7: FRIDAY, MAY 9

They had placed Alex's limp body on an air mattress in the front room of the school and sent all the other kids outside. His skin was grayish, the rise and fall of his chest so slight that at first Jill thought in terror that he must be dead.

Some detached part of her seemed to be observing from the outside. She found herself thinking: I'm handling this very well.

Alex's young teacher Dennis hovered, badly worried, over

the small, still form. "At least he's breathing."

"Why isn't the ambulance here yet?"

"Uh, I don't think anyone—" Dennis shook his head, took a deep breath. "No one knew what to do. We thought it would be best to wait until you got here."

Best to *wait?* For the first time in her life, Jill knew how it felt to be angry enough to lash out violently. Trembling, she told herself: Just stay calm. Do what has to be done. In her mind she drew a map of the surrounding area. St. David's on East 32nd would be the closest hospital, no more than a couple of miles away. Probably she could get Alex there herself more quickly than it'd take an ambulance to make the round trip.

Dennis plucked urgently at her arm. "Do you want us to call 911?"

"No. Ride with us to the hospital, Dennis. You can hold Alex on your lap."

Dennis nodded, picked up her son and held him close to his chest.

§

Driving as fast as she dared, halfway hoping a traffic cop would stop her and offer an escort to the hospital, Jill talked constantly to Alex, as if her voice could keep the life force from draining out of him.

"Mommy's here, sweetie. I'm here with you, Alex."

"I don't think he can hear you. He's unconscious."

"I'll keep talking to him, it might help." He's going to die, she thought, wondering why she was still so calm. She should be screaming, sobbing. Her son was going to die. She found herself praying for the first time in ages. Dear God, please let him be okay. Please give me back my little boy.

She focused on the street, acutely aware of the traffic around her, senses much sharper than usual. The unemotional observant part of her consciousness wondered what it would be like, to be no longer someone's mother. Dear God, please don't take him from me. Oh sweet Lord, she prayed, not that.

§

"I'm here with you, Alex." Jill held her son's limp hand and looked hopefully at his face. It seemed a little pinker than five minutes ago.

A swish of purple entered the room, a blur of motion, slender dark arms outstretched as Jill turned toward the door.

"Jill, oh my God! I came as soon as Clothile called me." Since their first year of law school, Carol Glassman had been Jill's best friend and confidante.

"Thanks for coming, girl." Carol now had her own family law practice, yet she must have dropped everything to be here so quickly.

"How is he?"

"They gave him an anticonvulsant drug. Doctor'll be back in a few minutes to check him again. Says his vital signs are all okay."

"Then...he's gonna be fine?"

"Yes. It's like a...like the most wonderful gift I've ever been given. He's going to be okay. Carol, I was sure he was dying. He was unconscious for almost half an hour. Then he just went to sleep a few minutes after we got here. It's weird how you can tell the difference just by looking. Alex, sweetie, Auntie Carol's here."

The boy's eyes opened briefly. "Head aches," he said faintly.

Jill gently massaged his scalp with her fingers. "Does that make it better?"

"No. Hurts."

"We'll ask the doctor if he can give you some medicine to make it better."

"Do you have any idea what caused it?"

"Not a clue. His teacher swears he didn't fall and hit his head, nothing like that, and the doctor says there's no sign of a head injury. They want to do an MRI. Don't know how I'll manage.

I'm already having trouble paying all the bills, and now I'll have to take unpaid time off from work. Naturally our HMO won't touch the MRI."

"Bastards. Can't you ask Keith to contribute?"

Lord knows, Jill thought, he's never given us a penny since Alex was a baby. The least he can do is help with Alex's medical bills. But she knew Keith. She sighed. "He's got a new family now, Carol...."

"Yeah, and makes two hundred thousand a year. You're gonna have to ask him, Jill. Alex is his son too."

"I feel so awful. I've been a terrible mother. Alex was having headaches. He complained about one last week, on his birthday, and I didn't listen, I just...." Jill burst into tears.

§

"We're keeping Alex here at the hospital overnight for observation," the doctor explained, already eager to be off to his next patient. "We fully expect him to be fine, Ms. Shannon."

"How soon can we go home?"

"Oh, tomorrow morning, I'd expect."

"Doctor, he had a *seizure!*"

"Childhood seizures are more common than most people realize," he told her, looking toward the ceiling. "In many cases, no one can say what caused the seizures, but the kids usually outgrow them in a year or two. If they do recur, they can generally be controlled with drugs. Your son should lead a more or less normal life." He looked at her directly. "You should rest, Ms. Shannon. Go home and get some rest. Alex will be just fine with us."

§

The sun had set by the time Jill drove into the parking space of her home on Fruth Street. Given her long work hours that was not unusual these days, but the house had never seemed as dark and empty as it did tonight. All the way from the hospital, she'd found herself turning toward the passenger seat to comment on an interesting car or building, or a song on the radio. She had taken Alex's presence so much for granted, she hadn't realized how greatly she'd come to rely on his company.

Jill pushed open the kitchen door and was greeted by an irate Miz Kitty and an eye-burning stench of runny cat shit. Locked in again. Never mind. Alex was going to be okay. That was the important thing. Thank you, dear God, thank you for letting Alex live. I promise I'll never take him for granted again.

An hour later, when Jill was convinced she had found and removed every pile and puddle of feline poop and forced down some food, she fell into bed fully clothed and cried herself to sleep.

8: FRIDAY, MAY 9

In San Antonio for his scheduled one day a week, Paul told Drew Chang about the way his auxosome mice were behaving. He'd anticipated a reaction anywhere from amazement to derision, and wasn't terribly surprised when Drew's response was faintly mocking.

"Gee, Paul, You've made yourself a little colony of Algernons."

"Algernons?" Maybe it was some sort of American thing an Aussie was expected to know without being told?

"Movie. *Charly.* That's *l-y,* not *l-i-e.* Super-intelligent mice. You'd like it. But take a clean handkerchief with you." He made dabbing motions at his eyes.

Paul shook his head ruefully and changed the subject. He considered himself incredibly lucky to be working even a single day a week with Drew Chang in a joint University of Texas-MJT Labs cancer research project. Dr. Chang was a slight young man with an intelligent face and straight black hair long enough to fall over his eyes, looking more like a studious teenager than an internationally acclaimed molecular biologist. He displayed a child-like fascination for his work, and Paul always drove home to Austin, ninety minutes north on the freeway, newly inspired and energized after a day in Drew's lab.

On his coffee break, Paul googled on the title. A site directed him to the novel that the movie had been based on (two movies, it turned out, not to mention a musical). A copy was listed in the UTSA library catalogue. What the hell, he thought. Drew wouldn't give me a bum steer.

Two hours later he left the John Pearce Library in a daze, still immersed in the tragic fictional world of Charlie Gordon. He'd intended to check out *Flowers for Algernon* and read it at home, but made the mistake of opening it, just to look at the first couple of pages. Somehow he had not been able to stop until he'd reached the end, eyes blurred with tears, throat constricted. Daniel Keyes' novel followed a sweet, remarkably motivated mentally retarded adult, Charlie, through experimental brain surgery trialed on a mouse named Algernon. The operation gave both man and mouse exceptional intelligence. Swiftly, Charlie Gordon learned to appreciate music and literature, understand math, read and write in many different languages, create music of his own and add to the science of neurology—but then, as in some terrible Greek myth of fate, his enhanced intelligence began to crumble, even as Algernon sickened and died. In the end, Charlie was worse off than at the beginning, thoughts and feelings blurred and muffled, yet haunted by vague memories of....

Of what?

Of having been *different* for a while.

Drew Chang had instantly understood the significance of those modified mice in Paul's lab. The results on maze running and manipulation of their environments went far beyond any data recorded previously. The implications were astonishing. By manipulating the genes in his own cells, using the same modifications, could he himself become the most brilliant human in history?

He walked in the spring evening, dazzled and appalled. What

would it be like, to learn new languages effortlessly, to compose beautifully complex music, to write sublime poetry, see more deeply into nature? Would he find, precisely because of his newly superior intelligence, that he'd become the most isolated and lonely man in the world? Worse—what if, like Charlie's, his brilliance were not permanent? Before reading the novel, Paul had felt sure that he would not hesitate to enhance his intelligence. Now that he was staring the opportunity in the face, he was scared shitless.

I have to find some way to get emergency funding for primate tests, he told himself. Damn, I'll see if I can talk admin into giving me a grant. Or get hold of some private money, pharma companies will go ape about this. He started to run, flushed with joyous excitement. Drivers making their way home stared at him disapprovingly. He didn't notice them.

9: SUNDAY, MAY 11

"Looks like he's doing fine now," Keith said. He stood by the kitchen window, watching Alex and his friend Daria play basketball in the back yard. "Unless he has another seizure, I don't really see the point of doing more tests."

You didn't see him lying there unconscious staring at nothing, and wonder if he'd ever wake up again, thought Jill. Her belly cramped. But she forced herself to remain calm. "It could be dangerous to wait, Keith. What if he has a seizure riding a bicycle? He could be badly injured."

"That's easy enough to solve—just don't let him ride a bike or take him swimming for a while."

"Damn it, Keith," Jill said angrily, "the seizure could indicate something like a tumor. The longer we wait the worse it'd get." She didn't for a moment believe it was a tumor, God would not be so cruel, but she wanted to be absolutely sure. "We can't take risks—"

But Keith had stopped listening.

"What *is* this, Jill? Pre-menstrual syndrome?" He wandered across the room, took a wooden box from the fireplace mantle and opened it, as though he owned the place.

Still the same charming man she'd divorced seven years earlier. It was infuriating, she realized, that he was right; her period was starting. And that fact was utterly irrelevant to *anything.*

He set the box down on the coffee table and gave her the benefit of his analysis. "Did it ever occur to you that the doctors are recommending all these tests to jack up their bottom line?"

Jill stared, shook her head in disbelief. "You're not serious!"

"This is quite a switch. I believe I've heard you say on more than one occasion that the medical industry is interested in money before health. I expected you to put Alex on some zany remedy prescribed by your local herb lady." At her furious look, he effortlessly changed tack. "Obviously I'll help pay for my son's legitimate medical expenses, even though it could be argued that you should have set aside some money for emergencies such as this. I'm just saying I have no desire to buy some neurologist's Padre Island summer house."

"Keith," Jill said, trying hard to restrain her anger, "I have an appointment with one of the best neurologists in the country. He's at the University of Texas Health Sciences Center in San Antonio. If his goal in life were to make money, do you think he'd be *teaching*? I've never asked you for help before. You and I both know I could file a Motion to Modify and get a court order for child support. I hope you won't make us go through that." She felt her stomach cramp again. Oh damn, it was. Her period had started a week early.

"Uh, I hate to disillusion you, Jill, but I think GWB has a little more clout than Miz Jill Shannon. Take me to court and I guarantee you, I'll take Alex away from you and stick *you* with paying *me* child support." He glared at her for a moment, then the tight muscles masking his face eased a little. "But look, Jill, there's no need for this to develop into a hostile situation. I'll talk to the doctor, okay? If he can convince me it's in Alex's best interest to have the MRI, of course I'll spring for it. He *is* my boy."

10: TUESDAY, MAY 13

Wayne walked down to the old farmhouse, Gretchen at his heel, carrying the paperback in the middle of a stack of old *Field and Stream* magazines. He'd sat down with the book several times but just couldn't get comfortable, knowing Fern might come home early from work and interrupt him.

She'd never disturb him at the farmhouse. Seemed to think the place was haunted or something. Once he'd asked her why she hated it so much, and she'd just stared at him. Tears had started running down her face and she walked away without a word.

Wayne pretty much avoided the old house himself. Not that it was haunted, at least not with ghosts. Unhappy memories got to him. Being the black sheep, the kid who never could do anything right. Robert was the son Dad had always wanted. One way or another, Wayne was always screwing up. Most of his childhood was an indistinct blur these days, and he counted that a mercy, but sometimes when he went down to the old house bits of his past would burst up with painful clarity. Well, he'd just have to risk an ugly memory or two to get privacy.

The gravel driveway, overgrown with grass and wildflowers, ended at a hedge that had taken over most of what had been the front yard. As a kid he'd seen a movie, *Sleeping Beauty*, about a princess who slept for a hundred years. Thorny bushes had grown so tall they completely hid her castle. It was like that.

No maintenance at all had been done on the house since way before Wayne's dad moved to the nursing home. It leaned at a precarious angle, like it would've fallen right over if there hadn't been a big old hackberry tree holding it up. The front door was jammed so tight Wayne couldn't budge it. He went around to the back of the house and found the kitchen door hanging by one hinge. The landing was rotted away to almost nothing, so he had to climb into the kitchen instead of walking up the steps. He settled down in the doorway, staring at the red, white and blue geometrical pattern of the floor. Dad yelled so loud it made Wayne's head ache. "You're gonna sit right here and think about what you done until you're good and sorry. No going to town for you this afternoon." And Rob's high, childish voice: "But Daddy, ain't Wayne coming to the picture show with us?"

Wayne took a deep, ragged breath. The linoleum under his butt had lost its colored pattern years ago. It was cracked and peeling, gray with too many years' worth of ground-in dirt and dust. He'd only imagined the colors. Too dark in here to read, anyway.

He sat himself down outside under the catalpa tree he'd helped Mama plant, been barely big enough to hold the little trunk upright while she shoveled soil over the roots. Now the trunk had grown big around as his torso. Leaves flashed a hundred shades of green and yellow; he felt the tension drain out of his body. The dog scratched in the wild untended bushes.

He opened *Awakening the Genius Inside You* and tried to read, but out of the corner of his eye kept catching phantom glimpses of his brother. Two year old Robbie running round and round the yard on plump baby legs. Six year old Rob effortlessly hitting the baseball over the fence. Seven year old Rob lying cold and still in his child-size coffin.

11: THURSDAY, MAY 15

Brightness filled the lobby of San Antonio's Garcia Health Sciences Center. Alex felt tired and cranky, irritated by the morning sunlight slanting through large windows.

"Look at this, Alex," said Mom. A big painting covered one whole wall of the lobby. "This mural was painted by children who were patients here." She was trying to be cheerful, but Alex could tell it was an act. He'd caught her twice today with her face scrunched up like she was about to cry, and both times she put on a fake smile when she noticed him looking at her. He wished she'd just cry; then he could cry too, and maybe they'd both feel better.

"I don't care about any stupid old mural. I'm tired." Suddenly his legs felt painfully heavy, and he plopped down on the floor. Ah! This was better. He considered stretching out, but the white tiles didn't look all that clean, up close.

"Alex! You're acting like a three-year-old. C'mon. Dr. Collins's office should be down this hallway." Mom tugged at his hand, trying to get him to stand up. When she put her hands under his armpits to lift him, he angrily shrugged them away. Why'd she have to treat him like such a baby all the time?

"I don't *wanna* go to the doctor," he whined. Probably wouldn't do any good, but if there was even a slim chance, it was worth a try. He couldn't remember ever wanting anything more than he wanted to get out of this place. "There's nothing wrong with me."

"You're probably right, sweetie. I just want to make sure."

He felt scared again. "Are they going to give me a shot?"

"I doubt it. They're just going to look at some pictures of your brain today with one of those machines we saw on the Internet. I don't think you'll have to get any shots."

"Well—okay." Alex stood up and followed his mother down the hall, sliding his feet along the polished floor.

§

A short balding man wearing a bright red coat strode into the waiting room.

"I need to see everybody's frangimuffles at once," he muttered, peering at Alex over the top of his glasses. "Yes, young man, I'm talking to you.

Dumb guy, trying to be cute. "I haven't watched The Carl Clueless Show since I was four years old." Alex noticed Mom giving him a warning frown and briefly stretched his lips into smile. It felt like a fake, but you had to be polite.

"Yeah?" said the little man. "Well, I'm forty-three and I still watch Carl Clueless. I'm Dr. Collins, by the way." He held out his hand.

Alex hated when people made fools of themselves trying to relate. I'll just pretend I don't see his hand, he thought. But Dr. Collins got a sort of hurt look on his face, like he actually cared if Alex liked him. Not wanting to hurt the man's feelings, Alex reached out and shook hands.

"Thank you so much for agreeing to see Alex on such short notice." Mom smiled at Dr. Collins, and the doctor's face lit up like they were old friends. Mom was always talking about how unattractive she'd become, but Alex thought she was beautiful, especially when she smiled. "And just what are frangimuffles?" She was looking at Alex expectantly.

"Oh, Mom, don't you know *anything*? Frangimuffles are the official money in Barrowsland."

"They also use them for currency in the computer game *White Dwarf*."

Hmm, Alex hadn't known this. He grudgingly gave Dr. Collins a couple of points. He was almost beginning to like the guy.

But then Dr. Collins spoiled it by saying, "What I'd like to do first—" Alex tensed and caught his breath, certain that a huge hypodermic needle would suddenly appear in the doctor's hand. "—is show you the machines we'll be using today and tell you a little bit about how they work. I think you'll be impressed with my toys." He grinned, and Alex relaxed a little. Dr. Collins opened the door to the inner part of the office, and when Mom hesitated, he said, "Mom's invited too—if that's okay with you, Alex."

"Yeah, I guess it's okay." Alex nodded casually. The last thing he wanted to do was admit how scared he was and how desperately he needed to have his mother with him.

"In this room is the MRI scanner. Don't worry, it's not turned on. You can walk right into the room." A white box with a large round opening in the middle took up almost all the space in the room. The thing looked a lot like a giant clothes dryer.

"This is the scanner. If the electric current were turned on, Alex, it would pull this right off your neck." Dr. Collins bent down to get a closer look at the round medal Alex wore on a chain. "Second place!" the doctor read. "What did you win that for?"

"Swimming. My swim teacher's gonna teach me to do the butterfly this summer."

"Excellent! That explains why you have such nice muscles."

Alex looked down at his right arm, flexed his bicep when he was sure no one was watching.

"MRI stands for Magnetic Resonance Imaging. The main working part of this machine is a magnet that's so strong, if you were holding a great big sledge hammer, the machine could yank it right out of your hands."

Alex cringed again, imagining the machine tearing his arms off. "Doesn't it hurt?"

"Nope. Before we put you in it, we make sure there's no magnetic metal anywhere in the room." Dr. Collins reached out and stroked the machine, as if it were a dog or a horse.

"I don't wanna get in that thing."

"Only your head goes in. See, you lie down on this table, and we just push it a couple of feet forward."

"Will the machine fix me up?"

"No, Alex. But it'll let us see pictures of the inside of your head. It'll show us what's wrong and help us decide on the best way to fix it." Dr. Collins turned to his mother and said, "Do you have any questions, Mom?"

Ordinarily, Alex would have hated it if an adult called his mother "Mom." But Dr. Collins did it so naturally it seemed as though he was simply calling her by her proper name.

"Can you give us a diagnosis today?"

"Sorry, no. We send the images to a radiologist. Before you leave this afternoon, we'll schedule a time for you to come back and talk about what we've found out. Probably sometime early next week." He put his hands around his mouth and yelled, "Nurse Snap! Nurse Crackle! You're *nee*-ded."

12: THURSDAY, MAY 15

Alex seemed so much at ease with Dr. Collins and his two nurses that Jill felt okay excusing herself to visit the snack room down the hall. When she pushed open the swinging door she found two youngish men and a slightly older woman sitting around a white Formica-topped table. She bought a bottle of apple juice and a candy bar from the vending machine, sat at a table near them, distracted herself listening idly to their animated conversation

"—aim for human testing to begin no later than the middle of next year." The slim auburn haired man crunched his paper cup and made a perfect pitch into the open trash can beside the snack machines. "What do you think, Drew, will Roberta go for it?"

Interesting accent. Unusual looking guy with intense eyes, unfashionably longish hair, beard a couple of shades lighter than his hair. She didn't like beards as a rule, but it looked good on him. He wore a white lab coast. Doctor, or maybe a research scientist.

"If she doesn't," the man added, "we need to look for some other source. BlickPharm, maybe, although I've heard some nasty stories about them."

BlickPharm? Her ears really pricked up. What sort of *nasty* stories? Blick Enterprises was exemplary in its support for environmental science. To add to her irritation, Jill couldn't quite place the accent. South African, maybe? Australian, that was it. She sniggered, briefly imagined him in shorts, wrestling a crocodile, mugging at the TV camera. Unaccountably, Jill felt her pulse accelerate.

The young Chinese man called Drew said, "You familiar with the PAHGE bill, Paul?"

"Prohibition Against Human Genetic Engineering." The Australian nodded. "More anti-science craziness, right?"

"The House is set to vote on it next month. Craziness is right. Here's part of the testimony some nitwit presented at a committee hearing." He handed across a crumpled sheet of paper. The woman intercepted it, read aloud:

"Protestant Perspective on Genetic Research, by Jack B. Price, Professor of Christian Ethics, The Parkland Baptist Theological Seminary, Fayetteville, Arkansas. Who said, blah blah, here we go.... 'I believe that the biblical texts of the Old and New Testaments apply to every possible situation we might encounter, including the one before us today. We first have to ask ourselves, "What is a human being?" The scriptures tell us that God created man in His image. To tamper with that sacred image, formed directly by the Hands of our Creator, is the sheerest blasphemy.'"

The Australian looked dumbfounded, shaking his head. "Wait a minute, Rachel. They're about to legislate on twenty-first-century scientific research, so they consult a document from Stone Age prophets?"

Drew said nothing. The woman said, "Hey, the Bible Belters deserve a chance to express their views."

"But surely your lawmakers don't pay serious attention to this fundamentalist drivel? They wouldn't back home in Australia, I assure you."

"The Reverend Price's radio program has a huge audience of devoted followers," Rachel told him. "Democracy in action."

"Yeah, but...but.... Look, when those people get sick, don't they go to the doctor? I mean, they'd drive straight to the emergency ward, not the nearest church, right? They get their tetanus shots and polio vaccinations, and so do their kids. I don't see anything authorizing *that* in the Bible."

Jill felt her teeth tighten. He might just as well have been speaking about her. Directly *to* her. She'd done precisely that. Yes, she had faith, but Alex deserved the best medical treatment on the planet.

"Paul," the Chinese guy said, "these folks see genetic engineering as different. And, well, it *is,* let's face it. Our work will lead to a permanently altered gene pool. Look at your mice!"

"But my God, Drew, so what? That's what natural evolution does all the time! We're not *hurting* people. These are treatments to keep people healthy and young. Nobody wants to die of horrible diseases. Don't these holy rollers postpone their own deaths, if they can?"

Drew smiled wickedly. Like a Devil's Advocate waiting to pounce, Jill thought. "Ah yes, but what if people with altered DNA *aren't human anymore?*"

The crocodile hunter sat forward, intent. He caught Jill staring at him, and looked carefully back at her. Flustered, she turned away, face burning. The woman doctor's beeper buzzed, and all three rose, walked quickly toward the exit, continuing their passionate discussion. The door closed. He was gone.

Oh well, she told herself, who cares. I'll never see him again and even if I did, so what. It's not as though I'm *interested.* Besides, even if there were the remotest chance he could find me attractive, I don't have *time* to spend on men at this point in my life. I have my work.

And Alex. His seizure had been like a frightening wake-up call. He'd get well, she was sure of it. Then he'd be grown up before she knew it. Seemed like only a couple of weeks ago he was a tiny baby. Fragile and ephemeral, life. I have to take more time to do things with Alex, she told herself sternly, while he's still young.

Jill rose to leave, and noticed that Paul had left a book on the table, half-hidden by paper napkin debris. On an impulse, she picked it up, paused beside a Coke machine to examine her pilfered prize. It looked expensive. Gold print on the spine. *Mitochondrial Function and Electron Transport Enzymes in the Brain.* Whatever that was. Inside the cover was an address label: "Paul Gibson, 34 Munro Street, Fitzroy, VIC." A shiver passed through her. She should hand it in at the front desk. Or maybe keep it safe for him, they'd probably misplace it, she could find him on the Internet. Jill hugged the book against her breasts and hurried out of the snack room.

As she walked rapidly back to Dr. Collins's office, she thought, God, I can't believe I've got an instant crush on a doctor. Keith is right about one thing. My attitude toward the medical profession has changed.

13: FRIDAY, MAY 16

"Here's your book back." Frowning, Wayne transferred *The Genius Inside You* to his undamaged left hand, passed the book to Nathan Pritchett.

"Thanks. Did you have a chance to read any of it?"

Wayne shook his head, looked at the floor next to Nathan's feet. "They try to get you to remember stuff about your childhood. Well, I couldn't remember anything, so I couldn't do it."

"Sometimes when people can't remember their childhood," Nathan told him carefully, "it's because of an unpleasant event when they were kids. Maybe too painful to think about."

Wayne stared at the floor, shifted his weight in the wooden chair.

"One of the things I do for people," Nathan added, "I help them remember. So they can deal with their past from the safety of the present."

"Just wanted to get my head straight, is all." Wayne's gaze flicked up, went back down to the floor. "No point dredging stuff dead and gone thirty years ago."

"Okay. Let's talk about more recent issues." Nathan wished he could send Wayne home again to finish reading the book. The triggers were there, the text aimed and cocked. No, it wasn't going to be that easy. "Let's get right to the heart of things. Tell me a little about your wife."

"She was the most beautiful girl in high school. The most beautiful woman in the world." Wayne did not smile, but his mouth underwent a transformation from stubbornly set to eager. "Everybody said she would forget all about me when I left to go to college, but she waited for me." He closed his eyes. "She waited for me."

Fern and Wayne had only been married for a little over eight years, according to the dossier. So he was talking about the first wife. Right off the bat. Nathan masked his excitement.

"Melody. My Melody. I would've done anything for her. I would've given my life. If only—" Wayne looked at Nathan as though seeing him for the first time. "You don't really care about any of this, do you? You're just sitting here listening to me because Fern paid you to listen."

"I do care, Wayne. I wouldn't have spent six years of my life studying psychology if I didn't care about people. I want to help you however I can, in whatever way you want. You said you'd like to improve your mind. Freeing your mind of distractions is very important. And one of the worst distractions is traumatic events that have never been put to rest. Another distraction is discord in your home life."

"My home life was fine before Fern started working at that freakin' hotel."

"Before we get to that. You were speaking about your first wife, Melody?"

"What's the point? They killed her."

"Who did that?" Nathan asked neutrally.

For the briefest moment, Wayne's face collapsed into anguish. Then the features shifted and hardened. "The doctors. Supposed to help her, but they made her live through the worst kind of hell. She didn't deserve that." Wayne's face flushed, his breath came in ragged gasps. "My Melody deserved Heaven. Not Hell," he said loudly. "Better if they'd taken her out back like a sick dog and shot her in the head!"

"It's okay, Wayne." Nathan spoke quietly, trying to establish a calmer mood. He would have given most clients a reassuring touch on the arm or shoulder, but he was terrified that Wayne would lash out at him.

"It's *not* okay! They good as murdered my wife."

"What exactly did they do?" Keep him talking about it. Encourage the rage and focus it, maybe that way lay breakthrough.

"They gave her chemicals that made her so sick she threw up every time she tried to eat. She looked like a skeleton. And her hair—her beautiful blonde hair—it just.... It fell out like a goddam mangy cat's fur. She was so weak at the end, she couldn't even talk to me."

"I'm so sorry, Wayne. I'm so sorry."

"That's what they said too. Sorry. And they were too. The sorriest kind of bastards. But them saying it didn't bring Melody to life again. Didn't give her a peaceful death." He was gasping, breathing in throttled gasps. "Pay them back for what they did. Make them see what it felt like to—"

Nathan waited, but his client fell silent, staring at the carpet again, face drained.

14: FRIDAY, MAY 16

Just west of the high drumming sweep of the McAllister Freeway, Boehler's Restaurant and Bar was definitely listing to the left. Paul stared in amazement. Drew had assured him the Victorian clapboard place served the best pork chops in San Antonio, but it looked ready to subside into the asphalt of Avenue A.

"There was a flood in 1920, and the building's never been the same since," Drew explained, grinning. "The city inspectors give it their blessing year after year. No danger of it falling down. My girlfriend got me in the habit of coming to this place when it was the Liberty Bar. She runs an art gallery not too far from here." Drew held open the door.

They ordered quickly, and Drew said, "Given any thought to what we were discussing this morning?"

Paul gave him a disgusted glance. "Yeah. Being human apparently means getting old and weak and dying." He flung up his hands. "Don't these ninnies know that most people today *already* live twice as long as they did when the Bible was written?"

The waitress placed slices of bread on the table, frowning a little at the outburst. "Mmm." Smiling, eyes closed, Drew savored a bite. "Nothing like freshly baked bread to ease the pain of living in an insane world. If it was just the Reverend Jack I wouldn't be concerned. But the OBD has come out in favor of the bill."

"Oh c'mon, Drew. You're not gonna tell me the OBD's in *favor* of an anti-science bill!" The Organization for Biotechnology Development was a lobby group representing the pharmaceutical industry. "It'd shut down half the research they're pushing."

"Yeah? Take a look." Drew found another creased paper in his briefcase. "Something weird's going on. Somebody's not playing by the rules."

Paul read:

> Daniel W. Rollins, Ph.D.
> PRESIDENT AND CEO,
> HEALTH-TECH BIOPHARMACEUTICALS
> PHOENIX, ARIZONA
>
> ON BEHALF OF THE ORGANIZATION FOR BIO-TECHNOLOGY DEVELOPMENT BEFORE THE SUBCOMMITTEE ON TECHNOLOGY COMMITTEE ON SCIENCE U.S. HOUSE OF REPRESENTATIVES
>
> EXECUTIVE SUMMARY
>
> Research is helping us learn how to work with DNA to grow different types of cells or create specific proteins. Such research can result in new discoveries that will lead to freedom from our most dreaded diseases, such as cancer and AIDS.

However, there are grave risks associated with the manipulation of human DNA. OBD agrees with the conclusions of the National Bioethics Advisory Commission (NBAC) that it is dangerous to engage in research involving the manipulation of human DNA except under conditions that have been approved by the FDA.

"Huh? Nobody's *asking* to do research that hasn't been FDA-approved." Paul's voice rose in frustration, and a middle-aged woman at the next table sent him an annoyed glance that he failed to notice.

"Keep reading," said Drew, and sighed. "Sometimes I wonder why we even bother. What's the point of burning ourselves out to give people better lives when they...."

Paul skimmed the rest. More talk of vague risks that might be associated with genetic engineering—but nothing of substance, certainly nothing to justify the final paragraph:

OBD recommends the enactment of legislation that will place strict limits on such research. This testimony includes our analysis of the legislation proposed by the Administration.

"Unbelievable. Ostriches with their bloody heads buried in the sand." Joining the enemy, trying to cover their lucrative, drug-selling asses, Paul thought.

Drew nodded. "When I first saw it on the Web, I thought I was reading *The Onion*. Then I figured some prankster must have hacked the OBD web site. But I confirmed it with Dan Rollins himself."

Many aspects of America still baffled Paul. The incessant patriotism and flag-waving, although the long enduring horror of September 11 helped explain that, even after the death of Osama bin Laden. The power and wealth of fundamentalist religion, with its flagrant denial of basic biological reality. This, letting some superstitious hokum rule, though—

"But, Drew, really, man," Paul said, battling his own reasoned cynicism, "the members of Congress, the people who make the final decision—they're intelligent, rational people. Aren't they, most of them? They wouldn't be swayed by rhetoric and non-sequiturs and...and general bullshit like this." He flipped the paper to the table, disgusted.

"They might not be swayed by it, but they could use it as an excuse to vote in favor of the bill. Maureen still keeps up with her old friends in D.C., still subscribes to the *Washington Post*." His girlfriend Maureen Baumgarten was a history major who had done a master's in political science then spent three years working in Washington D.C. before going into the art business. "She's convinced this bill is very important to someone, or several someones, with plenty of money and power."

Paul shook his head despairingly. Sure, law-making was rarely as honest as it should be. Still, he found it difficult to imagine that anyone would cheat and lie just to block research that could improve *everyone's* health, including that of the law-makers and their families. The fools trying to get this bill passed would suffer too, along with everyone else. It simply didn't make any sense.

"Drew, who the hell benefits from shutting down work that will help sick people?" He thought of the astonishing benefits his smart mice hinted at. Not just healthier lives—smarter, too! Of course smartness didn't always seem to be at a premium in this dismal world.

"If we could figure that out," Drew agreed glumly, "maybe we could do something about it." His mood improved abruptly. "Listen, Paul, I'm not supposed to tell you this yet, but I was talking to Roberta this afternoon."

"Yeah?" Dr. Roberta Treadwell had taken a few million inherited from her estranged grandfather, invested it wisely, and become vastly richer than the old bootlegger. She could have lived the remainder of her life in idle luxury, but she'd chosen instead to found MJT Cancer Research Laboratories. Because she had the ability to gather in brilliant people like Drew, her firm had prospered during all the tech downturns.

"I mentioned the work you're doing. No details, of course."

His heart started to race. "Oh?"

"She wants to talk you into coming with us when your UT fellowship expires. Maybe she'll agree to supply your funding needs."

Paul was speechless. The hope of a job offer from MJT had crossed his mind more than once, but he had hardly dared bank on it. "Man, thank you, I don't know what to—"

But mercurial Drew was frowning at him, back to being a worried man. "Thing is, Paul, if this damn stupid law passes, it'll stall everything my department's doing." He drained his glass, clinked it down angrily. "I could be out of a job myself."

15: SATURDAY, MAY 17

Once Alex was safely tucked into bed, Jill sat at the kitchen table going through files from work, making notes for interrogatories to be served on a former employee who had sued BlickPharm, alleging wrongful termination just one week before the rights to his pension vested. That was rather troubling, especially after the cryptic remarks about BlickPharm she'd overheard in the hospital snack room. Jill had promised to get the interrogatories done by Monday, but she could not keep her mind on her work. She was jittery but made more coffee anyway, then put the mug down on a book sitting on the edge of the table. Oh, yeah, that *Mitochondrial* thing. She felt sick with guilt, looking at it, and so her eyes tended to slide away. She forced herself back to it. She couldn't believe she'd lugged it from San Antonio back home to Austin. How the hell was she going to return it? It was heavy; the postage wouldn't be cheap. She should have left it at the Health Center.

She opened the laptop and went on-line. There was no listing in the San Antonio White Pages for a Gibson, Paul. Maybe he was only visiting for a short time.

Okay, Fitzroy was a suburb of the Australian city of Melbourne. Forty-eight Gibson, P. listings in the Melbourne, Victoria on-line White Pages. Google turned up ten pages of links, most of them posts about a heavy metal rock group. A few, however, seemed compatible with the subject matter of the book. She clicked on a post headed "The Role of the Basolateral Amygdala" and read:

> The nucleus accumbens appears to play a primary role in motivational circuitry. Dopaminergic afferents signal changes in pleasure inducing stimuli; glutamatergic afferents tie behavior to conditioned reward....

The email address of the author was pgibson@unimelb.edu.au. She searched the web. Okay. Unimelb must be the University of Melbourne. Had to be him. She found his Australian listing on the University of Melbourne homepage. This Paul Gibson was a postdoctoral fellow currently on transfer to here in Austin, hey, at the University of Texas Institute for Neuroscience. Research interests included molecular studies of neurotransmitter-metabolizing enzymes, developmental cascades, and neural mechanisms of reward through pharmacological and neurochemical means. The photograph on the site had been taken some years earlier when he had even longer hair and fewer wrinkles around his eyes. But it was clearly the man from the Garcia Center.

And zowie! No phone number was listed, but there was a UT Austin email link.

Okay, maybe like her he'd only been visiting the San Antonio Center. She clicked his address, and her email program opened up.

"Dear Dr. Gibson," she typed. Then she shook her head and backspaced. "Hi Paul, I have your book on Mitochondrial Function. You left it on the table at the Garcia Health Sciences Center the other day. I was going to turn it in to the front desk, but things tend to disappear in public places, so I decided to keep it safe for you. I'm relieved to see that we're both in Austin. I feel like a complete idiot. You can reach me at 512-462-5684. Jill Shannon."

I can't believe I'm going to all this trouble to chase some scientific genius who wouldn't give me a second look, she thought. She pushed the laptop away. Need to keep my mind on my work, or I'll have hell to pay Monday.

After a time, she found herself staring numbly at the words on her pad: "Thomason v. Miller, 555 S.W.2d 685, The knowledge of an agent is imputed to his principal." Such arid abstractions could be used to change the course of real people's lives, for better or worse, forever. She forced herself to concentrate, to decipher the parallels between the purchasing department supervisor at BlickPharm and a boss who was held responsible in 1977 for his employee's misrepresentation of the health of a bull. Aloud, she muttered, "Paul Gibson."

That made her grin. She liked the way it sounded. Letting her eyes close, she pictured his relaxed posture, the way his mouth curved when he smiled....

Disgusted with herself, she rose abruptly and went to the back door. The white trumpet-shaped flowers of Sacred Datura had opened, and a large Sphinx moth buzzed over them.

Your life is fine, Jilly, you moron, she told herself firmly. Don't screw it up by obsessing about a man who'll never be interested in you.

She sat on the ground, breathing the musky fragrance that had attracted the moth.

16: SUNDAY, MAY 18

Changing into his shorts on Sunday evening, Paul Gibson remembered the emails he'd let pile up. He shared this cramped, poorly ventilated office in Experimental Sciences with a woman graduate student but Rachel rarely came in over the weekend, had to look after her kids. Unless he needed to make long distance calls or change clothes, Paul usually avoided the place himself. A former occupant had smoked, and the stink still clung to the walls and furniture. His own apartment, barely less grim than his office, he used mainly for sleeping and showering. True, it didn't stink of dead cigarettes, but it lacked his office's high-speed internet connection.

He hesitated at the door, returned to the desk and hooked up the laptop. Odd. Nothing new from Drew; he'd expected a report on the latest fruit fly scans and hoped for word from MJT. Drew had seemed so moody, almost depressed. Paul hoped he was not losing enthusiasm for their research.

Hey, here was an email headed *Lost and Found: I have your book.* He'd almost deleted it as spam. Well, well, well. He picked up the phone.

"Hello, this is Jill Shannon." Classical guitar music played in the background.

After a pause to make sure he hadn't got a recorded message, he said: "Paul Gibson here. I got your email."

There was an equal pause at the other end. "Oh, yes. I have the book you left at the Garcia Center in San Antonio."

"Thanks for looking after it, that was careless of me."

"I know I should have handed it in to the front desk but I was afraid you might—"

"Not at all, who knows where it might have ended up? Some second-hand shop, probably. I'm in Austin at the moment. Could I come by somewhere convenient to you and pick it up? I see you have an Austin number."

"Sure. I'm at home, well, obviously, it's Sunday night...." Her voice trailed off. After a moment she added, "Right now if you want."

"Where are you?"

"Thirty-second and Fruth."

"Ah. I'm not far away. I can be there in...twenty or thirty minutes. Need to catch up on my running, this is a good opportunity."

"Fine. It's 3204, the white house with the stone wall around the front yard."

"Okay, see you soon."

17: SUNDAY, MAY 18

Jill started to put the handset down, lifted it again to her ear, gave an embarrassed laugh. "It's just as well you're not still in San Antonio, that'd be quite a long run."

But the phone was dead. He'd hung up. Jill felt her face flush.

By the time she tucked the covers around Alex, he was asleep. Was he tiring more easily? The seizure episode still frightened her. No, calm down, he'd simply been playing hard all day. But a sickened part of her was preparing to hear the worst when she and Alex next saw Dr. Collins. Jill lightly kissed the boy's forehead, quietly closed the door behind her. She glanced again at her watch. In less than ten minutes Paul would be here.

She started toward the kitchen to wash the dishes, hesitated, turned instead into her bedroom and critically assessed her reflection in the mirror over the dresser. It had been ages since she actually looked at herself. She tended to avoid mirrors these days. In her ragged cut-offs and one of Keith's old shirts, she looked about as enticing, she decided, as a street person. Well, at least the sloppy shirt partially concealed her extra weight. What the hell, might as well show off her most attractive feature. She pulled out the pins securing her hair in a tight knot, shook it loose, found her brush. Shiny honey-brown waves fell about her shoulders. She hadn't worn her hair this way in public, she realized, since the divorce.

Bringing her laptop and a file from work, along with Paul Gibson's book, Jill sat on the front porch so he wouldn't ring the doorbell and wake Alex. When the front gate clicked open she jumped, startled.

"Oh, hi!" Reaching for the book on the porch railing, she almost dropped her laptop. Paul bent forward on the walk in front of the porch, held his knees, breathing in deep, hard gasps. "Uh, are you all right?"

"Don't mind me," he said between breaths. "Cardiac arrest is one of my favorite hobbies."

"Sure you're okay?"

"Yeah. Overestimated my knowledge of the area. I should have slowed to a walk a couple of streets back." He sat down on the top step, close to Jill's feet.

"Here's the errant book." She handed it to him, then wondered if that was too abrupt. "Could I get you something to drink? Water? Tea?"

"No, thanks. I'll be running back." He opened the book, glanced at the minimal address label. "How'd you find my email address? I have a feeling we've met, but I—"

Should I mention actually seeing him at the Garcia Center? She felt herself flush. Nah. Sounds like stalking. "Google. Figured you had to be with the university."

"Yeah, I'm over here on a two-year fellowship."

"Studying what? Sorry, that's rude of me."

"Not at all. Well, I'm...." He broke off, searching for words.

"Poor non-scientist here, so short and simple?"

He grinned. "Let's see. Um, chemicals that control brain cell growth and operation. And influence how we feel and behave."

"Ah, the dreaded War on Drugs, I suppose?" Somehow he seemed less threatening in his sweaty tee shirt and shorts, sitting on her steps, than at the Garcia snack room.

"Well, yeah, these days you pretty much have to put that spin on it to get a fellowship." He shrugged. "My main interest's improving the brain's effectiveness and efficiency."

"Like, with drugs?" Sounded crazy and probably illegal, but there'd been an article in the *New York Times*.

"Pharmaceuticals might be part of it. Really, I'm concentrating on the genetics of intelligence. The inherited brain structures that support intelligence. But lifestyle, too—sleep, diet, and so forth. Training."

"Marathon runs for your brain?"

Paul smiled up at her from his step. "Exactly. Same principle as sports training. In fact, one of my colleagues in the psych department works with athletes to get the most out of their workouts by doing that—training their minds."

"So you're not a health expert?" Her pang of disappointment told her that she'd been hoping, absurdly, for something new and wonderful that might help Alex.

"Only in mice." He smiled ruefully. "Sorry for putting you to the trouble of lugging my book around." He glanced at her laptop. "Nice machine."

"For writing dry, legal documents."

"Ah, a lawyer!"

Silence fell. Jill sought frantically for some other topic, but Paul didn't seem to mind. He leaned back on his elbows looking up into the pecan tree canopy with a relaxed smile.

Oh God, he's so cute when he smiles like that, Jill thought. Sort of little-boyish. She felt her mind scurrying like a mouse in a cage, searching for something clever to say. But he was getting to his feet, stretching. He hadn't even asked her what she'd been doing in the Garcia building. Now he was leaving; she'd never see him again. "Look, this is pushy of me," he said, turning back, "but could I ask you a legal question?"

Ask me anything you want if you'll just stay here a little longer. "Sure."

"My landlord's selling the apartment building, and the new owner wants to raise the rent twenty-five dollars a month, starting next month. But I was supposed to have the apartment until the end of the year at my present rent."

"I'd have to look at the lease to tell you for sure, but your landlord probably has an obligation to pay you the difference between your rent under your contract and the new rent."

"Would you?" he asked.

"Would I what?"

"Look at the lease?"

"You have it with you?" Jill felt ridiculous even as she spoke. Obviously he did not have the lease with him. "Sorry, I—"

"I could bring it another day."

"Sure. That'd be fine. After seven is usually best for me."

"Thank you, Jill. And thanks again for taking good care of my book and tracking me down. Can't tell you how much I appreciate it." He gave a wave. "Bye, then, for now."

"See ya." The gate clicked and he was gone, picking up speed.

He's interesting, she told herself, he's smart, he's cute. I wonder what it would be like to— She leaned back in her chair, closed her eyes and pictured the two of them together on her bed. No, I can do better than that—walking along a deserted beach. We build a driftwood fire, spread our blanket, sit and watch the sunset. His arm is around me. I caress his face. He turns to me, and we kiss passionately.... She sat forward abruptly. Alex! Where's Alex while this romantic love scene's taking place?

Jill's shoulders slumped. Lusting after some guy was worse than idiotic. It was disloyal. Alex was her whole life, and now that he was ill.... Dear God, every possible moment was owed to him. Her heart clutched. How could she think of taking a single minute away from him? On top of that, Paul was obviously involved with precisely the kind of "conquest of nature" she'd been opposing for years, the sort of technological juggernaut BlickPharm were trying to counter.

Anyhow, she reminded herself with a snort, coming the rest of the way back down to earth: Fat chance someone like Paul Gibson would be interested in me.

18: TUESDAY, MAY 20

The Serenity Holistic Health Clinic now had neat white lettering and a logo that reminded Wayne of a bird's wings painted across the front of the window.

Dr. Pritchett seemed ready to get down to business today. The moment Wayne walked in the door, the pretty-faced little man started right in picking at him.

"I noticed you seemed to be uncomfortable in that chair last week. Would you prefer to relax in the recliner?"

None of your goddamned business, thought Wayne. He walked past the brown recliner and sat again on the wooden chair that had been pushed against the desk.

"Okay. Now, that book you borrowed," Dr. Pritchett said. "I'm wondering what you think of it so far."

Oh shit! He'd driven off without it. "I forgot to bring it back."

"Keep it until you finish." Dr. Pritchett waved a thin, delicate hand. "Have you had a chance to read any of it yet?"

"First couple of chapters is all. See, I'm not a very fast reader these days. That's one reason I wanted to read it. I was hoping it could help me to be a fast reader again, like before Melody...." Wayne could have kicked himself. It wasn't any of this guy's business.

Dr. Pritchett let a long, silent moment pass. "There are ways to improve your reading speed and comprehension. We can work on that, if you'd like to."

Thank Christ the guy wasn't asking a lot of embarrassing questions, like shrinks usually did.

"Yeah, okay." Wayne's stomach all of a sudden felt like there was a bumble bee buzzing around inside it. Same way he used to feel when he saw Melody walking down the sidewalk toward him when he was twelve years old, all nervous inside.

Dr. Pritchett went to an inner room and came back with a different book. "Here you are, Wayne. Start reading right here." The book was open to a point about halfway through. "Don't try to rush. Just go at your natural speed. This is not a test. It's just to establish a base reading speed so we can see how much you improve when you start practicing the techniques. Begin reading now and keep going until I tell you to stop."

"Okay." Wayne began to read. The words seemed familiar; Wayne was certain he had read this book before. Holding his place with a finger, he flipped the book closed, read the title on the spine: *The Swiss Family Robinson*. Some assignment in eighth grade, maybe, but he had no memory of actually reading it. And yet.... He remembered the story now. Pretending he was on a desert island, building a house out of driftwood. He'd found some lumber someone was throwing away, dragged it back to the side yard where no one ever went. He asked to borrow his dad's hammer, and his dad wanted to see what he was doing.

"That's not the right way to do things, Wayne. If something's worth doing, it's worth doing right. Now let me show you...."

It hadn't been fun anymore, not once Dad took over. He shuddered as memory caught him. The book tumbled from his lap.

§

Mama has baked him an angel food cake and when he gets home from school she wants the whole family to come to the kitchen to sing "Happy Birthday." Dad looks happy and excited and tells him, "Got a special present for you, son."

Wayne's more sensible side warns him not to get his hopes up, but he can feel himself grinning. I bet Dad got me the set of dumbbells, he thinks. Ever since seeing the ad in a magazine that promised a new body within a month, Wayne has dreamed of owning those dumbbells.

"It's out in the garage." Dad turns his back and heads out the back door. Feeling some misgivings now—Dad probably wouldn't have put the dumbbells in the garage—Wayne follows, dragging his feet as he approaches the side door of the garage, which Dad has left open. When he finally gets through the door he sees his father standing by a metal work table, beaming.

"It's a table saw, son. I'd have given an arm and a leg to have one of these when I was your age."

No, Dad, Wayne thinks, you'd have pulled a dirty trick on your only son to have one of these right now.

"Well what's the matter with you, Wayne? Don't just stand there like a deaf mutant. Don't you want to try it out?" Dad turns the thing on, a viciously sharp circle of steel whirring up through a slit in the tabletop. "See, Wayne," he says. "Here's how you do it." He pushes a board into the blade, and one end of the board falls to the floor with a sharp report. "Now you try

it."

Wayne backs away, scared shitless of the thing, but Payback likes the idea of cutting boards in two. He pictures himself ramming Wayne's daddy into that blade. Wayne drops away into a background of terror....

...and Payback takes over, steps up to the saw, pushes the board at the blade. Stinging pain, not much worse than being stung by a wasp, and red drops spattering everywhere, and Wayne's daddy yelling, "Look out, boy! What the hell you think you're doing?" Payback skips out again, leaving Wayne to deal with the bloody mess.

§

Payback raised his right hand and wiggled the sawed-off finger stumps. Hot damn! Back in control. After years of skulking in the background, he was It again.

"Wayne?" the little shit was saying, leaning forward with an anxious look. "Are you feeling okay?"

"All that fuckin' reading's given me a headache." One thing was for sure, he needed to get the hell outta this quack's office, no matter how much Fern shelled out for Wayne to come here.

The skinny little dude nodded. "Might be best to take it easy, go slowly." Just like everyone else, not a clue he wasn't talking to Wayne anymore.

"Listen, doc, no offense, but there's nothing wrong with me, and I'm a busy man." Payback stood, got his bearings, walked a little unsteadily to the door. He pushed out his chest, breathed deeply. One thing he couldn't stand about Wayne was the wimp's slouchy posture. "Nice talking to you, doc."

"See you next week." The little shit was scribbling something in his notebook. The hell you'll see me next week, Payback thought.

19: TUESDAY, MAY 20

Jill sat across the massive walnut desk from Les Collins, dreading what she was about to hear. Ever since his nurse called and asked her to come to the office, she'd known it would be bad news. Good news could have been shared over the phone.

"I'm afraid it doesn't look encouraging," the doctor said gently. "Alex appears to have a tumor."

Even though she was prepared for it, the words still hit her like a blow to the head. She was too stunned to breathe. Dr. Collins went on as though he did not expect her to say anything.

"Because of the location of the tumor, I cannot recommend radical surgery, even if the tumor is malignant. If we were able to get out all the affected cells—which is doubtful—too much of the brain would be damaged."

"You mean...." Jill's voice seemed to be coming from far away. "...Alex is going to be...a...he'll be...?"

The doctor shook his head. "That will not happen to Alex, because we will *not* do radical surgery."

"And there's nothing else we can try?"

"If the tumor is malignant, we could go a couple of ways. Let's cross that bridge only if we come to it. At this stage, the tumor might not be malignant. Alex could live out a normal life."

"But you said—"

Dr. Collins held up a hand, palm out. "True, the tumor appears to have caused Alex's seizure. We could see subsequent seizures. Alex will have to be more careful than most people when he engages in such activities as swimming and, eventually, driving. But with medication he could live a fairly normal life, as long as the tumor doesn't grow significantly larger."

"You think it's cancer, don't you?"

He searched her face for a moment. Finally he said, "Yes, Jill. I do. But I can't be sure yet. With very little stress to Alex we can do what's known as a needle biopsy. That'll tell us what sort of tumor we're dealing with here. I've already spoken with Dr. Arecchi, one of the best oncologists in the country. She can schedule Alex for a biopsy tomorrow."

Jill left Collins's office in a numb daze. She found herself obsessively recalling the afternoon she and Alex had spent together in the park shortly before the seizure. Even then he had been carrying the tumor around in his head, but they were both happy in their ignorance. She'd sat on a bench trying to get some work done, she couldn't remember what it was—something that seemed terribly important at the time.

"Hey Mom, watch this!" Alex had called. She looked up to see him climbing a knotted rope someone had hung from a tree branch.

"Wow! Look at you way up there. Be careful, sweetie!" She'd watched him for a few seconds more, then went back to her work.

"Hey Mom, look at me now!" He had climbed almost all the way down the rope and was using it as a swing.

"I can't watch you anymore right now, Alex." She barely registered the grin fading from his face as she bent over her book again. But it haunted her now. Maybe that had been one of the last times she and Alex would ever spend a carefree day together, and she'd blown it by making work more important than her son.

20: TUESDAY, MAY 20

From the highway, George Milton's place looked like a barely profitable sheep ranch that had been taken over in the middle of some now busted boom by a badly misinformed factory owner. An old stone house was dwarfed by cisterns and outbuildings, surrounded by fifteen square miles of sparse pasture.

The appearance was deceiving.

What looked like a group of linked factory sheds or outbuildings was a $1,900,000 house designed by a California architect, windows and veranda artfully facing away from the highway. The stone house had been built by George's estranged father, reputed in the area to be a reformed bootlegger, and George

Milton had spent his childhood there, nursing a driving ambition to get the hell out. The moment he finished high school he had joined the navy and after serving four years driving trucks across the United States had headed north, homesteading 160 acres in the Alaskan wilderness. By 1984 the wilderness had retreated, and the City of Fairbanks bloated outward to surround George's homestead. He refused to touch his father's ill-gotten gains, and twelve years of tax assessments forced him to sell out or forfeit his northern land.

George had always thought he would enjoy being a self-made millionaire, and perhaps he might have done had righteous riches come to him earlier in life. But city life soon bored him. He was disturbed by a new tendency to fall into deep depression whenever he passed by the construction project that had been his Alaskan home for more than a decade. So he took his $5 million and moved back south to the vacant family place near Sonora in west Texas.

No woman he'd met had been willing to spend her time holed up in a log house in the Alaskan wilderness, so George had never married. To his astonishment, when he returned to Texas he learned that he had a grown daughter, the result of a romp with Peggy Treadwell in the back seat of George's father's 1932 Dodge. Peggy had married James Johnson four months after the baby was born. While James had treated the girl as one of his own, it was clear for all the town gossips to see that Roberta Johnson was actually a Milton.

Because none of the remaining Miltons liked to talk about Roberta, George first heard the story when he was sitting around at Pelman's Café playing dominos and Shorty Moss got drunk enough to forget his manners. He looked George straight in the face and brought the subject up out of the blue.

"Say, Milton, I've always wanted to know why you knocked up old Peggy Treadwell and then run off and left her that way."

The other boys waited for George to haul off and bash Shorty in the face, but instead he just looked shocked.

"*What*'d you say, Shorty?"

"Hey, take it easy, Moss. Can't you see George don't know nothing about it?"

"She had a little gal." Shorty guffawed, and the others held their breath, but George was suddenly grinning as though he'd won the lottery.

"I've got a kid? I've got a little gal?"

"Well, she ain't so little no more. Took after your side of the family. Anyway, it's been more'n thirty years, George, nearer forty. She's all growed up."

"I've got a daughter!" He whooped. "Hey, Katy!" George gestured to the waitress. "Go up to the front, would you, and bring back cigars for all my friends. I've got a daughter!"

Truth to tell, George had been fretting quite a bit lately about having no offspring to pass his millions down to. The existence of Roberta Johnson was the best news he'd had in a long time, and his heart overflowed with paternal pride when he heard she was a big shot university professor. She did research, so George was told, on ways in which real people differed from the Rational Man assumed by most economists.

Like her father before her, Roberta had grown up chafing, living for the day she could break away from Sonora. She studied hard, kept her grades up, and moved west, first to Sul Ross University in Alpine, Texas, then to Stanford University in California where she earned a Ph.D. in economics.

Roberta's academic career, it turned out, had never really gotten off the ground, as her theories were ahead of their time, and few journals wanted to publish her work. Once her colleagues had caught up with where she'd been five years earlier, she'd gone ahead into the theoretical undergrowth, hacking another new path no-one wished to follow—at least, not just yet, until fashion chanced to sweep that way. And by then, Roberta had moved off again into the unknown. When George went to visit her with the good news that she was now a rich heiress, he found her teaching a course on *The Economics of Law* at the University of West Los Angeles, living in a ticky tacky house, and driving a twelve year old Volkswagen Golf.

Roberta was ready for a change of pace. She and George went back to Texas with a U-Haul trailer full of books and an architect.

George did not want to be bothered with managing his money, and since Roberta was an economist with an interest in the gritty and obstinate real world it seemed perfectly reasonable to turn that responsibility over to her. She did well. Within four years George's money had increased from the $3 million left over after building and furnishing the new house to $55 million. In 1989 Roberta started the G. Milton Foundation, which later became MJT. George was then 60 years old, and Roberta was 41, unmarried and childless. Both of them, in their different ways, felt the cool breath of time passing across the backs of their necks like a threatening knife blade.

Inevitably, perhaps, if eccentrically, her goal was to support research that would lead to an increase in the human life span.

Roberta had learned the value of hard work and perseverance from her mother and stepfather, the Johnsons. From her biological father she learned the virtue of taking time off to rest. Of a mid-week afternoon she felt her mind and her gaze wandering too often to the hills beyond the windows of her office, and at last had to admit to herself that it was time to stop work.

Her spirits rose when she heard Masie's musical Spanish accent on the phone. "Mister Milton's residence."

"Masie, tell Daddy I'm coming home this afternoon."

"Oh, Miss Roberta! We've missed you. I'll fix something special for supper."

More often than not Masie served the dishes Roberta had taught her to cook, fresh vegetables and lean meats, flavored with herbs rather than fats. But for occasions Masie considered special they had the country-style food George favored. Roberta herself had grown up eating that way in Sonora, and it pleased her to drape one of Mama's flower print table cloths over one end of the fourteen foot dining table and chow down like old times.

This evening it was Southern fried chicken, buttered yellow

squash, green beans with salt pork, and mounds of mashed potatoes. They sat down looking out at the courtyard, its vibrant colors exaggerated by the late afternoon sunlight. Sitka, the old Golden Labrador, padded in to sit at George's knee. "How was your day, Daddy?"

"Could've been worse, I guess. Don't look like yours was all that good. Pass the gravy, please."

She pushed the gravy boat across the table, wondering how much to tell him, how much to worry him. His hand shook as he took it; he looked ill. "Oh, I'm just a little concerned about MJT is all. Our research will be set back by this stupid, wicked legislation. No question about that. Here, Daddy, you want a biscuit?" He's really getting old, she thought, as he reached for the bread basket and almost knocked it out of her hand. She put a biscuit on his plate.

"Thank you, ma'am."

"Luckily, the Foundation's done well this year, but the stock market's down today. This damned recession's never going to end." Roberta frowned. The downturn could easily spread to the healthcare securities she had invested in so heavily.

"Yeah, I heard cattle was down, but I don't know about nothing else." Grease from the beans dribbled down his chin.

"Did you go to Jody's shop today?" She urgently wanted to take her napkin and wipe his face but could think of no way to do it without damaging his dignity.

"Yep."

"How's he doing? Here, Daddy, let me help you with that." She poured iced tea from a large pitcher into George's tumbler.

"'Bout the same. Ever since Nadine died he's just been marking time till he can go too."

"Does he still take flowers to her grave every day?" Roberta looked lovingly at the yellow and blue flowers on the tablecloth. She could remember gazing at those same flowers when she was ten years old, when Mama and Dad Johnson were talking about how business was down at the hardware store or how the garden was coming along. Now Dad was dead and buried and Mama in a nursing home, and poor George looked as if the twilight were closing down on his life. She'd rushed to get away, but sometimes Roberta wished she could go back to those Norman Rockwell days of her past.

George washed down a mouthful of chicken with a swig of tea. "Uh huh," he told her, eyes distant. He had his own memories, seemed increasingly to live more deeply within them. "Takes flowers every day. And he talks to her too. Thinks she talks back."

"Oh, that's so sad." She put down her fork and shook her head. Life seemed so pathetically short. What if Drew were right? Suppose a way was at hand—a scientific, technological, realistic way—to cure death? Drew Chang was one of the brightest, most sensible scientists she'd ever met, ever hired.

"Way I figure it," George said, crunching on a bite of chicken skin, "anything helps ease his pain is good. They were together fifty-four years. Must be hard for him to know what to do with himself with her gone. Anyhow, for all we know maybe she *does* talk back." He dropped a treat from the table to Sitka, who accepted it neatly.

For a few minutes the only sounds were biting and chewing and the ticking of the grandfather clock. A sheep baa'd in the pasture.

21: TUESDAY, MAY 20

Wayne was not the kind of guy Payback would choose for a friend, let alone a constant companion. When it came to school work and reading books, Wayne might have been smarter, back then, but when it came to the real world he was so out of it his smarts didn't do him a bit of good. Most of the time, Payback was glad Wayne knew nothing about him. There'd been times, though, when Payback would've given the rest of the fingers on his right hand to be able to explain a few things to this clueless shit-head he carried around with him.

From the first time he'd taken control of the body, back when Wayne was not yet five years old, Payback had been the one with guts. He'd taken the risks and done the scary shit that chicken Wayne passionately wanted to do.

§

Wayne's mama comes into the kitchen all smiley and says, "Wayne, honey, your daddy's got a surprise for you out in the garage." She grabs Wayne's hand, and they walk together out to Wayne's daddy's workshop. And there, in the middle of the garage, all shiny and red, is a bicycle. Wayne is so excited he wants to leap into the air and shout, but he's afraid of mama and daddy. One or the other will be sure to get mad and yell at him for making too much noise. He jumps and shouts inside, though. Wayne's daddy has a screwdriver, and there's a piece of paper on the floor with a diagram that shows how to put the bike together.

"It's your bike, son. Here, you put on the reflector." Wayne's daddy is as tall as a tree and as strong as Goliath. Wayne idolizes his daddy, wants more than anything in the world to please him. Eagerly, he takes the screwdriver, places the blade in the slot of the screw. This time, he'll get it right. He'll make Dad proud of him. He twists his small hand and sends the blade slipping out of the slot. It gouges a scratch in the shiny red paint.

"You stupid klutz!" Dad jerks the screwdriver from his hand. "I pay $65 for a brand new bicycle and the first thing you do is go and ruin it. What's the matter with you, Wayne?"

Wayne pinches his lips together tight to keep them from trembling, turns around and walks out of the garage so Mama and Dad won't see him crying. Just as he reaches the kitchen door, that's when Payback takes over and marches back into that garage. Mama's just standing there looking sorry. She never sticks up for Wayne, except sometimes when Wayne's daddy's hitting him she asks him to stop. But Wayne's daddy never pays any attention to her, and she just stands there like she's stupid or something, never lifts a finger to protect her son.

"Sorry I messed up the bike, Dad," Payback says. I'm not sorry at all, you big ugly jerk, he thinks.

Later that afternoon, when no one's around, Payback takes the steel rake from the garage and puts it right behind the back wheel of Wayne's daddy's car. Ralph Harlan from down the road gets blamed, and Wayne's daddy staggers down to the Harlans' house drunk as a skunk and tells Mr. Harlan if he doesn't pay to get a new tire, the sheriff is gonna be paying him a visit. They never hear the end of it, because he comes back with his nose swollen and bleeding. No money for the tire, neither.

§

The only thing Wayne ever did that Payback approved of completely was marrying Melody. Payback would've been happy to just stay in the background, maybe come out once or twice a year when he was feeling especially horny. And that's what he did, too, until Melody got sick. But then Wayne screwed up, the biggest fuckup yet, and let them kill the most beautiful woman ever to walk on the earth.

Payback had to step in and get whatever justice he could.

He got justice all right, but also almost got himself screwed bad. When that kid got killed by the bomb, he realized there'd be something worse than a beating to share. If Wayne went to prison for murder, Payback would be stuck inside right along with him.

Wayne had no idea what Payback had done, but some of Payback's fear must have gotten through to him, because for years Wayne never let down his guard, never gave Payback a chance to come out again. But the years of inner fighting took their toll. Somehow Payback's own private memories were sneaking their way into Wayne's dreams. Shit. It was just a matter of time before Wayne figured out he was not alone.

The trouble went from bad to worse. For Payback it was like being half stuck in a nightmare, not quite able to get free of it.

Stories started showing up on TV about new ways of treating diseases, even cancer, and suddenly the wounds left by Melody's death, wounds finally starting to heal a little, opened up again. When Wayne heard a Nature Forever speaker in the park talk about how medical science could cause the end of the human species, he starting brooding about what he'd like to do to the soulless bastards in white coats who took other people's lives into their careless hands. It was an opening for Payback, or the start of an opening. He sensed he was needed again, though he wasn't sure what he'd be able to do.

Well, now he was in control again, so he *had* to figure out what to do. Briefly, he wondered if he might try to enlist Wayne's help. Forget it. No, he had to do this on his own; Wayne would only screw things up. Let's start by using the Internet at the Delmar Public Library, he told himself, do some catching up.

22: WEDNESDAY, MAY 21

It was like preparing herself for her own death sentence.

Jill waited on a bench in the sunny Santa Inez courtyard, sick with anxiety. Somewhere inside the hospital, Dr. Arecchi was pushing a biopsy needle into her son's head.

When she was thirteen, Jill had sat in a hospital waiting room on an uncomfortable plastic sofa while doctors tried to save her father's life. She and Dad had just gotten back from their best camping trip ever. He complained of indigestion on the way home; the sausage they'd had for breakfast, he guessed. He was wearing a red and gray plaid shirt and that old brown cap he must have kept since he was Jill's age, and they talked about school and what they'd do on their next camping trip and whether to stop at the grocery store; all so ordinary. She'd seen no clue this would be the last time she'd ever be able to talk to her dad, that his failed heart would tear him from her. Of course she'd talked to him many times since then; but he was no longer there to hold up his end of the conversation.

Dr. Collins came to her in the courtyard, stepping from shadow into hot light. He did not have to tell her; she guessed the message from his slumped shoulders and sober expression.

"Malignant," Jill said, as if by saying it first she could divert some of the pain.

Dr. Collins remained standing. "We won't know for sure exactly what sort of cells they are until they're analyzed in the lab. But they're definitely cancer cells. I'm so sorry, Jill."

She was amazed by her terrible calm as she drove to a nearby cafeteria for dinner. Back at Santa Inez, sitting beside Alex's bed gently rubbing his back, she realized she could remember nothing about what food she'd eaten, which streets she'd driven down.

23: WEDNESDAY, MAY 21

Lauren and her dog were just starting out for a run when Paul pulled up to the curb. Beautiful as a model, she wore electric blue lycra and a matching headband to hold back her straw-blonde hair. Her face lit up with a smile as the battered Datsun clunked to a stop. No pouts today, he thought, winding down his window. Not yet, anyway.

"Hey stranger, where've you been?" she yelled. The dog yapped excitedly and strained against its leash.

"Working hard." He picked up a flat plastic case from the passenger seat.

"Well, aren't you going to get out?"

"No, I can see you've just started your run and I really just dropped by to return—"

"Now, Paul. You've got to come in. It's been a week since we've seen each other."

He looked at her through the open window. "You told me you didn't want to see me again."

"Oh, Paulie, I was upset. You know I didn't mean it!"

"No, I think you were right. It's better if we don't see each other for a while. I brought this for you." Nothing had ever been easy with Lauren, and clearly this was not going to change simply because he had decided to end the relationship. She had dazzled him when he first met her at Richard Ames's Christmas party, with animated talk of the book she was writing comparing the lives of Anais Nin and May Sarton. He had hoped they could open up whole new worlds for each other.

"You can't just hand me my goddamn diaphragm and walk away like that." Her eyes were watering up. The dog continued to yap.

Paul stepped out of the car. In the end, the only world Lauren had opened for him was the world of neurosis. She made no move to take the diaphragm, so he slipped it into his trouser pocket. One of Lauren's golden arms went around his neck and she pushed her body against his.

"You feel so good." She kissed his lips. "Let's not break up. We belong together."

Paul tried to take a step back but found that the dog had circled behind him, tying his legs to Lauren's with the leash. Her other arm wrapped him, and the leash slid across the back of his legs as the dog pulled free, dragging the leash behind it.

"Just stay here with me for a little while." Stepping back, she took one of his hands, began pulling him toward the house. Something wet his ankle.

"Lauren," he said, on the verge of laughter, "your dog just peed on my leg."

"Mister Teeny! You bad thing!" She scooped the dog up and turned to Paul, gushing on in the same high-pitched baby voice she used for the dog. "Come on, Paulie. I have some new bubble bath. You'll love it."

"Thanks all the same, Lauren, but I really have to go. I'll just rinse off with the hose. May I?"

"Shit, you can't just leave me like this. We have to talk about it. If you want to break up, we have to dis*cuss* it, get closure."

"I'll be glad to talk about it with you, but this is not a good time. Maybe we could meet for lunch one day next week." Lauren was beautiful and sexy, but it would be more fun to spend the morning with a tree frog.

She stood watching him slip back into the car as if she did not really believe what was happening. Her blonde ponytail swayed slightly in the breeze. As he pulled away he heard her scream shrilly, "Screw you, Paul Fucking Gibson."

24: WEDNESDAY, MAY 21

Evening was the weather's soothing apology after the vicious afternoon heat. Jill sat on the front porch, blinded by tears, hands automatically moving through scale progressions on her guitar. Alex must have wondered why I hugged him so desperately tight, she thought, when I tucked him into bed.

A yellow Nissan pulled up at the curb. Even in the twilight she recognized Paul Gibson. Heart suddenly pounding, she sprang up, wiping a hand across her wet eyes.

"Hello, Jill." He shut the car door as she opened the front gate. "Would've rung you first, but I was in the neighborhood, hope it's okay."

"Sure." She turned her face away from him, not wanting him to see she had been crying.

"So you're a musician as well as a lawyer, eh?"

She was still clutching the damn guitar. "Not really." With an embarrassed shrug, she put it aside. "I play a little. Music is a...a soul-relaxer. Come on in."

The front room was dark; she turned on a brass art deco floor lamp. It made a circle of light around two red leather easy chairs.

"Would you like some tea?" The kitchen had a 1940s gas stove and stainless steel countertops. Heavy copper and stainless steel cookware hung from a wall rack. Jill took cups from a shelf over the stove and lit the burner under the kettle. Shit! she thought. Wish I'd washed the dishes. "Carrot cake?"

"Sounds delicious."

"So, what brought you from Australia to Austin?" She set the cake and two plates on the table.

"Mainly the lab. And the library's brilliant. I have to get in a certain amount of official research, but in my spare time they let me use the equipment for my own purposes."

To Jill's surprise she was beginning to feel a little better. It helped, having a normal conversation. "I've read that certain herbs increase thinking power," she ventured. "Gotu kola, for example, and ginseng." But his hand moved back and forth, a kind of gentle denial. Oh no, she thought, now he thinks I'm some kind of New Age nut. Not that it matters what he thinks of me. He's here for free legal advice, certainly not because he's interested in me personally.

He said, "I know some research was done on ginseng, but I haven't studied it myself. I'm working with neuro-proliferators—um, clinical trials, you know, treating Alzheimer's disease."

"Senility, right?"

"Dementia, yes. Alzheimer's damages brain cells, kills them eventually. These proteins I'm working with activate neural repair and regrowth." She heard him hesitate. "What I'm most interested in is their effects on *normal* people."

Jill looked up sharply, nearly pouring boiling water on her fingers. "You're experimenting on human subjects?"

Paul smiled, shook his head. "Nowhere near that stage. Just mice."

She relaxed, found some humor in it. "Building better mice, huh? I hear there's a big demand for that." Then bit her tongue. Damn, now he's probably wondering if I'm a crazed animal rights activist.

"Better mice? Actually, yes, in a way. My guys can figure out the most amazingly complicated tasks."

"Maze running's a mouse favorite, I hear."

"Laugh if you will." His smile grew broader. "My mice have to open a latch, then go through a maze to find their food."

"You're underestimating your mice. I've had mice get into some places you wouldn't believe."

"Ah, these are tough latches, *two* distinct kinds. You can change the shape of the maze. The path to their dinner depends on the kind of latch. Ordinary mice never figure it out. Most of my guys have it down in a couple of days."

"Wow. Would that really work in people? Swallow a pill and remember more of what you read? I'd love to be able to do things I've never been good at before, like...." She trailed off, wondering what to admit to.

"Lumberjacking?"

She coughed tea. "I was going to say math."

Laughing too, Paul seemed to have snorted tea up his nose. "No one knows yet." He put the cup down and pulled out a handkerchief. "We've treated Alzheimer's patients with neural regrowth proteins. They start doing stuff they forgot how to do years ago—dressing themselves, you know, minor housework, making phone calls."

"Paul, those are just skills they learned as children. I mean, it's impressive, but why would it help a normal, healthy person?"

He shot her a keen look. "My best guess is, it'd boost your ability to pick up new skills. Possibly you *would* learn math faster and easier. What *is* this stuff?"

"Raspberry mint. I've always tried to have only the healthiest food in the house. Never let Alex eat too much sugar." She sighed, suddenly close to tears again. "All for nothing."

"Jill, I'm sorry, what's wrong?"

"I just found out today that my son has cancer."

"Oh my god, Jill. That's...." He shook his head, brows furrowed. "I'm so sorry."

"They say he might have less than a year to live." Despite herself, the words tumbled out, and the tears. "Dr. Collins and Dr. Arecchi—" After a moment, she said in a choking voice, "They recommend minimal doses of chemotherapy, but there's no guarantee it'll work."

"Les Collins?"

"Yes. You know him?"

"He's one of the best. That's why you were down at the Health Center that day?"

Jill nodded, relieved that Paul's opinion of Dr. Collins confirmed what she'd heard from others. She dabbed at her eyes, stood up. "Well, shall we go to the living room and apply the law to your lease?"

He looked desperately uncomfortable. "Maybe it'd be better if I bring the lease back another time."

"It'll help me to get my mind off things for a while. I want to try to be cheerful for Alex's sake. If he only has a few months to live, I'll make them as happy for him as possible. Here, take a look through the CDs and put on some music, but keep the volume down—he's asleep." Her CD collection was eclectic, everything from medieval dances to heavy metal.

She settled into one of the easy chairs, reading the six-page document. Muted, the Chieftains' *Celtic Harp* filled the space of the living room. "Ah, so you like Irish music too!" She looked up from the contract, relieved by his choice.

"It's always been big in Australia. Irish convicts, you know." Paul was investigating the book shelves that took up most of one wall.

"Did you realize this is a month to month contract?" Jill frowned.

"The rental agent told me it was for a year."

"No, it can be renewed for up to a year, but the owner has the right to terminate the lease at any time by giving thirty days' notice."

"So there's nothing I can do about it?" He grimaced.

"'Fraid not. Sorry."

"The bastard could actually throw me out if he wanted to?"

"He'd have to give you a month's notice, but it seems he's already done that."

"Yeah, certified mail."

"Well, twenty-five dollars more per month isn't so bad considering how low—" The door beside her chair swung open.

In his Spiderman pajamas, Alex blinked in the light, the top and side of his head heartbreakingly shaved for the biopsy.

"Mom, my head itches. I can't sleep." The child slid into the room through the barely open door, leaned against Jill. She gently stroked his back.

"I'm sorry, sweetie. I'll make you some special tea. Okay?"

Alex nodded, staring at the visitor.

"Paul, I'd like you to meet my son, Alex."

"I'm sorry you're feeling crook, Alex." Paul did not speak down to Alex as some adults did with children. The tone of his voice and the expression on his face were simply friendly.

"It's okay. My mom'll get me fixed up. You talk like my teacher Ms. LaTrobe."

"I'm from Australia. You know where that is?"

"Sure. The land down under. Do you have any money?"

"Eh?"

"Any Australian money? I have a money collection with money from all over the world. Wanna see?"

"Sounds interesting. Where is it?"

"In my room." Alex proudly led him through a hallway.

Preparing Alex's catnip tea in the kitchen, Jill could hear them talking.

"That's my alien space station. I made it myself."

"Well done, my good man."

Alex giggled with pleasure. "My coin collection's over here. My mom made the display case."

"That's very nice. Let's see, you have coins from England, and Mexico, and Canada, and look at this! One from Greece! Did you go to Greece?"

"No, I got it as a Christmas gift."

Jill took Alex in his tea. Paul was perched on the bed.

"I don't have any Aussie coins with me right now." Paul said. "People here don't like it when I try to pay for things with them."

Alex giggled into his tea, making bubbles. "Can you check and see? Maybe one got stuck in the bottom of your pocket. Sometimes things get stuck in my pocket and end up in the bottom of the washing machine."

"Well, I'll check the coins in my pocket, but I don't think we'll find anything but plain old American money." Paul delved into both trouser pockets, making a comic production of it. Out came a handkerchief, a roll of Peppermint Lifesavers, a billfold, a flat plastic case. "Oops."

"What's this?" Alex reached for the case.

"Oh that? Just something that belongs to a friend of mine." Paul glanced at Jill, who struggled not to laugh at his embarrassed expression. At the same time, she felt a stab of disappointment. Well, of course. What did you expect. Guys like him always have girlfriends or wives.

"Leave it, Alex," she said. "It's something grownups use."

"What for?"

"We'll talk about it another time. Right now, it's time for you to try to get some sleep. Let me tell Paul good night, and I'll read you a story."

In the living room, she handed Paul the contract and said curtly, "Sorry I couldn't give you better news."

"Oh well, best to know the grim truth. I appreciate your time. And thanks for the tea and cake."

I'll never see him again. "You're welcome." She tried to smile. He stopped at the door.

"Hey, would you like to go out to dinner with me some time? You and Alex, that is?"

Absurdly, she found herself hesitating. "Sure," she said finally, and her heart thudded. "That sounds like fun."

She watched him walk to his car, then gently closed the door, wanting to run, laugh, shout with glee. For a moment, she let herself feel optimistic about Alex. People did recover from cancer after all, and her son was young and healthy. Surely he would be cured! Forcing herself to walk calmly into the kitchen, Jill picked up the phone, pressed Carol's number. Her best friend was always urging Jill to get out and have a little fun.

Damn. The answering machine. "Carol," she said, "you're not gonna believe what happened. I've met a man."

25: WEDNESDAY, MAY 21

The Delmar Public Library was quiet this evening, and Payback had his pick of the three computers. He chose Wayne's favorite machine, set off by itself, back behind the bound copies of old magazines. Wayne belonged to several Internet forums, including Nature Forever and the Green Guerrillas. Payback found Nature Forever unbearably dull, with their ten page articles full of words he didn't understand. He usually slept or faded out when Wayne visited their web pages or laboriously read their bulletin board. Green Guerrillas was more interesting. They never came right out and told people to do stuff like spraying herbicide on test fields of genetically altered wheat or setting corn fields on fire, but they had a page that told you how to do it, even where to get the chemicals.

Payback had his own fish to fry. He had some catching up to do since he hadn't paid attention as much as he should have. Judging by what he'd seen Wayne do on the Internet, he should be able to use the Green Guerrillas' web site for his own purposes. Fuck genetically altered wheat. His interest was in cancer researchers, the bastards responsible for the horrible way Melody died.

He'd signed the library register as Wayne Elliot, but when he went to the Green Guerrillas Forum online, Payback registered as a new member, Earthsavior. He'd never used the Internet before, so he had to work slowly, but knowing everything Wayne did helped a lot, and Wayne was slow anyway. It'd just take a little practice. Without reading any of the other messages, he posted his own, picking out the keys and entering the letters one by one, using his left index finger:

> The earth is dieing at the hands of evil men who only want to pile up money and dont care who or what they have to kill to get rich. The very worst ones are the people that pretend to be working to save lives. Instead

what they are reelly doing is kill people. If they are not stopped they will destroy the whole human race. They made the final days of my beloved wife hell on Earth. The most important thing in the world to me right now is put a stop to their evil work. Does anybody out there know which companies are tampering with human genetic enjineering?

He clicked Send and waited. When he noticed he was tapping one foot nervously, he made himself stop it. A couple of new messages came in. Someone called margotlee talked about polluted rivers. Wolf443 advertised yurt kits. Payback was about to give up and leave when Linda Comstock posted a message:

> Earthsavior, your right. The genetic engineers are the worst. They want to mix animal genes with human genes. Did you ever see *The Fly*? Remember what happened Jeff Goldblum in that movie?
> To answer your question, I heard of at least 1 company bragging about some kind of cancer treatment using genetic engineering. I think somewhere in California.

Almost immediately there was another message from Ed Wedeck, whose name Payback recognized as a general know-it-all:

> I saw on TV about genetic engineering on the Discovery Channel couple months ago. MJT Labs in San Antonio TX is working on a cancer treatment that uses altered human DNA.

San Antonio! Less than a three hour drive from Delmar. He'd take Fern's car, tell her he had another appointment with Dr. Pritchett in Houston. Elated, Payback clicked on "Search" and typed in *MJT.*

26: FRIDAY, MAY 23

After the bright midday sunshine, Payback had to wait for his eyes to adjust to the dimness of MJT's main hallway. He walked slowly, the weight of his metal toolbox tugging at his left arm, and took careful note of the signs on the doors. *Mailroom.* Gerald Scarlett, *General Manager.* Roberta S. Treadwell, *Director.* *Stockroom.* Beyond the large double doors at the hall's end, the air smelled of chemical solvents; he had found the working part of the building. Acutely aware of the danger, proud as always of his daring, he walked briskly, a man with a purpose. On the doors he passed the signs were more stark, somehow menacing: LABORATORY 1, LABORATORY 2, ELECTRON MICROSCOPE, BIOHAZARD AREA. Some of the doors stood open, and he could see ominously unfamiliar machines with banks of control buttons and digital displays.

A hefty young black woman wearing a white lab coat left Laboratory 2 as he walked past. He was acutely conscious of her glance as she took in his green uniform, the heavy olive drab toolbox. She nodded absently, opened a door across the hall, was gone.

He began to relax. Security here was incredibly slack, but still, he had to establish a purpose for being here. He found the telephone system control panel nearby, next to an office with an open door. Someone inside the office was talking softly. Should he abort the mission? This visit might be his only chance; they'd get suspicious if a phone technician turned up twice. He took a quick peek inside. The man in the room was engrossed in a telephone conversation. Okay. Proceed.

He set down his toolbox on the heavy-duty vinyl tiles, opened the panel.Careful not to disturb the detonators in his toolbox, he took out an array of screwdrivers and wrenches.

Someone was looking at him.

He glanced up. The young lab worker again. She stood for a moment in the hall, hand on the door behind her. He nodded once, then ignored her, reached back into his tool box and drew out the cables from the old VCR Fern had stuck in the storage shed when they got the DVD player. He kept his right hand tightly curled. Even with his work gloves, the woman might notice the missing fingers. It was not the kind of detail he wanted the cops to know about if they interviewed her. She went inside and shut the door to Lab 2 as he pretended to jack the wires into the control panel's complexly tangled, color-coded innards. Footsteps from further up the hall. God *damn* it. He pretended to be hard at work.

The man having the phone conversation was getting excited; he began pacing the floor rapidly, talking loudly enough that every word was audible in the hallway. Payback wasn't paying much attention, but then his skin went cold. The man was talking about some filthy experiment. With horror and fascination, Payback heard him say, bafflingly, "Paul, there's no reason your retrotransposon should be limited to rodents. Exactly the same homeobox code, man or mouse." The man was quiet for a while, listening to the person on the other end. Then he laughed. "With a little luck, we could even upgrade an ordinary *Mus* wrangler like you into an Algernon."

Upgrade—what sort of language was that to use about his fellow humans? This was exactly the kind of disgusting shit Payback had to stop. Heart thundering, he took four steps away from the control panel so he could read the name on the door: Drew Chang, PhD. Boldly, Payback sneaked a look into the room. This Drew Chang was a little guy who looked as Chinese as his last name. "We've got to vector it past the blood-brain barrier," Chang said into the phone, listened for a moment then laughed again. He said something about mice. Apparently they were just using the drug on mice so far, not humans. *Re-wiring* mice. Payback shuddered. The man spit out a whole string of long words Payback had never heard of, like another language, only not Chinese.

The black worker came out again, heels clicking on the tiles, carrying a mouse in a small cage, and this time definitely challenged Payback with a suspicious glance. He ducked his head away, the brim of his AT&T cap hiding most of his face. He closed the box and moved on down the corridor, entered the first empty room he found and shut the door. He'd hide in here for a while, decide what to do next. Sure as shit wasn't going to be able to set up the bomb in Chang's room, not with that woman giving him the evil eye.

These homemade bombs were dangerous. Unstable. Drop one, treat it roughly, it could go off unexpectedly. It was amazing that the little dead girl had managed to haul one back to her Mommy's apartment. Every move Payback made had to be like a smooth, precision dance step. Sweating, he took one bomb from the tool box and checked to make sure the small receiver was still taped to the top. He had not expected the research labs to be filled with so many instruments, so many cell phones. The atmosphere must be filled with electrical signals of a hundred kinds. A stray signal could activate the receiver and set off the detonator. He calmed himself with the thought that the scientific instruments must be well shielded, or they'd interfere with each other during routine use.

With the greatest care, he placed the first bomb well back under a bench.

27: FRIDAY, MAY 23

Payback stood tensely on the crest of a hill, breathing the scent of juniper and limestone. At his feet, the lights of San Antonio spread like tentacles, revealing the path of its cancerous growth. The constant hum of night insects was a soothing mantra. Not too far away the song of a coyote cut through the background noise; an answering call came from farther out in the darkness. He relaxed a fraction, looked up at the stars.

Growing louder, the roar of a commercial jet engine overpowered the insect noises. His body stiffened, his breath came in irregular spasms. He looked up at the blinking red and white lights that moved in front of the stars. They'll never stop until they've killed the world. He shone the flashlight on the clock built into the small radio transmitter. 20:37. The drone of the plane faded. Insect sounds, and the ragged gasps of his own breath. Time to shit or get off the pot, as Wayne's daddy would've said.Payback shifted the transmitter to his undamaged left hand. Paused. Inhaled deeply. The button was slick with sweat. It took only the slightest pressure to push it.

28: FRIDAY, MAY 23

To the extent the security guard felt anything at all, he experienced surprise rather than pain. The police report, and Saturday's front page and TV stories, would state that when two bombs ripped through the Margaret Johnson Treadwell Developmental Biology and Molecular Genetics Laboratory at 8:42 P.M., Mr. Davis G. Broadbent, a guard with Walling's Alarm and Security, had died instantly.

29: FRIDAY, MAY 23

Roberta Treadwell had been interviewed once for a *People* magazine article on the private lives of the rich and famous. Under a picture of her dressed in shorts and a baggy shirt, hands dirty from pulling weeds in her garden, was the caption: "Just an ordinary person like you and me." She lived alone in a modest townhouse on San Antonio's Stone Oak area; her furnishings were elegantly comfortable but not extravagant. Usually she cooked her own simple meals and unwound after work by watching TV and DVDs.

On Friday evening she left work at 6:00, stopped at the grocery store and, on a whim, dropped by the video store next door and rented *All of Me*. By the time the telephone chimed she had finished supper, was stretched out on the sofa chuckling at the scene where Steve Martin tries to walk with Lily Tomlin controlling one side of his body. She let the answering machine take it.

"Ms. Treadwell, this is Booker Harding." The man spoke loudly and rapidly. "There's been a terrible accident."

30: FRIDAY, MAY 23

"Melody, I did it," Payback said in a low voice. "I did it for you, baby."

§

Memory twitches:

The air has a bite to it, the first really chilly morning of fall, and Wayne is feeling feisty as he walks into homeroom. He sees at once that something is different but it takes a moment to figure out what it is. A new girl is standing at Mrs. Dubois's desk.

"Class, I'd like to introduce a new student who has moved here all the way from Siloam Springs, Arkansas. This is Melody Neil. I know you'll all help her to feel right at home here at Lee Junior High."

Wayne is shy with girls, and he would have never had the nerve to talk to this pretty newcomer, but she happens to drop her History of the United States book on his foot as she passes by on her way to her desk at the back of Wayne's row. Without thinking—courtesy demands it—Wayne bends down, retrieves the book and places it on top of the stack she's holding in her arms. Their eyes meet. Hers are dark brown, as deep and mysterious as the night sky. Her face flushes, and she takes a step back, away from Wayne. But she smiles.

§

Her ravaged body is almost weightless when he lifts her to change the sheets on the bed. Her face has only the thinnest covering of translucent skin. When he lays her down, as gently as he can, she grimaces in pain; she tries to smile, but it is the grin of a skull. She is not able to talk anymore; when she tries it only causes her to cough and lose her breath. Her eyes are enormous in her wasted face. They are dark brown and as deep and mysterious as life itself. She speaks with her eyes: you have all my love forever, she tells him.

"Don't leave me, Melody. You can't leave me. You can't." Wayne buries his head in the bedding and sobs.

31: SATURDAY, MAY 24

Payback sat in a park in the morning sunlight, against a wall, reading about the explosion at MJT Labs. Security guy killed instantly. He was dreadfully tired; soon he must sleep. But if he slept, Wayne would be back.

Shit.

Payback was depressed, reading the article. Wayne the crybaby would've felt sick at his stomach, but hey—this was a war. Okay, he'd fucked up again; he hadn't intended to hurt the guy, just like he didn't mean to hurt that kid. But hell, it wasn't his fault. Collateral damage. Couldn't be helped. And anyway, the MJT sons of bitches were doing worse than killing one innocent bystander. That Drew Chang prick and his pals were going to fuck the whole planet.

The sun was in his eyes.

It went away.

32: SATURDAY, MAY 24

Wayne found himself sitting near a tree with his back against a brick wall. He was soaked with sweat and breathing hard. Newspaper sheets blew randomly near his feet. He had been sitting in Dr. Pritchett's office talking about how to read faster, like he used to be able to. Then there were nightmares. Huh? He wondered if the doctor had given him some sort of drug, that's what they did, that's what Dr. Rutherford—

Blank.

Breath burning. He must have left the doctor's office and wandered around and then fallen asleep here, wherever the hell here was. Must have been hours ago. Morning light. Fern was going to kill him. He'd borrowed her car for his appointment with Dr. Pritchett since it was doubtful his old truck could handle the trip to Houston and back. Where the hell had he left it? Not here.

He leaned his head against his raised knees, fighting dizziness. The nightmares had taken a different turn this time. "Just a dream." He spoke aloud, and the high pitched, shaky sound of his voice embarrassed him. A fat woman who had been dozing on a bench looked at him, looked away. "Nothing but a dream," he repeated, this time in deeper, more confident tones. The pounding of his heart slowed, his jaw began to unclench. He could handle it. This sort of thing had happened to him before, when he was younger. Lost time he simply could not remember. He could handle it now, as he had then. First step was to get up, start walking, figure out where he was.

"I have to phone Dr. Rutherford," he said aloud. No, what am I talking about? It's Pritchett. Dr. Nathan Pritchett.

No, Dr. Pritchett's office would still be shut at this hour; he rejected that avenue before it was fully formed in his mind. No matter what he decided to do next, the first necessary step was to find out how much time was lost, what he'd done during in the interval that was now a blank gap in his memory.

33: SATURDAY, MAY 24

For an instant, a wedge of memory opens:

One night in Wayne's despairing, drunker rage after Melody's death Payback beats another drinker savagely in a bar fight. The judge suspends his sentence in favor of aggression-control therapy for six months. He struggles to find work enough to pay for food and a cheap room in a sleazy rooming house. When his money is entirely gone, he takes the offer from the smooth Blick Pharmaceutical representative to participate in an experiment. The Marines want to try building a few better men. Dr. Rutherford—

Blank.

34: SATURDAY, MAY 24

Wayne opened the front door, found Fern waiting for him, eyes red and swollen, hair unbrushed. During the first second or two her expression flickered from relief to anger to furious rage. He stood paralyzed, unable to speak, one foot inside the mobile home, the other still out on the deck. Gretchen looked uncertainly from one to the other, then slunk away. Fern broke the silence at last.

"Just where have you been? Five days!" Although her tone was angry, Wayne exhaled with relief. He'd halfway expected her to shriek like a banshee.

"I went to Houston for my appointment, Fern, and the car broke down." The story had sounded pretty good when he rehearsed it; now it seemed embarrassingly ridiculous.

Fern glared at him. "Wayne Elliot, if you're going to tell me a pack of lies, you can just turn around and walk right back out that door. You hear me? I got a call from the DPS. They found the car, *my car*, Wayne, parked in front of somebody's house in San Antonio."

His first impulse was to turn around, get the hell out. But

he had no place to go. He'd stood by the side of the highway for two and a half hours, in increasing despair, trying to hitch a ride, wondering if the cops were looking for him because of something horrible he'd done. Vague scraps of memories had the quality of his nightmares: that Payback creature, as always, only this time he had set off an explosion. Killed people, maybe. A man shouldn't have to suffer such bad dreams.

They stood silently glaring at each other until Wayne couldn't take it any longer. "You wouldn't believe me if I told you the truth," he said lamely.

"Try me, Wayne. It couldn't be any more unbelievable than the whopper you just finished telling me." She held her hands belligerently on her hips, but her tight mouth eased, eyes grew a little less hostile.

Desperately he sought after something convincing, but his mind was entirely blank. Finally he shrugged. "The truth is, I *was* in San Antonio, but I have no idea what I did there." He hated exposing his weakness, hoped she would not believe him; he could see by her face that she did not.

"All right, Wayne. I think I understand. What an idiot I've been! All this time you told telling me you were looking for work.... You've been seeing another woman, haven't you?"

"No." It was an outrageous accusation, so unfair. "*No!* I...." He wanted to defend himself, but it suddenly struck him that for all he knew he *might* have been with another woman. Better screwing some tramp than killing—

"Do you care at all about me," she was saying, "about *us*, anymore?" She studied his face intently. "Because if you do, there are still some sessions left with Dr. Pritchett, already paid for. He also does marriage counseling, Wayne. If you still care at all, I'd like for us to go together. Try to work things out."

It was a form of reprieve. At least he would have a roof over his head, food to eat. He wouldn't be out on the streets where the police, even now, might be looking for him. "Okay, Fern. I'm willing to try." She kept watching him as if waiting for some obligatory password. "I love you, babe. I want to try and work things out." The lines of her face smoothed, her eyes filled with tears. She held out her arms to him.

35: FRIDAY, MAY 30

"No! Leave your hair down, you idiot!" Carol Glassman made a grab for Jill's hairbrush.

"I always wear it up except when I'm hanging around the house."

"Up is fine for a day at the office." Carol stepped back to admire her work. "Please tell me you weren't planning on wearing that."

"What's wrong with it?" Jill was wearing the same gray woolen skirt she had worn to work, but she had taken off the jacket and substituted a blue cardigan.

"Everything's wrong with it. Shit, girl, are you trying to look like my old sainted mother? Let's see...." Foraging in the closet, Carol reeled back, comically aghast. "Damn, Jill, when was the last time you went shopping for clothes?"

"I don't know. Four years ago?" Leaning against the dresser, Jill examined her acne scars in the mirror. Usually she avoided looking directly at her face, it was simply too depressing. "What difference does it make, anyway? My skin'll still look the same regardless of what I wear." When Jill's face first broke out after Alex was born, Carol constantly reassured her that it wasn't all that noticeable; once the inflamed pustules had faded, she generally chose to ignore Jill's complaints about her appearance.

"Your selection is sadly limited, but maybe we can—" Items started flying from the chest of drawers. "Ah! Here we go! Not perfect by any means, but it'll have to do." She brandished a bright red pullover sweater. "This with a pair of jeans. What do you think?"

"It's so bright. It'll make me look fat. Something more subdued."

"Jilly, why don't you try not looking like you're going to a

Puritan funeral. C'mon, girlfriend, get this sweater on."

Surrendering, Jill threw the cardigan on the bed. Despite her worries about Alex and the office work piling up during hour after hour of medical appointments, Paul Gibson strayed compulsively into her thoughts. I do want to look my best when I meet him at the door, she admitted to herself. Yet she felt stupid for trying, when it was impossible for her ever to look good again. "It's not a date."

"Okay," Carol said, "it's not a date. But you never know, maybe Mr. Right'll be sitting at the next table at.... Where?"

"El Gallo. Paul wants to try Mexican food. He's picking us up at six." Jill pulled the red sweater over her head. "Nobody goes on a date at six. Besides, you left out one minor detail. He's married."

"You don't know that. Did he *tell* you he's married? Did he have on a *ring*?"

"No. But he was carrying a diaphragm around in his pocket. Maybe not married, but a girlfriend for sure."

"Hmm. Still, he asked you to go out to dinner with him."

"Well, yeah. But in the first place, he may not have been thinking about it as a date. In the second place, you don't take an eight year old kid on a date."

"Maybe you do, if you happen to like someone who has an eight year old kid. So what does Alex think of Paul?"

"He keeps asking when Paul's coming back. See, that's another reason I shouldn't get too close. When the guy dumps us, Alex will be heartbroken."

Carol rolled her eyes. "You should write a book about how to have successful relationships, Jilly. Step one: work out a comprehensive dumping plan before the first date."

"Mom, it's past six." Alex was standing in the doorway. "*I Love Lucy* just ended."

Carol ruffled his hair. "You still like those ancient TV shows, huh Alex?"

"Yeah. Hey, Carrie, come see what I added to my space station today." He took her hand. Jill glanced at her bedside clock and frantically powdered her nose as a car engine drew near and stopped.

Carol's head poked back around the door. "I wonder who that could be?"

"How do I look? Oh, god, Carol. I'm so nervous. I haven't been out on a date in more than ten years."

"I thought you said it wasn't a date."

36: FRIDAY, MAY 30

Over the past few days, Paul had asked himself more than once why he'd invited Jill Shannon and her son out to dinner. He didn't ordinarily socialize much. Too busy. Besides, after being a skinny, bookish kid, he still had not gotten used to the idea that women found him attractive, despite Lauren's on again-off again infatuation. It seldom occurred to him to ask women out, unless they first pursued him, as she had. Anyway, he certainly wasn't *sexually* interested in Jill. But there was something very engaging and poignant about that poor child. Jill herself—well, she seemed intelligent, and pleasant enough to talk to. Made a change.

El Gallo was packed, and the hostess had to seat them in a booth at the back of the dining room, near the kitchen.

"Why don't you sit by your mum, Alex, and I'll perch over here where I can have this whole bench all to myself."

"Okay!" Alex bounced into the seat, and Jill offered a grateful smile.

"What do you recommend?"

"Sherbet!" said Alex.

"*After* the main course," Jill said.

"Yeah, yeah." The boy pointed to an entry on the menu. "The tamales are awesome."

"In that case, I'll try them," said Paul.

For the next half hour or so they ate more than they talked, and the talk was rather stilted. Once the kid had finished his meal, his eyes began to droop, and he leaned against his mother. "Sorry, I'm going to have to get him home pretty soon. He tires so easily these days." Jill looked fairly exhausted herself, arm protectively around her son. "A couple of weeks back he'd be going full speed ahead until at least 9:30. Since we've started the chemotherapy he's gone by 8:00."

Alex opened his eyes. "I have to take a pill every day," he said. "Dr. Collins said since I hate shots so much, he'd give me pills instead."

"How long've you been taking the pills, matey?"

Alex glanced at his mother, who said, "This is the fifth day; now he won't take any more pills for 23 days. Then the morning cycle starts again. Five days of pills, twenty-three days off."

"I'm sleepy, Mom." It was close to a whine. "Can we go home pretty soon?"

"Sorry, Paul." Jill's smile was strained.

"Hey, no need to apologize. I'm about ready for some fresh air anyhow. Alex, you feel up to eating that sherbet before we go home?"

"Sherbet? Yeah, I want lime flavor." The boy jerked his cropped head up and smiled, but his eyes still drooped.

On the way home he slept, stretched out on the back seat. For several blocks they rode without speaking; for the life of him, Paul couldn't decide if it was companionable or anxious silence. I wish there were something I could do to help them, he thought. Mice we repair immediately, humans take a little longer.

"I really am sorry about tonight," Jill said. "I don't blame you for being disappointed."

"Nah. I had no particular expectations."

"Of course not," she said flatly.

Now he'd offended her. What he had said? "You know. I've been here for months, but somehow I've never got around to trying Mexican food. I had no idea what to expect. Jill, I wasn't disappointed. Really, the food was quite good."

The sudden stiffness in her expression eased, and she glanced at him watchfully. "I meant disappointed about being dragged off home early. The kid. The distracted mother."

"Ah. No, not at all." He touched her shoulder lightly, wanting to reassure her. "It was hard to carry on a conversation in the restaurant anyway. Bit noisy." Had she flinched at his touch? Oh hell, in for a penny, in for a pound. "Has Les talked to you about the cancer research my colleague Drew Chang was doing? Before some crazed animal blew a hole in the lab."

"I read about that, it's terrible. Was Drew hurt?"

"Thank heavens, no. One poor bugger got blown to pieces, though, and the place is a shambles. It's set Drew's work back."

"What sort of research was he doing?"

"He's working on tumorigenesis at the molecular level."

"A treatment?" She was abruptly eager.

"Hopefully. It's a matter of stopping the things as soon as they begin. See, cancers start from a single cell, often a stem cell. It has to accumulate just the right random mutations in half a dozen or more nuclear genes. You know, the codes in the cell's nucleus. They control the cell's growth and reproduction."

She was listening. "DNA, yeah."

"Right. That cell starts growing out of control and eventually sends growth-stimulating signals to nearby healthy cells. That can lead to building a sort of rogue blood supply to the—"

He broke off. I'm talking too much, he thought. He often got carried away talking about topics that fascinated him and nobody else. But Jill was still gazing keenly.

"You're saying a tumor starts by accident?"

She *was* interested, then. "Yes. And it only goes malignant if growth-suppressing genes get damaged at the same time. We should be able to put a stop to all this madness by sneaking growth suppressant genes into the tumor cells." His lips twisted.

"Except?"

"Nobody's been able to reliably smuggle the repair genes inside the cells' nuclei where they're needed. Until now, if Drew's luck holds."

"My God." She was staring at him. "Dr. Chang's inserting genes right inside the...the DNA of damaged cells?"

"Exactly." He sent her a respectful glance; she was quick. "He's been transfecting the sick cells with a very specific retrovirus. It carries the repair code to targeted sites. Then the cells' own maintenance programs insert them and switch the gene on. That's why we're so excited, see, this could open up a whole new effective treatment for Parkinson's disease, just for starters. And some bloody lunatic decides to—" He cut himself short, hesitated. "Actually, as I said the other day, I've noticed something extra."

"Your mice are getting smarter."

"Seem to be." He paused again. It was hard to get this out, it sounded so far-fetched, so hubristic. "It's possible we could use the treatment to boost intelligence in humans, to increase the IQ of the mentally, um, challenged, and...well, maybe to turn ordinary people into geniuses."

"Wow! And this will actually work?"

Paul shrugged, not wishing to make exaggerated claims. "Well, on fruit flies and mice, but then they're not terribly bright to start with."

She brushed that aside. "No, but you were talking about cures for tumors. Alex—"

He felt wretched. "Unfortunately we're still at least a couple of years away from human testing."

"That might be too late...." Her voice wavered, and he saw her turn suddenly wet eyes toward the back seat.

37: MONDAY, JUNE 2

Fern perched on the chair edge, twisting her hands together in her lap. Seeing how nervous she looked, Wayne made a conscious effort to keep his own hands loose and relaxed. The Serenity Holistic Health Clinic now had an oriental carpet on the floor and three classy wooden chairs with leather seats. The brown recliner was nowhere in sight. Dr. Pritchett must be doing brisk business. Maybe he was tapping his own genius within.

"Now, Mr. and Mrs. Elliot," Pritchett said, smiling like a game show host, "I'd like to establish some very simple rules before we begin. First, I'd like each of us to agree not to interrupt each other. Everyone gets a chance to talk. Okay?"

Fern nodded; Wayne shrugged.

"Good. Rule two, we'll do our best to communicate with each other. Part of trying to communicate means being respectful of each other as human beings, even if we may not like some of the things the other person says."

Fern nodded again, but Wayne was finding Dr. Pritchett irritating. What were they, little kids or something?

"Wayne?" Dr. Pritchett and Fern were both looking at him expectantly.

"Yeah. Sure. I'll try to communicate." Wayne kept his eyes fixed on a fly that had landed on his boot, grooming itself with its front legs.

"Good. Fern, since Wayne and I have already gotten to know each other a little, why don't you start out by telling me what you hope to gain from our session."

"I want to save my marriage, Dr. Pritchett."

"Are there any specific aspects of your marriage you'd like to see different than they are now?"

"Well, Wayne hurt his back, and he's been getting disability, so he doesn't have to go to work. We thought it would be nice for him to be able to stay home and work in the garden, and he was going to add a room onto our mobile home, make it more like a real house."

Out of the corner of his eye, Wayne could see her glance over at him. He kept looking at his boot, even though the fly had departed.

Fern sighed, continued in a determined tone. "But then he started getting, like, cabin fever. So I was glad when he started going to the library. It was, you know, something for him to do to pass the time?"

Pass the time hell! It had been exciting, discovering the Internet. He wasn't an outgoing man, liked to keep to himself most of the time. When he did have to deal with others, it stayed on a hot-weather-we've-been-having level. So it was amazing to discover so many people out there on the net who shared his interests. Damned if he'd talk about that here. The Internet forums were his work, his mission.

Fern's voice went on and on. "Then Wayne started having these terrible dreams. He'd wake up screaming like the devil was after him. And last Thursday, he didn't come home from his appointment with you. If he even *had* an appointment with you."

Dr. Pritchett shot Wayne a brief, intense look, composed his face and nodded. "How did you feel when your husband didn't come home?"

"Well, I was scared! Like, afraid he'd been in an accident. But then I figured he would've called me, or the police would have, you know, if Wayne was hurt real bad or something. But nobody called me. Finally, the next day I got ahold of the police and reported the car missing." She paused, looked nervously at Wayne.

"Go on, Fern. You tell your side of things first. Then Wayne will have a chance to talk."

"Well, I didn't hear anything from the police that whole day. Then on Friday afternoon they called and said they'd found the car in San Antonio. And not half an hour after that, Wayne walks in the door and tells me he's been in Houston the whole time."

Dr. Pritchett said, "Uh huh," and then just waited. The silence stretched on. Wayne sneaked a look and saw that Dr. Pritchett was watching Fern, not smiling, not frowning.

Fern took a deep breath and for a moment squeezed her eyes tight shut. "See, Dr. Pritchett, Wayne stopped being interested in, in, you know...being intimate...about when he got interested in going to the library. I thought it was just because of his back hurting. But now, I don't know. I can put two and two together, and I'm pretty sure he's seeing another woman."

Wayne wanted to shout her accusation down, but God knows

what he'd been doing, that was the terrible thing. He shivered. They were both looking at him now, like they wanted him to say something.

"She doesn't believe me, but it's God's truth. I don't know what I was doing in San Antonio. One minute I was sitting here in your office and then...next thing I know, I'm in this park in San Antonio without any idea how I got there or where the car is. I figured I must've left the car in Houston."

"Wayne! You promised you'd—"

"Hold on a moment, Fern." Dr. Pritchett held up a hand. "Part of communicating is listening. Wayne, are there any other times you've suffered memory loss?"

"Well, I wouldn't really call it memory *loss*. I just couldn't say exactly what I'd been doing is all." Wayne cracked his knuckles. "Hasn't really happened since I was a little kid. Well, once or twice after my first wife died."

"I believe you, Wayne." The doctor reached toward Wayne as if to touch him, seemed to think better of it, turned to Fern. "Sometimes when people go through a very stressful situation—it could be some sort of disaster, or abuse suffered as a child, or a war—whatever the event is, it's something so horrible the person has to use extraordinary means to deal with it."

This guy's fulla shit, thought Wayne, disgusted. I didn't go through anything like that. Maybe when Melody died, but not before that. And I was forgetting things way before Melody died. But he kept his mouth shut. The doctor was backing up his story, that's what mattered right now.

"You'd hope that once the hurricane passed, or the child abuse stopped, or the war was over, then the person could go back to being the way they were before. But sometimes it doesn't work that way. Sometimes the horrible event just keeps happening over and over in the person's mind. We call it Post Traumatic Stress Disorder. One of the symptoms people sometimes have is just plain forgetting the bad things."

Fern's expression was pleading. "Can you fix it?"

I'm not a fucking wrecked car, thought Wayne. I've a good

mind to just get up and walk out. But he kept sitting there.

"There are things we can do to help. If that's what Wayne wants."

In an instant of freezing clarity, he realized he faced a choice. He had his land, and the disability payments were enough to live on. Barely. If he lived a very simple life. But he didn't want to be alone. He thought of the way it had been after Melody died. Crawling into bed at night, he never knew whether he'd wake up the next morning or a week later. Fern had helped him get his life back together. He didn't want to lose her. She was looking at him now, so concerned, like she really *cared*.

"Yes," he told them both, the words choking in his throat, "that's what I want. I'd like to figure out what's wrong with me so I can live a normal life, be a good husband." Long as I don't have to talk about certain things.

"Good." Dr. Pritchett smiled reassuringly. "I'll want to do a session or two with each of you alone."

"I can come in any time before or after work, depending if I'm on morning or afternoon shift." Fern smiled at Dr. Pritchett and tugged her skirt down over her knees.

"That'll be fine, Fern. Now I'd like you to take some material to read that I think will help...."

Wayne tuned out their conversation and looked around the room to see what else was new since last time. A picture hung on the wall, splotches of paint like somebody puked up their breakfast. Pritchett had a little light shining on it, looked like a bird perched up on top of the picture frame. If he squinted his eyes just right, the picture looked sort of like when you lay under the trees and looked up through the leaves at the sun.

"Will that be all right with you, Wayne?"

He jerked his attention back.

"Nathan wanted to know if you could come in next Tuesday at eleven." Fern was looking at him impatiently.

"Yeah." He nodded. So it's Nathan now, is it? "Yeah, next week is fine."

"Eleven in the morning," Fern said.

"I'll make appointment cards." Dr. Pritchett walked over to his desk.

"Thank you, Nathan." Fern followed Nathan, leaving Wayne to stare up at the painting again. He could almost hear the birds singing and the wind skittering through the leaves.

"But...I'm not sure we'll be able to afford this." Fern's voice seemed to come from a long time ago. Wayne forced himself to focus on her, homed in on her orange and brown blouse.

"Don't worry about it." Nathan put a reassuring hand on Fern's arm. "I'm willing to work with you on the fees. You can pay them out over time."

Wayne walked out holding hands with his wife for the first time in months. Sitting in the passenger seat, watching her adjust the rearview mirror, a horrible vision flashed across his mind: standing in his daddy's old workshop, putting together bombs. He had a chilling, nauseating thought. And dead people.

Maybe that was the thing hiding in the nightmares.

CHAPER 38: MONDAY, JUNE 2

If she could make it into her office without seeing anyone, she'd grab a few minutes reviewing the files before she handed the work off to Art. Through the small staff kitchen's open door, a nasal voice slashed at her. "Hey, Jill, not even a 'Good morning'?"

Ambushed. "Sorry, Becca. Didn't mean to be rude." The managing partner's secretary was sitting at the table, an open copy of Danielle Steele's *The Promise* face down next to an empty carton of pineapple yogurt with a spoon in it.

"Art wants to talk to you soon as you come in." Becca jerked her head toward the front offices. Silver earrings jingled, but her well-sprayed helmet of black hair remained locked in place.

"Let me just put my things away, and—" Jill edged away.

"Do you have the Reese Biotech files?"

"Yes. I took them home to work on them."

"Art wants me to get them from you." Becca smiled pleasantly, which did not bode well for Jill.

Jill shrugged, too tired to ask questions, set her briefcase on the carpeted floor beside Becca. "The files are in here."

Her head ached. She'd only gotten four hours sleep, after talking for two hours to Paul about cancer treatments, then staying up late to organize the files for Reese Biotech L.P. v. Blick Pharmaceuticals, Inc. She forced herself not to think about Paul. He was friendly enough, and gave her new hope for Alex, but there'd been no slightest indication that he'd ever see her as anything other than a pal. She felt a sudden craving for chocolate chip cookies.

§

The eastern wall of Arthur Sutton's office was almost entirely windows. Standing in front of Art's massive mahogany desk, Jill squinted against the glaring sunlight.

"Sit down, Jill," he said, without smiling. "How is your son?"

"Alex gets tired easily. I may have to take him out of school." The chair was so low Jill's head barely cleared the top of the desk. Executive Psychological Warfare 101. "We don't know yet how well the chemotherapy is working. I'm taking him in for a checkup next week."

"Good." He nodded, shuffled some papers and cleared his throat. "We, ah, think it's important to have a life outside of work, and we've always been generous with granting family leave to our staff." He looked down at Jill, pinching his lips together.

"Yes, you have." Jill suddenly remembered what it felt like to bring home a report card not good enough to please her mother. Now she had the same tightness in her chest, the same roiling stomach.

"We understand that you want the best medical care for your son, and it would be fine for you to miss a day or two of work now and then if you were a student law clerk. But it's just not acceptable to reschedule depositions and mediation sessions, as Becca tells me you've done."

"Art, I asked to reschedule *one* deposition from 10:00 in the morning to 2:00 in the afternoon. In any event, I shouldn't have to take much time off from now on. I can take Alex for his appointments on weekends."

Art looked doubtful. "You're a good lawyer, Jill. We all like you, and we're willing to be flexible within reason. We'll see how it goes over the next few weeks." He carefully wrote in the open file that lay on his desk. Jill found it difficult to take in what she was hearing. At a seminar she had attended the previous year one of the speakers had discussed the procedures to be used when firing employees. Progressive discipline. Warnings, all written down in the file.

Art looked up, told her, "There's something that could be even more serious. You're aware, of course, that BlickPharm is being sued by Reese Biotech for patent infringement."

"Of course. I was organizing the files last night for the depositions this afternoon."

"Are you aware that the oncologist who has been treating your son, Dr. Arecchi, is on the Board of Directors of the corporate general partner Reese Biotech?"

What? "No, I wasn't."

"Well, now you are. Technically there may not be a conflict of interest." He shrugged his eyebrows. "I'm sure you can imagine how it would look if word got out that one of BlickPharm's professionals was using the services of someone associated with the opponent."

She was dumbfounded by the blatancy of it. "No, really I can't, Art. It's not as though Dr. Arecchi is a party to the lawsuit."

"Look, Jill. I'd love to spend the morning arguing the fine points of legal ethics with you, but unfortunately I have previous engagements. Mr. Blick wants you off the case. It's that simple."

She'd heard rumors that Bruce Blick had snoops and spies checking up on anything he considered his business. Until now she had never quite believed it. BlickPharm were the *good* guys.

Yet how else could they know which doctors were treating Alex?

"I'm sorry, Art but I didn't think—"

He raised his voice very slightly. "Thank you, Ms. Shannon. We'll see how things work out. Getting rid of the Reese case should help you get caught up with everything else. If you're able to keep up with a normal workload for the next couple of months, I'll feel comfortable going back to business as usual. But we are not a charitable organization. As was explained to you in your first interview, we have no choice but to require a minimum number of billable hours from our professional staff. We'd be in bankruptcy if we didn't. Ms. Shannon, as much as I wish it were otherwise, if you cannot meet our standards, I'm afraid we're going to have to let you go."

"Oh." Jill was too dazed to argue.

"By the way," he went on, as though unaware that he had just snatched the rug from beneath Jill's feet, "since you won't have to worry about the Reese case anymore, I've volunteered you to help Preston Bowie with a class action suit he's putting together. You can even do some of the work on Allen-Hoffman time. That should bring you up to forty hours per week."

How generous, she thought bitterly. Preston would load her down with enough work for two people and expect her to get it done on her own time. She took a breath, opened her mouth to protest, but Art Sutton was looking at his watch.

"That's all." He removed his eyeglasses and stood up, extending his right hand. "I do wish you the best of luck, Jill. You and your son."

39: SATURDAY, JUNE 7

A car pulled up to the curb as Jill was weeding her small herb garden.

Alex, dozing in the hammock, suddenly came to life. "Mom, look! It's Paul!"

Peering out the window of his dented yellow Nissan, Paul

was grinning as if he or the car were some huge joke. Jill felt a rush of gladness. He called, "Hey, guys, feel like going for a ride? I'd like to show you something."

"I...." Jill looked down in dismay at her baggy jeans and stained yellow tee shirt. "I need to change my clothes."

"Not at all. What you have on now is perfect."

"Me too? Can I go too?" Alex surprised Jill by running across the yard. She hadn't seen him display this much energy in a long time.

"Absolutely you too."

"How do you like my cap?" Alex struck a proud pose.

Paul walked behind Alex so he could see the front of the cap. "Texas Longhorns. Showing the old school spirit, eh?"

"I have to wear it since my hair fell out. To keep from getting a sunburned head."

"Looks good on you." Paul leaned over, opened the passenger door. "You don't mind sitting in the back, do you, buddy?"

"Nah. I can lie down and rest."

"How you going?" he asked as Jill settled into the passenger seat.

"Not wonderful, actually," she said. "My managing partner gave me a hard time about taking Alex to Dr. Arecchi."

"Huh? How's that any concern of theirs?"

"Dr. Arechhi's on the Board of Directors of a company that's on our largest client's shit list. One of their products is giving our client a run for its money." She shook her head wearily. "So now I'm on the client's shit list as well. I think the firm's looking for an excuse to get rid of me. They've also assigned me to do a bunch of pro bono work for Preston Bowie."

"Hey, I saw him on television. A major Green advocate, right?"

"Yep, and one of the world's biggest assholes. It would be awfully convenient for them if I quit. That way I wouldn't be able to apply for unemployment comp."

"Damn!"

"Oh well." Enough of this gloom and doom, Jill, she told

herself. "So how's your research going?"

"More fascinating every day. Keep this to yourself, Jill, but it looks as though we're onto something that can...." He broke off, took a deep breath, gave her a dazzling, wildly excited grin. "Well, um, let me put this as modestly as I can. Something that should be able to tune up an ordinary human into a genius. But wait, there's more. Along with the extra set of steak knives, we'll throw in a life span of a hundred and fifty years or more."

He was joking of course. Hard to tell. Australians were weird.

"Smart mice, and now a century and a half life span?"

"This is the most amazing part yet. In fact, I'm not sure I should tell you—you'll think I'm nuts."

"No, come on, Paul. I promise not to call the men in white."

Apparently he was regretting his manic outburst. "You really should come by the lab sometime and see for yourself. I'll bet Alex would get a kick out of seeing the mice."

Jill turned to the back seat, but Alex was lying down, asleep.

40: SATURDAY, JUNE 7

Paul parked at the top of the hill, just in case. The old car was getting more crotchety by the day. The rocky land sloping down to the creek was brilliant with yellow wild flowers after recent rain.

Jill looked down toward the creek, smiling radiantly. "It's lovely," she said. He realized, with a shock, that her illuminated face was quite beautiful, somehow more deeply affecting because of its imperfection.

"Alex?" He watched her reach into the back seat and gently touch the top of her boy's head. "We're here. Do you feel like going for a walk?"

"Sure." The boy sat up, rubbing his eyes.

"Let's go then," said Paul. "I want to show you something wonderful down in the creek bed. This way."

Alex stumbled once or twice. Paul squatted down. "I've been

told I make a pretty good horse. Grab hold around my neck and let's see how it goes."

"Hey, good view from up here!" Alex said happily.

They walked the rest of the way to the creek mostly in silence. Paul pointed out plants that had been used as food or medicine by the hunter-gatherers who had lived in the area over five hundred years ago. They rounded a curve of the creek bed, saw the paintings on the rock.

"Wow!" Alex whispered.

"How remarkable! I had no idea there were paintings like this in Texas!" Jill's amazed reaction was all Paul could have hoped for.

Despite the bright sun, this desert air held a touch of chill. Paul stood beside a small pool at the bottom of a sinkhole formed when the ceiling of an underground cave gave way thousands of years ago. On the other side of the pool, higher than eye level, gracefully abstract men and beasts roamed through hills and forests, rendered in black and various shades of red, yellow and orange.

"When those paintings were created," Jill said, shaking her head in awe, "ground level must have been four or five feet higher."

He rubbed at the bristles of his beard with the back of his hand. She was obviously as swept up in the enchantment as he'd been when he first found this hidden place. An anthropologist friend had told him about the people whose names and language had been forgotten long before the Spanish began to explore Texas. All that was left of them were a few flint tools, their paintings, and their middens, preserved by the dry air of the caves for hundreds of years.

Paul smiled. Don't get too carried away, he told himself. Probably Jill would be disgusted if she knew what had first drawn him here. Lauren certainly had been, after one disastrous conversation. Analyzing the refuse of these ancient people—stems and seeds of plants, animal bones, human feces—anthropologists had learned that they used medicinal herbs to treat diarrhea. Inevitably, Paul had found himself wondering if these old paintings might contain clues to other medicinal plants.

"This is *wonderful*," Jill said. "You continue to amaze me, Dr. Gibson. Mild-mannered research pharmacist by day, bold paleoethnobotanist on the weekend."

He grinned back at her. "Well, you know, I *am* fascinated by the ingenious ways ancient peoples used plants.' He paused, looking for the right words. "I was...well, captivated by the spiritual mood of the place. On my first visit, I sat here hardly breathing for the longest time, not wanting to break the spell."

She closed her eyes and let the silence stand. "I wonder what sort of music they had," she said, then. "What their language sounded like.... And they must have had some form of commerce. And, you know, law."

"Right. The pigments they used in the paintings came from a couple of hundred miles east of here." Alex was leaning against his leg. "Hey, kiddo, you look sleepy. Time to head home?"

"If I can have a ride on my horsie again," Alex said. He sounded exhausted but at ease.

§

Paul turned the ignition key. Nothing happened.

"Watch this." He pushed in the clutch. "No engine, Ma." The car began to roll down the hill, picked up speed. He released the clutch. With a shudder, the engine caught.

"Good thing you knew what to do." Jill laughed in rueful admiration. "Long walk to the nearest bus station."

That's why I like being with her, Paul realized. She's interested in the world around her, and she's a good sport. She's just...fun to be with. And so's the kid. God, he thought, it's so damned unfair. In three or four years we'll finally have some meaningful cancer treatments through phase three trials. It's going to hurt like hell, watching that kid die, knowing we're on the very edge of a cure, not being able to do a damned thing about it. Or worse: being *able* to, but not being *allowed* to.

41: SATURDAY, JUNE 7

Wayne pushed the pillow away from his face, rolled over and squinted at the alarm clock: eleven o'clock. Fern had left for work hours earlier. He'd been asleep for fifteen hours. Wasn't there something important he had to do today? He couldn't remember.

When he sat up the room seemed to rotate under him. Just go back to sleep. No, he needed a drink; his mouth felt as dry and sticky as a peanut butter sandwich without the jelly. He eased himself out of bed, leaned against the nightstand to keep from falling, shuffled slowly to the bathroom.

A splash of cold water on his face and a long, cool drink worked wonders. It came back to him. He was determined to read *Awakening the Genius Inside You,* even if it took all day and night to do it. A cup of coffee, and he'd be ready to tackle it. With the book's help he would strengthen his mind enough to fight off this madness threatening to take over his life.

Exercise 2-1: Recapturing the Power of the Child

The purpose of this exercise is to help you reach back in time and experience how it felt to be a little child just learning to walk. If it's possible for you to revisit the actual place where you lived as a child, this is often very helpful. Or perhaps you have toys you played with as a child, maybe a favorite book your parents used to read to you. If none of these is available, you can still reach back in time, but it might be more difficult.

Choose a time for this exercise when you can sit quietly and concentrate without any fear of interruption....

Wayne closed his eyes and tried to relax every muscle in his body, beginning with his head and working down to his toes. He imagined himself drifting backwards through the years of his life, growing younger and younger. I am only a year old, he told himself.

Nothing happened, except that he developed an intense itch on the bottom of his right foot. The hell with it.

Important! This is an interactive book. You must do the exercises as they are assigned. Skipping the exercises and reading ahead in the book will void the guarantee we made to you in the introduction.

Shit. He might as well walk down the road to the old farmhouse, try again. He could sit in the front yard instead of the back. Maybe he'd be able to capture the spirit of his child-self in the front yard.

§

Through the odors of rotting wood and dust he could smell the memory of sugary vanilla and chocolate.

I guess houses are haunted by memories of the living, Wayne thought, as much as by ghosts of the dead. His father was in the nursing home in LaGrange. His mother, far as he knew, lived somewhere in South Dakota, at least that's where she was last time he got a Christmas card from her. But she was here in this farmhouse too, standing by the kitchen counter.

"Happy birthday to you, Happy birthday to you." *The enthusiasm in Mom's voice made up for her inability to carry a tune.*

She's made his favorite cake, angel food with chocolate frosting. Wayne smiles, reaches out for the plate Mom holds out to him. The heavy sound of Dad's step in the hallway causes Wayne's whole body to tense up, and he forgets to take the plate.

"Got a special present for you, son...."

"No!" Wayne said aloud. He crossed the kitchen, passed

through the door his father had entered all those years ago. It was dark and smelled bad. The dog had stayed outside, spooked as always by the place. He turned on the flashlight so he could find his way along the hallway. First door on the right would have been Rob's room. Wayne felt the warm, gritty little-brother hand holding his own, tight and trusting, crossing the highway to check the mailbox. In memory he smelled newly mown grass and bluebonnets. Mom left Rob's room untouched for years, like someday he might turn up and say he'd only been joking and wasn't dead after all. Now, Wayne saw, Rob's room was almost empty. Dad had donated a lot of stuff to the church when he went into the nursing home. A couple of Rob's baseball posters still clung to the wall. One had fallen, leaving a darker rectangle where it had protected the wallpaper from fading. Mom had yelled at him to get out of her baby's room. Like she thought it was Wayne's fault. When he tried to tell her he wasn't even there when Rob drowned she started crying and told him to keep quiet.

The flashlight flickered in the gloom. Mom and Dad's bedroom. Wayne walked quickly past without touching the door. Four years old, he'd woken up in the middle of the night with an ear ache so painful he thought his head was splitting in two. He'd knocked on Mom and Dad's door. No one answered. He gathered up his courage, turned the knob, pushed the door open just enough to squeeze through. Dad yelling, jumping out of bed, hands lashing. Next thing Wayne knew, it wasn't night time any longer, he was sitting up in bed eating a bowl of Campbell's Chicken Noodle soup.

That was me, someone said.

Wayne shuddered, and the flashlight beam swayed crazily. Nobody. He hadn't heard anything. The place was empty, had been empty for years. Just his imagination. He stopped at the last door on the right, his room. Vines had grown over the windows, filtering the sunlight to a dim greenish glow. He stood in the doorway, just looking. When he closed his eyes it was exactly the way it had been when he was sixteen: twin bed against the wall to the right, brown and white bedspread with cowboy motif that he'd had since he was five years old, dresser against the left wall, wooden box under the window. Toy box when he was a little boy, treasure box when he was older. It was hard, though, hard to put himself into the room.

"Gotta remember being a little kid," he thought, concentrating on the exercise from the book. "Gotta recapture the power of the child learning to walk." It was hard, hard to remember back that far. About the earliest memory he could scrape up was Dad teaching him to shoot a gun. Wayne must've been about six or seven.

"This finger on the trigger, keep your eyes on the spot you're aiming for." Wayne felt slightly nauseated, remembering.

I came then too, the voice insisted. Would've blown off his ugly head if I thought I could get away with it.

Shit, stay focused, Wayne told himself, swaying in the doorway. What had it been like to be a little kid, looking around at a fresh new world? Mommy and Daddy standing out in the front yard. He'd been lying in bed...right...there. Daddy hit Mommy's face. Blood running down Mommy's chin. He'd climbed out of bed and run to the front door as fast as he could go. The chilly memory of the soles of his feet on the wood floor as he toddled down the hallway, going to rescue Mommy.

Daddy's as big as a giant, and Wayne remembers the story Mommy read to him about Jack and the beanstalk. Jack ran from the giant, but Wayne runs smack into Daddy and pummels the huge legs with his tiny fists.

"Don't you hurt my mommy!" he screams. Daddy lifts him by his pajama top and flings him against the wall, and a pain more horrible than anything Wayne has ever imagined shoots through his head and down through his back.

"Mommy!" he cries. But she does not come. A giant hand rises up, comes down against the side of his face.

"Don't you ever hit me again, boy. You understand?"

Wayne tries to stand up, but his legs don't work right. A feeling inside him says wordlessly, someday we'll get even with him. He deserves death. Someday we'll kill him.

Trembling and sick, Wayne walked back down the dark hallway, leaned against the back door, taking huge, gulping breaths of fresh air. Fuck the power of the child, he thought. Fuck this whole book.

The voice in his head shouted at him: You can't get rid of me so easily.

42: MONDAY, JUNE 9

The death sentence was imposed on her little boy in soft, apologetic tones. Jill thought she had prepared herself for the worst, but she was wrong.

"The chemo isn't working as well as we had hoped. The tumor has grown slightly since the last scan."

Jill nodded mechanically, thinking: No! This can't be right.

"We often see some tumor growth during the first few weeks of low-dose chemo. But in Alex's case, the tumor cells don't seem to be affected any more than the normal cells. We could increase the dosage, but Alex's immune system is already compromised."

"How long, Dr. Collins? How much longer will my little boy live?"

"We can't predict with anything with certainty, Jill. Alex could live for another year, or he could have as little as three months."

"Oh god, isn't there anything else we can do?"

The doctor looked at her with sympathy, shaking his head. "I'm sorry, Jill."

Her stomach knotted, but it didn't feel like the period she was expecting. As she left the room, tears clouding her eyes, she reached into her handbag for a Tampax. But when she visited the bathroom, she put it back. Not her period after all. God, if I'm not early I'm late. She shook her head. At least it's not because I'm pregnant, she thought with a certain bitter resignation. Keith had two new children; she had only Alex.

43: MONDAY, JUNE 9

Alex lay on the floor in Dr. Collins's kids' room, waiting for his mother to come out of the office. Maybe I'm going to die soon, he thought. It was not a particularly alarming thought, although he would miss his mother.

Someone larger than his mother came into the room and stood near the door.

"Paul!" He sat up too fast, made himself dizzy.

"Hey Alex, my man, how's life?"

"It's okay." The room spun around a little. "I got a checkup today, and Mom's in the office talking to Dr. Collins."

"If you feel up to it, and if your mom has time, I'd like to show you guys an experiment a friend of mine is working on."

"I feel fine." It was true. He did feel fine, now. He hoped mom would say yes. He was pretty sure she would, because she liked Paul a lot. He could tell by the way she laughed and looked happy all the time she was with him.

"How's summer camp?"

"Mmm, it's okay." Alex shrugged. "I get tired, though. The teacher told my mom I'd have to quit going if I don't get better." He felt bad, remembering how serious his mother looked when the teacher said that. Mom was worried about him, but also she was worried about losing her job if she had to stay home all day and take care of him, Alex knew, because he heard her talking to Aunt Carol on the phone when she didn't know he was listening. He tried not to act tired at camp, but sometimes he just couldn't hold his stupid looking bald head up any longer.

"Most people feel better after the chemotherapy is over with." Paul poked his head out the door. "Here comes your mom."

The grownups all said "Hello, how are you" to each other. Mom looked tense but she wasn't crying, so Alex guessed Dr. Collins hadn't told her he was going to die next week or anything. When Paul asked Mom if she'd like to visit the lab, she said yes, if Alex wasn't too tired.

"I'm not tired at all," he assured her, and she hugged him. But her eyes were sad. Dr. Collins must not have had good news.

44: MONDAY, JUNE 9

Paul seemed as proud of the place, she thought, as if he owned it. "UT Health Sciences is working in partnership with MJT Labs," he said. When she cocked her head enquiringly, he said, "That's a private research lab. Part of the deal is, they get to use our microscope. See, a good scanning electron microscope costs hundreds of thousands of dollars, so it makes sense to get as much use out of it as possible."

The electron microscope had a room of its own. The device took up one whole wall; it would have resembled a desk with an ordinary computer monitor and keyboard except for the boxlike specimen chamber and three foot high electron gun.

A slight young man with an intelligent face and straight black hair rose from the chair in front of the monitor, smiling. She remembered him from the snack room down the hall. My god, she thought, was that only three weeks ago? "This must be Jill and Alex. Paul has told me so much about you both, it's nice meet you. I'm Drew."

He smiled shyly, giving Jill's hand a firm shake. She instinctively liked him.

"Let me put up something interesting on the display for you. Would you like to sit down, Alex, so you can see it better?"

Jill nodded her permission; Alex sat in the chair while she looked over his shoulder.

"This is the optic lobe of the brain of an ordinary fruit fly, magnified 5,000 times," Drew said.

On the screen, miniature leafless trees grew along the inside of the bowl of a golden chalice.

"Now...." Drew reached over Alex's shoulder to enter instructions on the keyboard. "Here's the same thing from a fruit fly I treated with the artificial chromosome pair Paul and I are working on. Notice anything different?"

"More squiggly lines," Alex ventured.

"Yes." Drew shot him a rewarding smile. "Those structures are called dendrites. They're involved in transmitting electrical impulses from one brain cell to another."

Jill found herself becoming interested. "So would this fly see better than the untreated one?" It made a welcome distraction from her overwhelming anxiety about Alex.

"Frankly, we don't know yet. It's difficult to design an experiment to test the visual acuity of a fruit fly. So I asked Paul here to help me out with those pet mice of his. He's told you about the mice?"

"That they've gotten smarter? Yeah," Jill said. "Extraordinary."

"We'd expected it, since the genes we're studying are pretty much identical in a wide range of organisms, from fruit flies to humans. They're conserved by evolution, you see? It's very exciting to see our predictions validated in the lab. But the thing that's really blowing our minds is the lifespan extension. Has Paul told you about that?"

The century and a half thing? Good grief. "You mean you really weren't joking?"

"I was afraid you'd think I'm a complete loon." Paul smiled, halfway serious.

"I'm still reserving judgment. Tell me more."

"Look, why don't you and Alex visit my lab in Austin and meet my Algernon mice? If you arrive after five, you can park in the lot and they won't tow you away."

"I don't know." Medical science was not high on her list of favorite topics right now. Chemotherapy had failed Alex. Maybe the Nature Forever people were right after all. "Raincheck, okay?"

45: MONDAY, JUNE 9

Every time Wayne dozed off, he found himself in a circular metal vault with only one way out, a locked door. Enclosed in the vault with him was a creature Wayne was afraid to look at.

But sleep crept up on him, and the monster approached with slow, sly, terrible steps. Wayne shuffled away, scuttled sideways so he could watch the monster out of the corner of his eye. The horrible thing kept pace, maintaining a consistent distance between them; but Wayne knew that the instant he fell asleep, the thing would be on top of him.

He broke into an all-out panic-stricken run. The creature's breath fell cold upon the back of his neck, an odor of dead fish. He tried to scream, to reach out for Fern. His arms wouldn't move, his voice was a hoarse squeak.

He ceased to exist.

"Wayne, honey, are you okay?" Fern put a hand on his arm.

Payback drew back, as from a slimy crawling thing. "I can't sleep," he said. "Think I'll go for a walk." He could hear her crying softly as he left the room. He dressed quickly in the bathroom, pulled on Wayne's boots, went out into the night. When Gretchen nosed curiously at his foot, he kicked the dog away.

§

Payback liked the old farmhouse with its squeaky floor boards and musty odor. He especially liked being here at night. When him and Wayne were kids, he used to prowl around when everyone else was asleep. In the night he was king of the place. He'd tell himself that if Wayne's daddy ever caught him, he'd kill the old coot on the spot.

Tonight he had no time for aimless prowling. He went straight for Wayne's childhood bedroom. His most vivid memory of this room was of Wayne whacking off under the bed covers, worrying that it might be true that you'd go blind if you did it too often, or turn into a moron. Payback snorted to himself. Wayne had turned out so fucking stupid it wasn't even funny!

The secret place in the closet had been Wayne's, but Payback knew all about it, as he knew everything about Wayne. You pushed at a section of the door molding from several different directions, gradually working it loose. When a gap widened enough to slip a knife blade in, you gently pried the molding out, and there was a hole big enough to hold several *Hustler* magazines and other more personal secrets.

Shining the light into the hole, Payback angrily thought for a moment that the hiding place was empty, pilfered in his absence. No, wait, it was still there, curled and faded with age, the color photograph of a pretty teenage cheerleader caught in mid-leap, her mouth open in laughter, wheat colored hair fanning out like smoke around her head, well formed legs spread wide. A bright red megaphone rested on the ground beside her. Along its length, white letters spelled out: GO TIGERS! Signed at the bottom of the photo in peacock blue ink, barely legible now: *To Wayne, My love forever, Melody.*

Payback wept over the photograph. Even though Melody never even knew he existed, he loved her.

"I'll make them pay, baby. Like I did before."

Time to go to work seriously on Doctor fucking miracle medical science Chang.

46: WEDNESDAY, JUNE 11

High ceilings, green tiled walls, and an overpowering odor were Jill's first impression as she pushed open the door of the Experimental Science Building. A guard sat in the entryway behind a sign that advised "All Visitors Must Sign In."

"What's that smell?" Alex wrinkled his nose.

"Acetone, I think."

"What's acetone? Oh, look, Mom!" He pulled Jill toward a colorful display on a bulletin board as the guard handed her an

ID badge. Grinning, she followed him. These days Alex spent so much time lying around listlessly, it was wonderful to see him interested in something. The chemo had knocked the poor kid around, and he got depressed every time he saw his bald reflection or heard some other kid sniggering at the way he looked.

He pointed to a series of photographs of white mice and read aloud, "'How To Make a Knockout Mouse'.... Hey Mom, look at this! They're changing the DNA in this mouse." He seized her hand, "Dr. Collins says I got cancer because some of my DNA got messed up. He says scientists like Drew and Paul are trying to find ways to fix it up again. They'll figure out a way to make me better, Mom, I know they will."

"I think you're right, sweetie." Guiltily and conflicted, Jill remembered the petition she had drafted for Nature Forever, asking Congress to outlaw the very research that might yet save her son's life.

They rode a creaky elevator to the third floor, found the open door to Paul's office partially hidden between two large wooden crates labeled with low-level chemical hazard signs. Jill paused to collect her thoughts, fingers dragging through her hair, but Alex barged in gleefully.

"Alex! Where's your Mom?" She watched Paul set aside the paper he had been reading and put an arm around her son.

"I'm right here." Hearing his voice, seeing his affection, Jill was suddenly optimistic, confident that she could deal with any problem. Paul had that effect on her, she realized.

"We've come to see the mice!" Alex shouted.

"Well then, let's go to the lab."

47: WEDNESDAY, JUNE 11

The lab Paul used was in the pharmacy annex, a much newer building than Experimental Sciences, with spotlessly white walls and highly polished vinyl flooring. In a white, somewhat stained lab coat, Paul showed them the built-in room-sized cooler, the warm room, and his lab bench, cluttered with plastic and glass bottles.

"Science labs are only neat and tidy in the movies," he told them. "This is what they look like in real life."

"Where are the super mice?" Alex asked impatiently.

"This way." Paul opened a door at the end of the lab. "We have stricter housekeeping procedures for this room. With so many animals living in a relatively small area, we need to keep it very clean to minimize the danger of infection. Right now each mouse shares a pen with another mouse, because we're watching to see how their auxosome treatment affects social behavior." Two walls of the room were lined with stainless steel mesh pens. "You know what that means, Alex? How they get on with each other."

"Can I pet them?"

"We prefer not to handle them any more than necessary, Alex. We don't want to cause stress."

"Well, I wasn't planning to *hurt* them."

"Of course not. I know you weren't. But imagine how you'd feel if a hundred foot tall giant reached down and picked you up. Even if it was the nicest giant in the world, it'd be scary."

"Like King Kong."

"Exactly. Tell you what. You can help me feed them and give them fresh water. Watch me do the first one, then you can try it."

"He's looking at me!" Alex laughed delightedly. "Come 'ere, Mom!"

Jill peered into the pen. A brown mouse was standing on its hind legs watching Alex, nose quivering.

"I think it likes you, Alex." Jill felt a burst of happiness.

"You know, I believe it does," said Paul. "I've never seen the mice so excited. I think they realize they have guests they've never met before. Since they've been getting the retrotransposon, they seem to crave novelty. I should set up a telly for them to watch." He laughed.

"What's that lump in its neck?"

"That's the osmotic pump, Alex. We use it to deliver exactly the right dosage to the brain at constant levels."

"Doesn't it hurt?"

"No, I'm glad to say. As far as we can tell the mouse can't feel it at all. But we're working now on a better way to get the synthetic chromosomes into the mouse's brain cells. Then we won't have to use the pump at all." He stepped to the end of the block of pens. "These mice in the pens with the red tags are special. I found these five very old mice—"

"How old do mice get?"

"Well, these ones'd be sort of like eighty or ninety year old people. Not expected to live much longer."

"Like me," Alex said in rare burst of bitterness.

Looking uncomfortable, Paul reached out and squeezed the boy's arm. "Don't give up just yet, mate. Most of the untreated mice in this group already died of old age. These guys've been getting treatment for three weeks so far, and something surprising's happened. Look closely at them. Do you see anything strange?"

Like the rest, the five mice in the specially marked pens seemed excited to see their guests. A couple stood on their hind legs, poking eagerly twitching noses through the wire mesh; another ran back and forth across the front of its pen.

"Look just the same as the others to me," said Alex, his thin face still dreary.

"Indeed. That's what's strange. Before I treated them, the hair around their faces was losing its color. Two were getting quite bald. They'd all lost muscle mass—you know, they were skinny, even though I gave them plenty of food. And they had very little energy. Mostly they just lay around. See the white one there?"

Alex nodded, suddenly smiling as the mouse in question jumped into the exercise wheel and set it spinning.

"That old fellow had a tumor on his stomach the size of my fingernail." Paul held out a pinky.

Alex squatted down and peered into the pen. "I can't see it. He's running too fast."

"You wouldn't see anything even if he were standing still. Tumor's gone without a trace."

"That's amazing!" Jill glanced from the mice to Alex. "When will you be authorized to try it on people?"

Paul gave her a bleak glance. "Not for a while, sorry, we shouldn't get our hopes up too much. I'll need to watch these animals for at least a year, if they live that long. It's the only way to check the long-term effects of the drugs." He rubbed at his beard, peering into the cage in front of him. "There are another two teams trialing this general method at other labs. What's strange is, they report some retardation of the aging processes, but neither of them mentions reversing it. Jill, these animals are showing every sign of getting *younger*. Genuine rejuvenation." He coughed, rolling his eyes. "I speak loosely, you understand."

"I won't quote you in court, doctor. What's causing the difference—the artificial chromosomes, right?"

"That's my strong suspicion. I expected the auxosome to boost their intelligence by stimulating brain cell abundance, but the effect seems to have generalized. The gene enhancements seem to reverse at least some parts of the aging process. Might be the mitochondrial proof-reading. Sorry, mitochondria are—"

"What's an 'oxuh-zohm'?" Alex asked, still watching the lively mice. "Does it make them as strong as an ox?"

Paul laughed with delight. "Where have you seen an ox, cobber? On TV?"

"At the petting zoo," the boy said blandly. At Paul's momentary

double-take, he shrieked with laughter. "Hey, gotcha!"

Comically rueful, Paul reached down and shook Alex's hand. "Well done, my good man. It's a word I made up. 'Auxo-' is Greek for 'growth'." He looked at Jill across the top of the cage. "We synthesized a double chromosome strand. An auxiliary string of genetic code that does what the preacher ordered. Is that an American phrase? I think I heard it in a movie."

"What's a chromosome, Mom?"

"A set of instructions that control the way the cells in your body grow," Paul told him. "Billions of them."

"Like DNA?"

"Exactly. In fact, chromosomes are made of DNA and protein."

"Dr. Collins told me about DNA. He said my DNA gave me my blue eyes."

"Yep. We get a set of 23 chromosomes from our Mom and another set of 23 from our Dad. The two sets match up and work together, but they're not exactly the same. That's why you can inherit your Mom's eyes and your Dad's hair."

Alex frowned, his fingers tracing an imaginary diagram. "What does the auxosome match up with?"

"Excellent question! We built a pair of auxosomes, matched with each other. In this case, they carry the same genetic information on both chromosomes. That makes it easier for proof-reading enzymes to repair any genetic mistakes. They can compare one against the other."

"Paul, this will be incredible if it works," said Jill. "But what if it doesn't. God, what if it goes wrong? Isn't it possible you'd be releasing a horrible plague?"

"If the auxosomes did turn out to offer any danger to future generations, we could just edit them out from germ cells. Besides, Reba Jenkins at the University of Pennsylvania has developed a technique to selectively activate or disable inserted genes, even in somatic cells."

"And you'll own the patents?"

"Well, we've done most of this on our own time."

"My God, Paul, if this works you'll be filthy rich! Richer than Bill Gates!"

"Don't think the idea hasn't crossed my mind—but that's the least of it." His gaze was bright, and he smiled at her, and at Alex. "Staying young and healthy for a hundred and fifty years interests me more than any amount of money." In an obvious effort to restrain his own enthusiasm, then, he shrugged. "Let's not get too excited just yet. The mice might suddenly fall over dead. Just have to wait and see." He put a hand on Alex's shoulder. "Ready to go to work, sport?"

48: THURSDAY, JUNE 12

"Good night, sweetie."

"Night, Mom."

Reluctantly, Jill kissed Alex on the forehead and closed the door. It was getting harder to drop Alex off at summer day camp in the morning and to leave him alone in his bed at night. Each moment with him had become precious, and she longed to quit her job and spend every hour of the day with him, in case... just in case. Being required to spend her evenings organizing Preston Bowie's sloppy files didn't help a bit.

I should call Keith, she thought, ask him to help out while Alex is sick, so I can stay home with him. For three days now she had been putting it off; the longer she waited the harder it got. She started toward the kitchen, detoured to the bathroom to apply a herbal facial masque. Plastered with a thick layer of green goo, she could think of nothing else to do, no more excuses for putting off the call.

Resolutely, she sat down at the kitchen table, phone in hand. She entered Keith's number, got up, went quickly out into the backyard, in case Alex was not yet asleep. Not the sort of conversation she wanted him to overhear.

April answered the phone.

"Hi April, it's Jill." Silence. "Jill Shannon."

"Keith is in the shower," April said curtly.

"Could you please let him know I called? It's about Alex."

"I'll have him call you."

"Oh, and...." Shit. The bitch had hung up on her. Fuming, Jill went back inside, opened the laptop and went online. A friend of Nancy Buchanan had told her about an herbal anti-cancer treatment known as SMV-9b; when Jill had asked for the details on how it worked, Nancy's friend supplied the patent number.

The patent information came up on the USPTO web site.

Under the summary, she read: "It has been found as described in the examples below, that the compound can slow or halt tumor progression in vivo." It went on and on. After struggling for half an hour to decipher the technical language, Jill sent an email.

> To: Paul Gibson
> Subject: Help!
>
> Hi Paul, are you online? Would you consider interpreting a cancer treatment patent for me?

Five minutes later she had her answer:

> Give me a few minutes to wrap up a discussion I'm having with Drew, and I'll jog over and look at it with you.

Coming here? Now?

"Okay. See you soon," she typed. Then she raced to the bathroom to rinse the hardened green masque from her face and brush her hair.

49: THURSDAY, JUNE 12

Paul slowed to a walk two blocks before Jill's house so he wouldn't be completely out of breath when he arrived. The run had cheered him up. Must be the adrenalin, he thought, a good antidote for despondency. Drew seemed to be slipping ever farther into depression as the so-called "Frankenscience" hysteria grew; the MJT bombing had worsened his anxiety, understandably. The police report suggested that one of the explosives had been positioned near Drew's office. Today he had threatened to quit his job at MJT Labs, buy some land in the country and become a hermit.

At Jill's kitchen table, Paul alternately read the patent application and sneaked peeks at her while she made tea. Hanging above the refrigerator was a large monochrome photograph of a tall slender woman with straw hat and bare shoulders. With a shock, he realized it was Jill. Without thinking, he found himself blurting out, "You look a lot different in that photo, when was it taken?" He regretted the words at once; from her crestfallen expression, he knew he had hurt her.

"That was before I had Alex. Before my divorce. You know those magazine stories about Demi Moore and Elle McPherson, how they spring back to perfection after childbirth? Didn't happen to me."

"I'm sorry, I didn't mean to—"

"In high school my friends envied me, because I never had a zit. But after Alex was born, I got post-partum acne. My face looked like it caught fire and someone tried to put it out with an ice pick." She touched her fingers to her cheek, self consciously. "The doctor couldn't prescribe medication, because I was breastfeeding. Then Keith got involved with one of the secretaries from his law firm. After that, I started eating like a horse to, you know, *console myself*...." She sighed, placing mugs on the table. "After a while he wasn't interested in me anymore. And really, who could blame him for trading off the damaged goods for a new model?"

Damn! What woman wouldn't feel furious? He sought after something he could say to neutralize his carelessly cruel question. He wanted to tell her that Keith was a jerk. That any man who would walk out on a woman like her was a fool. No, shit, probably better to keep quiet rather than risk making things even worse. He turned his attention back to the patent, hoping to find some scrap of good news. What he read was not terribly encouraging; the owners of the patent made bold claims for their product, but the experiments described were not well designed and the results were questionable at best.

"Doesn't look as though it'll do any harm," he told Jill, "and it *might* do some good. But that's not saying much. I really wouldn't recommend it." He longed to tell her more about his own research but dared not get her hopes up. His auxosome work would not be ready to test on humans for at least five years. Gloom settled back around him like a shroud. By that time, Alex would probably be long buried.

50: FRIDAY, JUNE 13

"Morning, Wayne." Old Miss Janichek leered at Payback as he slouched into the library. He hated it when people called him Wayne. He knew the old biddy expected him to smile and make conversation the way Wayne always did, but Payback was a busy man. No time for small talk with small town librarians.

He scribbled "W. Elliot" on the Internet sign-in sheet and took his place at Wayne's favorite computer. Wayne had started to fight him again; Payback had to work fast and do what needed to be done before Wayne locked him out of control again.

Payback did a web search on Dr. Drew Chang, the prick he'd heard on the phone in the MJT labs. According to the news, he and the rest of the scientists working there were unharmed by the bomb. The first item that came up confirmed what his gut had told him. Payback didn't even attempt to read it—every other word was something he'd never heard of. The title was enough: "Genetically Engineered Mice in Cancer Research: Modifications to the Genome Utilizing Direct DNA Insertion."

There was no time to make another bomb, even if Wayne's wallet had contained enough money to buy more materials. Direct action was called for.

51: FRIDAY, JUNE 13

Paul drove aimlessly, considering endless variations on the same questions. When he found himself outside Jill's house the sun had gone down. Too late to knock on the door? The kitchen light was shining through the side window. To avoid waking

Alex, he walked along the side of the house, pushed open the gate into the back yard and tapped on the back door.

"You startled me," Jill said, but looked glad to see him.

"Busy?"

"Yes. But I'm ready to take a break." She stepped on to the porch. "Mind if we sit out here?"

"How's Alex?"

"A little stronger, I think."

She pulled out one of the wooden picnic benches, but Paul felt jittery, full of energy going nowhere. Alex's swing set was next to the picnic table; he grabbed the upper bar and began to do chin-ups.

"Dr. Collins enrolled Alex in the research program for SMV-9b. We started the treatment four days ago," Jill said. "He seems to be feeling a little better already."

Probably feeling better because they stopped the chemo, thought Paul. But he smiled down at her and said, "Glad to hear that, Jill."

"You're certainly energetic tonight." Her voice was tired.

Breathing hard, he dropped to the ground and squeezed into one of the swing seats. "Ever been in a situation where you had a chance to accomplish something great—but to do it, you'd have to risk everything?"

"I've never come that close to greatness," she said with a wan grin. "When I realized I wasn't ever going to be a famous film-maker, I thought I could do wonderful things with a law degree. You know, do my part to make laws setting limits on pollution and destruction of farmland. Once I got out into the real world, I discovered that most environmental lawyers spend their time finding ways for land developers to get around EPA regulations." She sighed, pushed her hair away from her lowered face.

"Okay, fair enough. But suppose you really *could*—" He broke off, then let the words spill out. "What I was talking about before. Take a drug to make your brain work more effectively. Maybe make you the smartest person in the world?"

"Like your mice."

"Right." He sat down beside her, leaned back against the edge of the table.

"You really think it'll work on people?"

"That's the risky part. I'm not sure. And I can't afford to test the auxosome on primates. Chimps are incredibly expensive, and now MJT won't be able to help out any time soon. Besides, these days there's all sorts of protective protocols." Quickly, he added: "And a good thing too."

Jill pondered silently for a time. "When I can't decide what to do," she said thoughtfully, "I ask myself: what's the worst thing could possibly happen one way or the other?"

"If I inject myself with the auxosomes? Jill, it could fry my brain. Burn me out. I could end up psychotic, or...." He cleared his throat. "Retarded. You ever read *Flowers for Algernon*?"

"Uh, don't think so. Wait a minute, wasn't that on television a few years ago? A retarded man called Charlie, right?"

"Yeah, but the book's more impressive. I read it last month when I first started thinking about this. What if I trial the auxosome treatment and it works—but only for a short time? How could I bear it? I mean, to remember being brilliant, knowing I couldn't ever experience such clarity and sweep again?"

She frowned in the dimness. "Paul, I read a magazine article about a woman who tried to gas herself. She didn't die, but her brain was badly damaged."

Grim, he nodded. "Insufficient oxygen."

"She had to settle for some shit menial job, but it's like you said, Paul—the most horrifying thing is that she could *remember* speaking several languages and using complex math, all the skills she'd lost."

He thought: Jill instantly understood what's frightening me. God, it's good to have someone to talk to. He sat down next to her on the bench, wanting desperately to put an arm around her. He didn't dare to, not yet. "Right. I could end up stupid. There's no evidence of that happening to the mice, but I still don't fully understand how the gene tweaks work. Of course, maybe if I increase my brain power, even for a little while, I'll be able to figure it out. All I have to do is beat evolution."

"But your mice are okay?"

"So far. Problems could show up in a year's time, or in their offspring. And the homeobox package might work differently on humans. I doubt it, though. The latest genome maps show a common basic mechanism in both species. All the auxosomes are doing is.... How can I put it? Kick-starting the dormant machinery that grows healthy new tissue and proof-reads and safeguards germ cells. You know, sperm and ova."

"Paul, suppose there *has* to be a trade-off? I mean, you're saying human intelligence could be boosted just by manipulating a few genes. Surely evolution would have come up with the same trick during the past 100,000 years?"

"No, it's more than just a few genes, and besides, natural selection doesn't plan ahead, Jill."

A little sharply, she said, "I do understood that. I'm saying that maybe for a mutation to work in one direction—enhancing cleverness, say—it has to steal resources from existing parts of the brain. Coarsen other abilities or feelings. That happens with autistic savants, doesn't it—they can hear a piece of music once and play it faultlessly, or list 200 prime numbers off the top of their heads, but they can't tie their own shoelaces—that sort of thing?"

He got to his feet, pacing. "I agree. There's a technical term for that, 'antagonistic pleiotropy.' But look, we've worked out how to beat tissue rejection in organ transplants, and that's something nature never managed."

"Okay, and I suppose anesthetics is another example. Why didn't perfect pain control get evolved?" She paused, thinking about it. "I suppose pain is too useful. Lets you know when to pull your hand back from the hot stove."

Paul sat back on the bench, this time a bit nearer to Jill. "Yeah, but you're right, selective anesthesia could've occurred as a natural mutation and then been conserved. Not to *obliterate* pain, just mute it. Tune agony down to dull discomfort. Surely pain doesn't need to be so disabling."

"That's what I mean. We use pain killers all the time these days and it doesn't bother us."

"Right. So a mutation that increased our voluntary control over really bad pain needn't be a disadvantage. It just didn't happen to happen, that's all." He grinned. "Sheer chance. Same with improved intelligence, maybe. Species get trapped in what biologists call a 'local optimum.' To try a totally fresh track, their offspring would have to do *worse* before the next generation can mutate in interesting ways."

Even in the darkness her eyes were bright with the excitement of this intellectual chase.

"Like when you're stuck at the top of a hill," she said, nodding, "and there's no direct way across to a higher peak, right? You need to climb down again and start again at the foot of the new hill. You're saying evolution mightn't produce extreme intelligence by itself because it can't see ahead, can't see the value of it."

"Ex*act*ly. A species can only make a giant leap by risking almost inevitable failure. But science *can* look before it leaps. We beat blind evolution every day."

"Like...surgeons performing heart transplants," Jill said, "even though natural selection frowns on it."

Paul grinned at her. "Well, you've got to admit, you hardly ever find heart transplants happening in the wild."

"But suppose it *is* like that book, it only works for a short time, then you're worse off than before."

"Yeah, but *Flowers for Algernon* wasn't a scientific report of an actual experiment. It's just a beautifully crafted work of fiction. And its heartbreaking power *depends* on its tragic conclusion."

"Hmm. I guess logically Charlie Gordon *could* have found a way to mend his poor brain. But then the movie wouldn't have made me cry."

They fell silent, gazing at each other. He was excited and encouraged. A touching and tragic work of sheer fiction had nearly overwhelmed his own intelligent assessment of the prospects. That should have been a clue, he thought. The very process of reading a book.... It'll ruin your damned eyes, his parents had nagged him, get outside and kick the football around. The irritating scientist inside his head started to nag: maybe his parents weren't so dumb after all. If you keep your gaze fixed on pages of print for hours at a time when you're a kid, you really *might* screw up the developmental pathways that work perfectly well in the environment we're adapted for, the hunter-gatherer world that's swiftly vanishing from the face of the Earth. Paul laughed out loud.

"What?" She leaned forward, as though anticipating a treat.

God, he thought, her face becomes tremendously appealing when she's interested in something. "All that reading really *does* ruin our eyes, just like our mothers warned us," he said, teasing her to see her lips curve into a smile. "Poor vision mostly doesn't kick in until we're past our reproductive prime, so mutations that could correct the problem just don't get selected in. But intelligent intervention can fix things in one fell swoop. I agree, Charlie *didn't* have to get stupid again."

"All right, already. I'm convinced."

Well, maybe; he wasn't really so sure. Tormented by the possibility, he continued to rack his limited human brain for an answer, but there was no way to find the truth except to perform the experiment.

"My God, Paul," Jill was saying, "I wonder what it would be like to be that smart?"

"Hard to say. Almost like becoming...something different. A meta-human. A post mortal. We'd conquer death in an afternoon." He smiled at her in the half-darkness. "PMS. Post mortal syndrome."

"If you were that much smarter than everyone else, who would you talk to? Wouldn't the rest of us seem very boring to you?"

"That's one of the risks I'd be facing."

Her face fell. "It's as if you're talking about leaving and never coming back."

Finally he put his arm around her. She tensed but did not move away. "It could be very lonely. I don't think I want to risk it." Even as he said the words, he mentally argued with himself: it would be worth any risk to experience life as intensely as possible, even if only for a year. To be an Einstein, a Murasaki, a Goethe, a Kandinski, a Beethoven...a Groucho Marx. To soar. To caress the universe. To make the whole world laugh with hilarious joy. And what if I weren't the only one to take the journey? What if Jill would come with me?

They were silent for a long moment, a companionable silence rather than an awkward one. "It must be getting terribly late," he said at last. "I'd better go so we can both get some sleep."

When he rose to leave, Jill got up too and put a tentative hand on his shoulder. The kitchen window shed a triangle of light on her face, revealing one glistening eye. He moved toward the warmth of her body and then stopped. She seemed too vulnerable; this was not someone who'd enjoy intimate fun for a night or a month and then go on with her life without looking back. He gave her a friendly pat on the arm and said, "See ya later."

Before he could turn away, her hands were moving up the bare skin of his arms to his shoulders, through his hair. Reflexively, his arms closed around her, pulling her closer. She slid her hands down his back, under his shirt, turned her face away so that he kissed her jaw instead of her lips, buried his face in the soft fragrance of her hair. A mosquito whined close to his ear as Jill lifted her face and kissed his lips.

"Let's go inside," he said.

He felt her nod against his chest. Arms around each other, they walked to the house, paused awkwardly at the screen door, unable to pass through the opening together but not wanting to separate. Finally, Jill stepped away from him. Taking his hand in the darkness, she led him into the kitchen.

They stopped and kissed in front of the refrigerator, and then again just inside her bedroom. She clicked on a small lamp beside the bed, sat down to pull off her sandals. He kicked his own shoes away, peeled off his socks, then raised her up again, pulled her tee shirt over her head and kissed her neck as he reached around to unhook her bra. The clasp seemed to be stuck.

"Um. You don't happen to have a pair of scissors to hand?"

Giggling, she pushed his hands aside, easily unfastened the bra and flung it aside. The smell of her intoxicated him. In the dim golden light, he found it hard to read her expression. Would she regret this and hate him for it later? At the moment it didn't seem to matter. He slid her shorts down to her ankles, she stepped out of them.

"Maybe we should close the door," he said, moving away from her. "Alex."

"Yes."

When he turned back to her she was on the bed, leaning against the headboard, her knees raised, slightly apart. He pulled off his shirt, let it fall to the floor, lay down beside her. She shuddered as he ran his hand along the inside of her thigh.

She sat up. "We can't do this. I'm not on the pill," she told him. "I'm assuming you don't carry condoms around with you?"

"No, sorry. But you'd surely hate me if I did." Lauren's diaphragm had been riding around in the glove box of his car for a couple of months now. Dare he mention it?

Jill's gaze was longing, and she was playing absently with his zipper. Maybe he dared.

"Um, Jill?"

"Hmm?"

"Remember that diaphragm Alex pulled out of my pocket?"

Her jaw dropped. "You can't be serious!" She shook her head. "I couldn't possible use some other woman's— Paul, that's a *disgusting* idea."

"No, no, Jill—she hasn't *used* it. Lauren liked to be prepared. It was a spare diaphragm she left at my place a couple of weeks ago. And we weren't—We argued all the time, we hadn't— Still, yeah, sorry, it was a bad idea."

But she was swinging one leg over and kneeling, straddling him. "Diaphragms," she commented with a remote, scientific air, "aren't more than seventy-five percent effective."

"You read that in *Cosmo*, right?" He could hardly breathe. All the oxygen in his body seemed to be trapped with the blood surging into his penis.

"If you must know, yes. Would you prefer a citation from *Nature?*"

"Seventy-five percent is better than noth—"

"But that's only if you don't use a spermicidal jelly with them." Jill leaned forward and toyed with his nipples.

He closed his eyes, waiting incredulously. Good god, she was going to go for it. Lauren would kill him. Still, maybe he could give the thing a good wash. Could you boil a diaphragm? It'd go all out of shape, surely. They must have some way of—

"I have some herbal stuff." Jill mused, moving her murmuring lips over his mouth and driving him crazy. "It's supposed to kill head lice—" She snorted, and he wondered if he'd explode or burst into maniacal laughter.

"It's not crabs I'm worried about, Jill."

"If it kills head lice, it'd probably work on sperm, don't you think?"

"And other delicate organisms," he said with a shudder. The blood was quickly running back where it belonged.

"It's very gentle," she assured him. "Guaranteed not to irritate the...skin."

"Sure," he told her. Anything for science. "Let's give it a try."

Delicately, she swung her leg over and stood up.

"You go get the diaphragm and I'll find the louse treatment."

Paul pulled his trousers back on and felt his way through the darkness of the living room, almost upsetting a flower pot atop a fern stand, went out to the car. Under his bare feet, the street's pavement felt cold. With a brief stab of guilt, he withdrew Lauren's unused diaphragm from the glove box. But after all, he had tried to give it back to her, and she wouldn't take it. He'd have to purchase a replacement for her. Did they come in different sizes? Of course they did, they had to be fitted. Was there a model number on the case?

When he got back, Jill was examining the contents of a small glass jar. He handed her the diaphragm, and she scooped a yellow glob from the jar.

"I hope you won't find it offensive if I offer a suggestion," he said. "I mean, it's not as though I've ever inserted a diaphragm. But it seems as though you might want to apply the spermicidal *after* you've inserted the thing. Isn't the ointment going to make the diaphragm very...slippery?"

Too late. Jill had already applied a liberal quantity of the yellow stuff.

"Turn around," she said. "I'd rather not have you standing there watching me."

Paul turned his back with gentlemanly consideration. She didn't say anything more for a long time. Something like a bat flew past his ear, hit the ceiling, bounced off.

Jill gave a ghastly, embarrassed laugh. "Oops."

He poked around in the half dark, trod on something dank and disgusting with his bare foot, yelped. The dank thing slid away under the bed. Bending, craning, he fished it back out. It had picked up a dust bunny. He held it out toward her like a giant furry oyster. Convulsed with horror and mirth, Jill took it and stood naked by lamplight.

"I'm going to the bathroom." She regarded the diaphragm in her hand. "I'm going to wash it off and try putting it in before I apply the treatment."

Paul took off his trousers. There was a book on the dressing table, *Galapagos* by Kurt Vonnegut. He picked it up, opened it to the middle. Jill's muffled voice interrupted his studious reading. "Oh my god.... Fuck!"

He got up and tapped lightly on the bathroom door. "Would you like me to help?"

"I think maybe we shouldn't do this after all." She flung open the door and burst out, the diaphragm, now beardless, clutched in one fist.

Paul gently stroked her back. "We don't have to do it if you don't want to," he said in his most soothing tone. "I'll be happy just to cuddle up with you." It was true, too, he thought. He could get off just looking at her. But still. "If you'd like, I can try to insert it for you. I might have better luck since I'll have a better view."

She grabbed him and gave him a slurpy kiss on the mouth.

"We could call Lauren and ask her how to do it." Jill handed him the diaphragm, laughing, revealing her white, perfect teeth.

"Oh shit! What's happened to it?" With dismay he saw that the formerly pink diaphragm was now stained with dark blotches.

"It's the louse treatment. It was yellow in the jar, but it turned purple when I rubbed it on."

Oh well. It wasn't as though he and Lauren were ever going to be best friends anyway.

"Let's forget about the diaphragm and just go with the louse treatment." She collapsed against him, pulled him on top of her, wrapped her long legs around him.

No turning back now, he thought.

§

As they lay with their bodies still pressed wetly together, she asked, "Why were you carrying your old girlfriend's diaphragm around in your glove box?"

"I haven't seen her for a while. Hadn't got around to giving it back to her."

"Well, maybe you could just mail it to her."

"I could do that. Yes, maybe that's what I should do." He thought about that for a while. "Of course I'll buy her a new one."

"Tell me about Lauren. What's she like?"

"Gorgeous. Smart. Critical of almost everything I said or did.... I took her to see the cave paintings, and she complained the whole time. It was too hard to walk in the tall grass. It was dirty. Her shoes would be stained. It was boring."

"And you liked her...why?" Jill raised her eyebrows.

"I used to ask myself that, and one day I realized that I got tense whenever I was with her. She didn't seem to like much about me either. I thought she'd be relieved to end it."

"But she wasn't?"

"Hard to say. She yelled at me, said some nasty things. But I hear she's been going out with an investment banker. He's probably everything I'm not—good dresser, member of the country club, all that."

Jill lay relaxed against him, and from her regular breathing he guessed she was asleep; he was beginning to drift off himself when she said, "You should go now, Paul. I don't think it would be a good idea for you to be here when Alex wakes up. It would be too confusing for him."

As quietly as he could, he slipped out of bed and dressed, kissed Jill softly. This time she was truly asleep.

52: SATURDAY, JUNE 14

Jill stretched luxuriously and sat up, feeling happier than she had in a long time. It was nice to be touched, she thought. She stopped smiling. Where was Paul?

On the kitchen table crossed by the long early morning light, she found a sheet of notebook paper with her name scrawled across the top. "JILL, I enjoyed last night. Will you and Alex honor me by coming to my hovel for dinner tonight? I promise it'll be interesting and maybe even delicious." She kissed the note, laughing joyfully.

§

Paul's apartment was less than a mile from Jill's house, on the second floor of a rambling stone house that had been divided into six apartments. Built in the early twentieth century, before the little boxes all the same, the place had high ceilings and large double hung windows that created a feeling of spaciousness.

"This is no hovel, Paul! It's totally charming." Jill admired the large windows that lent a spacious feeling to the room, took in the M.C. Escher print opposite the futon sofa.

"Hey Paul, can I look at this?" Alex had already pulled the *Pictorial Atlas of the Solar System* from the built-in bookcase.

"Sure. Make yourselves at home. Which means take a look in the fridge and see what you'd like to drink."

"Whatever you're cooking smells wonderful." Suddenly shy, Jill stood in the open doorway to the small kitchen.

"I promised you something interesting. Every dish contains at least one wild ingredient, harvested fresh just this afternoon."

"Really? From where?"

"Right around here. Try a bite of this. It's Turk's cap sauce for the cake."

"You made cake?" She took the spoon he offered, sampled the sweet red sauce. "Yummy."

"I have to confess, I bought the cake at the bakery." He leaned forward and lightly kissed her lips. "Would you mind bringing the white wine from the fridge?"

53: SATURDAY, JUNE 14

Wayne felt something wet on his face, opened his eyes, straining to see through the darkness. He could barely make out the shape of a square railing and beyond that a car. Fern's car. He twitched, startled, as something loud began rhythmically thumping behind him. Gretchen. He relaxed. The wet thing he felt on his face must have been his dog's nose.

"Hey girl." He reached in the direction of the thumping and groaned. His back was stiff and sore from lying on the wooden planks. What was he doing lying out on the deck at night, anyhow? Where was Fern? With great effort and pain, he sat up. Gretchen pressed her head under his arm, wanting him to pet her. He ignored her, got shakily to his feet and tried to open the front door. It was locked. What the...he and Fern never kept their door locked. She couldn't have shut him out!

"Hey, Fern!" He beat on the door with his fists, stopped at a horrifying thought. Something bad had happened to Fern. What if he had.... But no, now he heard her moving around inside the trailer. The light came on, the door flew open, and she stood there in her white nightgown glaring at him.

"What the hell do you think you're doing? How dare you stand there banging on the door at three in the morning?"

He didn't want to admit to her that he had no idea. He remained mute.

"Where have you been with my car this time?" Fern seemed perfectly willing to talk for both of them. "Did it never occur to you that I might lose my job if I didn't have any way to get to work? Did it? Look at you standing there like a complete idiot! You don't give a shit about my job, do you? You don't give a shit about anything or anybody but yourself." She blocked the doorway. His first impulse was to push her aside, but he felt too...broken. What did she mean about missing work? The last thing Wayne remembered was going to sleep in his own bed.

"Fern?" He took a deep, shuddering breath. He had to know. "What day is this?"

She turned without a word and walked away from him. But she left the door open. Wayne followed her into the bedroom, shutting the door behind him. Outside, Gretchen gave a mournful, lonesome howl.

54: FRIDAY, JUNE 20

Nerves shrilling, Nathan Pritchett watched the man named Wayne Elliot saunter past him into his office. Because it wasn't Elliot, not exactly. This man was trying his best to hide nervousness. Understandably. So what was he doing here? Why take the risk of revealing himself?

"I don't believe we've met," he said.

"Name's Payback."

That made him blink. Not an instant's evasion. Nathan forced himself to breathe easily, to find his own center.

"That's an unusual name."

Gravel voiced: "Well, my real name's something different. But I'm called Payback."

Much as this fragmented personality dislikes needing my help, Nathan decided, he's chosen to face the facts: there's now no one else to turn to. Maybe I'm the first person he's ever known, including both his wives, who didn't mistake him for Wayne.

Nathan settled into the chair facing the man who was not at this moment Wayne Elliot. The hair on the back of his neck was bristling; this was a distinctly dangerous situation.

"Like a nickname?"

"Yeah."

"Good to meet you, Payback. I'm Dr. Pritchett."

"Yeah. I know. Listen, Nathan, I need your help. Wayne's been thinking about killing himself."

Again, Nathan was shaken. He felt the polite look stiffen on his face. In a scratchy voice, speaking with deliberate simplicity to the demented child across from him, he said, "Do you think there might be anything you can do to help Wayne, so he won't feel like killing himself?" That was an outcome he needed to head off at the pass.

"That's what I came here to ask you. If I already knew what to do, I wouldn't be here."

"Sometimes the most useful thing I can do," Nathan heard himself saying, on self-protective automatic pilot again, "is to help you unlock knowledge you already have. Do you know why Wayne's thought of killing himself?"

Payback shrugged. "He thinks he's going nuts."

"He's found out about you?"

"Maybe. See, up until just lately I knew everything about Wayne, but the moron didn't even know I was here. Whenever I was in control of things, Wayne just sort of blacked out. Know what I mean?"

Nathan nodded, holding expression from his face.

"So a month or two ago, Wayne started dreaming about stuff I did a long time ago, stuff he never knew about, and now sometimes he can hear me. Not out loud, you know, but inside our head."

"Could you tell me more about what he's dreaming?"

"Just dreams, dude. Stuff happened when we were kids. And when Melody died."

"Your wife," Nathan said carefully.

"Our wife. Wayne's wife." The terrifying man got to his feet. Nathan knew what must be going through Payback's head: *Damn shrink, poking into all sorts of things that are none of his business.* That insight calmed his hammering heart. He declined to tell Payback to sit down. I'll show the cocky devil one of my cards, he thought.

"Wayne has many of the signs of having been abused when he was a child."

"His daddy was a real asshole. Beat the shit outta him over the least little thing."

Not that it took any great insight to recognize the origins of dissociative disorder this explicit.

Payback shrugged, sat down again.

"And some of the dreams are about his daddy?"

"Maybe."

Try as he might to keep a poker face, Nathan felt his eyes dart away from Payback's for a split second. Damn. "I see. Would it help, do you think, for Wayne to talk to me about the dreams?"

That suggestion badly frightened the madman. Jesus, what the fuck has he been up to? If it was bad enough, Payback would do anything to prevent Wayne merging with him, seeing into his own suppressed history. Nathan was glad he had a can of Mace ready in his drawer. He felt his hand slip of its own accord toward the right side of the desk, locked it in place by sheer will power. They give you a hard time for fucking your patients, but they're even less sympathetic when you Mace them.

"Look, doc, I gotta take a leak." Payback was on his feet.

"Maybe I could come back some other—"

Hastily, Nathan rose, opened the door to the utility areas at the back of the small office. Not now, not when he was so close. "Through there." Doubtfully, Payback went into the dim corridor, eyes jumping from side to side. After a time, the toilet flushed. He returned, wiping wet hands on his trousers, and sat down again.

"I was hoping you could give Wayne some kind of drug to calm him down," Payback said.

Nathan cleared his throat. Since the recent unpleasantness, no pharmacist was permitted to prescribe drugs of any kind for him. He said, "Yes, I work with a psychiatrist who could prescribe medication. But even when medication is used, the best results are almost always obtained through a combination of the medication and talking."

"Long as I'm in control, everything's fine. But you let Wayne take over...no telling *what* he'll do."

What *Wayne* might do? "It might help Wayne if we could... introduce you to him, explain to him what's going on, so he won't think he's going nuts. I get the impression you're stronger than Wayne. Emotionally, I mean."

"Smarter too."

That was highly unlikely. But allow him his delusions of omnipotence. "Maybe if you could share your greater strength and intelligence with him—"

"How can I do that if he thinks he's going nuts just hearing my voice?"

"I believe explaining things to him would help. Could we ask Wayne to come out and talk to me now, Payback? Since you know everything he knows, you'd have a better understanding as well."

"Fuck, no! If Wayne takes over he might kill us. I told you, you dumb asshole, he's obsessing about suicide."

"Payback, are you concerned that he might talk about things you'd rather leave alone? That would be understandable but—"

Shit, busted flush. "Listen, Dr. Rutherford, I gotta go now."

Payback sat forward on the edge of his chair, muscles moving in his shoulders. "It was a mistake coming here. Should've known nobody could help."

Hastily, Nathan said, "I'm not going to ask you to stay if you're uncomfortable here, Payback. But I do want you to know one thing." He paused for a solemn moment, meet the man's eyes. "I understand your fury about Melody's terrible death. There are bad forces at work in the world. You could be a savior for this damaged world, Payback." Was this the moment for one more touch of the needle? Let's see. "By the way, my name is Pritchett, not Rutherford. You might think about that."

Payback hesitated. Fascinating! He hadn't even registered that slip of the tongue. The man looked dead on his feet.

"How long have you stayed awake, Payback?"

"Smart little shit, aren't you?"

"I do know that you can't keep Wayne quiet indefinitely. How long, Payback?"

"Don't push me, pal. Forty-eight hours straight, this time, and I've got plenty more in me. Things to finish and miles to travel."

"Maybe not." Nathan leaned back in his chair, a show of command, probably unconvincing. This thing needed to be behind bars. "You know you can't keep it up much longer."

"Yeah, well." The defensive personality watched him warily, then abruptly rose. "Whatever. I have stuff to do, Doc. You'd better unlock the door."

Hastily, Nathan slid out from behind the desk and saw Payback on to the street. He deadbolted the door and started shaking. After five minutes and a stiff jolt of bourbon, he found Fern Elliot's work number

"Fern, this is Dr. Nathan Pritchett. No, not at all, my pleasure." Something rattled out back. He peered around the open door, saw nothing. Of course, there was nothing to see, he was safely alone now. "Mrs. Elliot, I'm afraid there's something we need to work through together. No, no, your husband is in excellent health—physically, at any rate. I'm rather concerned, though, for his state of mind." A footstep? Jesus, I'm jumpy, he thought. Don't be ridiculous, there's nobody else in the place, I've got the damned door deadbolted.

He cut through Fern's witterings. Time to cover his ass. "Well, the truth is, I'm rather fearful that he might harm himself. Normally I would be obliged to preserve your husband's confidences absolutely, but I must inform you that he is suffering a... well, call it a deep depression. Well yes, that's what disturbs me, too, it's possible that he might. I must ask you to let me know if his conversation does ever turn to suicide, or to violence against others. Now Fern, please don't be alarmed, I'm sure we'll handle this stressful situation together." As quickly as he could, he got the weeping woman off the phone, sat back, chair squeaking.

His nerves shrilled. Jumpy as a cat, he stood, went to the door, tested the deadlock. A shadow fell over his desk. Oh shit, he thought, appalled. The bastard unlocked the goddamn back door when he was.... Shrieking in terror, he leaped sideways, cracked one shin painfully against the desk corner. The Payback creature's face was covered with a dripping handkerchief. Oh Jesus, he was prepared for Mace!

"Don't hurt me," Nathan shrieked. "I'll tell you everything I—"

"You interfering scum," the man said, voice muffled. "You're one of them. You say your name is not Rutherford, but I tell you it is."

Payback moved, then, like a leopard. Nathan Pritchett felt a spike of excruciating pain as his neck was broken. A face hovered scowling just over his own; it shifted, like an image in a funhouse mirror. Nathan saw that it was his wife Lisa, whom he had betrayed so often and so bitterly, come back to find him after all these years. He opened his mouth to say her name, but couldn't form the word, only a gurgling sound that echoed into darkness. She took him in her arms and rocked him.

55: FRIDAY, JUNE 20

Except for the air conditioner's low drone and the sounds of Drew Chang's own movements—tapping the keyboard, the occasional squeak of his chair as he shifted his position—MJT Lab 2 was whisper quiet. An abrupt beep from his cell phone was jarring.

He picked it up, pushed the talk button without shifting his eyes from the monitor. "Drew here."

"Hey!" Maureen's voice had an edge to it. "You haven't forgotten our dinner date?"

Drew blinked, tried to shift focus.

"Tonight at eight?" His girlfriend certainly didn't sound happy, and who could blame her. He gritted his teeth and felt like slapping his forehead in a meaty Homer Simpson *D'oh!*

"Oh my gosh, Maureen! I'm so sorry. Ed got those tumor specimens prepped for me this afternoon, and I completely lost track of time—Damn, what time is it?"

His watch had stopped working a week ago, and he hadn't found time to buy a new one. Once he'd have purchased a battery instead of a whole new watch. Disposable nation. A small part of his mind tutted reproof, an echo of his moralizing father.

"It's almost 7:30," Maureen told him.

"Listen, I'll finish up here and be there in an hour—if you'll forgive me for being late."

"I'll cut you some slack this time—if you'll stop on your way here and pick up a quart of ice cream."

"Vanilla. Chocolate topping."

"Perfect!"

"See you at 8:30." Drew put the phone down and was immediately absorbed again in the image on the monitor, a tumor section magnified 25,000 times.

56: FRIDAY, JUNE 20

Payback stood tensely behind sheltering branches, leaning on the baseball bat his father had given Wayne for his ninth birthday, lenses held to his eyes. Payback could remember how the old fart had made Wayne practice hitting the ball and had grunted scornfully when Wayne swung and missed.

"You ain't never gonna make the major leagues, son, that's for sure," the old son of a bitch had said. Later, Payback had come out and used the bat to break one of the windows in the old man's shop. When the prick had shown up swinging his long leather belt, Payback had ducked out and left Wayne to take the whipping. Poor dumb Wayne, never had any idea why he was being punished.

There was only one vehicle in the parking lot besides Drew Chang's, and it was not yet 7:45. Of course a large part of the place was still a mess, with clean-up work turning it into a trash heap of broken concrete and steel. It was a wonder any work could be done inside at all. But the damned papers said at least one of his bombs had failed to detonate. For three days Payback had watched the damaged but doubly guarded MJT Lab Building, using binoculars. Chang usually worked until at least 9:00 or 10:00, so there was a good chance this was the break Payback had been waiting for.

57: FRIDAY, JUNE 20

Drew gathered his loose papers from the console and turned to his laptop to make the final entry of the day into the log that recorded each step of his research. He had been so engrossed in his work he had forgotten about eating and drinking all day; his throat and mouth were parched. The air in the hallway still stank of floating dust and concrete particles. He walked to the Oasis dispenser, filled a paper cup, walked back to his chair. I should be going, he thought. Maureen's going to be really pissed if I don't show up. I'll just check the data printouts, then I'll go.

58: FRIDAY, JUNE 20

One of the two lighted windows in the MJT lab building went dark. Payback's pulse raced as he watched the outer door, waiting to see who would come out. If it was Drew Chang, he would have to wait for another chance. Dr. Rutherford had always given him strict orders to be careful, not take any risk of getting caught, and that meant not trying to grab Chang if anyone else was around. But it won't be Drew Chang, he thought. Chang had been staying later than this.

A security guard passed in front of the door, speaking on a radio.

59: FRIDAY, JUNE 20

Out of the corner of his eye, Drew saw something move in the doorway and looked up from the computer printouts he had been reading.

"Oh hi, John. Calling it a night?"

"Yeah, I'm meeting Susan and a couple of friends for drinks. Care to join us?"

"Thanks, but I promised Maureen...oh shit! Do you have the time?" Drew glanced at his bare wrist.

"Eight-oh-three."

"Damn, I've gotta finish up here and get going."

John stood in the doorway for a moment longer as if waiting for Drew to walk out with him, then shrugged. "See ya Monday."

"Yeah, have a good weekend." Drew barely glanced up from the printout. He read until the phone rang again. Caller ID showed Maureen, calling to make sure he'd left. She knows me so well, he thought with a rush of fondness. Rather than waste time answering the phone, he stuffed the printout into a drawer and walked out, locking the door behind him.

He nodded to the guard at the main door, left the building, entered his car, headed for home. At the exit from MJT's main drive, a figure loomed out of the shadows. With unbelievable speed and brutality, the man smashed his side window into a rain of shattered fragments. Drew Chang cried out, but a rough hand had him by the hair, a knife jabbed at his throat. "Undo the fucking belt," a voice said. Terrified, he unclipped his seat belt. As the strip of fabric withdrew, the carjacker had the door unlocked, wrenched open, and Drew fell into stinging gravel. All of this in a blur of panic. Then nothing.

60: FRIDAY, JUNE 20

It was nine-thirty in the evening before Paul remembered to check his voice mail and found a message from Roberta Treadwell, the third since Monday: "Seems as though we're doomed to play telephone tag forever. Please call me, home or office, any time night or day."

He hit Reply and she answered immediately.

"Dr. Gibson! I thought we were never going to hook up. Can you bear with me just a sec?" Through the speaker phone, he could hear running water. "I found a puppy abandoned on the highway. Poor little thing was covered with fleas." Roberta soothed the puppy. "Be still, just a minute longer. What shall I call you? Basil, I think.... That's a good boy. Wasn't so bad, was it? No, get down, Sitka, play nice. Okay, Dr. Gibson, I'm with you. Thanks for waiting."

"No worries. Call me Paul, Dr. Treadwell. I'm very sorry about what happened to your facility."

"That's Roberta. We're dealing with it, Paul, not letting it stop us. Have to work around the mess. Luckily the most critical instruments were shock-mounted and came through okay. Paul, here's the thing. Drew Chang has been talking you up every chance he gets. He was excited about a memory boosting treatment you've been testing on mice, and last week he gave me a preliminary paper you'd both written on a synthetic vector."

"Yes, I've had some promising results." He cleared his throat. How much should I tell her? Be bold. "Actually, memory enhancement's just a side-effect."

"I'm impressed with what I've read. I'd like to discuss bringing you here to work at MJT. If you're interested, maybe you could come down to San Antonio, meet everyone, take a look at what we're doing. Mess and all, I'm sure we could find you some space."

"I'm very interested." Was that too eager?

"Good. I don't know what my calendar is like for the next couple of weeks, but you pick a day and I'll try to work everything else around it."

He opened the *Daytimer* on his laptop. "June 26 would be good. Thursday."

"Around ten?"

"That would work."

"I look forward to meeting you, Paul."

"I'll see you then." He sat perfectly still for a fraction of a second, letting the reality of Roberta's invitation sink in, then flung his arms wide in a shouting gesture of triumph. News this good had to be shared. Jill, Jill. He'd seen her twice already this past week, when she brought Alex back to the lab and when they'd both come over to his apartment for supper. While Alex was absorbed in feeding the rats or looking at *A Pictorial Atlas of the Solar System*, Paul and Jill had managed some playfully passionate embraces and gropings.

"Hello?" Jill sounded tired.

"Hi, I hope you weren't asleep."

"Paul!" Less tired now, and happy. "No, but I've been reading some articles for CLE-continuing education credit, and I'll tell ya, they should sell these things as sleeping aids. How was your day?"

"Until a few minutes ago, uneventful. Remember my telling you about Roberta Treadwell and MJT Labs?"

"Place that got blown up, where Drew works."

"She's invited me down to interview for a research position."

"Really, Paul? That's great!" The excitement in her voice was gratifying. "You'll be able to spend full time on your auxosome research."

"If I get it, yeah."

"You'll get it. When word goes out about your research, you'll be able to take your pick of positions. When're you going?"

"Thursday next. Gives me time to read up on the work everyone's doing there, so I can impress them with my instant intuitive grasp." He chuckled. "Hey, I don't want to keep you. I should let you finish your own work so you can have carefree fun tomorrow. We're still on for Lake Buchanan, aren't we?"

"Definitely."

"Maybe we can do rude things together while Alex takes his nap." Visions rolled through his head, Jill emerging nude from the water.

"Mmm, I should hope so."

"See ya at nine."

"Okay. Goodnight, Paul."

§

He was pondering the positive direction his life seemed to be taking when he heard banging at the door.

"Paul, are you there? It's Lauren."

Oh *shit!* He could pretend not to be home, but Lauren might well park herself by the door and wait for him. He opened the door, tried to smile politely.

"Hello, Lauren. It's late."

"Paul, we have to talk." She pushed her way into the room. "You can't pack me off to the attic and forget about me. I deserve better than that. "

"We've talked, Lauren." Sighing, he sat down on the edge of a chair and motioned her to the sofa. "Our relationship wasn't working—"

"For *you*, maybe."

"Hell, judging by the number of hours you spent berating me for my failings, it wasn't working for you either. Anyway, I heard you had a new boyfriend."

"We were talking about you and me. Don't try to change the subject. I *berated* you, as you call it, because I *cared* about you. I wanted to improve our relationship by *talking through things* that bothered me instead of *holding them inside*." She was a wise soul speaking patiently to a foolish teenager.

"Lauren, everything about me bothers you. You don't like the way I dress or the sort of car I drive, or my opinions of books and movies, or the sort of work I do. I'm curious, Lauren. What is it you *do* like about me?"

She shook her head sadly. "This is you all over, Paul, trying to turn this into an intellectual discussion. Why are you afraid to talk about your *feelings*?"

He was tempted to confess that all he felt at the moment was an intense desire never to see her again. No. Unfair. For the sake of the pleasant times they had enjoyed together, he owed it to her to hear her out. "I'm not afraid to talk about my feelings, Lauren. I didn't enjoy spending hours on end listening to your assessments of my faults and weaknesses. Not fun."

"Not fun? That's all you think about? Having *fun*? Sometimes we have to go through discomfort to reach a higher level of emotional maturity. Did it ever occur to you that through my willingness to point out your weaknesses and work with you to correct them, I was offering you a priceless gift?"

"Actually, no." Good god, what would it be like to live inside that head?

"Well, think about it now, Paul. Any fool can sit simpering and telling you what a wonderful big strong man you are. But I was willing to do more than that. I was willing to be completely honest and forthright. Aren't deep insight and candid discussion worth more than empty smiles?" She leaned forward, gazed into his eyes, touched his arm with her pink porcelain fingertips. "Aren't they?"

"No doubt. But it makes more sense to spend time with people who like me as I am."

"So, do I hear you saying you have no desire to improve yourself? You'd rather spend your time with people who have low standards? People who can't discriminate between the coarse and the refined? Your scientist buddies, I suppose."

He groaned inwardly. As always, it felt as though he and Lauren spoke different languages. When they first met he had been able to overlook this lack of verbal rapport, enraptured briefly by the perfect lines of her neck, the graceful way she moved her hands, the delicacy with which she pursed her lips. Now, her physical perfection left him unmoved; the thought of intimacy with her actually revulsed him.

"I don't know." Luckily, there was no need for in-depth responses on his part. He shifted uncomfortably on the hard wooden seat; his backside had gone numb. "Could I interest you in a glass of wine, Lauren?" He slouched to the kitchen and pulled a full bottle of cheap California Chablis from the fridge.

"That would be nice, thank you." She insisted on them clinking glasses, then there was a refreshing moment of silence.

Recharging, so she can continue the vocal battery, he thought.

§

Paul glanced at the kitchen clock as he poured the last of the second bottle of wine: Just before two o'clock in the morning. "I know you, Paul, better than you know yourself." She sipped at her wine with a tight little smile. "You're the kind of man who goes blindly through life and then wonders, at the end, why it all seems so meaningless when you look back on it."

Dear god.

"Lauren, I'm really very tired, and I don't think we're getting anywhere. Let's call it a day." It was at least the fourth time he had made the suggestion.

"Funny how you always suddenly get tired when we get around to the psychological issues."

"We've been talking for almost four hours. I have to get up at 8:30 this morning."

"Oh! I had no idea it was so late." She upended her wine glass. "But now that you mention it I *am* sleepy. Would you mind terribly if I stay here tonight?"

"Okay." He went to get sheets and a blanket from the closet. By the time he got back to the living room Lauren had disappeared. With trepidation he pushed open the bedroom door. She was curled up in the middle of his bed, clothes strewn across the floor. Quietly, he closed the door and made himself a bed on the sofa.

61: SATURDAY, JUNE 21

It was a perfect morning, like a day remembered from childhood with all the tedium and unpleasantness distilled away and only the intense beauty and wonder remaining. Jill bounded up the steps to Paul's apartment and threw open the door. A gorgeous pouty-mouthed woman sat at the kitchen table brushing her long blonde hair. A completely naked woman, who was now scowling at her.

Oh my god, Jill thought, confused, I'm in the wrong house. Her gaze skittered about the room for familiar objects. Yes, there was the grey leather sofa, the M. C. Escher print on the wall, the *Pictorial Atlas* on the coffee table where Alex had left it. And next to it, two empty wine bottles and two glasses.

"Who the hell are *you*?" the naked woman demanded as Paul walked out of the bedroom, buttoning his shirt.

Speechless, Jill looked from Paul to the woman, back to Paul.

"Hi Jill," he said cheerfully. "Uh, this is Lauren."

"Lauren?" Jill said stupidly. Oh my God, it's the diaphragm woman.

"Have you been seeing other women this whole time?" Lauren screeched incredulously.

"Don't worry," said Jill coldly. "He won't be seeing *this* other woman again." Grabbing Alex's hand, she turned around and started for the stairs. When the boy didn't move quickly enough, she picked him up bodily and carried him.

"Jill! Wait! It's not what you think."

"You bastard!" Lauren's voice rose above Paul's. "This whole time, you've been—God only *knows* what kind of diseases you've given me."

As she stumbled under Alex's weight out the front door of the building, Jill heard the crash of breaking glass and more screaming from Lauren, which gave her a small measure of satisfaction.

"Mo-om, what are you doing?" Alex wailed, struggling. "I thought we were going to the lake with Paul."

"You and I will have more fun today by ourselves."

"No, Mom! I want Paul to go too!"

In her haste to get away, Jill practically flung Alex into his car seat.

"Ouch!" His tone was indignant, but his eyes were confused and frightened.

"Paul has company, Sweetie. He can't go with us right now."

"But you said he was coming too."

She jumped in and slammed her door as Paul, barefoot, wearing only a shirt and underpants, came running from the building. "Jill, hang on!"

She started the engine.

"You don't understand!" His mouth opened and closed as he tried to find some excuse. She threw the car into gear as he reached the car. He leaned on the door, gulping air, his wry, crestfallen expression framed by the open window. "This is completely innocent, Jill. *She's my mother!*"

Jill gave a gulp of angry laughter. "Just leave us alone!" She floored the accelerator.

After a moment she reached over to comfort Alex, who was confused and upset. I should never have brought the facetious lunatic into Alex's life, she told herself in rebuke. But no, be fair. Paul had *helped* them, had told her about the growth hormone treatments. Her mistake had been to change the nature of their friendship. She should never have believed him when he said his relationship with Lauren was over. But her lips curved into a reluctant smile. Mother, indeed!

Alex sniffled, and as cheerfully as she could manage Jill said, "You and I will have a lovely time at the lake. Shall we stop by Daria's house and see if she can come with us?"

"I guess so...Mom?"

"Yes?"

"Why didn't you stay and talk to Paul?"

"I was angry with him."

"Because he had company?"

"Yes."

"Why? How come you were mad at him for having company?"

"Because he promised to go with us to the lake today but instead he was...entertaining a guest."

"You mean that lady with no clothes on?"

"Yes."

"She wasn't really his mom, right?"

"That was just a silly joke. What do you want to do at the lake today?"

"Swim. Why couldn't Paul bring the lady to the lake with us?"

"She didn't want to go."

"Oh." Alex sounded unconvinced. "But we can still go to Paul's lab to feed the rats, can't we Mom?"

"We'll see." As the shock wore off, Jill wondered if she had been unreasonable. Perhaps she should at least have listened to what Paul had to say. But no, damn it! What was going on was painfully obvious. She found herself wondering if Paul and Lauren had used the blotchy diaphragm.

62: SATURDAY, JUNE 21

Wayne found himself in the dark, stopped on the shoulder of a deserted country road slumped behind the wheel of the blue Impala, with no idea where he was or how long he'd been away from home. Fern would be mad as fire that he'd taken her car again. He flicked on the dim interior light. His watch read 2:47—obviously A.M. but he had no idea of the date. He'd woken on the front deck, stumbled into the bedroom, fallen asleep almost as soon as his head hit the pillow. It was the last thing he remembered. Well, he'd blacked out before and come to in some strange place. He could handle it. I'll just drive until I come to a road sign, he thought. He started to turn the ignition key and stopped stock-still, chilled to the bone. On the seat beside him was a leather binder, smeared with something dark as blood. He looked into the back seat. Nothing. Slowly, he opened the door and, dragging his feet, walked to the back of the car.

Somehow knowing in advance what he would find, he opened the trunk. The body of a slim young man, head covered in matted blood, lay curled like a dead cat where Wayne himself must have placed it. Once, he'd questioned whether the horrible dreams were real. Here was the end of all doubt. Hesitantly, as if touching a hot stove, Wayne laid his hand on the man's chest. To his vast relief, he felt movement

I have to get this man to a hospital, he told himself. I have to get him there before I—Pressure grew inside his head. He held his head in his hands, rocked back and forth. The pain was unbearable.

"Stop it!" he screamed. "I'll kill myself. I swear, I'll get in the car and drive it into a tree."

You moron idiot! The voice sounded exactly like his dad. What if you don't kill us? What if we end up as a paraplegic in a fucking prison. Is that what you want? Loser. You've always been a loser. You'd even manage to screw up killing yourself.

"No!"

You listen to me, Wayne. You're gonna get in the car and drive it home.

"But...."

Shut up and listen. You're gonna drive home and put this man in the old workshop.

Wayne tried to speak, but the pain was too intense. He whimpered faintly.

The voice told him: The man in the back of this car is an evil murderer. Dr. Rutherford wouldn't lie about that, would he? This man is like the ones who killed Melody. Do you want to let him get away with it? Do you want him out there turning the lives of innocent girls into a living hell?

"I'll get in trouble."

What, you think you won't get in trouble if you show up at a hospital with this guy? Gimme a break, Wayne. You can't be *that* stupid. Now look. If you listen to me and do as I tell you, everything's going to be okay.

Wayne nodded. The pain in his head began to subside.

Shut the trunk, the voice instructed. Get in the car and drive home.

63: SUNDAY, JUNE 22

Before he'd started out for San Antonio, Payback had decided to bring Drew Chang to the old farm house. He would turn his father's old workshop into a hospital room. Show Chang what it felt like to be a guinea pig. The place was safe. Fern would never dream of coming down here, after the way he'd scared her off in the past.

The air in the workshop was dank; its smell was unchanged after all these years—bare earth, motor oil, turpentine. Even at noon on a cloudless day, only dim light came through the small, dusty window at the top of the wall opposite the workbench. Payback had made the workbench into a bed by covering it with a patched sheet he'd taken from Fern's linen cabinet.

So far, except for the brief interval when Wayne took over, everything had gone like clockwork. Chang had been slipping in and out of consciousness during the whole trip east from San Antonio to Delmar. He didn't look to be in any condition to try escaping, but Payback kept him tied up just in case and left the duct tape over his mouth. Chang was such a weedy guy, it was pretty easy to drag him from the car to the workshop and lift him onto the table.

"Hey, fella. Time to wake up." Payback slapped the side of Chang's face. The little man groaned and his shallow breathing speeded up. The eyes stayed shut. *I hit him on the head too hard,* Payback thought. *Well, shit, maybe if I let him rest he'll come around after a while.*

He sat down on the stool next to the workbench. Wayne had sat here, watching his daddy puttering around, pounding hammers, drilling holes in things.

§

"You're never going to amount to anything," Wayne's daddy says. "Why can't you be more like Rob? Now there's a boy who's gonna grow up to be somebody."

Wayne sits there hating himself, wishing he could be more like his younger brother who is strong and cocky. And then a sneaky little thought works its way into his mind. Maybe something'll happen to Rob. Then Dad'll have to love me, because I'll be his only little boy.

§

Chang opened his cracked lips, moaned something unintelligible. *Probably asking for water,* Payback thought. He had squirted water into the scientist's mouth less than an hour ago, but instead of swallowing it, the little bastard had choked on it and spit it out. Payback wanted to keep him alive for a while.

"Come on now, you're gonna die if you don't swallow your

water." Payback poked the tip of the water bottle between Chang's teeth and squeezed. "Swallow it, damn you!" Payback punched Chang in the face. He regretted it even as he was swinging his fist, but he couldn't stop himself.

§

"Eat it, damn you!" Wayne's dad leans across the cheap eatery table, scoops up a spoonful of food and shoves it at Wayne's mouth. "I paid a buck sixty-five for this food, now you better eat it."

"But Daddy, I can't eat it. It hurts my mouth." Wayne turns his head to the side. Watching from behind Wayne's eyes, Payback can see the thick brown gumbo. He can certainly understand why Wayne does not want to eat it.

"Don't give me any of your lip, boy. I'm gonna count to three, and if you ain't shoveling it in by then, I'm gonna take you outside and let my belt teach you a little lesson. One...two...."

Wayne lets his father push the spoon into his mouth. The gumbo is spicy like fire. Wayne gags. We're going to throw up, have to do something. Payback pushes himself to the front of Wayne's head. After a blank moment, Wayne times out and Payback has control of the body. Without thinking twice about it, Payback shoves the plate toward the edge of the table. It teeters there for a fraction of a second then crashes to the floor. Payback notes with surprise that the mess has splattered all the way to the next table. The woman who is sitting there reaches down and rubs a glob of gumbo off her leg.

§

Chang seemed a little more alert after his latest gagging and coughing fit. He stared up at Payback with fishy eyes. Maybe he knew in his heart why he was being punished.

"You helped to kill my wife," Payback told him. "I loved her ever since the first time I laid eyes on, and you people did your experiments on her, and it was a lot worse than the cancer. Why didn't you leave her the hell alone?"

Payback spoke for Wayne, but also for himself. The little scientist looked up, his face scrunched as though he was making a great effort to understand.

"Look up there." Payback pointed to the wall behind the work bench where he had tacked up the curled, faded cheerleader photo from Wayne's secret hiding place. *To Wayne, My love forever, Melody.* "That's why you're here. That's why I have to punish you."

But Chang would not turn his head to look at the picture. He stared at Payback. Screw him. Let him lie here by himself for a while and think about what he did. Find out how Melody felt when she was too sick to eat anything and just lay there in the hospital day after day. No need for the duct tape, at least. Little bastard was too weak to make much noise.

§

When he returned Chang was still breathing, but his skin was very pale. Payback didn't feel much better than Chang looked. He couldn't think straight enough to deal with Chang. Too tired. Have to get some rest. But the second he fell asleep Wayne would be back, although he'd be just as exhausted. Gotta do *something*. He couldn't think what, except kill Chang slowly and painfully. Had to be more than that, some better revenge. He couldn't spend the rest of his life killing the bastard scientists one by one. He started to nod, caught himself with a jolt. Felt as stupid as Wayne. That conversation he'd overheard between Chang and the guy with the English accent. Some drug could turn ordinary men into geniuses?

"That's what I need to do," Payback said aloud. "I need to take some of that fucking drug. The Genius Within." He would sacrifice himself by taking the drug, use its power against its creators. What happened to him after that didn't matter, he'd been dead since the death of his beloved Melody. Saving the world was all that mattered now. He shoved Chang roughly. Little shit was still too out of it to be any help.

Earlier he had opened Chang's binder and found inside it a report of some sort with two names at the top. Now an idea came to him.

Numb with fatigue, he shuffled out to the car, opened the binder. There it was: Paul Gibson, University of Texas at Austin. He was pretty sure the English guy's name had been Paul. Okay, drive up there to the University of Texas and make this Gibson fuck give him some of the genius drug. Then he'd have no trouble figuring out what to do next.

Without going back into the workshop, he got into the car and drove up to the mobile home Wayne shared with that lump Fern.

64: SUNDAY, JUNE 22

Unbelievably, Wayne's battered old suitcase was open on the bed when Fern followed him in after a long stewing silence. She stood watching wordlessly as Wayne pulled newly washed shirts from hangers in the closet and folded them carefully. At last, beside herself, she forced calm into her voice. "Honey, will you please tell me what's going on with you? A police officer called here yesterday and told me—" She swallowed hard. "Told me Nathan Pritchett is dead. He's been murdered."

"Tough shit," Wayne said. "Guess you've blown the money you gave him. Why'd the cops call here?"

"They think he died sometime after your appointment. Some criminal. They wanted to talk to you, find out if you'd seen anything suspicious. It's a rough part of the city, they say."

Wayne grunted.

"I told them I had no idea where you were. I've just about had it with you, Wayne. I don't hear a word out of you for two days and you drag in looking like a dead man yourself. Lucky I didn't have to work this weekend, or I'd have lost my job for not showing up again." He wasn't even paying attention.

"I have to go take care of some things." He did not look up at her.

"Wayne, this is getting serious. I talked to poor Dr. Pritchett, it must have been just before—" Her voice trailed away.

"I'm trying to get better, Fern. Can you just trust me this one time? I promise, this will be the last time I'll ask to use your car."

Regaining her resolve, she said, "You've told me this before, Wayne. But it never gets better. It just keeps getting worse. Do you have any idea what you look like? You're right, Wayne. You need to take care of some things."

"Don't you raise your voice to me!" For the first time since she had come in, he met her eyes. She felt her face contort with anger.

"Wayne Elliot, as your wife, I'm entitled to know what's going on with you. I'm *afraid* of you, do you realize that? Half the time you don't even seem like you're in your right mind. Do you want to know what I talked to Dr. Pritchett about?" Fern stepped closer, too angry herself to be afraid of him.

Wearily, he sat down on the edge of the bed and held out his arms. "Listen, Babe. I promise you on my honor, I'm going to get better."

Not quite ready yet to relax, Fern stepped into the circle of his arms and leaned her head against his. "Wayne, honey, I want to believe you."

"You know what I dream of? Growing old here with you, sitting and rocking on the front porch. But I have to work out some things first."

"What things, Wayne?" A current of fear passed through her body.

"I can't—Someday you'll understand." Not unkindly he pushed her away, got up, continued packing his suitcase.

"I don't know what to make of you. Take the car. Do what you have to do. But you should know that Dr. Pritchett thought you need to be in a hospital, to keep you from hurting yourself." She regarded him with fright and weary concern. The good Lord preserve us, it couldn't have been *Wayne* who killed Nathan? Could she be sure? She added, trembling: "Or somebody else."

"First I gotta get some sleep," he said.

65: MONDAY, JUNE 23

Jill opened her eyes, stretched, smiled at the sunlight streaming through her bedroom window. For a few seconds she was sure this was going to be a good day, until she remembered that Alex was dying, and Paul was a cheating bastard. No, that was unfair, he'd never promised— Moaning, she buried her head under a pillow, wishing she could fall back into sleep, forget about getting up and going to work.

Even with Alex's friend Daria along, Saturday's trip to the lake had been a dismal failure. The two kids had quarreled on and off throughout the day. Jill had found herself fighting to keep from crying.

She and the boy had both moped around the house Sunday. When Jill went into the office in the afternoon Alex tired himself out by whining some more, slept for a couple of hours, and woke up in an even worse mood, threatening to run away from home. But he had eaten a good dinner and laughed at all the right places when Jill told him a bedtime story.

She dragged herself out of bed, made a strawberry smoothie, Alex's favorite breakfast, and somehow found the strength to smile cheerfully when she went in to wake him.

"Morning, Mom." He smiled up at her. "I dreamed I was a ten foot tall plastic fork."

"What was it like being a ten foot tall plastic fork?"

"A sixty foot tall boy was setting the table for dinner and tried to put me next to a spoon." Squeaky with laughter, he rolled out of bed, and Jill decided with relief that the worst must be over. But when she let him off at summer day camp, the last thing he said before he walked away was, "Can we go feed Paul's mice this afternoon? I love those little mousies, Mom."

"We'll see."

66: MONDAY, JUNE 23

If there hadn't been so damned many people around, and if Payback hadn't been so nervous, the University of Texas campus would be almost pleasant, what with all the trees and even a creek. Months ago, Fern had given Wayne her credit card "for emergency use only"; Payback bought himself a light weight jacket and backpack at the University Co-op Store. With this get up on, maybe people would think he was a student. That wasn't much of a plan, but better than nothing. Find Gibson, maybe talk to him, maybe use force; play things by ear.

He called campus directory assistance. They told him Dr. Gibson's building and office number. A campus map and an hour or so wandering around took him to the Experimental Science Building. A guard was posted on duty at the door, but Payback walked around to the side of the building, found an exit door that hadn't closed properly. Absolutely no sense of security. That was okay; made his life a whole lot easier, even if he was nervous as a dog with three tails. He stepped inside, snicked the door shut behind him. The small sound echoed in the stairwell. Payback leaned against the nearest wall, eyes closed, counted to a hundred. As his pulse slowed, his fright receded. He opened his eyes, took a deep breath, climbed one floor, opened another heavy fireproof door into an antiseptic hallway. No one in sight.

He turned right, walked the length of the hallway, looking at the names on the doors. Like the ones at MJT, these doors had big labels: DANGER! RADIOACTIVE, BIOHAZARD. WARM ROOM. Footsteps behind him. He turned, seeking for something to say if the person asked him what he was doing here. Unnecessary. Payback could have been invisible or something; the young man opened a cabinet door and rummaged around. Either he was deliberately ignoring Payback (smartass scientists, even when they were students, too good to pay attention to lesser mortals), or perhaps the guy was so preoccupied he wasn't paying attention to anything around him. Shit, Payback could have snuck up behind him and cracked him over the head, and he'd never know what hit him.

Payback took the stairs. Offices on the next floor showed names on the doors. Two older men walked out of one into the corridor. Absorbed in their conversation, they gave Payback only the briefest glance. He began to relax. Easy. Going to be easy.

Finally he located Paul Gibson's insignificant office on the third floor, next to the stairwell. The door stood open, but no one was there, just two empty desks. Payback found a straight backed wooden chair and sat down to wait, running possible scenarios through his mind, planning what to say if Paul was friendly, what he would do if Paul tried to run out on him or call the cops. He was desperately sleepy and wished he could go outside into the open air and sun and walk around for a while. No, if he did that he might miss his chance, and he couldn't afford to spend another day in Austin. Twice he slumped forward, caught himself, jerked back upright.

Someone was hovering over him. Fern? He lifted his head, tried to remember where he was.

"Hey! Did you want to see me?" A brown haired woman was standing next to him, looking exasperated.

"Paul Gibson. I'm looking for Paul Gibson." Payback's throat was dry, his voice hoarse.

"I'm his office mate. He's probably up in the lab."

"Oh, okay. Thank you." His mouth felt gummy. "Um, could you tell me how to get to the lab?" What the hell. This person had already seen him here. She might as well tell him what he needed to know.

"Stairs up one flight, turn right almost to the end of the hall. I'm not sure what the room number is, but you should be able to find Paul once you get there."

"Thanks." Payback cursed himself for nodding off. Hey, once

he'd taken the drug he'd be smart enough to avoid the police even if this bitch gave a good description of him. He was just lucky as hell Wayne hadn't taken over while he was asleep. As he turned to leave, she asked if he was working for Paul. Still groggy, Payback mumbled, "A friend, y'know?"

"Well, cool, but no one's supposed to come up here without an ID badge. Visitors are supposed to sign in and get a name tag." Her own tag, he noticed, said she was RACHEL GROSSMAN (BIO).

"No one told me. Maybe I should go back down and get one."

Grossman shrugged. "Whatever."

A clock in the hallway showed the time as 5:06. Shit! He must have been half-dozing for hours. Gibson might already have gone home for the day. Well, what the fuck, Payback told himself. I can spend the night in the lab if I have to.

67: MONDAY, JUNE 23

Alex was all smiles when Jill picked him up from camp late in the afternoon. "We're going to the lab, right?"

"Okay, Sweetie. I'll take you to the lab." She felt her own mood lift at the thought of seeing Paul. "C'mon. Let's go." She took his hand, but he shook it off, too old for that. They walked across the parking lot, Alex running ahead like any eight year old kid eager to get somewhere. She signed her name and they accepted tags from the bored guard at the front desk.

68: MONDAY, JUNE 23

The third floor seemed to consist entirely of laboratories. Four doors opened off the end of the hall, but none bore a sign or a name. Payback considered walking boldly into one of them and asking for Paul Gibson but decided against it. Even if he'd soon be a genius, no reason to go out of his way to make things harder for himself. Made a lot more sense to look around without drawing attention. He put his hand into his pocket to feel the comforting hardness of his 9 mm Luger pistol.

At the first door on his left, he bent down, hidden by the work bench nearest the door, and slowly moved into the room, concentrating on keeping each footfall silent. He reached a tall cabinet he could hide behind, peered around the edge without standing up. Nobody else was in the room.

I'll just stay here where it's safe for a little while, he thought. This could be my last day to live. Something could go wrong. What if this guy Paul has a gun too? What if he gives me poison instead of the drug? What if he gives me the drug but it kills me instead of making me smarter? Those people said they'd only used it on mice. This is like when Melody went to the hospital. They were supposed to cure her, then she died. She died, the careless, heartless bastards killed her. Now *I* could die. What if he tries to run and I have to shoot him?

He heard footsteps and laughter; people coming down the hallway. As they passed the door to the room where he was hiding, one of them—sounded like a kid—broke into a run.

"Paul! I've come to take care of the *Mus musculus!*" a boy's voice called. The odds were not high that more than one Paul would be up here; Payback had found his man. But damn it, this was not the way he had planned things.

"Alex!" A man, presumably Gibson, came to the door of the lab next door. "Hello there, buddy! Come in, both of you."

"Couldn't let the mice go hungry." A woman. She sounded nervous. Payback could surely relate to that.

They moved away from the door, and he could no longer hear what they were saying. Now what? He had counted on finding Gibson alone. Wait until these newcomers left? But what if they all left together? Of course they would. It must be Gibson's wife and kid. Payback cursed his bad luck.

He should do it now, even if it meant killing another kid. It was a trade-off. Two adults and a kid in exchange for the world. But what if he wasn't able to handle three people, if they overpowered or tricked him? A kid was no threat to him physically, but still, that made it three to one. One of them could get away and go for help. Christ, maybe there was a fourth person in the lab, just not saying anything yet. He'd heard of lone gunmen terrorizing large groups of people, sure, but those guys had automatic weapons, high powered rifles. He nervously touched his one handgun.

His mouth tightened. He knew what Wayne's father would think of him, standing here scared shitless about facing one man, a woman, and a kid. No question. The bastard would say that Payback was a cowardly loser.

This time he couldn't afford to screw up. Too much was riding on it. Just go for it, play it by ear, figure out what to do as he went along. He looked at his watch: 6:36. His heart was thundering. He'd give the visitors until 6:45 to leave. If they weren't gone by then, they'd pay the price. Again he gripped the pistol in his pocket and waited.

69: MONDAY, JUNE 23

"Paul?" Alex called from across the room where he was filling the food dispensers.

"What is it, my man?"

"This brown mouse looks sick."

"Yes, I gave her a dose of something new I'm working on. It makes the mice a little sick at first, but after that, they seem to be healthier—and smarter—than ever. Someday this might help get you better, Alex." He looked at Jill, lowered his voice. "I think the auxosomal proof-reading enzymes might even be able to fix multiple mutations. They'd find the insertion or deletion, snip it out, and reinsert—"

Someone was standing in the doorway. Turning, Jill saw a stocky man with short, dark brown hair. His face, though not unattractive, would have been easy to forget except that the eyes were terrified.

"Looking for someone, mate?" Paul jumped off the stool.

"You Paul Gibson?" the fellow said between clenched teeth.

"That's me." The two stared at each other for long seconds, until Paul broke the silence. "And you are?"

"Call me...." He hesitated. "What the hell. Payback." The man locked the door to the lab behind him, then stepped over to the mouse pens. With a little cry, Alex ran to stand beside Jill.

"Well, what can I do for you, Payback?" Paul didn't seem particularly concerned, but Jill was aghast. She put her arm around Alex and pulled him close; with no further notice, Payback lunged at her. Horrified, Jill saw that he was pointing a large handgun at her.

"Everybody hold still, or I'll blow this little lady's head off." Payback's left hand, holding the big gun, was shaking, and Jill feared he might squeeze the trigger by accident. Her best hope for staying alive might be to calm the guy down.

"My purse is over there on the table," she said slowly. "There's some money in my wallet, which you're welcome to take."

"I didn't come here for money. Are you stupid or something? Why would I come all the way up here to steal someone's wallet?" But he crossed to the table, rummaged through the purse, emptied the wallet. Keeping the gun fixed on Jill, he pocketed the cash; for a moment his eyes flicked down. Oh shit, her driver's license.

Alex began to cry, and Jill saw that when Payback had shifted his focus, the gun shifted too, so that now it was pointing at her son. Slowly, so as not to alarm the man, she moved until her body was between Alex and the gun.

Paul cleared his throat, and Payback jerked his head around. "I'm serious, man. You so much as move an inch, this lady's going to die."

"Just relax, mate." Arms hanging loosely at his sides, Paul spoke in his normal calm voice, as though he dealt with mad gunmen every day. "No need to hurt anyone. Why don't you tell me what you want, and I'll try to help you. But we don't have any narcotics in this lab."

"I want some of that smartness drug. That stuff that turns

people into geniuses. You know the stuff I mean."

After a shocked moment of palpable disbelief, Paul shrugged and nodded. "The auxosome? Okay. No worries. I can do that. Hang on just a moment and I'll fix some up for you. Really, there's no need for the weapon, won't you please put it away? You're terrifying the little boy."

He'll get some sort of tranquilizer, Jill thought in a daze of hope. He'll load the hypo up with some major shit that'll knock this Payback creep out until we can get the police to the lab.

"Oh, one more thing." Payback added. "Make up two doses of it, one for me and one for you. That way I'll know you're not trying to poison me."

Paul stared back silently for what seemed a long time. Finally he said, "Look, Payback, you need to understand something. The auxosomes are still in the experimental stage. They've never been tested on people. Never. Only on animals. When they're given to the mice, the mice get sick at first."

"I just heard you tell the kid that after they get over being sick, they're healthier and smarter than ever."

"That's true with the mice. So far. But it might make people a lot sicker. We don't know."

"I'm willing to take the risk, and you better be too, if you don't want to have a bloody mess to clean up off your nice clean floor." Payback poked at Jill with the barrel of the gun.

"Don't you hurt my mom!" Alex struggled to free himself from Jill's arm.

"Well, aren't you a cocky little runt. Lady, you'd better teach your kid some...." Looking closely at her son for the first time, seeing Alex's patchy hair, he fell silent; a spasm of disgust crossed his face. "Somebody already run an experiment on you, kid?"

Fury. Rage. Terror. Just stay calm. Breathe slowly. Jill realized she was squeezing Alex so tightly he must be terribly uncomfortable. She loosened her grip, thinking bitterly of how today might have been her last chance ever to touch Paul as well.

"All right, Payback. I'll make up two doses of the drug."

"Make up four. More the merrier. We'll start with the kid."

She screamed. "Paul, no!"

"It'll be okay, Jill."

"You fucking prick," she yelled at Payback, spray bursting from her lips. Never in her life had she been so icily furious. "You'll inject my kid over my dead body. Go on and shoot me, I don't care."

Paul said in an absurdly calm voice, "Jill, Alex needs his mother to take care of him. Please don't do anything."

"Everyone gets the drug," Payback said. "Alex first. That's your name, right, buddy?"

"Mom?" Alex whispered. "I'm sorry I talked you into coming to the lab."

"Shut up!" Payback drew back his lips like a growling dog. "Hey, Paul, I'm keeping an eye on you, man. You make any move except to get the drug ready, and Miss Pizza Face and her baldheaded kid are history."

"We have to do what he says," Paul was murmuring in a soothing tone. "Jill, look, I'm ninety-nine percent certain we won't suffer any bad side effects from the auxosome. Not compared to getting shot dead, anyway. Sorry, bad joke." To Payback he said, "I need to measure the bolus based on body weight, Payback. How much do you weigh?"

"One eighty-five."

"Okay, same as me, roughly. I'm going to walk to the other side of the room and take four bottles from the warm room. That's where I keep the auxosomes, because there's a very narrow range of temperatures at which the viral vector remains stable."

Payback nodded his head curtly. "Do it. Get what you need, but don't try anything clever. It better be the drug you give me and not just water or something. I want you to show it to me."

Time slowed down, dragging on and on. Payback fidgeted, switching the gun from left hand to right. The tip of the fourth finger and over half of the pinky on his right hand, Jill saw, were gone, nothing but ugly scar tissue.

"Quit staring at my hand!" Payback kicked hard at Jill's ankle, and she tightened her grip on Alex again, afraid he would again try to defend her. "You won't be making any police reports, bitch."

At last, Paul turned toward them.

"It's ready." Paul walked slowly toward Payback, holding a tray with four thin, one-use hypodermic syringes.

"Shit, no, I hate needles, man. I want to swallow mine with water."

"It has to go directly into the bloodstream."

Payback hesitated. "I need to think." His eyes were fixed on the syringes, but he kept the gun pointed at Jill. "Do the kid."

"Chin up, son," Paul said, kneeling down beside the trembling boy. "Lean over, I'm going to give you a little shot in the leg, your arm's too thin. It'll sting a little bit, but you'll be okay in a moment."

"I hate 'jections, like he does."

"Can you be brave?"

The boy's eyes were filled to overflowing with tears; he nodded.

"Okay. Deep breath." Paul eased the tip of the needle beneath the skin of Alex's right thigh, withdrew it, dabbed with a medicated square of gauze. "You alright, honey?"

"Sure." Alex was crying silently, but he nodded.

"Give me your arm," Paul told the gunman.

"I'm not an idiot," Payback said. "You two first. I'll tell you which needles to use. But first we wait for half an hour. I want to see what happens to the kid."

"The janitors might walk in on us. Let's get it over with. You can choose one of these two, Payback. Your weight's close enough to mine."

"The door's locked."

"They have keys, you know."

After five endless minutes, with Alex visibly unhurt, Payback reserved one of the syringes with shaking fingers, more agitated than ever. "Okay, inject her and yourself," he said, still pointing the gun at Jill. Paul rolled up one sleeve, swabbed the skin of his left arm with an alcohol patch, took a syringe from the tray, flicked it with a practiced finger, slid the needle in.

"Go on! Inject it!"

Paul pushed the plunger. After a moment, he swabbed Jill's arm, injected her.

"Now me. Hurry!" Payback held out his arm and winced, his face going pale, as Paul injected him with the drug. Jill wondered in a wild moment of hope if Payback were going to faint.

"Mom?" Alex whispered. "I need to go to the potty."

"I thought I told you to shut up." Payback reached around Jill and grabbed the front of Alex's shirt.

"Don't you touch him!" Jill pushed at Payback's arm; there was a deafening blast of sound, and Payback's body was jolted backwards. Jill could see Alex's mouth wide open, screaming, but she could hear nothing but a low-pitched roar. It took a moment for her to realize that Payback's gun must have gone off. Paul, face bloodless, turned to look at her, took a step toward her, stopped when Payback, hands shaking, pointed the gun at her head.

Alex went limp in her arms, then jerked convulsively. Her first thought was utterly desperate: he had been hit when the gun went off! No, thank god, that couldn't be right. A bullet would have hit her first. Her son's face was ashen, his lips blue, his jeans stained with urine. If he slid to the floor he might injure his head, but she was afraid if she moved to lower him more gently Payback would panic and fire another shot.

She swung her face up toward Payback, tried to make him meet her eye, but he stared fixedly at the top of her head. "My boy is very ill," she told him, barely able to hear her own words over the roaring in her ears. "You must let me call an ambulance. He might die! Please. Kill me if you have to, but please let me call a doctor for my little boy." Surely someone must have heard the gunshot, she thought. These labs usually had a couple of students or researchers, even in the evening, people wandering in to check on their experiments, tending to the animals. Why the hell wasn't anyone trying to get in here to see what had happened?

"Shit!" The gunman's face was a livid mask of fear and hatred, staring at Alex's sagging body. "You asshole! You've poisoned us all!"

"Alex has cancer, you fucking moron!" Her voice was ragged, edging toward a scream; she didn't think she would be able to remain still much longer. "I've got to get him to a doctor. I think he's dying."

Paul caught her eye. "Payback, you need to let Jill take care of her son. He's seriously ill. He needs to lie down. She's not going anywhere. Just let her put the child down."

Payback studied Jill and Alex for a few long seconds and finally said, "Okay."

"Thank you." Jill gently lowered Alex to the floor, and a little color returned to his face. His heartbeat was weak, but regular.

Paul was saying, "There's something else you need to know. Another two injections are required, two weeks apart."

"Bullshit," Payback said. "You're making it up."

Damn it, Jill thought at the same moment, why bring up the need for extra treatments? Then she understood: he was providing an incentive, a motive to stop Payback from killing them immediately, as the gunman surely intended.

"Call them booster shots. Genetic regulators. Look, the auxosomes will start to multiply very fast inside our cells, like a virus. But they won't harm us. They regress some of our body and brain cells back to stem cells, how they were in the womb, and force others to build new cells."

"Extra brain cells," Payback said.

"Many more than we need," Paul told him with terrible, contained calm. "It's what happens in the fetal brain...." He paused, plainly searching for words. "There are two processes that put the brakes on neurogenesis. On nerve-building, right? That's the process we just kick-started. One's called apoptosis—" He paused again. "Call it nerve pruning. Like cutting brambles back, see? Without the two regulator shots, our brain cells might just keep multiplying in an uncontrolled way. I can't make any guarantees." In a hard, angry tone he said, "*Fuck* it, this was *years* away from human clinical testing." Paul glanced sideways, then, as though he heard something. Instantly, his face was impassive. Jill, ears still ringing from the gunshot, didn't catch anything until a fraction of a second later. Raised voices in the hallway.

The voices were getting closer. Jill could make out some of the words now. "...check this one...clear...of the building."

A rattling sound: someone trying to turn the locked door-knob.

A masculine voice shouted, "Police!" Something crashed against the door.

Panicked, Payback looked wildly around the room, ran to the nearest window and climbed out, moving amazingly fast. Paul ran toward him, blocking Jill and Alex.

There must have been a ledge under the window. The intruder faced the room, raised the gun, pointed it at Paul. As a second crash brought the door down, he fired the gun.

LIFE

70: MONDAY, JUNE 23

Wayne hurt real bad. He tried to move, and couldn't. It was the worst physical pain he had ever experienced. The weight of something burned in his cramped right hand. He forced open his eyes, looked down. Sinews stood out on his bare arm; he was clutching a gun.

Fuck, he thought, I finally found the guts to do it. Shot myself. Must be dying. It was strange. He'd always imagined death would come more quickly, if you did it that way. Stick the gun in your mouth, pull the trigger, then nothing. This wasn't nothing. Hell, no. This was way worse than nothing.

Why aren't I tasting blood? He ran his tongue over his aching, bullet-shattered teeth, and they weren't shattered—all his teeth were there, and hurting like a son of a bitch, like they do when you're five days gone with the worst case of flu. Impossible that you could fire a bullet into your skull and leave your teeth intact. Maybe they give you your body back in Hell, the better for you to feel the torture.

He groaned out loud. Maybe he hadn't shot himself after all. Maybe he'd jumped out of a high window. When he forced his eyes open again, he blurrily saw a limestone wall to his left, a thick cover of leaves to his right. If you jumped out of some building, he asked himself, why the hell are you holding the gun?

As his head began to clear a little, another possibility occurred to him. While he was in the bad place, the dark hole where he did things he never remembered, maybe he'd used the gun to murder someone. The law might be pursuing him—or pursuing someone he'd rather die than meet up with, someone hungry for payback. Flat on his back, he took inventory. Both his hands worked, and the fingers flexed. Arms were bruised, but he could still use them; he levered himself up to sitting position. Whole head seemed intact, aching as though he'd banged it hard again and again against a brick wall. Okay, he could move his right leg; oh, shit. Through the pain, more pain, sharp and localized. The left ankle was either broken or badly sprained. When he tried to move it, agony jolted up his leg. Looked like he was just going to have to lie slumped here, a sitting duck for whatever pursuit might be after him.

Using his arms and the good leg, he pushed himself toward the wall. Like he'd be any safer there. He cried out as his left leg scraped against a concrete collar. Its rusty manhole cover was slightly ajar. Like a wounded animal, Wayne began pushing away from this obstacle, then stopped.

Use your brains, man. Maybe, if he drew on every bit of his will power, he could shove the cover off and climb down the manhole. Sprains or not. Some sort of ruckus not far away. Rapidly moving feet clattered. Police radios crackled, hissing. Someone shouted an order to close off this part of campus. Not for a moment did Wayne doubt that they were after him. His worst fears had come to pass. Well, almost the worst: at least he hadn't blown his own fucking head apart. Breathing deeply, he got up on all fours, pushed on the cover, saw it move an inch, pushed again. The grating noise of it appalled him.

Hopefully the cops were making too much noise themselves to notice the harsh sound. The heavy brute of a thing didn't want to move. When he had created an opening barely wide enough to squeeze through, Wayne took a steadying breath and lowered his legs into it, lips clamped tightly so no sound would escape. Inside he was screaming fit to bring the whole crew down on him.

There was no way he could put his weight on the messed-up left leg, so he had to prop on the steel rung, all his weight bearing on his right foot, brace himself as best he could with that leg and his right arm as he pulled the cover back in place with his left. Adrenalin coursed in his blood stream; with its aid, and cursed prayers to some god of the doomed, he climbed down the steel ladder, lowering himself with painful jolts one rung at a time.

71: TUESDAY, JUNE 24

The previous evening a hospital orderly had set up a cot for Jill in Alex's room, offering a pill to help her sleep, but at 11:45 in the morning she still sat beside her son's bed, holding his hand. Even in his sleep he moaned and clutched at her hand whenever she tried to pull it away. She felt confused and sick and still didn't quite understand what was happening. All she knew for sure was that she'd followed the paramedics when they put Alex on a high-tech stretcher and carried him away. And she knew—she saw again and again in awful memory—that after the gunshot Paul had fallen from the window. Hospital staff offered only vague assurances that he was alive. Imagining the worst, she alternated between tears and determined calm, for the benefit of Alex.

Her cell phone vibrated; she gasped, startled. "Hello?" I sound like a frightened child, she thought.

"Jill, it's Paul. How are you?"

"I'm so glad you called." She covered the mouthpiece with her hand so he would not know she was crying.

"I tried to get in to visit you and Alex, but they said no visitors other than family until he's feeling better.... Are you okay, Jill?"

"Yeah, just a moment." She reached behind her for the box of tissues on the table beside the bed, wiped her eyes and nose, took a deep breath. "Okay. Better now."

"How's Alex? They said he'd be okay but wouldn't give me any details."

"The doctors think the shock must have brought on a seizure. He could've *died*, Paul. So could you."

"I'm all right. I wasn't shot, Jill." He gave an embarrassed laugh. "I passed out."

"Good thing too, perfect timing. They say Alex'll be okay, he's coming out of it. Planning to keep him one more night for observation and release him tomorrow morning. What about the auxosomes, Paul? Are we going to be all right?

"I feel a little—well, to be frank, comprehensively under the weather. Low grade fever, headache. I'm pretty sure that's what caused me to faint. How are you?"

"My stomach hurts. Muscle pains everywhere."

"I thought of filling the syringes with saline solution," Paul said in a wretched voice, "but the prick was watching me too closely, and he seemed crazy enough to kill someone if he thought I was trying to put something over on him. I was expecting the onset to be slower, since I injected us subcutaneously rather than into a vein. So far, I haven't noticed any changes in mental capacity."

"Me either, unless it makes you anxious and terrified. Um, that was a feeble attempt at humor."

Paul laughed dutifully. "But look, Jill, I think there's actually a chance the stuff'll help Alex recover. Don't expect anything drastic for a while, though. The artificial chromosomes have to make huge numbers of copies of themselves and then infect sufficient cells before they start to edit and correct our DNA errors. We'll just have to wait and see." He hesitated. "Have you told anyone about the auxosomes?"

"No, not yet. I was pretty shaken up when they first brought us to the hospital, so the police said they'd talk to me later. A nurse gave me a pill. Said it would relax me. Haven't really talked to anyone about what happened at the lab."

"Let's not tell the quacks or the cops about the auxosomes. Not just yet. It'd muddy the waters. I mean, what could they do?

This is uncharted medical territory."

Jill thought about that for a while, hugging the phone against her ear. "You're right. If Alex is okay tomorrow, I don't see any reason to go into details. Have the police caught that guy?"

"No. Son of a bitch got away."

"Oh my God. He's still out there somewhere."

"You and Alex should be safe. It's the regulator shots he'd be after if he came around again, not you two. I'll just need to be very careful for a while. I told the cops he was a junkie looking for a fix so he got angry when I didn't have any narcotics in the lab."

"Paul, they'll notice the used hypodermics. You must have dropped them when the gun went off."

"Bugger, you're right. I'll say he interrupted me working on the animals. Unfortunately, if they assume he's not coming back they won't bother posting extra guards there. Maybe I shouldn't have told the bastard about the regulator doses, but I wanted to make sure he didn't kill us all immediately."

"I think that's exactly what he planned, just kill us all on the spot. My God, Paul, he nearly shot you anyway. Where did the bullet end up?"

"Went through the wall out into the hallway. Good thing no one was standing there, they were all trying to break the door open. But look, I don't really expect to see him again. He'd hardly try to shoot me if he's all that concerned about follow-up doses."

"That was then," Jill said, in a terrifying burst of insight. Abruptly she felt cold and sick. "He's going to be a different man once the enhancement effects kick in, isn't that right? He'll be smarter, Paul. He has to come back. And I think he knows my address, he was staring at my driver's license. Paul, I can't go home."

"You're right, of course. You can stay at my—"

"Oh no, Paul, I couldn't possible impose—"

"You take my apartment," he said firmly. "I'll camp for a few weeks in my office. Believe me, I've done it before."

"No, if Alex and I move into your apartment you should stay with us. Safety in numbers."

What would her old friends at Allen Hoffman and Nature Forever think? Moving in with the enemy. No, she *was* the enemy now—a genetically modified human. Wasn't genetic engineering against God's will? But people had once said that about airplanes, too, and blood transfusions. She'd been taught all her life that God was a God of love. Surely God's will wasn't for people to suffer and die unnecessarily. After all, He had given people brains to think with. Wouldn't it be against God's will not to make the best possible use of His gifts? If they worked right, Paul's auxosomes would repair broken or worn-out DNA; how could something like that be against God's will? It didn't make sense. She couldn't believe it was any more against God's will than using antibiotics or taking vitamin supplements.

72: TUESDAY, JUNE 24

Afternoon light fell in golden bars across the executive office. In one fluid motion, Art Sutton brushed a speck of lint from the sleeve of his dark blue, custom tailored Tom James suit, gestured Jill to one of the chairs grouped around an antique tea table across from his desk. His shirt's crisp whiteness, the neatness of his silvery mane with every hair in place, the faint hint of cologne made Jill acutely aware of her own disheveled appearance.

Although a nurse had loaned her a hospital gown and wrapped her in a blanket as she sat beside Alex's bed, there'd been no time to go home and change into something fresh. It had seemed more sensible to come straight to the office from the hospital, where she had left Alex playing backgammon with one of the volunteers. Yesterday's silk blouse was wrinkled, and her white skirt was smudged with dirt. Becca had intercepted her as she grabbed a couple of files to work on at home, informed her that Sutton wanted to talk to her right away.

Art seated himself across from Jill. "How's your boy?"

"He's better today. His doctor wants to keep him in the hospital another day for observation, but we should be able to go home by Thursday, Friday at the latest. I planned to take my files home and work on them there."

Art cleared his throat. "Jill, you recall the chat we had a couple of weeks ago."

"Yes, and it's been working out very well. I haven't had to miss any work since then." Seeing Art's lips tighten, she added, "Until yesterday."

"Right. Until yesterday. And today. And it sounds as though you'll be missing tomorrow and Thursday as well. Maybe Friday."

"Art, for heaven's sake, Alex and I were threatened by a crazy man with a *gun*. The thing went off only a foot from my head. Do you have any idea what that's like? I spent hours yesterday at the police station going over the whole thing, answering hundreds of questions...."

"I'm sure it was a difficult experience for both you and your son, and you have my heartfelt sympathy. But the fact remains that you are not currently capable of doing the job we hired you to do."

That caught Jill completely unprepared; she gaped at him. It had never occurred to her that Art would not understand; she had expected him, in fact, to be grateful that she was conscientious enough to take work home under such atrocious circumstances.

"The other partners and I discussed it yesterday evening, and we agreed. We're going to have to let you go, Jill. I'm very sorry." He held a properly serious pose for a moment, then brightened. "We will, of course, allow you two weeks' severance pay, and once Alex is better, we'll be happy to help you find a new, less demanding job."

It was impossibly unfair, impossible to take in. "You're just... *firing* me? Just like that?"

"Not at all, Ms. Shannon—helping you to relocate. Aside

from the personal problems you've had in connection with your son, you've been an excellent employee and," he smiled magnanimously, "we're prepared to give you glowing references."

"Uh...don't you want me to finish drafting the Leigh Partnership Agreement? I'm right in the middle—"

"Thank you, Jill, that won't be necessary. We've already reassigned all the files you were working on. Javier has some boxes and will help you pack your stuff and carry it out to your car. Oh, and we'll need the key to the front door and to your office." He held out his manicured hand.

With trembling fingers she slipped them from her key ring, placed them on the glass top of the tea table, ignoring his open hand. Offended, he reached down and took the keys. They clinked against the glass. She wanted to throw them in Art's face, yell every bitter insult she could think of at this uncaring machine of a man, but that would not change his mind, would only excuse his contempt. It must be contempt he felt; how else could he act like this?

"Goodbye, Art." With as much dignity as she could muster, she turned and walked away.

"So long, Jill. Good luck."

Luck? It'll take a damn *miracle*, Jill told herself in despair, for Alex and me to get through this with no money coming in. In the hallway she pulled her cell phone out of her purse and entered Paul's number. "Alex gets out of the hospital tomorrow," she told his voice mail. "Still want a couple of roommates?"

73: WEDNESDAY, JUNE 25

Wayne guessed it was at least two days since he climbed down the manhole, but it could just as easily have been two hours. He had found himself in a tunnel barely high enough to stand up in. One side was a walkway, the other was filled with pipes and electrical conduits. He had crawled along the walkway until he came to a point where the tunnel widened to form a small room containing a boiler that did not seem to be in use. He had hidden himself behind the boiler, curled into a fetal position, drifting in and out of consciousness. This place was his home now; the idea of leaving was terrifying. Gnawing hunger had given way to a sort of chronic numb emptiness. But he could no longer ignore the thirst and the need to pee.

He unfolded himself slowly and carefully, like working a rusty pair of pliers. He stood, leaned against the moisture beaded wall to keep from falling over. His hurt ankle had swollen but he could put a little weight on it now, which indicated it was not broken. He had no plan, since he had no idea where he was. The cops had been yelling about closing off part of campus, so he could be at a school. He'd dreamed about a chemistry lab. Sometimes in the dreams he was a grown man, other times a little boy, screaming in protest as his father held him down so the doctor could give him a shot.

He walked very slowly, leaning against the wall, finally found a ladder. Not the same one he'd come down. This one was much shorter, and he was pretty sure he could climb it without falling. Maybe the cops had given up looking for him by now and he could melt away into the city. What he'd do then he had no idea.

At the top of the ladder was a wooden trap door rather than a manhole cover. He poked his head through the opening: he had come up into a long hallway with green walls. He pushed himself free and scanned his surroundings. He seemed to be the only person around. A clock on the wall read 3:10. Must be A.M.

Ignoring the pain from his ankle, Wayne shuffled down the empty hallway until he found a toilet. His foot looked awful. Farther along was a sign on the front of an unlocked door marked "Student Lounge." Inside, he found a water fountain and more: a half eaten hamburger someone had left on one of the two Formica-topped tables. Rapturously, he took a very small bite to make the pleasure of eating last longer. He could remember no food that had ever brought him such tremendous pleasure.

74: THURSDAY, JUNE 26

The Four Seasons Hotel was built just above Town Lake, with terraces overlooking the parklike riverbank. Although his auxosome-induced nausea and headache had passed, Paul still felt too weak to run and instead had gone for a walk on the trail winding around the lake. He sat on the edge of the lower terrace, for the first time in his life totally captivated by a landscape.

A Rose of Sharon hedge was in bloom. Its unusual shade of reddish purple caught his eye. Bending to look more closely at one of the flowers, he was struck by the pleasing composition of shrubs and stone work. Had he ever seen such depth of color before, all the myriad shades of green, broken here and there by the contrasting reds and purples of flowers? Not since childhood, he realized. Not since wondrous, goggling infancy, besotted by the mystery and beauty of every patch of light, rich scent, sweet or sour taste on his hungry baby's tongue. Those forgotten baby memories burst up through him, nearly over-whelming, bringing prickling tears to his eyes. Looking down at the wall, built from local limestone, he noticed the fossilized remains of sea animals that had lived in this place millions of years ago; he found the juxtaposition of modern and ancient life forms powerfully moving.

A young woman jogged by, and Paul marveled at the play of light through her hair and the movement of her muscles under sleek, tanned skin. A week ago, he realized, he'd have reacted with brief, routinely lustful appreciation but now, as he watched her pass by, he felt as well the thrill he experienced solving a particularly challenging theoretical problem or suddenly grasping new insights in the lab. With something close to awe he watched a drop of sweat on her face refract sunlight in a burst of rainbow colors.

Uh-oh, he thought then. The auxosomes in my brain tissues starting to kick in.

In his late teens he'd tried LSD once, had reveled in the

sensory blitz, the roller coaster ride of weird perceptions, but this wasn't an acid trip. He was seeing the world whole, for a moment. He had anticipated that the neural enhancements might gradually improve his memory or help him reason more clearly, but he had not expected his perception of ordinary things to be intensified. Jill will love this, he thought, smiling. Alex too, although that lovable scamp probably lived in a world like this most of the time.

With a jolt, it occurred to him that Payback was probably going through the same thing. Despite the anger he felt at the man for violating their privacy, endangering their lives, Paul found himself wishing, improbably, that he and Payback could talk, compare notes on this remarkable change they were going through. I might get my chance to talk to Payback, he thought, if the bastard comes back looking for a second injection. But surely he won't come waltzing back into the lab.

Paul continued on his walk, and the fluid flow of his muscles delighted him. I wonder what he'll do. What would *I* do if I were in his place? He stopped, struck by a terrifying certainty: If I were in his place, I'd grab Alex. Oh God, I've got to warn Jill.

75: THURSDAY, JUNE 26

"Alex and I are staying here at Paul's for a while," Jill said. "Hold on a moment, Carol." She put her phone down, juggled a box of files onto the table, retrieved the phone and kicked the door shut. "I feel reasonably safe here, the apartment's on the second floor." She gave her friend the address.

"But you're okay? There's nothing I can do?"

"We're fine, really."

"Let's be practical, Jill. I'm worried for you. Any prospect of another job?"

Jill shook her head in fond exasperation. What was this, "tough love"? Maybe so: Carol forcing her to confront the hard options.

"Not immediately."

Carol paused. That was unusual enough to alert Jill.

"You know, you could sell your house."

The suggestion floored her. Dryly, she said, "Rather a drastic solution."

"Sweetie, the guy tried to *murder* you and Alex."

"I know. Carol, I gotta go, so much stuff to be done before Paul gets back."

"Take care. And give Alex my love."

"You bet."

Carol's suggestion seemed less preposterous by the time she stopped at the pharmacy to fill Alex's prescriptions. Someone had left a GreenSheet Weekly Advertiser on the counter next to the lip balm and breath freshener, and Jill leafed through it while she waited for her order to be filled. Surprising how much prices had climbed since she and Keith bought the house on Fruth seven years ago, even allowing for the recession's burst real estate bubble.

A plan was coming together by the time she got Alex settled into bed, where the doctor said he must spend most of his time for the next few days. From the Yellow Pages, Jill chose a realtor who claimed to specialize in selling residences in the Hyde Park area.

"A two-one on Fruth Street? I have a couple of free hours. I can come over and take a look at it now."

"I'm not actually at the house right now, and it would be hard for me to meet you over there. My little boy is sick, and I can't leave him alone. Could you drive by Fruth Street and look at the house, then meet me here at 2456 San Gabriel?"

Within the hour, Blanca Mendoza, licensed broker, was seated in the living room with Jill, pen poised over a Listing Agreement. "If you're looking for a quick sale, I'd say don't ask more than $375,000. Of course I'll have to do a full inspection, but the house looks in excellent condition and has curb appeal. One bath is a drawback, and so is the lack of a garage. If you could live with $375,000 I have a buyer I think might be interested. The housing bubble has well and truly burst."

Jill did a quick calculation: after she paid off the mortgage and the realtor's commission, that would net her almost $150,000. Enough, maybe, to supplement income from part time work for two or three years.

"Shouldn't we ask for more than I actually expect to get?"

"Tell you what." Blanca smiled agreeably. "We'll list it at $400.000."

"Okay. Sounds good." Jill began studying the agreement.

"I'd like to take someone by this afternoon, if that would be all right with you. This is exactly the sort of home he's looking for."

Oh. Eager. Well, eager is good. "That would be fine." She handed over her spare house keys.

After Mendoza had left, Jill squeezed oranges so Alex could drink fresh juice when he woke up, then realized she had nothing else to do. She started toward the refrigerator to engage in her usual default activity but realized she had no desire to eat. Her gaze fell on the three cardboard boxes she had brought with her when she moved to Paul's. One of the clerks had bought them in as she was being escorted from Art Sutton's office. They contained the personal contents of her office; everything had been cleaned out. It was made icily clear that she would have no need, ever again, to return to the office that had been hers for the past two years. Might as well go through the boxes now, she thought. If anything's missing I'll give them hell about it.

The first two boxes held books and binders she had collected from continuing education seminars. Looked like everything was there, though she couldn't be 100 percent sure; she hadn't kept a record of everything she'd taken to the office.

In the third box was a collection of stuff from her desk: her calendar, a photo of Alex, a folder of notes for a paper she wanted to write for a legal journal. Several items, though, didn't look familiar. Curious, she pulled out a green file folder labeled "Violet Crown Estates: Plaintiff Interviews." It was the class action lawsuit she'd been working on with Preston

Bowie. A land developer had decreased the value of neighboring homes by badly polluting a creek. But she had never seen these particular files before. She'd have to get them back; poor Clothile had probably searched every cubic inch of space in the building by now, looking for them. She pulled out two more files. Both Violet Crown Estates. The next file did not have a label; "Correspondence" was scribbled across the front in pencil. Preston Bowie's scrawl. Uncertain that she should, Jill opened it.

The first sheet bore Blick Pharmaceuticals letterhead. At the top, boldly printed with a black marker:

Tom, I don't need to tell you what the introduction into the market of a superior SSRI antidepressant like Luminol would do to our bottom line. Take care of it. BB

She had seen that same handwriting, those same initials on Blick Pharmaceuticals memos about their pet Green foundation, Nature Forever. Nobody named Tom worked in her office. Underneath, written with a ball point in a different hand:

Preston, you need to get your people to work up a no holds barred campaign in support of H.R. 117. Bruce will make it well worthwhile. Tom

Jill frowned, puzzled. She was not naive. Money could buy political power, and often did—but surely Nature Forever stood for something different, something better than the usual sordid deals. I shouldn't be reading Preston's personal correspondence, she realized, feeling cold. I should get this back to him immediately.

Despite herself, she reached for the next letter in the file. As she read it, her stomach tightened sickeningly. At the top of the dot matrix printout was the heading *Green Guerrilla Message Board* and several sentences, the last unfinished, from a Usenet posting:

MJT, Incorporated is a hideous bleeding sore on the body of Gaia. This corporation would attempt to control the creation of life itself. This corporation and others like it were responsible for my wifes death. Tonight I did my sacred duty as one of Gaias soldiers against the cancer of Homo

Below was handwriting she recognized from the memo:

This is Rutherford's S 54B from the Ebuflex programming trials in the early 80's. Calls himself Earthsavior now.

That last note was not signed, but she recognized the handwriting as BB's. Bruce Blick. She was still sitting there, too stunned by what she had read to move, when Blanca Mendoza called with the good news:
"I've got a full-price offer for you on your house!"
As she hung up the phone, eyes filling with tears, Jill told herself: This is one of the defining moments in my life. Her job and house had both been a larger part of her self-image than she had realized. Now her house was gone, and the very integrity of the job that was no longer hers had been snatched away. It was as if she'd lost her footing and were falling helplessly out of her life and into someone else's.

76: THURSDAY, JUNE

I'm changing, Wayne thought. I must have fallen and hit my head when I smashed up my ankle. He had discovered the library the night he'd gone poking around looking for more food, and somehow his mind felt far hungrier than his stomach. Reading became a compulsion; he slept during the day and spent his nights furtively crouched in the library. Half the time he'd get so wrapped up in his reading he forgot to eat. He knew he'd have to leave this place eventually, but it was too dangerous now with the cops out to catch him for whatever horrible crime he had committed. Keep a low profile, that was the thing. No way even to call Fern, they might know his identity, have his home phone bugged.

At first he had picked up books at random, read until he felt restless. Soon, though, he found himself developing an interest in certain topics, seeking out extra background information in other books mentioned in footnotes and bibliographies. Whenever he stopped to think about it, he was amazed at how quickly he was gulping the books down, how much of the information he'd absorbed. The second night, he got interested in brains. It turned out the individual components of a human brain were almost identical to those in a mouse. The difference between him and a mouse was really no more than the number of brain cells and the number of different ways those could link with each other. Synapses, that was what the scientists called the connections.

As if recalled from a dream, fragmented bits of overheard conversation played themselves over in his memory. He'd been given a shot! Someone had loaded him up with some fucking drug! A treatment that would cause extra neurons to grow, forcing them to build new connections. That's what this damned treatment was doing. He had no idea how he knew it, but it was so. Dizzy, he hunted for information on neurons, reading eagerly. When he noticed it was almost time for the library to open for the day, he gathered up as many books as he could carry and took them back with him when he returned to his underground refuge, where he continued to read under the dim utility lamp overhead until he fell asleep.

He hadn't felt this way since he was a kid, a small fry, when he and his friends went exploring, climbing on the roofs of houses under construction, poking around in Old Man McNutt's junkyard, watching tadpoles grow into frogs a little each day. Eventually, even his manic craving to learn gave way to exhaustion, and he slept for a few hours.

§

Even as he stands beside his father, watching the strong, sure hands push the plank into the whirring saw blade, Wayne knows he is dreaming. He sees the scene as if he is standing slightly above and behind himself, hears the malevolent shrieking of the blade as if from a vast distance.

His father turns to him as one end of the plank clatters to the floor. "Now you try it."

Wayne draws back, away from the cruel thing that lies in wait, ready to hurt him badly. Without any conscious thought on his part, his older, dreaming self steps into the scene. The little boy is gone. He directs the murderous rage he feels for his father into his hands. Grasps the wood, begins to push it into the blade, as his father has done. He feels a stinging sensation. Bright red drops spatter on the wood, the table, his own arms. He feels triumph.

§

Wayne sat up, suddenly and completely awake, stared at the ugly stumps of his fingers. He had never known how it happened. His father had shouted at him, calling him careless, blaming him for not paying close enough attention.

"How the hell could I've known what I was doing?" Wayne muttered aloud, angry at the past. "You didn't bother to teach me. I wasn't ready. You made me do it when I wasn't ready." The fury he felt toward his father shocked him as much as the memories that came crowding into his mind like a barrage of baseball cards raining down on him, burying him. The rock flung through the workshop window. The honey in the gas tank of his daddy's car.

"You were too much of a fucking coward," someone said in his daddy's voice. "So I had to do it for you."

Chilled, he knew that the words were coming from his own mouth. He lurched back against the cold concrete. "Who are you?" God, was he going nuts, hearing voices?

"Just call me Payback." His father's voice.

"You're part of me." He was shaking.

"I'm no part of you. People all the time calling me by your name, but I'm no part of you."

This was the one who'd done those things he was too terrified to recall. But now he *had* to remember. Staring down into the pit of memory was the only way he could make himself whole. How else could he make amends for whatever vile things he had done? He willed himself to remember those things, those horrors that had come to him in dreams:

§

Lying unconscious, dark hair spread across the brown and yellow-stained mattress, the bitch looked more like a schoolgirl than a grown-up cancer researcher with a fancy medical science degree. Like Melody when he'd first met her, before she'd got sick. Payback waited, watching. He would not touch her until she woke up. He wanted her to know exactly what was happening to her—and why.

He glanced at the Mason jar sitting atop the dusty wooden crate that served as a bedside table. The surface of the dark layer at the bottom of the jar rose and fell in jerky waves.

The cancer doctor stirred, put a hand to her forehead, moaned.

"Well, it's about time. You'd think I gave you a whole bottle of sleeping pills or something, 'stead of a little tap on the head."

She opened her eyes a slit and made as if to sit up.

"Not so fast there." He shook his finger. "First you have to find out what it feels like to be the guinea pig."

Now she was fully awake, her eyes round with surprise and dawning fear.

"It's time for payback and you're going to make the first installment. You owe—" He found himself panting slightly, hand trembling a little. "What you people did to my wife—no, don't bother trying to get yourself loose." He had her tied down to the bed with stout hemp rope from his daddy's workshop. "Don't you be getting any ideas about yelling either, you understand?"

Only hours ago, her lips had haughtily issued orders. Now they were parted and trembling, ready to scream. Payback liked seeing that. But there was too much risk if she made a lot of noise and attracted attention.

He stuffed deep into her mouth a dirty rag doll with yellow yarn hair, taped it in place with silvery duct tape. Something he'd found on the floor of the trailer when he first moved in. The sight of the doll's droopy legs straddling the woman's chin was so comical he wanted to laugh, but this was a solemn occasion. A time of retribution and instruction. She began to gag, and he jiggled the doll's head, pushed it in again but not quite so far. He picked up the Roselli hunting knife from the top of the crate, tested its scalpel-honed sharpness with his thumb, lifted her blouse.

"It was right about here," he muttered to himself, and touched her spasming abdomen. "I'd stop that squirming if I was you. It's gonna to hurt more if you don't lie still."

Her eyes were huge now, terrified, and she was making blurred, frightened sounds. He ran the knife lightly along her skin, just below the navel, plotting the course. He moved his hand back to the starting position and retraced the line, bearing down hard enough to part the skin. At first the cut was clean; then it filled with blood. Payback glanced up at her head. She was twisting from side to side, spilling tears from her eyes, grunting, moaning.

Payback pulled at both sides of the skin, slashed through the lumpy yellow fat, exposing the shiny peritoneum, carefully positioned the knife. The woman arched her back and jerked her midsection up; the knife sliced into the guts, spilling foul-smelling semi-liquid into the tightly packed darkness of the abdominal cavity. The stench, like shit and vomit stirred together in a warm bowl, disgusted him.

"Shit! You stupid klutz! I told you to lie still." When Payback had imagined his revenge, he'd thought it would be easy, like gutting a deer. But a dead deer didn't move around and cause you to screw up and cut into the bulging intestines. "This is just gonna make it take longer and hurt worse." He looked up to see if she was paying attention to what he was saying. Her head had fallen back on the pillow, eyes closed. Damn! He briefly considered trying to revive her but decided it would be better to finish what he was doing while he could count on her lying still. He picked up the Mason jar, upended it into the wound. A seething mass of June beetles fell into the abdominal cavity between the protruding coils, tiny claws grappling for purchase in soft, bleeding tissue.

§

It was too much to ask of himself. Everything blurred, lurched sideways.

77: THURSDAY, JUNE 26

As Drew Chang swam effortlessly, warm water massaging his body, he could see bright red and green coral formations only a few feet below, as clearly as if he were viewing them through crisp mountain air. A school of small, arrow shaped fish surrounded him, flashing neon yellow and purple in the sunlight. He marveled at the clarity with which he could make out the flow patterns over and around each individual fish as it moved swiftly through the water.

He couldn't stay here. People were counting on him. Roberta Treadwell, Paul Gibson. And Maureen. She was expecting him for dinner. He had to call her, let her know he would be late. The water was cold, murky, as he swam upward toward the surface. So cold it hurt his head, made his throat burn. He broke through the surface and found himself staring up at dimly lit wooden rafters. He remembered disjointed fragments of talk that made no sense, the mutterings of a psychotic. Quickly he closed his eyes. The crazy man might see he was awake, strike him again. But the air did not smell as it had when the lunatic was close by. The man had an unpleasantly sour body odor, now absent.

Drew opened his eyes a slit, turned his head, fighting dizziness. He was in a room with bare studs and rafters and an odor of damp earth and motor oil. In his right hand he loosely held a water bottle with a little straw. He was horribly thirsty. The first small sip set off a wave of nausea, but he fought it down.

Dim light fell from a small, dusty window directly above him. All he could hear were chirps of birds and a discordant scraping, maybe branches dragged by the wind back and forth across the roof. Drew began sinking into his warm, beautiful ocean, jerked himself back into alertness. I'm dying, he thought. I've got to stay awake, however painful that is. He wondered if the lunatic had brought the binder where he kept his cell phone. Oh God, I'll have to get up and look for it.

Slowly...slowly.... With the greatest effort of his life, Drew sat up, fell against the wall at his back, breathing in shallow gasps. He was sitting on a plank table about four and a half feet above the floor. Was that his leather binder, on a chair half-visible in the gloom? I have to reach it, he thought. He didn't need to know where he was, thank the good Lord, because 911 dispatchers could pinpoint the location of callers using cellular phones.

He planned his journey from the table to the chair with the sort of precision he used in writing a proposal for a scientific research project. He would slide to the edge of the table. Rest until he felt strong enough to move. Make a half turn so that he could hold onto the table with his hands as he slid off. Rest. Ease himself to the floor, supporting his weight against the table. Rest. Once he was on the floor, he could crawl on his hands and knees, taking as long as he needed to reach the chair.

The plan worked as he anticipated. Excellent scientific analysis, he thought approvingly, head swimming. By resting each time he exerted himself, Drew managed to conserve his strength. He reached the edge of the table, paused to catch his breath. He felt dizzy, but by fixing his eyes on his goal and taking slow, deep breaths, he kept his balance. Slowly and deliberately, he put his weight on his left hip and pushed against the table top with his hands, rotating his body until he lay on his stomach, legs extending over the side of the table. He was relieved to note that he was less dizzy in this position than he had been sitting up. Once a friend had talked him into trying sky diving; now, calling on the same reserve of courage that had allowed him to jump from an airplane 5000 feet above the ground, he began to push himself backward into space.

Something happened that Drew had not built into his plan. The table had been made by nailing planks across a frame. For years the roof had leaked, rotting the plank on the front edge of the table, rusting away the nails. His weight snapped the rusty nails. The plank tilted. Drew lost his grip, crashed heavily to the floor.

Pain speared his left arm. A thought began to form: "Oh shit, I've broken my fucking arm." Confusion, then, and the slide through darkness.

78: THURSDAY, JUNE 26

The Margaret Johnson Treadwell Laboratories were housed in an attractive building of steel, concrete, and glass, located near the top of a hill on the western edge of San Antonio. It was drought-hot. Paul stood for a long moment, admiring the dramatic view of the hills, intense blue of the sky, myriad shades of white in the clouds forming as the earth absorbed heat from the climbing sun. From here the world was a glowing Van Gogh painting.

A security guard checked him through, wanding him. The starkness of the reception area's gray slate floor and white walls was relieved by electron microscope images mounted in chrome and glass. Two Mies van der Rohe chairs, a glass topped table, and the receptionist's desk were the only furniture. Paul barely had time to glance at a couple of the framed images before Roberta Treadwell came out to greet him. She was a tall, angular woman with a square jaw and an almost masculine face, formidable until she smiled. But her smile was so openly friendly that Paul lost any trace of nervousness about making a good impression on the MJT people he'd be meeting.

Touring the labs, seeing the plastic-sheeted damage, meeting the fifteen scientists who struggled to sustain their work with part of their equipment in ruins and not yet replaced, Paul lost track of time. After what seemed no more than a couple of hours, Roberta looked at her watch. "You're not a vegetarian, are you, Paul? I'd like to take you to the Texas Steakhouse for lunch."

Given Roberta's wealth, Paul expected a chauffeur-driven limousine but she slipped behind the wheel of a tiny brown English Morris Minor, laughing at his unguarded expression. "I would've driven something more dignified, but I forgot you were coming today until I was halfway to the office. I'm so sorry."

"Not at all!" Paul folded himself into the passenger seat. "I feel quite at home riding in a car that has the steering wheel on the proper side."

"Ah, that's right, Aussies drive on the left hand side of the road." A touch of the starter brought the engine to life. "I collect antique cars. And a few not so ancient."

"Someone surely did a beautiful restoration job on this one."

"Thank you."

Paul sensed personal pride. "You do the work yourself?"

"I hire out the body and paint work, but I do the engines myself. My dad was a mechanic, and I spent a lot of time watching and learning about cars when I was a kid. Helping out down at the shop beat the heck out of doing housework with my mom. My dad was always trying to talk me into taking up a more sedate hobby, like needlepoint, but I find working on cars relaxing."

Paul laughed. He could easily imagine Roberta in greasy overalls sliding out from under a car. "I wish I could say the same. My car's in desperate need of T.L.C., but aside from changing the oil and checking the tires, I'm afraid cars are a mystery to me."

"Maybe I should offer you a new car as an incentive to join us at MJT. What do you think, Paul? Would you be interested in, say, a three year contract? You'd have the freedom to choose your own research.... No need to make a decision right now. I'm not trying to rush you."

"I'm very interested in the position," Paul told her, and left it at that. It would not be good form to accept on the spot, before compensation had been discussed.

"We can go over the details when we get back to the office." She turned into a parking lot, pulled into a space near the front door of the restaurant. The smell of charcoal grilled steak and freshly baked bread told Paul how hungry he was.

Seated, orders placed, Roberta leaned toward him, speaking in such a low voice he could barely hear her. "There's something else I need to tell you," she said with a worried frown. "Drew Chang has disappeared. Has he said anything to you? I know he was particularly upset by the bombing."

That was strange. He hadn't heard from Drew for the best part of a week. "Have you checked with Maureen?"

"John Gilbert was the last person who saw him Friday evening. We spoke to Ms. Baumgarten, of course; she was expecting him for dinner that evening, in fact she gave him a call to hurry him up. He never showed. Next morning his car was found abandoned in the driveway leading to the parking lot."

"The police—?"

"Don't have a clue. Well, they're assuming he didn't just wander off into the sunset—the window was smashed on the driver's side. They're investigating various possibilities. We were told to keep the news to ourselves for the moment. Paul, I don't mean to alarm you, but you need to know that they are looking into terrorist groups and environmental extremists opposed to scientific research. The FBI was called in yesterday."

Paul didn't trust himself to speak.

"It would set our research back years to lose Drew," said Roberta.

"He's the best friend I've made in this country," Paul said, realizing it for the first time, slightly chilled by her detachment. "They should have called me. Someone should have told me."

Roberta reached across the table and squeezed his wrist. "The police are working through a list of everyone he knows, but they'd start with his colleagues here and his family. I'm sorry nobody thought to contact you, Paul. They think there's a good chance he's still alive. If some terrorist or radical group kidnapped him, they'd want to use him for publicity, maybe for some sort of ransom."

"I don't understand these people!" Paul said passionately. He found himself voicing the same question he'd posed to Drew. "How can they *obstruct* something that'll make the lives of their kids longer and healthier?"

"With most of them, I think, it's a lack of knowledge and understanding. Their idea of science comes from what they see in bad movies. But there are some who should know better, and that scares me badly, Paul. Frankly, I think that deep down they hate people, themselves included. Have you been keeping up with the legislation on genetic engineering?"

"Not as well as I should." Paul tried to focus on this new topic. Good god—Drew, a hostage to some crackpot militant group?

"I started to get really worried when the Prohibition Against GE bill passed in the House. They're having committee hearings in the Senate now, and if the committee recommends it, I'm afraid the Senate will pass it too. Unless it's drastically amended, MJT will face major obstacles. I can't imagine they'd pass it with the provisions that prohibit basic research, but— Until we know what's going to happen, it'll be difficult to write an employment contract. We could put in some sort of contingency clause."

"Roberta, I'd assumed this new law would only restrict federal funding, or products from going on sale. You're saying these idiots want to shut down *basic research* as well?" He really should get up to date on this kind of thing, damn it, the university was probably abuzz with rumors. Then again, being shot at made a complete hash of work-related small talk. Not to mention the distractions of slowly having your nervous system rewired from the inside out.

"I'm afraid so. As it's written, it'll ban any research related to modifying human DNA. You should read it at once, Paul."

"I'm ashamed of myself." Certainly he couldn't mention the auxosome procedure at this point, let alone the fact that he was an unintended guinea pig for it. Leave it for now, let's not muddy the waters. "I've been so engrossed in research that I haven't read a newspaper for the past month, other than to skim the headlines on Google News. Roberta, the fact is, I find it difficult to believe that intelligent, civilized people could prohibit basic research."

"I know," she said bleakly, looking up from the menu. "It denies the importance of truth." She grimaced. "I do appreciate people's anxiety about rapid change, but most people seem way too concerned with short term comfort. They crave the false security of denial. Well, we're just going to have to work around it." After a moment, she said, "Please, if Drew gets in touch with you—"

"Of course. Immediately. And vice versa, please?"

79: THURSDAY, JUNE 26

Fern felt like she was committing a sacrilege, snooping with Linda around the old farmhouse where Wayne had spent his childhood. Before they got married, he'd said to her, "Honey, I'm fixing to share all my worldly goods with you till death do us part. But there's one thing I need to keep private, and that's the old home place. The mobile home is ours, but that house is my private property, off limits, even to you."

Most of the time Wayne acted like he didn't even know the place existed, but every now and then he'd get into one of his moods. He was like a different person at those times, withdrawn, rude even. He'd go off to that old house by himself, sometimes spend a couple of days there doing Lord knows what. The first time he did that, Fern got worried about him and went down there to check on him, make sure he hadn't been snake bit or fallen and hit his head and passed out or something. He'd just about taken her head off, told her she'd better not dare even go down to that part of the land again, ever.

"Gate's locked, and he always keeps the key with him." Fern halfway hoped Linda would decide it wasn't worth walking all the way down the driveway. But no such luck.

"Well, then, we'll just climb through the fence and get ourselves some exercise." Linda put a foot on the middle strand of barbed wire and pushed up on the top one with her hand. "You go on through first, Fern."

"What if he's *there*?"

"You said he's been gone three days, right? He couldn't have been down at that old house all that time. Besides, he took your car."

The gravel driveway, overgrown with grass and wildflowers, ended at a hedge that had taken over most of the front yard of the farm house. It was kind of restful.

"How the hell do you get inside?" Linda's insistent nasal voice spoiled the mood.

"Don't ask me. He wouldn't let me near the place."

"Looks like a gap in the hedge over here...yeah, he's made a path."

Squeezing through the hedge, they stood and stared at the crazily leaning house. Linda was doubtful. "Think it's safe to go in?"

"We could just look through the windows. Oh my god, what's that?" A creepy rustling sound, something in the workshop. Fern halted, terrified. Maybe Wayne *was* here, had been out here the whole time. Linda's face had turned pale, and her eyes were big as saucers.

"Let's get outta here!" Fern turned to run, but Linda's shaky laughter stopped her.

"It's nothing but some old pigeons, Fern. C'mon back. We shouldn't let this place spook us out. I swear, you'd think we were stuck in *The Blair Witch Project*. Come on now, looks like the garage is in better shape than the house."

"The garage is where they had the workshop. Where Wayne got his fingers cut off."

Linda giggled nervously. "What if we find the fingers in there, all dried out and brittle?"

"Oh stop it, Linda." Fern took a deep breath, prepared for the worst, and pushed open the small door to the right of the large doors meant to swing up and let a car pass through. To her surprise, it opened easily. They stepped slowly into the room, footsteps almost silent on the earth floor. In the dim light it was a mess, hand tools scattered haphazardly on the shelves and floor, thick dust coating everything but the workbench under the window; the stench was foul.

"What the hell's he been doing in here? Keeping pigs?" Linda's voice seemed too loud. They should be whispering. At any moment Wayne might appear. What would he do if he found them here? Fern saw the bloody baseball bat, then, and backed away from it, unable to utter a sound past the tightness in her throat.

"Oh shit." Linda reached toward the awful thing, stopped. "We probably shouldn't touch stuff, Fern. The police'll want to have everything left just like we found it."

"No, Linda." Fern said hoarsely. "We don't need to call the police. He probably went hunting. Killed a rabbit or something. I always wondered what he ate when he stayed down here."

"You don't hunt rabbits with baseball bats, Fern." Linda's voice shook. "It wasn't a rabbit, and you know it. Look at this." She was pointing to a dark mass on the floor next to the bench.

"What is it?"

Fern shook her head. "A pile of old clothes."

Boldly, Linda approached it, poked it with a foot. Her scream rattled the windows, went on and on. Fern just wanted to run out of the room and keep on running until she was away from this place, away from what her life had become. Start fresh someplace else. She didn't think she could move. Her mind had got detached from her body. But she was moving, she was shining her flashlight on the thing by Linda's foot. A pale human hand protruded from a shirt sleeve that looked as though it had once been white and was now reddish brown. She raised her trembling arm slightly and found a face with the beam of light. Lips parted in a grotesque snarl, eyes rolled back in their sockets. She gasped as she saw that the hair was filthy with dirt and what looked like clotted blood or...she felt vomit rise in her throat... could it be bits of brain oozing out of a cracked skull? The room began to reel. She caught herself on the workbench, retching painfully.

Linda's screaming stopped, and in the silence it felt like the world had ended. Then Linda took a noisy breath and said, "Fern, your hubby's got himself into some real trouble this time. We gotta get outta here and call the police right now. This is no pile of old clothes. It's a body."

"Wait, let me think for a minute."

Fern had always felt she owed her first loyalty to Wayne, come what may; abruptly, she had a sinking feeling that everything she'd ever believed was wrong. She was overwhelmed by the need to talk to someone about it. But not Linda. Someone who...what? Someone more sensible and reliable. Panic filled her, and her thoughts fell away in a jumbled mess.

"Let's just get out of here, Linda. I can't think straight, can't breathe." She was able to move her feet. She bolted from the room, but just outside the door her legs collapsed, and she sat down heavily on the ground, fighting nausea. Linda sat down beside her. Linda's hands were shaking, and her face looked white as a sheet.

"Promise not to talk about this to a soul," Fern said when she was finally able to speak again. "Not until I make up my mind what to do."

Linda shook her head, looking down at her lap. "I don't know—won't we be, like, aiding and abetting a murder or something? Fern, your own life might be in danger. Shit, mine too. What if he comes back and figures out we've been in here and saw what he did?"

Fern nodded, tears rolling down her cheeks.

Somebody groaned.

80: FRIDAY, JUNE 27

Still a little weak from the initial effects of the auxosome injection, Jill sat at the picnic table while Alex played with his Gameboy. Hope followed by bitter disappointment would be too terrible to bear, and yet.... Her son seemed more alert, less fatigued. Both she and Paul had been a bit under the weather for days with mild flu-like symptoms, but Alex bounced back practically overnight.

It had seemed worth taking the risk to come by their house to pick up some clothes, and she had given in when he begged to visit the back yard "one last time." Hard to believe she'd sold the house. So many memories. Dominating the small backyard was the mimosa tree she and Keith had planted when it was a foot-tall sapling no bigger around than her finger. The Mexican Oregano was a gift from her mother, and Keith had given her the rose bush when Alex was born. The datura was her graduation gift from Carol. She hoped the new owners of the house would love the place as she had. I'll start crying if I think about this too much, she told herself. If she let herself start, she wouldn't be able to stop. With an effort, she directed her thoughts else-where, to Preston Bowie's letters. Anxiety replaced mourning.

Should she simply give them back and go on about her life? Did she have a moral duty to expose Bowie and Blick

Pharmaceuticals? As a lawyer, she was obligated to maintain the confidentiality of her clients' affairs—unless doing so endangered human life. In this case, Nature Forever was her client. Still, at least she could inform the Nature Forever board of Bowie's relationship to Blick.

Or she could simply return the box to Allen Hoffman as if she hadn't read the letters. Surely the easiest solution, perhaps the safest. Bowie and Blick seemed to be involved in a deadly serious game, probably with millions of dollars at stake. If they came to think Jill was a danger to them, her life could be in danger. She shook her head. Oh, come on. Let's not get carried away with paranoia, she chided herself. Crazy Payback certainly was much more of a threat than a lawyer and the president of a pharmaceutical company.

But she could not shake off the fear.

"Come on kiddo," she told her son. "Time to get our bones back to the apartment."

§

Alex spent the rest of the morning bouncing off the walls, begging to go outside and play. Jill kept him in, afraid of what could happen. It was a relief to get out again in the afternoon, and Alex was thrilled at the prospect of spending time with Paul at the lab, seemingly unfazed by the terrible thing that had happened last time he was there.

"I'll be okay, Mom," he assured her as they rode the elevator up. "This is probably the safest place around. There are cops everywhere."

Paul was clearly glad to see them, but his face was troubled.

Once Alex was set up feeding the mice, Jill asked, "What's wrong? Worried Payback might get in again?"

Paul shook his head. "He'd have to make himself invisible to get past the extra security guards and video cameras. No, I just heard from Roberta that Drew Chang has been found. He's in Methodist Hospital in Houston, the intensive care unit.

Not expected to live, and even if he does, he may have suffered permanent brain damage."

"Oh my God, Paul. What happened?"

"If anyone knows the details, they haven't told me. Looks like someone grabbed him right there out of the MJT parking lot, and they're looking again at the bombing."

"I feel like no place is safe anymore."

Paul glanced over at Alex, who was standing still, intently studying two of the mice. "Alex and I will be okay here, love. There's no way Payback could get past the extra security."

§

Hurrying, still nervous about leaving Alex, Jill took Bowie's "Correspondence" folder to Kinko's and made copies of each letter, frequently glancing over her shoulder to make sure no one was watching, starting a couple of times when someone walked by a little too close to her. She had still not decided what to do, but knew she must keep proof of what she had seen. On her way back to the lab she used her cell phone to call Keith. She'd phoned April from the hospital, and had been wondering rather angrily why Keith hadn't even bothered to call to ask after his son. They exchanged awkward polite greetings.

"Alex has been better the past few days."

"Oh? I'm glad to hear it." Keith's tone added the unspoken query: And why bother calling me with this fascinating information?

"He's back home from the hospital."

Keith's manner altered sharply. "Hospital? What happened?"

"Well, the seizure. But he's improving."

"Another seizure! If you'd let me know, I'd have sent flowers or something."

April hadn't even told him! This was way beyond the woman's usual bitchiness.

"Keith, I called April. Alex almost *died*. We were...." She stopped. If she mentioned the gunman Keith would probably accuse her of negligently exposing Alex to danger. "Alex could have died, and you wouldn't have known until.... I can't *believe* April didn't give you the message. Look, Keith, Alex is sick and needs me to be with him. The reason I'm calling is...." She took a deep, shaky breath. "To ask for some child support. Just for a while, until I can find another job."

"You don't work for Allen Hoffman anymore?" Irresponsible and unstable, his tone said.

"They fired me for missing work when Alex was sick. As soon as I can arrange nursing care for Alex I'll look for another job." Too apologetic, she thought. If I were doing this on behalf of a client, I'd be much more forceful. "I've sold the house, Keith. I'm just waiting for the closing."

"You've *sold* the *house*?"

"I didn't have a whole lot of choice. The mortgage payments were more than I could afford, and the prospects of getting another full time job don't look too bright as long as Alex...until Alex gets better. He was enrolled in a research program and was doing much better, but—"

"A research program? Last time I talked to you, you told me he was going to be fine. What do you mean by a 'research project'? Some untested procedure?"

She was angry now. "It seemed better than just watching Alex die of cancer and not trying to do anything," she said hotly. Sure as heck better not mention the herbal treatments. "But the chemotherapy wasn't working—"

"Die of *cancer*? Why was I never told?"

"Keith, it's not *my* fault your damn wife refuses to pass on my messages."

"You should've called me at the office."

"I *have* called you at the office. Okay? Your son has cancer." She spoke with exaggerated clarity. "I enrolled him in the best program of treatment I could find. The treatments seemed to be working, but Alex's last MRI showed that the tumor is still growing." She paused, waited for Keith to say something; for once, he was speechless. "As a result of the tumor, Alex tires easily, so I couldn't keep him in summer day camp.... If I'm to go out and look for work, I'll need a trained caregiver to look after him."

"Jill, my secretary just passed me a note—I have a call on the other line from someone I've been trying to reach all day. Naturally, I'm willing to help you and Alex. You're still living at Fruth Street for right now?"

For a moment Jill hesitated. Well, she could meet him at the Fruth Street house. She certainly didn't want to have to explain to Keith about their flight from Payback.

"Yes."

"I'll come by this evening after work, and we can talk about it."

"Okay. Thanks, Keith."

She entered Paul's number. Alex answered the phone. "Laboratory of Dr. Paul Gibson." From his voice, she never would have guessed he was ill.

"Hi sweetie. How are the mice?"

"They're fine. I'm helping Paul clean out their pens. He can't take the phone right now, because his hands are shitty." He giggled. Jill decided to let it slide.

"Listen, instead of me coming to get you at the lab, maybe Paul could bring you to our old house." She heard Alex relay the request and, in the distance, Paul's cheery, "No worries."

81: FRIDAY, JUNE, June 27

"Wow! You've got a *Humvee*?" Alex stared in amazement as Paul opened the door for him.

"Correct. An ex-military high mobility, multi-wheeled vehicle. Very politically incorrect."

"Did you buy it?"

"Nope! 'Fraid I don't have that much money. My new boss loaned it to me. Said she was afraid my yellow car wouldn't make it back from San Antonio."

"Well done, my good man." When Paul sent him a startled look, then burst out laughing, Alex added, "You must have a nice boss." He smiled back at Paul.

"Yes, she is. You know what else? She's invited all of us— you, me, and your mom—to spend a weekend at her ranch some time."

"Are there horses at her ranch?" Alex pictured himself galloping over the open range.

"I'm sure there are. A swimming pool too."

"Cool! Hey Paul, let's pretend we're soldiers."

"Okay. Which side are we on, and who are the bad guys?"

"Um, give me a minute to think about it." Paul was *fun* to be with!

82: FRIDAY, JUNE 27

A night-blue Mercedes, Paul saw, was parked in the drive-way of Jill's house. When the door opened, a tall blond man in a conservative business suit stood there. Instantly Paul's body went into cortisol alert; he pushed Alex behind him, holding tightly to his hand. An instant later his brain caught up with his instincts. This wasn't Payback and, from Jill's description, it wasn't Preston Bowie either. So who the hell was this character, answering a knock at Jill's front door at this hour of the evening? He forced himself back into calmness.

"Hi! Jill in?"

"I don't think she feels like—" The blond bloke glanced down at Alex, surprise registering on his face. "Hello son, I'm sorry to hear you've been ill," he said stiffly. Putting a hand on Alex's shoulder, he guided the boy into the house while blocking Paul's entry.

"Who is it, Keith?" Jill's voice came from somewhere in the house.

"Please tell her it's Paul." Keith, eh? The estranged husband. No, not estranged—divorced. Long gone. Remarried. Then what was he doing here now? Come to visit his son? Not before time. Relaxing, Paul moved closer to the door.

"Paul who?" Keith didn't seem willing to give an inch.

Footsteps sounded on the wood floor; Jill, eyes puffy and red, peered from behind Keith's shoulder. "Oh, Paul! Come in. Where's—"

"Hi, Mom! Paul brought me home in a Humvee." Alex hugged his mother, and she kissed his upturned cheek.

The ex-husband continued to stand firm in Paul's path. For a moment the two regarded each other silently. Good looking enough, Paul thought, in a remote, faded photograph way. Can't imagine him and Jill together.

Finally Keith moved away, turning his back. "If you were planning to entertain a...guest...perhaps I should come back another time to finish our discussion."

Ignoring this, Jill said firmly, "Keith, I'd like for you to meet Paul Gibson. Paul, this is Keith Hindle, Alex's dad." They shook hands uncomfortably. "Keith, I think we've probably discussed all there is to discuss. The only thing left to do is for you to say yes or no."

"I've already told you yes. I'll be happy to help you and Alex. But if I'm going to be helping, I'd like to have some say in how you're raising him. April is a stay-at-home mom, you know. Alex should spend more time at our house. And *you* should be out looking for a job."

Jill's jaw visibly went rigid, but she merely nodded. "I've been sending out resumés, and I'd be delighted for you to spend more time with Alex."

"Good." Sitting down in one of the red leather chairs, Keith made a big production of taking out his check book, making out a check, rising to hand it over.

"Thank you, Keith. I appreciate it." She held the door open. The bloke shot a hostile glance at Paul then turned to Jill. "I'll have April call you tomorrow to arrange a time to pick up the boy." He left without another word.

Leaning against the closed door, Jill looked pale and tired.

"In between visits I forget how difficult he can be to deal with."

"Never mind," Paul said. "I have news. I've got a neurologist pal at the Institute, Betsy O'Reilly."

"Ah," she said wanly, "now it comes out—"

Paul grinned. "Betsy's motherly, you have no worries on that count."

"Hey! *I'm* a mother, you know!"

"Yes, but not a *motherly* mother. I mean—" He cleared his throat and gave her a desperate, theatrical look, making her smile. "I told Betsy about the auxosome treatments. Obviously I swore her to secrecy, but we absolutely need to get checked out by an expert. Appointments for tomorrow. Hey, you look exhausted." He put an arm around Jill's waist. "How's about I take you and Alex out to dinner?"

"Now that you mention it, I haven't eaten anything since breakfast. I'm starving. But I should probably get Alex home to bed."

"Tell you what. You take Alex home and get him settled. I'll stop *en route* for some takeout. Give the local kids a thrill when they see the Humvee roar up. You don't see one loose in the wild much anymore."

She gently pulled his head toward her and kissed his lips. "Takeout would be great."

"What would you like?"

"Surprise me."

83: FRIDAY, JUNE 27

Nearly a full week after he disappeared, the police had told Maureen regretfully they did not expect to find Drew alive. Angrily, she had denied them. She had refused to give up hope. Until now.

Dispassionately, gazing at the waxy body that lay on its back, plastered arm elevated, chest moving rhythmically at the command of a respirator, she said aloud, "This is not Drew."

The Methodist Hospital emergency room resident frowned.

"I'm sorry, Mrs. Chang, I realize this is difficult for—"

"We're not married. I'm Maureen Baumgarten," she told him.

"Miz Baumgarten, Dr. Chang's employer made a positive identification this morning. This is definitely—"

"That's not what I mean." The monster who did this had taken away the most important parts of her beloved Drew—his sharp intelligence, his love of life. She remembered his amazing ability to make people laugh even when they were feeling blue. To make her laugh.

"Oh, I see." He obviously didn't have a clue. His fresh-faced competence infuriated her; he looked about 15. But then so did Drew, sometimes, in the mornings, with his tousled black hair and almost no need to shave. Tears, stinging, filled her eyes again. It felt as if she'd spent the whole week crying.

"It looks as if everything is intact," the resident said, coming to stand beside her, making a notation in his chart at the foot of the bed. "All his major organs are functioning properly—"

"Except for his extraordinary brain," she cried.

"Now, now, we can't be sure of that yet. He apparently called out for help when he was found, although he's remained unconscious while he's been under our care. I can tell you that his cranial wounds are healing normally. We had to re-fracture his arm to reset and pin it correctly, but he should make a complete physical recovery."

His words turned into meaningless mush, like the hushing repetition of the respirator. I need to accept that he's gone forever, she told herself. Even if he regains consciousness, he'll never again be the man I love.

Someone entered the room, a short middle aged woman with stylish tinted reddish hair. Alyssa Chang, Drew's mother. With an effort, Maureen composed herself. They'd only met once before, when Drew received his doctoral degree, and hundreds of families and friends buzzed about smiling and chatting and taking pictures. They had talked on the phone a couple of times, but she knew the woman disapproved of her son going with a non-Chinese. It was bitterly awkward, being here when Alyssa Chang saw her son like this for the first time.

Alyssa, she saw, shrank with grief as she took in the mass of tubes and wires, the machines with their blinking lights, the pale, still figure they tended. One hand reached out toward him, was withdrawn without contact, as if she were afraid she might harm him further with her lightest touch.

"Oh Maureen, I can't believe this is happening!" she said, voice breaking. Without quite knowing how, Maureen found herself in Alyssa's arms, both of them sobbing.

At last, Maureen said, "You must be tired, Alyssa, driving all this way. Won't you sit down?"

"But that's your chair, my dear—"

"No, no, I've been sitting here for hours, it'll do me good to stand."

"Ki was in Colombia when we heard. Couldn't get a flight out until tomorrow." Alyssa sank onto the chair, holding back her tears, visibly gaining control of herself. "You look exhausted yourself, honey. Do you want to go home and get some rest? I'll sit right here and call you the moment there's some improvement in his...condition."

84: FRIDAY, JUNE 27

Wayne propped his head on a pale yellow evening gown and stretched out on the pallet he'd made from other clothing he'd found on one of his exploratory trips through the tunnels. A flight of stairs had opened into the backstage area of a large auditorium. Through an unlocked door, he'd found a roomful of costumes.

"You got to get off your butt and do something about that follow-up shot," his father's voice said, insistently.

He didn't know whether he'd been here for hours or days listening to that voice, his father's voice speaking through his own body, sometimes in words, more often chunks of memories, or sometimes only small fragments, no more than an impression of a face, or a single sentence spoken by someone from his past. Mama calling out to Daddy, "I put 'em with the dirty laundry." Payback/Wayne lying flat on his stomach, the raised pattern of the bedspread digging into his face, listening to Neil Diamond on the radio. Inconsequential moments in the grand scheme of things, but they were *his*.

"Goddammit, asshole, why can't you get it through your thick skull? We're both gonna die if you don't listen to me and do what I say."

Wayne would have run away from the increasingly urgent words if they had not been coming from his own mouth. He tried to space out, sink far down into the peaceful hiding place he had made for himself inside his head.

That won't work anymore, dumb ass.

This time the voice spoke only inside his head, slowly, calmly as if it did not want to frighten him.

I'm stuck with you and you're stuck with me, no matter how much we wish it wasn't so. You gotta listen to me, Wayne. Be quiet and listen.

Wayne saw himself in memory, holding a gun, ordering people around; felt a little thrill of power. They were afraid of him, doing what he told them to do.

"Pay attention to this part," his father's voice ordered, speaking aloud this time. A man in a white lab coat was saying something important. "...too many brain cells...pruning them back like brambles...without the regulator injections...."

"We'll die," his father's voice said aloud. "Our brain cells will keep growing and growing until our fucking head explodes. I can feel it happening already." Wayne touched his head, massaged his temples. The blood pounded there. Yes, he thought, alarmed; it ached, it felt tight, as if the bones of his skull were pushing outward.

"What the heck can I do? The police are looking for me." He found himself on the verge of angry sobs. "Because of what you did."

"No point blaming me. We're in this together. If you'll listen to me, I'll tell you what to do. Just shut up and listen. I saw the bitch's address."

85: MONDAY, JUNE 30

A half hour's walk around Jill's neighborhood paid off for Wayne. During the day, university students parked their cars along the side of Fruth. There was a constant flow of people coming and going. The apartment complex opposite her house was large and anonymous; Wayne noticed that most of the occupants walked past each other with at most a nod. Few people seemed to know each other by name. No one paid the slightest attention to the middle-aged woman sitting against a concrete column in the covered parking area, reading a book. Just another student, older than average maybe, but there were plenty of older people going back to school these days. Wayne had felt horribly self-conscious at first, going in public dressed as a woman, but after a couple of hours he settled into his role. He even had to admit that the A-line skirt was more comfortable than trousers.

By the end of the third day, he had learned that Jill and the kid were no longer living in the house, although they came by once and carried away some clothes and stuff. The kid was in the back yard by himself while the mother was inside. Wayne had almost made a move this morning when she put the kid in the car and ran back inside. But she was back out again before he got across the street. Damned high heeled shoes. Never mind. Time was on his side.

Sitting there all day gave him plenty of time to think, to capture more of the bits and pieces of his shattered life, try to fit them together like a four-dimensional jigsaw puzzle. He had become more adept with practice and was able to view his life almost like a movie.

At first, revisiting his nightmares had been too terrifying—a dark haired woman lying on the bed, the skin on her abdomen peeled back, blood seeping onto the yellowed sheets. Slowly he grew bolder, dared to view the scene from beginning to end. Yet whenever he tried to move forward or backward from that horrific scene, he slammed into a blank wall.

By the afternoon of the third day the headache had bloomed into a vicious pounding that subsided for short periods of time and came back worse than before. The slightest movement of his head brought on waves of nausea. I'm going to die, he thought. I'm going to die right here in this parking lot. They'll find out who I am, they'll call Fern. She'll think I was a transvestite. That's the way they'll remember me in Delmar forever. Wayne Elliot, Mike and Denise's son, the cross dresser. The headache tore back in full force again, and he wished he could die right now, anything to stop the agony. Through the relentless pain, he saw himself, a younger version of himself. Twenty-three or four, maybe. He sat in a room with dull metallic walls. Big, comfortable chair, one arm stretched out straight in front of him. He got the impression he'd been sitting like that for quite a while, wondered how his arm was able to float effortlessly like that. Was this what they called hypnotism?

"Let your arm float down now. I'm going to read you something from the newspaper, Wayne."

That's right, another person was in the room with him, a big, robust man with a handsome face and neatly combed hair. White lab coat over a dark suit.

Wayne saw his younger self slide down a little in his chair. The arm drifted down, rested lightly on his thigh.

"Sit up. Listen closely. You need to pay attention," the other man said. "This is a newspaper article from the *Houston Chronicle*, September 5, 1982:

WOMAN DIES IN TRAILER BLAZE
Delmar, Texas

Members of the Delmar Volunteer Fire Department
pulled the body of an unidentified young woman from
the blackened interior of a mobile home that burned
Monday near Delmar.

Through the fog of his headache, Wayne watched himself
in memory. It was like light bursting through a sudden opening
in a sky covered by black clouds. When the pain eased, when
he could think clearly again, he stated it to himself in words:
They made me do it. Dear Lord in Heaven, I wanted so badly
to pay those fucking doctors back, get even with them for what
they did to Melody. He shook his head in denial. But I never
would've *done* it.... Maybe I *didn't* do it, he told himself desperately. Maybe it was just garbage they fed me under hypnosis,
like in all those movies. They brainwash you, everyone knows
that.

He started to unravel, sitting there in the street in women's
clothing, and spun into the past.

§

*"Wayne, you need to get out more, circulate. Melody wouldn't
have wanted to see you this way." Wayne's old school buddy...
what's his name? Ted, right?*

*The thought of her last days takes him to the brink of tears.
He jerks his mind away; can't let Ted see him cry like a woman.*

*"Go to the lake, man. It'll do you good." Ted sounds genu-
inely concerned.*

*"Can't. Social Security bitch lined me up for this research
project. They're interviewing this weekend."*

*"I saw that. Some pharmaceutical firm. Hey, man, that's
risky shit. You wanna be a lab rat for a few bucks?"*

"See, maybe I can get a reference from them later. Help me

get back into school." Melody's funeral used up all the money
he's saved. The thousand bucks BlickPharm is offering volun-
teers could make the difference between school and the street

§

Could that be it? He'd forgotten the drug tests completely.
They did something to me, he thought. Maybe I didn't do...that...
after all. Dear Lord in Heaven, could it all have been a fabrication? Suppose someone at BlickPharm mindfucked him into
believing he committed those unspeakable crimes. Who could
have done that? And why would they? Rutherford, he thought.

§

"Sit up! Listen closely. You need to pay attention." The voice
was a razor, cutting him. "This is a newspaper article from the
Houston Chronicle, *September 5, 1982."*

WOMAN DIES IN TRAILER BLAZE
Delmar, Texas

Members of the Delmar Volunteer Fire Department
pulled the body of an unidentified young woman from
the blackened interior of a mobile home that burned
Monday near Delmar.

"Young man, you're letting your mind drift! Sit up straight,
focus on my voice. Now listen: This is from the report filed
by Cody R. Thibodeux, Harris County Coroner September 5,
1992, same date as the newspaper article."

The decedent, a white female 35-40 years of age, was
observed in the rear bedroom, in full rigor, unclothed
except for a pair of white athletic socks. She was lying
on her right side, her legs drawn up toward her chest.

Most of the flesh was gone from the hands and lower arms; the nose, lips, and eyes had been burned from the face. Some dark brown scalp hair remained, pulled to the back of the head and held by a rubber band. The forearms and hands were badly charred, the torso burned but intact. There was a partially healed abdominal wound around three inches long. The wound appears to have been sutured with nylon fishing line. The lower legs appear to have been under a sheet or blanket and show little damage from the fire. Both right and left ankles exhibit extensive laceration and bruising consistent with having been bound with rope. Some of the binding abrasions are healed or partially healed.

"Stop that! Move your hands away from your ears. If you don't listen now, we'll have to go through the whole procedure again later. You don't want to do that, do you? This is from the Autopsy Report filed by Harley Watson, M.D. Medical Examiner for Harris County, September 6, 1992."

The abdominal cavity is filled with pus and contains a number of foreign objects, including the putrefied body of what appears to be a mouse, and six June beetles.

"Nurse! I need you to come over here at once and clean up this vomit."
"Yes, Dr. Rutherford."

§

—Blank.
"Maybe I didn't do it," he said aloud, hoping desperately it was true, terrified it wasn't, weeping. A passing kid looking at him in fright, ran past. "Maybe I didn't do any of that."

He recalled the other one, then: the young scientist, Drew Chang. He lay on his pallet, drifting in and out of sleep.

§

Payback waits patiently for the young woman to wake. Lying there asleep, she looks more like a schoolgirl than a scientist. But appearances can be deceiving. Dr. Rutherford showed Wayne the article in that journal. Payback will not begin until she is ready to understand what is happening to her. And why.

She stirs, touches her forehead, moans softly.

"Well it's about time. You'd think I gave you a whole bottle of sleeping pills, 'stead of a little tap on the head."

The young woman opens up her eyes.

Payback shows her the knife before he uses it. Wayne's daddy's hunting knife, nice and sharp. She tries to writhe away from him, but he has her tied down good and tight. He passes the blade over her abdomen, lightly the first time, then with more pressure. Blood oozes from the cut. Payback peels back the skin, exposing the shiny abdominal lining. What was it Wayne's fancy books called it? The peritoneum or something like that. He slices through, and the intestines spill out. Payback is a little surprised to note that human insides look about the same as an animal's. Glancing up at the woman's face, he sees with disappointment that she has passed out.

§

Wayne sat up, crying out in the dark. The same terrible nightmare, and Fern was not here to soothe him back to sleep. Was it a nightmare? Had it really happened? Sitting there, jolt after jolt of uncovered memory coursed through him like poison. Killing his father—No, no, he was still alive in LaGrange, that had been Dr. Rutherford. Then that poor feeble schmuck Nathan Pritchett.

Sick with confusion and remorse, his impulse was again to

take his own life before this thing growing in his head killed him. He acknowledged now that he had been pushed and prodded and deformed and programmed by that devil Rutherford, but after what he had done he didn't deserve to live. And now there was the poor fool Chinese scientist that Payback had taken to the old workshop. Surely he'd be dead by now.

If there's even the smallest chance he's alive, Wayne told himself, in his own voice, I have to go back there and.... Christ help me! I'm dying myself, and the police are looking for me. I *have* to get that shot. Maybe I could just call this Paul guy. No. He'd report the call to the police. Maybe they'd have his phone under surveillance.

I have to take the kid. It's my only hope.

86: MONDAY, JUNE 30

As far as Dr. Betsy O'Reilly's assistant knew, it had just been a routine exam. Betsy took them into an inner office, closed the door. "Well, looks like y'all get a clean bill of health. The MRI scans don't show anything unusual in any of you."

Unable to believe what she was hearing, Jill said: "What about Alex's tumor?"

"There's a small abnormality in the frontal region. Since I have no previous scans to compare it with, I can't say much about it."

"Small? How small?" Jill found herself grinning at Paul, hardly daring to hope but filled with hope anyway.

"Under three millimeters. About the size of the pellet you use in a BB gun."

"I knew it!" It took all Jill's willpower to keep from jumping up and down like an excited child. "He was only over at Keith's house for three days this time, but I could see the difference when he came back home. How can it possibly be working this fast?"

Betsy said, "I have to admit I'm amazed myself. But a tumor

is an aberration. The auxosomal repair mechanisms obviously have an antiangiogenic—" She paused. "They've cut off its blood supply and begun to tear down the messed up cells. What concerns me more is the excess growth of healthy brain tissue and synaptic connections. Repairs are one thing, re-optimizing a human body is quite another." She gazed frankly from Paul to Jill. "I hope to hell you know what you've let yourselves in for. This could be the breakthrough of the century—or it could be lethal."

87: MONDAY, JUNE 30

"Who wants to go first?" Paul set down the tray with its three hypodermic syringes, each loaded with a precise bolus of regulator proteins.

"I will." Alex stepped forward. "I'm not scared anymore." He looked away as Paul slid the needle under his skin, grimaced but did not cry out.

"My turn." Jill felt buoyant with hope. Alex would stay at Keith's house for at least another week. He'd be safe there from Wayne. Once Jill got another job, life could go back to normal for them both. No, much better than before, with her new love as part of their lives.

Paul was glancing toward the door. "You know, I can't help thinking about Crazy Payback. I wonder where he is, how he's doing. Wish there was some way we could get hold of him."

"Surely you wouldn't be willing to help him after—"

"He may be an entirely different person now from the madman we saw two weeks ago. Besides, the kind of torture he'll go through if he doesn't get the regulator injections...I wouldn't wish it on *any*one."

88: MONDAY, JUNE 30

Patience, his father always said, is one of the primary virtues of a hunter. That gift had never come naturally to Wayne. Another day squandered watching Jill's house had him squirming with frustration. Time to try a more direct approach.

He walked down the street and crossed well to the south of the house, ankles hurting in these stupid women's shoes, prepared to break into the house and take both Jill and Alex hostage if necessary. Let's see about getting in through a window. Certainly looked possible. No dog in the yard, and if he was lucky, no alarm system. The house wasn't low rent, but it didn't look as if it'd been outfitted with anything elaborate. Still, after his earlier attack in the lab, maybe they'd have stepped up precautions. Probably not. She was sleeping somewhere else, wouldn't have seen a need to do anything special here.

He was passing by on the sidewalk for a closer look when she showed up with some guy in a pickup truck. Not that scientist Gibson, either.... Bitch must be putting out on the side. That made Wayne feel better about what he might have to do to her, but damn! This guy's presence was definitely a complication. Wayne drifted back over to the apartment complex to wait it out some more.

Not more than five minutes later, another guy came running up. Paul Gibson. Uh oh! Gonna be trouble now. Wayne waited, expecting at any moment to hear shouts, maybe gunfire. But no, in a few minutes, out comes the first guy, hauls a ladder from the pickup, leans it up against the house and starts scraping paint. Hired help, okay. He kept this up until it was almost dark; then he got into the truck and drove away. Jill and Gibson were still inside the house.

For a moment Wayne considered grabbing Gibson, but no, way too risky doing something like that right out in the open. Besides, Paul Gibson seemed like the type of guy who wouldn't give in all that easy just because the gun was aimed at his own head, look at the way he'd behaved last time. The kid was the one to grab, wherever the hell he was. Well, maybe he didn't need the kid. Maybe Jill would do.

He hid himself in the shadow of a large, untrimmed shrub, waited for what seemed hours. Finally the light went off in the front room. Desperation drove him. They must be going to bed. If it had been him, he would've been all on top of the foxy little— He broke off, angry at himself. Unfaithful to Fern and the sacred memory of Melody, and anyway it just wasn't true. His mind, he was coming to realize, swarmed with these stupid tags of macho, jock bluster, as if his very thoughts had been infected over the years. It made him want to squeeze his head with his hands until his skull cracked.

Pull yourself together, man, he chided himself. Keeping to the shadows, he moved closer, slowly and precisely, until he was only a few feet from the wall of the house.

A faint glow came from one of the windows. A night light probably. A stuffed giraffe and a toy robot perched on the window sill. Good choice. Since the kid wasn't there, no one was likely to come into that room. It would make a hiding place. He pulled his flashlight from his pocket and examined the edges of the window. No sign of an alarm system. With a sharp, tearing noise, Wayne slit the screen vertically with his pocket knife.

89: MONDAY, JUNE 30

Amid a clutter of boxes and kitchenware, Jill plopped down on a stool and sighed. "I sort of wish I'd thrown in the furniture and kitchenware as part of the sale. I'd forgotten how much trouble it is to move. Don't think I could've done it without your help, Paul."

"We're almost done in here. What do you say we take a break for a few minutes?"

"Love to. Let's sit outside."

The backyard was still the same, a segment of the past

preserved for one last moment. Jill sat on the picnic bench, relaxing for the first time since the gunman's intrusion in their lives. Alex was getting better, and seemed happy enough staying for a few days with his dad. The financial wolf had been driven away, at least temporarily, from the door. And Paul was here with her. She stretched her arms above her head, trying to relieve muscles that ached from lifting furniture and boxes. "You know what I'd like more than anything right now? A back massage."

"That can be arranged, but you need to lie down for the full effect." Paul ran his hands over her shoulders. "Too bad we can't bring the couch out here."

Wincing as he kneaded her tight neck muscles, Jill sighed. "There's an exercise mat."

"Perfect. What is that incredible fragrance?"

" Star jasmine. The vine with the white flowers over on the fence. Isn't it wonderful? I thought it was lovely before, but it's ten times better now. Have scents been different for you? Since the auxosomes?"

"Yeah, way more complex. The jasmine, for example—it's not just sweet, there's a sort of...I dunno, tart aspect."

"Yes!" Jill agreed enthusiastically. "Everything has more depth. Before, I was just looking at pencil sketches of the world. Suddenly I see everything in three dimensions and living color." She fell silent, surprised by what she found herself saying. "Gosh, that really is true, you know. These past couple of weeks I've been so upset I haven't really stopped to notice it until just now."

"Wait'll you have a chance to listen to music. Not just wallpaper background—really listen."

"Oh, yes!" In her mind's ear, Bach spoke complex melody. "Maybe we should go inside and put on a CD."

"In a little while. Let's just relax here for a few minutes."

She stretched out on her stomach, eyes closed.

"Have you weighed yourself lately, Jill?" Paul ran his hands easily under her jeans. "You're getting skinny."

"No scale at your place," she mumbled. "Now that you mention it, the zipper seems to go up a lot easier these days."

"And down, luckily."

The neighbor's air conditioner fan came on, and in the low hum she identified a fugue of separate frequencies reflected in the motion of Paul's hands, moving from muscle to muscle on her shoulders, arms, lower back, like water flowing over and around her. The cycle of water: liquid, gas, liquid. The cycle of the universe...what had Paul said?...forever expanding. Forever undergoing creation, she thought.

While she could clearly distinguish where her body ended and his began, it was fascinating to realize that the motion of his hands somehow followed the rhythm of her own body, as the rhythm of Alex's body had followed hers when he was a tiny seal swimming in her miniature sea.

She drifted, almost fainting in the joy of it.

90: MONDAY, JUNE 30

Wayne waited quietly for a moment, afraid they'd hear him if he made any more noise. After a while, he got his nerve back again. Knife positioned to make the horizontal slit that would allow him to open the screen fully, push up the window, and step into the room, his hand jerked as a kind of wail came from the rear of the house. Animal? No, definitely human. What the hell now?

Slowly, taking care to slide his clumsy shoes to avoid stepping on a fallen tree branch, Wayne eased along the side of the house. A rickety wooden fence stopped him; he probed it carefully to see if he could climb it, maybe get in through the back door instead. It creaked ominously. Leaning against the house, straining to see through the darkness, focused on the sound of breathless laughter, he finally made out two pale naked bodies moving slowly together on some sort of pallet on the ground.

A woman's voice, between gasps: "It's never been like this

for me." Definitely her voice.

"Me either. Not even close."

More laughter and rolling around. Wayne wished it were not quite so dark.

"I think we're starting to process more sensory inputs simultaneously," a man said. Now Wayne recognized Paul Gibson's voice.

"I wonder if pain would be more intense too?" The woman sat up, and a shaft of light from the house fell on her breasts, her curly brown hair. Jill Shannon, yes, but she looked slimmer than in the lab.

"The potential'd be there, but maybe we'll be able to distract ourselves from it."

"Like my contraction pains when Alex was born.... Want me to give you a hard pinch, check your theory, Einstein?"

"Actually, to my certain knowledge, Einstein never published in the pain physiology journals. You mean Hilgard."

"Who's he?"

"He and she, actually. Experts in hypnosis and pain control."

"Is there no end to your mysterious Antipodean wisdom? Ouch. Hey!"

"It didn't work, then?"

"I was distracted. Oh god, that feels good. No, don't stop." More laughter.

Half-watching, half-abashed, Wayne hesitated before going back to the bedroom window. Something long-buried was surfacing from his memory. His wedding night with Melody. Although they'd Done It several times before, that had always been furtive, rushed and tinged with fear of pregnancy and disgrace. Being joined together as husband and wife, with the community's blessing, took some of the thrill away, but knowing that he and this wonderful woman were bound together for life had brought him, in an explosive release of emotion, into a greater intimacy than he'd ever felt before with another human. He had pressed his face into her shoulder and wept. That should have been excruciatingly embarrassing. Somehow, with Melody, it was okay; it brought them even closer together. He had never allowed that sort of intimacy between himself and Fern.

Blinded by sudden tears, Wayne took a step backward, stumbled, grabbed the fence to keep from falling. It made very little noise, but Jill turned her head.

"What was that? Something over by the fence."

"I'll check."

Shit! Paul, naked, approaching the fence. Wayne crouched low, held his breath.

"Can't see anything."

"Miz Kitty maybe. The next-door neighbors have been taking care of her for us, asked if they could adopt her. But she keeps coming back here. I'm jumpy lately." Holding her jeans in front of her, Jill had joined Paul by the fence. "Let's go in and make some tea."

Wayne could hear them with total clarity as they paused for a passionate kiss. He could *smell* them; his dick swelled against his pants, but he remained absolutely still until he heard them walk away across the grass, heard the back door close behind them. He rose, then, and made his way uncomfortably back to the kid's window.

91: MONDAY, JUNE 30

Eyes glistening, lips curved in a happy smile, Jill raised their clasped hands and kissed the backs of his fingers. One hand fell again, wandered.

"What's this?"

"Well, I know it's unusually large, but—"

"No, you idiot. *This.* The little fringe. I thought you told me you were circumcised?"

"Oh my god. I thought it felt a bit— My *prepuce* is growing back. Hey, Jill! You know what this means?"

"Another visit to the Mohel for bris? Ouch."

"I'm not Jewish. But look, it works!"

"I can tell that it *works*. Here, let me just—"

"No, the auxosomes work. They're regenerating our tissues, Jill. I'm growing a new foreskin! The auxosomes are turning back the clock."

"It's the wonder of the age!"

"Not that quite that, although as I say I do acknowledge that it's unusually—"

"The *auxosome*. Kiss me, my fool."

"Mmmm. Yum. Jill, I love you, you know that, don't you."

"Nice to be told, though. Kiss me again. Mmm. I love you too, Paul. Let's never be apart again."

"Come back, you."

They kissed again. After a time she drew away. "Paul, I could do this all night, but really we can't. Mustn't. Would you mind putting the kettle on? I'd better get started on packing up the stuff in Alex's room."

He released her hand reluctantly, and silently appreciated the curve of her shoulder as she walked away from him. He had filled the kettle, reaching for the valve to feed gas to the burner, when he heard her frantic scream.

92: MONDAY, JUNE 30

He stood in the kid's room, readying himself for his next move, when the woman from the lab flung open the door. He was so startled by her abrupt entry that he lost the advantage of his greater size and weight. In the pressure of the moment, he was a second too slow to raise his gun. She didn't miss a beat.

"You *mother*fucker, what are you doing in my house?"

Before Wayne knew what hit him, she was on him, and had smashed him in the cojones with her knee. He fell forward, screaming his pain, barely able to breathe. It was impossible to move. Her fists smacked at his bowed head, stinging, but his bruised balls were all he could think about. Somehow he picked himself up, crabbed for the window, fell through the tattered wire screen head first. He heard Gibson in the room shouting, "What's going on? Are you okay, Jill?"

"It was that Payback asshole from the lab. Dressed as a woman."

"I'm going after him. Is he armed?"

"No, the bastard dropped his gun," he heard her shout back.

Shit! Wayne's eyes blurred with tears. The pain was excruciating. On top of everything, his elbow had smacked something hard when he landed and he'd scraped his shin on the window sill.

He tried to find a less painful posture, dragging himself along the side of the house. He would have traded the title to his land for a bottle of Tylenol. He tumbled over a tree root, groaned as his weight fell on a particularly tender spot on his left elbow.

Behind him, he heard Gibson yelling. Despite the pain, he forced himself to his feet. The front door banged open; he turned back, instead of running out to the street, and with difficulty clambered over the tall fence into the neighbor's yard. New agony. He crossed the back lawn, pulled himself over their back fence and was running clumsily down the alley, keeping in the shadows.

In a confused haze of pain he made it safely back to his underground hideout and dropped to his pallet, shoeless and utterly exhausted. Within minutes he felt pain crying out from places he hadn't even known existed. He must have strained every muscle in his body diving out that window. To make matters worse, the headache was starting again. Hopeless, he thought. I'm a dead man. He found himself breaking down into wrenching sobs that made his body hurt worse than ever. This setback would have him laid up for three or four days. Worse, now that they knew he was still hunting them, Jill and Paul would be constantly on their guard. Blood pounded in his skull like liquid lead.

93: TUESDAY, JULY 1

It was a strange feeling, walking into Allen Hoffman as an outsider. Stranger still when the receptionist, whom she'd known for years, treated her as though she were an unwelcome stranger. Jill wondered what gossip had made the rounds in connection with her being let go.

"I'm here to see Clothile."

"Did you have an appointment?" the young woman asked suspiciously.

"Anne, for goodness sake, I'm returning some files and papers. No. I don't have an appointment, but I'm sure Clothile can spare two minutes to talk to me."

"I'll have to ask Mr. Sutton," Anne said doubtfully. Luckily, at that moment Clothile herself came down the stairs.

"Jill! How good to see you! You look *fantastic*!" Smiling warmly, she held out her arms for a hug, Jill's supposed involvement with the enemy seemingly forgiven.

"I've brought some papers that look like they belong to Preston. The day I left, Javier picked up a box that wasn't mine." Jill glanced at Anne, who nodded her approval. Good. The last thing Jill wanted was a little chat with Art. "I would've returned it sooner," she said to Clothile, "but Alex has been in the hospital."

"You poor thing!" Clothile's sympathy seemed genuine.

"Thanks, Clo. Look, I'd better not stay. Art seemed so eager to get me out of here, I'm sure he wouldn't be thrilled to have me hanging around." She had to escape before Clothile asked about her life.

"Wait just a sec, Jill. While you're here...a letter came for you yesterday, hand delivered. Don't think it has anything to do with the cases you were working on—it's labeled personal and confidential. I called you right away, but your answering machine wasn't working. Hey, what the heck," Clothile nodded toward the closed door of the conference room, "Preston's here for the day. You can give him his stuff in person."

Instantly Jill's mouth went dry. Could she keep her face impassive, knowing what she now knew? Stop being silly, Jill, she told herself. Relax. Still, she could not make herself move toward the door. "Has he said anything about...the files?"

"Um. No." Clothile shrugged, looked a question. "He asked where you were."

Jill forced herself to walk to the door, open it, say, "Hello, Preston."

"Come in, Jill."

Was she imagining it, or were his eyes hostile, despite the upward curve of his lips? Heart racing, she set the box on the conference room table. "Art instructed one of the runners to pack up my stuff when I...left. They put this file in my car by mistake. Just glanced at the file headings, looks like these are yours." I'm babbling, she thought. Shut up shut up shut up.

"I see." He opened the box, flipped through the files. "I hadn't even realized these files were missing. That runner should be fired. Who was it?" Before Jill could answer, he said, "Did you look through the files?" His gaze cut into her.

Sure that her face had betrayed her, she rejected outright lies. "Just a glance, why? I thought maybe some of my own personal files might be in the box. Naturally, once I saw that this wasn't the case, I brought the box back."

"Naturally. Why did you wait so long to bring it back?"

"Preston, my son has been gravely ill. I've had to stay home with him."

"Have you told anyone else about...the information in the files?"

He knew. Her nervousness had betrayed her. "I'd rather not discuss this with you right now, Preston." If she answered yes, he might accuse her of breaching client confidentiality. If she answered no, he might—what? Call someone to arrange a hit-and-run in the parking lot? She concentrated on breathing steadily.

"Fine. But you should know that if you reveal any information obtained from my personal papers, which of course you had no right to read—" A bitter, brittle edge entered his voice "—your current problems will seem very small indeed."

"I understand."

"For your sake, I hope you do." With one hand, he gestured for her to leave; she slunk from the room.

94: TUESDAY, JULY 1

Bruce Blick, naked except for a black robe of the finest silk, sat on the marble floor, dangling his feet in warm scented mineral water that bubbled up from the bottom of the hot tub.

When Franz the butler solemnly ushered Tom Gebhardt into the bathing court, Blick greeted him without rising. "Sit down, Gebhardt, and take off your shoes. There is quite possibly nothing more relaxing than soaking the feet in hot mineral water."

It was an order rather than an invitation, and Tom obeyed, though he would have preferred not to. No doubt his trousers would be wrinkled from being rolled up in the damp atmosphere, and probably stained from the water as well.

"I had a chance to look over the P&L earlier this morning," Blick told him. "Providol is doing even better than we'd expected. The advertising and promotion are finally paying off, just as you said they would."

Tom smiled, glad for credit where credit was due, unusually.

"If we can keep the sales figures climbing at the same rate, we'll break even on the advertising sometime within the next six months and cover the R&D within a year or so." Bruce Blick raised his head and stared, somewhat glassy-eyed, at the arched window in the wall on the other side of the steaming pool. Following his gaze, Tom saw a sunny hillside carved into vegetable gardens and vineyards and, some distance away, a village of white houses with red tiled roofs clustered around a rustic church. None of it real, thought Tom. By pushing a button or two, Blick could change the scene to a lunar landscape. The sunny hillside was framed by a vine that had been trained up and around the window; the sweet scent of its salmon colored flowers filled the room. The vine, at least, was real.

After an uncomfortably long pause, Blick continued, "Naturally, if another company were to begin marketing a competitive product—"

You mean a *better* product, Tom thought testily. Our sales would crash, yes. A drug currently with the potential to be one of our best sellers could easily fail to cover the costs of development and marketing.

"It's a pity the Jolly Green Giant, or whatever he calls himself, didn't finish his self-imposed task with MJT Labs," Blick said.

"Earthsavior. I'm convinced it's the late lamented Rutherford's madman. One of their scientists *was* attacked—"

Water flicked from Blick's toes, some of it soaking Tom's rolled trouser legs. There was no malice in it, but Blick's agitation was evident. Tom looked sharply at his boss, but Blick was gazing off through the window, into the virtual distance. Back before Tom had joined the corporation, it evidently had seemed like a good idea to contract with the military, using certain psychologically disturbed individuals whose frantic, unpredictable rage might be...bent and shaped to useful ends. The drug and trance work decades earlier by the CIA and Army harnessed that rage, but their methods stalled, crippled by the limitations of the first primitive generation of pharmaceuticals. By the Nineties BlickPharm had better drugs available, and even better ones now. But Rutherford had lost control of his subjects, or perhaps he'd never had it in the first place.

"Enough about the bad news," Blick said. "To the best of my knowledge, MJT isn't anywhere close to human tests with their gene-mod products, so there's no need for panic. We need to stay on top of things, that's all, keep our intelligence lines open. When the time comes, we can make an offer to buy the rights from them. Meanwhile, we stir the pot now and then and let Nature Forever take its course."

Tom chuckled politely, then resumed his serious, business-like pose. "I do have something new on MJT, actually. This young research scientist Gibson that Roberta Treadwell plans to take on seems to be, uh, doing one of our long-time Nature Forever volunteers."

"Oh?" Blick looked at him keenly. "You feel she might be approached for information?"

"Unfortunately, that's no longer likely. Allen Hoffman terminated the young woman on our representative's recommendation. She's split with NF too. Some sort of falling out between her and Preston Bowie, probably," said Tom. "Bowie was a little vague on the details. I suspect he put moves on her."

"Trust Bowie to screw things up." Bruce frowned. "I never have understood what you see in that sleazy asshole."

"He's...loyal."

Blick shrugged. "Can we place someone to watch this person? She sounds to be in the right place at the right time. Could end up being of some value after all."

"Bowie's stuck in Austin for the time being, doing the scut work she was taking care of before he managed to alienate her. I'll tell him to keep an eye on her." Tom Gebhardt gloomily pictured the press getting even a hint of Rutherford's flawed work. Bruce, he wanted to say, imagine the shitstorm we'll be in if our crazed Mr. Earthsavior Elliot harms this woman in any way. Let alone her young child. But he remained silent, watching Blick's attention drift away behind the rising steam.

95: TUESDAY, JULY 1

She drove a short distance and parked on the street to open the envelope Clothile had given her. It bore the return address of Keith Hindle's law firm. From where she sat, she could see the blue and white umbrellas that shaded the tables on the patio of Chez Bubba. A month ago, she might have stopped there to enjoy a salad or lemonade, but it was now far beyond her budget. She pulled the cover letter from the envelope.

> Re: In the Matter of the Marriage of Keith M. Hindle and Jill P. Shannon and in the Interest of Alex Shannon, a Minor Child

> Dear Ms. Shannon: Please find enclosed a copy of the Motion to Modify In Suit Affecting The Parent-Child Relationship in the above styled case, filed today in the District Court of Travis County. An emergency hearing has been set for Thursday, July 3

The envelope fell, unnoticed, as she read the document that Grady Bridges, representing Keith Hindle, had filed in the state district court. Among other things, it stated that Jill was an unfit mother, that in future Alex Shannon should live with his father.

Jill sat staring stupidly at the papers, as though by looking at them long enough, reading them over a sufficient number of times, she could understand why Keith would do something like this. With sudden cold clarity, she realized that Keith had sent the papers to the Allen Hoffman offices knowing she no longer worked there, certain that she would not receive them until after the hearing. He and April could say whatever they wanted in court without Jill cross-examining them, presenting her side of events.

In the two days since she'd last seen Alex, Jill had called Keith's house twice a day, asking to speak to her son. Each time, Keith or April had assured her Alex was fine; he was sleeping, or taking a bath, or eating. It'll be the same thing this time, she told herself, but still she picked up her cell phone and entered Keith's number.

"Hello?" Still the bright, friendly tone Jill remembered from the days when April was a secretary for Keith's law firm.

"Jill here, April. May I please speak to Alex?" Jill tried to keep her voice natural.

"He's playing with his sister. I don't want to interrupt their game."

"I'm sure Alex won't mind interrupting his game to talk to his mother."

"I have to go. I'll have Keith call you later."

"Listen, April—" A click on the line. The bitch had hung up. Sweating with rage, Jill was trying to decide what to do next when the phone rang.

"Hello!" Jill shouted.

"Mom?"

"Alex!"

"I heard April on the phone. Are you mad at me, Mom? I wanted to call you, and April told me you didn't want to talk to me...." His voice was trembling.

"Of course I'm not mad at you, Sweetie. I'm sorry I sounded so cross when I answered the phone just now."

"I want to come home, Mom. I don't like it here. Daddy and April yell at each other all the time."

"Honey, is April going to be upset with you for calling me?"

"She doesn't know. I waited until she went outside."

"What were April and Dad yelling at each other about?" Jill felt a stab of guilt for encouraging Alex to gossip, but it might give her a clue about the motive for filing the motion.

"She was mad at Dad for giving money to you. She said it wasn't his fault if you weren't able to hold down a job. I don't like her, Mom. When Dad's not around, she tells me to shut up and leave her alone. Will you come and get me?"

"Alex, I don't think I can right now, but I'll call your dad and ask him to bring you home." She could think of nothing else to say that wouldn't make things worse for Alex. She could hardly share with him her fears about the crazy gunman who was stalking her, or her anxiety about getting Alex back in time for the final regulator injection.

"Please, Mom. Please come and get me." Alex began to cry.

"Honey, listen to me. I promise you I'll talk to your dad. I want you to come home too, Sweetie. I've missed you so much."

She was beginning to cry herself and had to work to keep her voice steady.

"Gotta go now. She's coming inside." Alex was still weeping when he hung up. Jill was too angry to cry for long. The same instinct that drives a mother wolf to risk her life by attacking a cougar that threatens her cubs impelled Jill to do whatever it might take to get Alex safely home. The first step was to fight the motion Keith had filed. Jill pressed Carol's number.

96: TUESDAY, JULY 1

Preston Bowie had drunk the better part of two bottles of Chateau Ausone Cabernet Franc during the afternoon, but he could not stop himself pacing anxiously from room to room, out to the deck, back into the house. Impending doom. Why the fuck had he left those letters in the office?

On impulse, he picked up the phone and entered Tom Gebhardt's private number.

"Hey, Bowie. What's up?" Tom sounded distracted. Bowie could hear battle sounds in the background.

"Got a problem with that woman we were talking about last time. The one who's been seeing Paul Gibson."

"Uh huh."

"She, ah, I think she broke into my house and went through my drawers looking at my private papers." The story sounded absurd to Bowie even as the words fell like lead out of his mouth.

"Uh huh." Frantic screams in the background on Tom's end.

"I think she knows about Bruce's interest in Nature Forever and probably about that nut case Wayne Elliot too."

"Wha'd you say?" Tom suddenly seemed very interested.

Bowie repeated himself with some satisfaction; at least he'd diverted Tom's attention from his damned DVD.

"How the hell do you figure that, Bowie, unless you pointed it out to her?"

"I just told you, Tom. I think she broke into my house and

went through my drawers. When I wasn't here."

"Oh for Christ's sake, Bowie. Can't you stop bullshitting even for two minutes? You left papers lying around the office?"

"I said it was at my house. *My house!*" Bowie's voice rose an octave into a whine. "Please don't accuse me of lying," he said in a lower voice.

"Give me a break." Tom sighed. "What's important is how we deal with it now it's happened. Bruce is not going to be at all pleased. In fact, Bowie, I wouldn't be surprised if this was the last chance you ever get to fuck up."

"I couldn't help it, Tom. How was I supposed to know she'd go poking around into things that were none of her business? She'd been missing work, her fucking sick kid, I didn't even think she was coming in that day. The damned office boy. I can't help the kind of half-brained help they hire."

A pause, then silence. Tom had turned off the movie. "I gotta go, Bowie. If I were you, I'd move away and try to start a new life someplace else. Under a new name. Priscilla maybe."

"It wasn't my fault." But Tom had hung up on him. Bowie threw the phone across the room.

97: TUESDAY, JULY 1

Paul's Personal Assistant icon popped up on the screen. "Excuse me, Your Excellency, there is news about the Prohibition Against Human Genetic Engineering Act." Despite his fatigue, Paul laughed out loud. He'd complained to his office mate Rachel that the computer showed him no respect; she must have done a bit of reprogramming to his new PA when he wasn't looking.

"Show me." Paul had been so engrossed in combing his data for anything he might have missed that he'd lost track of the time.

"Gibson, you in there?" Rachel, knocking at the door.

"Yeah, hang on." He got up, slightly dizzy after sitting for so long. A new policy for the Pharmacy and Experimental Sciences building called for keeping doors locked at all times.

"Just thought I'd stop by and tell you the news, in case you hadn't heard."

"What news?" Paul glanced at his watch and was surprised to see it was already past 7:00. Good grief. He'd been at his desk for eight full hours. He realized he was starving.

"The assholes in Congress have passed the anti-GE act. As of today, half the work I've done for my dissertation is worthless. I'm gonna have to practically start over."

"Fuck a duck! That's what the PA was trying to tell me." The small pop-up on his monitor displayed the headline: *Anti-Frankenscience Bill to Become Law.* "I knew they were blathering about it, but I couldn't believe they'd really do it." Beneath the pop-up, his DNA sequencing results kept rolling on the main screen. He remembered his last conversation with Roberta. Neither of them had credited Congress with the stupidity to pass a law banning basic research. Well, the unthinkable must have happened.

"I feel like getting stinking drunk," Rachel said, leaning in the doorway. He could smell her faintly sour breath in the confines of the small room. Or maybe it was his own. "Care to join me?"

"Thanks, but I promised Jill I'd bring pizza tonight."

§

Angry voices as he opened his front door. The television set? A tense, frowning Jill greeted him, her friend Carol, equally angry, was sitting on the couch. Were they having an argument? Paul stood in the doorway, uncertain.

"Hi, Paul." Jill was sullen. Was she angry with him?

"Hi, Jill. Carol. Something wrong?"

"Just as I'm beginning to think things are getting better, Keith files a Motion to Modify our divorce decree. It was served on me this afternoon. He wants an emergency hearing to give him temporary custody of Alex. He claims that I've provided unwholesome living conditions and inadequate medical care because we didn't go with standard surgery and radiation treatment. He's refused to bring Alex back."

"Surely Keith can't do that! Can't you just go over and bring him home?" Paul still stood in the doorway, the cooling pizza forgotten.

"I advised her not to," said Carol. "They've got a hearing set for Thursday. Really, I know how angry you feel, Jilly, but it won't hurt Alex to stay there for another day, and it could be very hard on him to see his parents fighting over him. Plus," she told Paul, "Keith and April could conceivably accuse Jill of trespassing if she goes onto their land."

He felt his mouth gaping, and closed it. "Christ, Jill, I'm so sorry this is happening." He urgently wanted to hug her, but wasn't sure she'd welcome an embrace. Never before had he seen her so angry.

"Carol's been good enough to sign on as my lawyer."

"We're gonna make 'em sorry they fucked with Jill and Alex."

"Then you're fairly sure you can win?"

"Nothing's ever certain," Carol said. "Keith has the best family lawyer in the city."

"His firm contributes heavily to all the judges' campaign funds," added Jill.

"But two of Alex's teachers will testify what a good mother Jill is and Dr. Collins is willing to state that the standard treatments wouldn't have helped, in fact would have made Alex's final days much more painful." Jill's eyes filled with tears. Paul felt a burst of protective anger. Did Carol have to put it so bluntly?

Numb, Paul set the pizza on the coffee table. "But what if you do lose?"

"They're asking for custody."

"So Alex would be obliged to go and live with his dad?"

"Yeah." Jill looked wasted. "I'd only get to see him once

every other week. The poor kid will be heartbroken."

"But Alex still needs his second—" He broke off.

The attorney looked sharply from one to the other. "Needs what?"

Jill spread her hands, palms up.

"Nothing," Paul said.

"Uh huh." Carol turned to Paul. "There's something you guys don't want to tell me?"

Paul got up and took three plates from the shelf next to the table. "Pizza's getting cold. Might as well eat while we talk. Hey, Jill, I'll bet you haven't eaten all day. Have some pizza. Something to drink? Coke? Beer?"

"I'm not hungry, thanks."

"I am." Carol reached to open the box. "C'mon, Jilly. You gotta keep up your strength. Now answer me. What haven't you told me? You know I don't like surprises in the court room."

Jill nibbled at a slice of pizza; Paul shot her a questioning glance. After he'd given up hope of her ever speaking again, she said, "There's something we didn't tell the police about the crazy guy that shot up Paul's lab."

Carol raised her eyebrows. "I'm waiting."

"This insane man forced Paul, at gunpoint, to inject all four of us with an experimental drug."

"Alex too?" she said in disbelief. Jill nodded, and Carol put a hand to her forehead, shaking her head slowly. "Oh God," she sighed.

"No, it's all right, it's *helping* Alex, Carol."

"How do you *know* it's helping him? He hasn't been *living* with you."

"We've seen scans. He was already much better before he left for Keith's house. And I've talked to him on the phone since then."

Carol looked as if Jill had just assured her that Paul had a method of bringing the dead back to life. "Don't you think it might have been advisable to...not to conceal evidence from the police?"

"It's our only hope for Alex," said Jill. "The police think the gunman was trying to steal narcotics. If we'd told them about the injections—" She looked pleadingly at Paul, then back to Carol. "I'm sorry," she muttered wretchedly. "I was wrong. I should've told the police about the auxosome injections."

"Uh huh." Carol turned to Paul. "You actually think this will *cure* Alex? Are you making plans to visit Stockholm, Paul?"

Before he had a chance to defend himself, Jill said fervently, "The change in Paul's mice was incredible, even after just one injection."

"Mice. Wonderful. You say it's experimental? Not approved by the FDA?"

"True." Paul forced himself to take another slice of pizza. Let's keep the temperature down. "Look, conventional medicine can't do anything for Alex. Why not let the kid have a fighting chance?"

"The court certainly wouldn't see it that way. Jilly, remember Brockman and Brockman?"

"The vet case. Yeah. Oh shit."

"Um hm. Paul, the Brockman child was terminally ill with a type of tumor that had responded in animal trials to experimental reovirus treatment."

"I've heard of that," he told her, "but surely it's still in Phase I clinical trials?"

"Yeah, but the treatment's been approved for veterinary use. Worked on mice and dogs. Killed 90 percent of all the tumors by infecting the sick cells and leaving the healthy ones alone, something like that. Or 100 percent cure in 90 percent of the animals, whatever. But as you say it wasn't yet available to be tested on humans. So the father made back-door arrangements with a veterinarian friend to treat the kid with the virus. Mrs. Brockman found out, raised hell. Nobody's gonna do Frankenscience experiments on her baby."

"It hurt the child?" Jill cried anxiously.

"No. The kid started to improve miraculously."

"But you're saying the father *lost* the case?" Paul was incredulous. But the law here even granted patents on genes....

"Yep, and his veterinarian friend lost her license. They were lucky to avoid jail."

"That's insane!" Paul jumped to his feet, paced in agitation. "If people are terminally ill anyhow, why not let them try experimental treatments? No, no," he waved his hand, "I know the arguments. But surely the court'll see reason if you present a strong enough case."

"Not a chance."

Paul was bitter. "Because Keith's lawyer contributed to the judge's campaign fund?"

Carol tightened her lips. "No need to be so cynical. It's just... it's not up to a family law judge to make the FDA's decisions for them."

"Expert witnesses—"

"Yes, they could testify for us, state that Jill had good reason to believe what you two planned is in Alex's best interest. Then Jill might keep custody of Alex, but only if she promises to stay the hell away from experimental drugs in the future. The judge is legally bound to uphold all federal and state laws. She can't say it's okay for someone who isn't a licensed physician to use treatments that haven't been approved by the FDA."

"It's worse than that, actually," Paul said slowly. "The new bill means that my auxosome work is now illegal, since it involves genetic engineering."

Carol squinted at Jill under raised eyebrows. "Jilly, we've been friends for...what?...almost ten years now. I know what you're thinking of doing. But don't, okay? Please don't do anything that would make the situation worse than it already is."

§

After Jill had kissed Carol goodnight at the door, with thanks but a certain mutual chagrin, Paul said thoughtfully, "Illegal or not, I have to finish my work. It's too dangerous to stop now."

"You can bring a supply of the regulator protein thingees

home here, can't you, for safekeeping? Or is that being too paranoid? They're not going to kick down your lab door, surely."

"Heaven knows. A lot of craziness is getting built up right now by the media. 'Frankenscience'!" He shuddered. "Imagine basing your national public health policies on bad horror movies from the 1930s. Movies that were based on a book written by a teenager in 1817! It's—it's—" He caught himself. "Still, I do have to make absolutely certain that what I've designed *isn't* some kind of hazardous plague."

Jill stared at him, open-mouthed.

"Paul! You assured me—"

"I know, I know. But what if the auxosome hooks itself up inside our bodies with an *E. coli* bacterium, or some rhinovirus? We could see people catching it every time we sneeze!"

She sat down with a thump. "Well, would that be such a bad thing? The world could use some more intelligence."

He looked at her, looked away. "Don't forget the need for regulator shots."

"Oh. Oh." Her voice was very faint. "If people *caught* an auxosome infection, they wouldn't be able to control—"

"Exactly. Neural growth runaway." He seized her hand, trying very hard not to think of lurid horror movies with people's heads exploding. "It's extremely unlikely, but that's why I need to finish my current project. But I'm more worried about *populations* exploding."

Jill blinked, nodded, following the logic. "Oh God. If mice or cats or heaven forbid people catch it and it really does make them deathless—"

"Yes. And their children, and *their* children...."

She shuddered. "Billions and billions and billions," she said in Carl Sagan's accent, but without the trace of a smile on her face.

"Right now I'm trialing three methods for inserting the regulator operons directly into the primary auxosome genome. The mouse models look good so far. I'm adding a version of what the Greens call a Terminator gene. It'll temporarily shut down the reproductive system in both males and females, just to be safe." He was bleak. "Let's just hope the lunatics in charge of the asylum don't nail my lab door shut before I've finished my trials."

98: WEDNESDAY, JULY 2

Bruce Blick forced himself to make three circuits of the garden, walking slowly and savoring the colors and forms of the flowers, breathing their perfume, keeping his mind otherwise empty. By the time he sat down on his favorite bench his mind was free of anger, and he could think clearly.

Tom was proving to be something of a disappointment. Not that Bruce had expected a flawless performance, but allowing a man like Preston Bowie access to sensitive information had shown a surprising lack of thoughtful analysis. And now Tom was complaining that there was nothing he could do, because the police were watching both Shannon and Gibson.

Blick considered these facts calmly, as nothing more than data. The best thing to do under the circumstances, he decided, was to leave Tom nominally in control but to call the shots himself. He opened his notebook and began making a to-do list.

Preston Bowie was keeping a low profile at a friend's mountain hideaway in Montana and would cause no further trouble, at least not for a while. He could safely be ignored for the present time.

Jill Shannon was an unknown. She could be a disaster, she could be harmless, or she could even turn out to be an asset if she could provide useful information about her boyfriend Gibson. At the very least, Blick needed to have her interrogated.

Paul Gibson and Roberta Treadwell were definitely problems. Once before, BlickPharm had attempted to buy patents from MJT Labs, but Treadwell required provisions forcing Blick to market the products at or below a certain price. Evidently she saw herself as some sort of crusader. Gibson might be easier to work with, but somehow Blick doubted it. If Gibson moved to MJT Labs, he probably would surrender the rights to the products or processes he developed. Blick considered himself a non-violent man, but in this case there was no evading the fact that the most effective way to deal with Treadwell and Gibson would probably require sharp, brutal force. Police reports indicated some kind of recent drugs break-in to Gibson's lab. That would provide a useful cover, perhaps.

The latest word from Blick's main Austin contact was that Jill Shannon's ex-husband had filed a lawsuit alleging Shannon had exposed her child to an experimental cancer treatment. Was it possible that the treatment in question was based on Gibson's DNA research? Unlikely, but worth considering. Apparently the child now lived with its father. Blick made a note to have Tom look into the logistics of acquiring the child.

Finally, Rutherford's live wire. Blick blinked, then, two facts fusing like crossed electric lines. *Of course.* The supposed drug addict who had shot up Gibson's lab was Wayne Elliot. Too bad he hadn't taken out Gibson. Would've saved everyone else a hell of a lot of trouble. Elliot had disappeared from sight years ago, and Blick did not even try to predict what the former asset might do next. Futile waste of time, trying to analyze the behavior of the insane, as Rutherford should have realized at the outset.

Blick contemplated these pieces on one small corner of his strategy board, mentally composing possible paths they might take, searching out points of weakness where a small action on his part was likely to trigger a major reaction, tapping out notes for himself. At length he set the notebook aside and called his executive assistant to order his lunch. He would eat a leisurely meal first, then move steadfastly into action.

99: WEDNESDAY, JULY 2

The one good thing about staying at Dad's house, well two things really, were Sherry and Tamara. Alex's little half-sisters worshipped him, followed him around like faithful puppies.

"Alex, will you read to me?" Four-year-old Sherry leaned against his shoulder, thrusting a book in front of his face.

"Not right now." He gently pushed the book away. No time for distractions—he felt some part of himself reaching outward into...what? The bubbling empty spaces around him. It was like the pressure of water when you swam in a pool, or hot water pouring into a bath. He turned on an imaginary faucet and felt something flow, passing into the battered machine in his hands. It seemed to be coming from outside but moving through him. He guessed it was something the auxosomes had done. What else could it be? But Paul hadn't said anything about that. He told his sister, "Don't you want me to finish the present I'm making for you?"

The little girl plopped down on the floor next to him. "You can't give me my *own* horsie. A present's gotta to be something new."

"Just wait'll I finish."

Sherry pointed. "What's that thing?"

"It's a part I got from that old VCR Dad set out for the trash collectors."

"Why are you putting it in the horse?"

"Patience, little sister. You'll see in a minute."

"Is it a present just for me?"

"We-el. Maybe you could let Tamara play with it sometimes when you're not using it."

"She might break it."

"If she breaks it, we'll fix it. Okay? Now watch this." Grinning, he set the toy on the floor in front of Sherry and pressed a button on the VCR's remote control. The toy horse advanced toward Sherry, all four legs moving. As Alex worked the buttons, it turned away at the last second to avoid running into her. The little girl shrieked, delighted.

"Can I try it, Alex? Can I do it?"

"Sure. Here you go." He handed her the remote control. "Push this button for forward, this one for left, and—" The quick step in the hallway told him that April was coming, and he found himself looking around for a place to hide.

"What in the world are you two doing sitting here in the closet?" April shot an irate glance at Alex. She never missed an opportunity to let him know that she considered him a bad influence on her daughters, unworthy of playing with them. "What have you done, Alex? Why did you break the little horse's legs?"

"He made the horsie run, Mommy! Look!"

"Alex, I've told you, you're to leave the girls' toys alone. Do you understand me? From now on, every time you break one of Tamara's or Sherry's toys, I'm going to take one of your toys away from you."

"But Mommy, look! He made the horsie run." The little girl pulled at her mother's skirt.

"Stop that, Tammy! Alex, I want you to pick up this mess right now and then get yourself cleaned up. It's almost dinner time." She picked up the toy horse. "Look at what you've done!"

"No, Mommy, where are you taking my horsie?"

"It's broken, Tammy. Alex broke it. Broken toys go in the trash can."

As the clicking of April's heels receded along the tiled floor of the girls' playroom Alex leaned toward Tamara and whispered, "Don't worry. I'll fish him out of the trash later on, and we'll find a hiding place for him and only take him out when the coast is clear. Wait'll you see what else I'm working on, Tammy."

"What? What?" Her tears were forgotten.

"I'm making a flying machine that really flies."

100: THURSDAY, JULY 3

Jill was not a complete stranger to Associate Judge Mary Patterson's courtroom. She had assisted Art Sutton with a couple of divorce cases, although her own divorce had been uncontested. At the time, Keith had convinced her it would be a waste of money for them each to hire a lawyer, that the judge's signature on their agreed divorce decree was a mere formality. God, she'd been naïve.

Being here as a party in a contested matter, for the first time, made a chilling difference. "Just pretend it's someone else's case," Carol had suggested. Good advice, but hard to act on it when the outcome might have a significant effect on Alex's life—indeed, on his very lifespan.

§

Keith, called as the first witness by Grady Bridges and dressed in conservatively cut suit, presented the perfect picture of the successful young lawyer. At once refined and masculine, his features were composed into an expression of deep sincerity.

Grady swiftly went on the attack. "Did anything out of the ordinary lead to your filing the motion that brings us here today?"

"I was shocked to discover that my ex-wife has moved in with a man she's only known for a very brief time." Carol jotted in her notebook. Keith looked directly at Jill; she stared back at him in disbelief. "Alex is staying with my family, and I didn't like the idea of sending him back to an unwholesome environment."

"During the years since your divorce, how often have you seen Alex?"

"At least once a month, usually more often." His open, honest expression never faltered as he lied under oath.

"That son of a bitch! Jill whispered furiously. "He never—"

Carol laid a hand on her arm. "We'll get him on cross."

"What was the nature of your son's illness?"

"As I learned belatedly, he was diagnosed with cancer several months ago. The usual course of treatment would have been surgery followed by radiation, but his mother chose to take him to a—" Keith did not say the word *quack* but his expression made it clear what he thought of Dr. Les Collins "—an unconventional doctor who used some sort of experimental low-dose chemotherapy."

Grady was shocked. "Had Ms. Shannon consulted you about Alex's medical treatment?"

"No, I never would have agreed to it. But I doubt if anything I could have said would matter to her. My ex-wife has very strong opinions."

Grady actually shuddered. Don't overdo it, thought Jill. You're not playing to a jury today.

" Did Ms. Shannon explain why she had moved in with this man?"

"She hasn't been able to hold down a job lately, can't afford the house payments. I've been helping her out as much as I can, but I have my own family to take care of. She's moved in with this man, who isn't even a permanent resident of the United States, and plans to sell the house that was awarded to her when we were divorced."

"Did you discuss any of your concerns with Ms. Shannon?"

"I tried to, but she insisted that Alex and this man get on well and that the chemo treatments had nothing to do with my son's deteriorating condition. I think under the circumstances it would be far better for Alex to live with us—my wife and me and our two daughters, Alex's sisters."

"How do Alex and his sisters get along?"

"Very well. They'd be devastated if they were separated. And the boy's condition improved dramatically since he's been with us. I think our stable family life is good for him."

§

Carol Glassman rose for the cross examination.

"I wonder if you could tell me, Mr. Hindle, which kindergarten Alex attended?" She asked the question with a casual air.

"Jill never told me." For the first time, Hindle looked uncomfortable.

""It was a long time ago."

"Yes, it was."

Glassman paced towards the judge, turned back. "So which school did Alex attend last year."

"I don't know. I generally see Alex on the weekends."

Carol left that hanging. "You testified that when you picked Alex up from his mother's house, he looked much worse. When was the previous time you saw Alex before that day?"

"The exact date? I don't know, but no more than a month earlier. I've always tried to see Alex at least once or twice a month."

Glassman assumed a thoughtful pose. "Why did you have notice of this hearing delivered to the offices of Allen Hoffman and Flory when you knew Jill Shannon no longer worked there?"

"It was the last known—"

"You hoped Jill would not know about this hearing until it was over?"

"Of course not!"

"You've stated that Mrs. Hindle would look after Alex if he lived with you. What special qualifications does your present wife have to care for a child with cancer?"

"She's a very nurturing person," Hindle said, glancing at his lawyer.

Carol raised her brows ever so slightly.

101: THURSDAY, JULY 3

Kept up most of the night by the pounding in his head, Wayne had finally dozed off around four. When he woke at ten, the violent headache had been replaced by a dull pressure, uncomfortable but bearable. At least his swollen, bruised balls were less painful now. The bitch had packed a kick like a mule. He tested his limbs; his aching muscles, too, had recovered more quickly than he'd expected. It's now or never, he thought. No time to mess around feeling sorry for myself. I need a car.

From the jumble of returning memories, Wayne was pretty sure he knew where Payback had left Fern's car, but he was afraid to drive it, if it was even still there, since she might have reported it to the police as stolen. He'd have to steal a car as soon as he could.

102: THURSDAY, JULY 3

When the judge called a recess for lunch, Jill was treated by Carol at The Granite Garden, a favorite restaurant, but she found herself unable to eat more than a couple of bites. For the first time it was starting to seem sickeningly real: They might take Alex away!

When the hearing resumed, Carol presented their side. Two of Alex's teachers testified that he seemed a happy, well adjusted child, that Jill was a loving mother. Neither had ever met Keith; as far as they knew, he had never visited Alex's school. Grady had no questions.

"Okay, girlfriend." Carol patted Jill's shoulder. "Your turn."

To her surprise Jill felt quite calm, settling into the leather chair on the witness stand. Carol led her briefly through a history of Alex's childhood, the doctors he had seen, the treatments prescribed.

"Could you tell the court how you made the decision to take Alex to Dr. Collins at the University of Texas Health Sciences Center?"

"I'd read their literature, and done research on the Internet, and it seemed to me they were offering the best chance for my son to get well. I discussed the treatment with Dr. Collins. Weighing all the pros and cons, we decided the potential benefits of the treatment far outweighed the risks."

"Were you in the habit of consulting Keith Hindle about Alex's medical care?"

"He'd never shown any interest in Alex's school or medical care or anything else. The few times he saw Alex were when I called him up and suggested it. I'd always wanted Alex to have a father as well as a mother, but Keith was usually too busy. Before his dad picked him up last week, Alex saw Keith a total of three times over the past two years."

"How do you know exactly how many times Alex has seen Keith?"

"I keep all my appointments in my daytimer. Yesterday I went through it and counted the number of times Alex went to visit his father."

On cross examination, Grady asked, "Did you consult Keith Hindle at all about Alex's medical care when you found out Alex was ill?"

"As a matter of fact, I did try to call him the night before we left for the first interview with Dr. Collins. His wife answered the phone and told me he was in the shower and she'd let him know I'd called. He never returned my call."

"Are you a physician, Jill? Do you have any medical training?"

"No, but I've read a lot of—"

"Have you at any time in the past been associated with a group called Nature Forever?"

"Yes." Oh no! Dear God, please help me get through this. Heart pounding, she tried to steady her breathing. "I did volunteer work for them, and also worked on some of their files when I was at Allen Hoffman."

"How long did you do volunteer work for them?"

"A little less than a year."

"Um hm." Grady nodded as if this confirmed everything he'd previous stated about Jill Shannon's character. "Tell the court, Ms. Shannon, some of the projects you worked on as a volunteer."

"One Saturday morning a month, handing out literature at

the Balcones Mall Farmers' Market. All the employees were expected to do some volunteer work. It sort of went with the job."

"And where was your son Alex when you were spending your Saturday mornings in this way?"

"Either with a babysitter or in daycare."

"Um hm." Grady nodded confidently. "You did additional work for Nature Forever, didn't you? You drafted a petition to send to Congress?"

"Yes."

"Could you speak up, please, Ms. Shannon?"

"Yes, I drafted a petition."

"And what was the general nature of the petition you drafted?"

"It was to express support for PAHGE."

"And that is?"

The contradictions of Jill's life were bearing down on her, leaving her little chance of escape. "The Prohibition Against Human Genetic Engineering Act."

"So you were well aware of the dangers inherent in doing medical experiments on human subjects?"

"Objection!" Carol was on her feet, glaring at Grady. "You're asking the witness to express an opinion. She's not an expert in the field of medical research."

"Objection sustained."

"Ms. Shannon, did you believe there could be dangers associated with medical research?" He said her name with a little sneer, drawing out the word "Mizz."

"In certain cases, yes. But—"

"In fact, you believed this strongly enough to canvass for a bill to protect people from such dangers."

"Alex's chemotherapy didn't—"

"Please just answer the questions, Ms. Shannon," said Grady, and added with a smirk, "You're a lawyer. You should know how to behave in the courtroom."

Jill held back her anger with difficulty, meeting his mocking gaze.

"Okay, Ms. Shannon, you've stated that you believed medical research could be dangerous. And yet you subjected your son to treatments that involved giving him experimental doses of chemicals, without informing the child's father. How was it you didn't believe your son was entitled to the same protection you desired for everyone else?"

"You're completely distorting the truth! You're making it sound as though we loaded Alex's system with chemicals."

"Just answer the questions, please."

"The doses in Dr. Collins's treatment plan were *lower* than usual. Chemotherapy was Alex's best chance."

"Was it helping him? Is that why he had another seizure and was close to death—until he went to live with his father?"

Jill stared down at the wooden rail at the front of the witness stand, thinking helplessly of the auxosome injection.

Carol rose. "Objection! Calls for an expert medical opinion."

"Sustained."

"I believe we've already established that Ms. Shannon is not a medical expert," said Grady dryly. The judge glared at him. "Now, Ms. Shannon, suppose you tell the court what else you did for Alex."

Jill knew what was coming and wished a great hole would appear in the floor and swallow her.

"Did you and your son visit an establishment known as the Wellness Center?"

"Yes."

"While at the Wellness Center, did you purchase a product known as SMV-9b made by a company called...ahem...Eden's Bounty?"

"Yes."

"Was this product administered to your son Alex?"

"Yes," Jill said miserably. "But...."

"Just answer the questions, please, Ms. Shannon." He stared blandly at her. "Now, Ms. Shannon, had Alex's doctor prescribed this SMV-9b?"

"We enrolled in the program with his approval."

"And did your son Alex have a seizure after taking SMV-9b?"

"It's a herbal *nutritional* supplement. I don't believe it had anything to do with the seizure, and neither do the clinic physicians." If only Les Collins could have been here to testify as an expert witness!

"Answer the question, please. Did your son Alex have a seizure after taking SMV-9b?"

"Yes but...."

"Thank you. No further questions, your honor."

Jill's heart sank.

Carol did what she could, introduced an article from a medical journal into evidence as proof that Jill had rational grounds for believing their treatment would benefit Alex. Still, as Jill stepped down from the witness stand she feared she had come across as a wishy-washy flake who deserved the epithet "Unfit Mother."

To her surprise and vast relief, Judge Patterson gave her a sympathetic look. "It's obvious from the testimony I've heard today that you love your son very much, Ms. Shannon, and want the best for him. I'm very much aware of how difficult it is to balance work and family life." Jill sagged with relief. The judge, though, was not finished. "I can also understand your concerns, Mr. Hindle. Before making my decision I'd like to speak with the child privately."

"I'll phone my wife to bring him in," Keith told her.

103: THURSDAY, JULY 3

Alex and Tamara were sitting together on the floor looking at books when the girls' mother barged in without even knocking on the door. He could tell by the rapid way April was walking that she was nervous, and he hoped he had not done anything to upset her. Once you set her off, she could keep yelling at you all afternoon.

"Come on Alex, we have to go." She grabbed his hand and

jerked him up. It hurt. He winced, said nothing.

"But Mommy, Alex's reading *Les Misérables* to me."

"Don't be silly, Tamara. Alex can't be reading that book. He's too young. He wouldn't understand all the words. Here. Get Pearl to read *Little Lost Puppy* to you."

"But I want to hear more about Cosette. And Alex does too understand the words! He tells me what they mean."

"Pearl! Come in here and look after Tamara. I have to take Alex down to the courthouse."

§

Judge Patterson seemed to be a pleasant person who liked kids, unlike so many adults who seemed to think kids were nothing better than a nuisance. A big framed photo hung on the wall behind her desk: the judge standing in the woods with a good-looking man and three children. On her desk Alex saw several smaller photos of the children at various ages.

"I need your help here today, Alex," she said, smiling kindly. "I asked your stepmom to bring you in to talk to me, because there were certain things none of the grownups could tell me. Is it okay if I ask you a few questions?"

Alex nodded and glanced around at April.

"Mrs. Hindle, if you wouldn't mind having a seat in the hall—"

April made a brief grunting sound. Maybe she felt insulted at being asked to leave, Alex thought. He wished *he* knew a way to make her go away. She walked out and the door clicked shut.

"Now, Alex." Judge Patterson leaned across and smiled at him again. "You've been living at your dad's house for the past week, is that right?"

"Yes, your honor," Alex said, like he'd seen it done on TV.

"How do you like living with your dad?"

Alex shrugged. "It's okay. But I'd rather live with my mom."

"How did you feel about you and your mother moving in with Paul?"

"Well...." He hesitated. Probably he should say he was happy about moving to Paul's apartment, but really he didn't like it there all that much. He had no friends in the neighborhood, and Mom was so worried about that Payback guy he hardly got to go outside at all. It wouldn't have mattered when he was too sick to get out of bed anyhow, but now.... Mom had always stressed the importance of telling the truth. "I like living with my mom," he said at last.

"Do you and Paul spend a lot of time together?"

"He lets me help take care of his mice. Experimental mice, that is. In his lab."

"That sounds like fun."

"It is. Paul's making the mice smarter."

The judge smiled and nodded, just being nice, for sure— not believing or even understanding what he'd just said—then looked more serious. He had to get through to her, had to *explain.* "I hear you've been pretty sick, Alex."

"Yeah. I had cancer, but I'm much better now. I gained four and a half pounds last week. See, the auxosomes are rebuild—" Oops, too *much* information. Alex clamped his mouth shut, heart sinking.

"What's that, honey?" The judge looked down at him, sympathetically, but at the same time intently, trying to figure it out. Maybe if he was evasive she'd change the subject. Mom and Paul had insisted that nobody must know about the auxosomes, but Mom had also taught him never to tell straight-out lies. Ethics was hard.

"I just don't like to talk about, you know, medical things." No, that just made it sound worse. He bit his lip hard.

"Is there something someone told you to keep secret?"

Alex stared miserably at the floor. He was going to have to disobey his mother, either by lying or by telling the judge about the auxosome treatment.

"What did they ask you to keep a secret?

It was a crime to lie in court, so probably it would be best to tell the truth even though that meant revealing the treatments to the judge. And didn't lawyers and judges have an obligation to keep secrets to themselves, like priests?

"My auxosome shots," he said reluctantly

"Those are the treatments you had with Dr. Collins in San Antonio?"

He could say yes, but that would be a bare-faced lie. "No, the ones I had here in Austin."

"At the Wellness Center?"

"Um. No."

"What other sort of treatments did you have here in Austin? Who gave you the shots?"

"Paul."

"Dr. Paul Gibson?"

He couldn't meet her gaze. "Yes."

"Were the shots the only things Paul and your mom told you to keep a secret?"

"Yes, your honor." It was a relief to find that Judge Patterson didn't seem upset. Maybe everything would work out okay after all.

When Mom came in he was so relieved to see her he couldn't sit still. He ran to her and threw his arms around her. "I missed you, Mom!" He didn't ever want to turn loose of her.

"I've missed you too, Sweetie." Mom bent and kissed his upturned cheek. Dad walked in behind Mom, but April stayed outside, to Alex's relief.

"Very smart boy you have there, folks," said the judge. "Just a couple more questions for you, Jill. Alex said that Paul gave him some sort of shots here in Austin and that you told him to keep it a secret. Could you shed a little more light on this for me?"

Alex felt Mom's body go stiff.

"Judge, it's—" He felt her take a deep breath. "A week ago, an armed mentally ill man came into Paul's lab when Alex was there feeding the lab mice."

The judge made a whooshing noise with her mouth. "Oh-*kay*. That's what I've been trying to remember. I saw a report in the paper. That *was* you two? And your son, he was there too?"

"I'm sorry, your honor, I had no intention to deceive you by—"

" One moment, Ms. Shannon. Wasn't the intruder looking for narcotics or something?"

"That's what we thought, too, but then he pointed a gun at my head and threatened to kill me if Paul didn't inject him and the three of us with a...an experimental treatment Paul... Dr. Gibson's developing. You have to understand, Paul *had* to inoculate us or the crazy man would have shot us down in cold blood. He ended up firing his gun at Paul!"

Dad burst out shouting at Mom. "Good *God*, Jill! You never told me any of this!" He sounded so mean Alex took a step back, away from him. He added, "My apologies, your honor, but this is just *outrageous.*"

Mom said, "You can check with the police about the gunman—"

"It's true! Mom wouldn't tell a lie." Alex stepped forward again, between Mom and Dad; he disliked Dad shouting at her that way.

"No one has accused your mom of lying," said Judge Patterson, but she was frowning and didn't seem as friendly. "We're just trying to get a clear picture of what happened. Now Alex, when we were talking a few minutes ago, you mentioned shots, plural, more than one. Did Paul give you another shot after the one you had when the man was pointing a gun at your mother?"

Maybe he could pretend to pass out. No, that would only delay the inevitable. "Yes," he answered faintly.

"Can you speak louder, please, Alex?" Judge Patterson leaned toward him.

"Yes, I've had another shot." He clutched his mother's hand.

"Jill, am I understanding this correctly? You voluntarily allowed Alex to have a second injection of this completely untested substance?"

"No, your honor. Alex and I received a stabilizing injection, a biochemical regulator. So did Dr. Gibson, of course."

Judge Patterson shook her head in amazement. "I can hardly believe what I'm hearing. I have no choice but to grant Keith's petition."

Alex hid his head against his mother, trying hard not to cry.

"Judge, please!" Mom sounded as though she was about to cry too. "You need to understand. This was like taking an antidote after some lunatic has forced you to swallow poison."

Oh no, Mom, you're making it worse.

"Not that it *was* poisonous, of course, but—"

"That will do, Ms. Shannon. These are only temporary orders. If you can present convincing evidence at the final hearing that these repeated treatments were in the child's best interest, that will influence my final decision."

Dad looked like he was about to burst. "Judge, I had no idea about this, or I'd have asked that Jill be limited to supervised visitation. How do I know she won't try to shoot Alex up with something else when he's with her over the weekends? I'd like to make a motion at this time that Ms. Shannon be limited to supervised visitation on every other Saturday."

The judge sighed. "I'm going to grant Mr. Hindle's motion. Let's go back into the courtroom and get this on the record. Again, Ms. Shannon, these are only temporary orders, in effect until the final hearing."

Alex realized, with absolute clarity, what was happening. Supervised visitation meant he could never be alone with his mother. No chance to conclude his treatments. "No!" he cried. "The auxosomes fixed my tumor, but the new cells have to be pruned back just right! It's called apo— Apoptosis. What you're doing amounts to depriving me of my right to life."

Both Judge Patterson and Dad stared at him.

"Jill trained you to say that," Dad said. "Or was it Gibson?"

They were just like April, telling Tamara that he was too young to know how to read *Les Miserables*. They thought he was stupid, just because he was young. "Nobody told me!" He stepped away from Mom and looked into the judge's eyes. "It's obvious! The new cells have to be kept under control!"

"Someday when you're older, Alex, you'll understand that your father is doing this to protect you," Judge Patterson reached out to pat him on the head. She had seen nothing, understood nothing. He stepped away from her hand.

"Judge, I won't *live* to be very much older if you prevent me from having—" But the judge wasn't listening anymore.

"As I told your mother, Alex, this is only a temporary order. I'm going to set a final hearing for a month from today. This will give your mom time to prepare a case proving that she was acting in your best interest."

"Come on, Son. You're going back home with April."

"No! I want to go with my mother."

"Alex, darling," Jill said softly, "you do need to go with your father for now. We'll figure out something. Maybe your dad will let us talk on the phone sometimes."

"*She* won't let me call you."

Dad laughed in a way that implied Alex was being preposterous. "Certainly April will let you call your mom. Maybe not just as we're sitting down to dinner or going to bed or taking a bath, but you can call your mom any other time."

"Sweetie, you'd better go with your dad for now." Mom bent her knees so that she could look Alex in the eye. "I love you, sweetie. Remember that." He held his head up, feeling tired and sick, and tried to smile at Mom, to make her feel better.

Dad put a hand on his back to guide him out of the room. "Your mom loves you, Son, but she has some very dangerous ideas, and sometimes she acts in ways that are not very smart."

I'm going to *die*, Alex thought. It made him feel cold and horrible. After all this, I'm still going to die. And it's their stupid fault.

104: THURSDAY, JULY 3

On the way to the parking lot Alex had thought hard and quickly, and asked permission to get his Sega-Genesis games and some extra clothes from his room in Mom's house. Dad had already gone back to work from the courthouse, and Mom agreed to meet April at the house. April pulled into the driveway of 3204 Fruth Street, behind Mom's car.

"You wait here," April told him. "It'll just cause a scene if you go in with me."

"Okay." Alex smiled agreeably.

"I'm locking the doors so you'll be safe."

The boy nodded. "Don't worry. I'll be okay."

A workman on the front porch was painting the woodwork. April spoke briefly to him and headed toward the back door. The moment she was out of sight, Alex flung off the buckle of his car seat, got a grip on his backpack, opened the car door and slipped out. He was already hidden across the street behind the shrubbery at the apartment building when Mom came down the driveway. He heard her cry out when she saw that he was not in the car.

He forced himself to keep still and quiet as she walked anxiously around the yard calling, "Alex! Where are you, Alex?" I'll wait until April's left, he thought, then go find Mom. The moment she disappeared around the side of the house, he took the opportunity to run into the covered parking area under the apartment building. To his surprise, someone called his name softly, a strange looking woman in a long orange skirt. His breath was cut off by a strong hand pressing against his nose and mouth. He kicked wildly, and the woman cuffed him sharply across the back of the head.

"Listen carefully, Alex." A man's voice, not a woman's. Payback's voice. Alex felt his bowels about to loosen, and clamped down tight. "Do as I say, no one gets hurt. You make a lot of noise or give me trouble, you and your mother will pay the price. Understand?" A man's face, under the wig.

Completely terrified, Alex nodded. He caught a glimpse through withered shrubbery of April running from the side of the house.

"God*damn* you," Mom cried. Her voice came clearly from across the street. "I told you not to leave him alone."

"But the car doors were locked. I told him not to open them."

"You left the boy shut up in the car on a hot day like this? Of course he opened the door. He was about to suffocate in there."

"Oh, he was not! I wasn't gone for more than three minutes."

"Time enough for my child to disappear."

"You know he's around here somewhere. He's just playing games with us. Alex! You come out right now!"

"You fool. This is no game." Mom ran to her car. "Get your goddamned car out of my driveway so I can get out of here."

"Shouldn't we look for Alex?" April sounded frightened.

"I mean it, April. Get your car the fuck out of my way, or you're gonna need to have it towed home."

"Okay, okay. But where are you going?"

"I'm going to look for the madman who's kidnapped my son."

105: THURSDAY, JULY 3

Seated at the conference table in Roberta Treadwell's office, Paul thought of Jill for the hundredth time that day. Carol had assured him he could do nothing to help at the court hearing, and when Roberta called an emergency meeting of the MJT scientists whose work would be affected by the new law, Jill had urged him to go.

"This will definitely put a crimp in our plans to expand here in San Antonio, which have already been somewhat compromised by the terror attack," Roberta was saying. "I'll be working with our attorneys over the next several days to determine exactly which of our projects has to be modified or put on hold entirely. They tell me some of the provisions are so poorly worded that no one will know for sure what the law means until the Supreme Court decides somewhere down the line."

What a strange nation this is, Paul thought. A news article on the Internet the night before had extolled the law as a victory for morality. They regard themselves, he thought in disbelief, as the world's standard bearers for science and industry, yet they make laws based on ancient ignorance and superstition. It was quite obvious from reading the text of the new law that whoever had drafted it didn't have the faintest clue what genetic engineering actually did. These poor rich barbarians, he told himself in despair, simply hadn't understood what they were throwing away. People in China, Singapore and Latin America would snatch up the spoils. Meanwhile, he thought, my auxosome research is set back, and with it the hopes of the whole human race.

"We're now looking seriously into setting up a branch of MJT in another country, or moving out of the United States entirely," Roberta said, confirming his private assessment. "I've spoken this morning with Ramón Li at the University in Guadalajara, Mexico. He's interested in a joint project." She keyed a note into her PDA, rose. "Thank you all for taking the time to meet with me today. I'm sorry we've reached this point. The general public apparently doesn't welcome research that will make life longer and healthier for every human on Earth. But I'm glad we're at least in a position to continue. Someday, perhaps, we Americans will come to our senses and this ill-conceived law *will* be struck down."

As the meeting broke for coffee and pastries, Paul sought Roberta out, asked for a word in private. They stepped into her office.

"I'm concerned for the safety of my mice," he told her.

"I thought you'd sacrificed all your auxosomal models?"

"All but two of the originals. I'm retaining those as controls. But I have a new batch transfected with modified auxosome. It's coded with its own regulators plus the sterilizing Terminator, so there's no need for additional inoculations."

She looked up sharply. "I understood that you were keeping those experiments separate from your work here?"

"That would have been desirable, but under the present circumstances—" He shrugged, spread his hands. "I couldn't be sure how much time we had left before the law steps in. The new batch is responding well to their treatment."

"Paul, I'm impressed and gratified by the success of your research efforts," Roberta said, shaking her head, "but you know we can't condone blatant breaches of the—"

"Of course." He gave her a winning smile. "My lab associate will retain several under observation in her home. I'd be very happy, however, to make you a gift of four former laboratory animals, which your children might enjoy as pets."

She smiled back. "You know perfectly well I don't have any children. Very well, bring them here and we'll find a place for them." She rose. "I'll keep an eye on them myself. I do realize that these might be the most important mice the world has ever seen."

106: THURSDAY, JULY 3

Payback's unyielding grip on Alex's neck would not be obvious to passersby, but there was no way Alex could break free. Three weeks ago he'd seen the gunman fire off his weapon at Mom and Paul. He had no doubt he'd be dead in a moment if he tried to yell or get away. Probably end up murdered anyhow, but the longer he could stay alive, the more chances he'd have to escape.

He tightened his own hold on his backpack. Things in there might come in handy—if he survived long enough to use them.

Matter of fact, he told himself, this weird guy in the dress might have done him a favor. If he could just get through the experience alive, escape, find his mother without getting recaptured, maybe he could disguise himself the same way. Change his name to Matilda or something, and never have to see April again. He guessed he'd never see his dad again either—not that he'd seen him all that much anyhow, even living in the same house. Dad mostly left him with April. It'd be pretty much okay not seeing Dad again, especially if Mom and Paul got married. I'd way rather have Paul as a father any day, he thought, than Dad. He liked his step-sisters, though. He'd miss them.

Payback hustled him along, stopped beside a red car parked on the street, shoved Alex inside, snickering when Alex grabbed at his seatbelt and tried to fasten it. Probably wondering why I'd bother, Alex thought, when I'm going to be dead anyhow in a little while. His fingers felt numb, and he couldn't get the belt fastened; he hoped Payback was a good driver.

As Payback opened the door on the driver's side, Alex heard his name being called. The man shoved him down painfully, hand pressing the top of his head. He could barely see over the dashboard. But that was Mom's car coming slowly down the street. Driving around looking for him. He took a breath to shout out to her, but fingers clamped cruelly on his skull. Maybe if I concentrate really, really hard, he thought in panic, I can make Mom look this way.

"Keep your fucking head down!"

Mom had pulled even with Payback's car, passing by slowly. Payback had his engine started, taking his hand away, maneuvering out of the parking space. Alex pulled himself up, wriggled to see over the back of the seat. Mom's car was turning around in a driveway. She must have recognized Payback, maybe even seen Alex. She was coming!

Payback hit the accelerator, throwing Alex painfully against the back of the seat. Mom was right behind them.

"Sit *down*, you little prick." The car swerved sharply around a corner, and Alex lurched against the door.

"Get down on the floor." Payback swatted at him.

Curled up on the floor, arms over his head, Alex was flung about as Payback accelerated, braked hard, careened around corners. "God damned bitch." Alex guessed Mom must still be behind them. Maybe she had her cell phone and was calling the police. He hoped not. The police would make him go back to April's house. Battered and bruised, he was feeling sick at his stomach from all the bouncing around. He pushed up from the floor, struggled back into his seat. They were on the wrong side of the road, aiming at an intersection. The lights up ahead switched from green to red. Instead of slowing, Payback pressed his foot to the floor. A car came at them from the side, swerved, horn blaring. Behind Alex's nostrils, acid burned. He couldn't keep it in. As he vomited, metal tore with a terrible noise behind them. He was flung across the floor of the car, onto the man's feet in their ridiculous women's shoes.

Payback ignored him and his stinky puke. "Holy shit!" he shouted gleefully. "Bitch ran the red light too and got totaled."

107: THURSDAY, JULY 3

In the Humvee, Paul checked his voice mail. Nothing new from Jill, but Carol had left a message asking him to call. She answered the phone herself. "Law Office."

"Carol, it's Paul. How did it go?"

"We had it won, but I'm afraid Alex let a rather wild cat out of the bag about that, uh, Stockholm research you were doing. The judge didn't like the sound of it, she's signed an order appointing Keith temporary managing conservator."

"Oh, bloody shit."

"Oh shit indeed." Her voice grew stern, even pissed-off. "I have to tell you, Paul, I'm not happy about this. April's gone over to Jill's house to get some of Alex's things, and Jill left without saying much more than see ya later. Mind filling me in on exactly what's going on? You've been holding out on me. Jill confessed you'd given Alex a *second* injection of that experimental substance."

"Roughly speaking, yes, but under the care of an Institute neurologist, Dr. Betsy O'Reilly. MRI scans, full blood work, the lot."

"Why the hell didn't Jill tell me up-front? There's nothing worse than a client who gives her lawyer only half the story. I can't *believe* she did this to me."

Paul felt wretched. Really, how could they both have been so stupid? Poor Alex, he must be feeling terrible. "She didn't want to involve you in it, I guess."

"But how can I represent her adequately if I don't know what's going on? Jill knows better than that. Well. So Keith has temporary custody of Alex, and judges tend to like to keep kids where they are, especially if it looks like a stable family situation. You guys better come up with some damned good proof that this auxosome shit is safe and legal."

Paul grimaced. "I do think it's safe, with the regulator shots, but—" He took a heavy breath, let it out. "In fact it's illegal under the new law."

"Oh, that's just great!" The lawyer's tone was bitingly angry. "Keeps getting better and better. When you see Jill, please tell her to give me a day or two to cool off, and then call me. I may see things differently tomorrow, but I'll be honest, Paul. Right now, I'm not sure the judge didn't make the right decision today."

She clicked the phone off in his ear.

108: THURSDAY, JULY 3

Pulled over to the curb, motor running, Wayne looked back up the street. A crowd of people gathered around the intersection where Jill's car had been broad-sided. The vomit-reeking child lying against his left foot revolted him. Maybe he's having another one of those fits, he thought. This is bad. I need the kid alive to get the second and third stages of treatment from Gibson.

But it was more than that: he didn't want the little guy to die. Without stopping to question his motives more closely, Wayne scooped the kid's mouth out with his fingers. That's what you're supposed to do, isn't it? he thought. Keep unconscious people from choking on their vomit. He wiped his fingers, then poured the contents of a three quarters empty can of Coke over the kid's face.

"Hey, kid, time to wake up." The boy moved his half-shaven, patchy head, moaning. Wayne propped him back up on the seat, placing his own blue and red checked shirt over the center console to make a pillow. "Listen to me, Alex. You hit your head and got knocked out. But you're gonna be okay. Hear me?"

Alex groaned, barely nodded.

"Now I know you're in some kind of trouble yourself. I saw you run away and hide from your mother and that blonde lady. You help me, I'll help you. We're in this together. Okay?"

Alex nodded again, but his eyes stayed closed.

"The cops could be after us any minute now, so we have to get outta here. Have to ditch this car soon. They'll be looking for the license number." As he talked, Wayne eased the car back into the traffic.

Originally he'd planned to drive calmly to a place he'd picked out and call Paul Gibson from a pay phone. If Jill was dead in the crash, his plan might still work. She was the only one who knew he had the kid. But he couldn't count on her being dead. He needed to put some distance between himself and the car. Change of plan, then. If he could figure out an inconspicuous way to transport the kid to the tunnels, his home for the past three weeks, he could telephone Paul Gibson from one of the offices once everyone went home for the day. Gibson could meet him right there at the university. The kid could be left in an office or storage room, tied up if necessary.

They drove through a low-rent residential neighborhood. Little kids ran around everywhere, women pushed younger kids in strollers. Hmm, Alex was way too big for a stroller, but if he could find a wagon, it just might work. Three blocks farther along, he found a house on the left side of the street with a faded "For Sale" sign angling out of an overgrown front lawn. He pulled into the driveway. No garage, but the drive curved behind the house, so the car wouldn't be visible from the street.

Even after they stopped, the kid just lay there. Wayne leaned over to check; the boy's eyes were open, staring at him. A slight shiver went through him, but he gritted his teeth and made the speech he'd prepared.

"Here's the plan, Alex. I'm gonna go find something I can push you around in so you won't have to walk. Then we're gonna go and find your pal Paul Gibson. I want you to wait here until I get back. We're in the shade, so you won't get too hot, and the sun will be going down pretty soon. I'm gonna lock the car doors. If I come back and find you gone—" Wayne stopped. Threaten his mother? Not the kind of thing you'd say to a partner, especially a boy, and under the current plan he needed the kid's cooperation to pull things off. "Well, I *won't* come back and find you gone, will I? I'm just locking the doors to protect you, 'cause this is sort of a rough neighborhood."

"About my mom," the kid mumbled. Wayne realized Alex must be worried because of the accident, and wished he'd kept his mouth shut back there when it happened.

"Your mom's gonna be fine. When we talk to Paul, he can tell us how she's doing. Now I want you to just rest until I get back. Are you hungry?"

The kid shook his head.

Wayne locked up, pulled the wig tight, and tottered into the street in his stupid goddam women's shoes.

109: THURSDAY, JULY 3

Paul's answering machine had collected three messages, increasingly frantic.

"Hello, this is Keith Hindle. Please give me a call as soon as you can. 472-3754 or cell phone 861-5728."

"Paul, this is Keith again. If Alex turns up at your place, please contact us."

"Paul. Keith again. Jill was in a car accident. She's been

taken to Seton Hospital. Alex has disappeared, and the police are looking for him. Please call immediately if he shows up at your apartment."

Paul's hand shook as he picked up the phone. Before he could instruct it to call Seton Hospital, it beeped to announce an incoming call.

"Paul Gibson."

A kid's voice. "Hi Paul, it's me."

"Alex?" His heart lurched with a palpable thud. "Where are you?"

"I'm safe, but Mom was in a car wreck."

"Are you at the hospital with your mom?"

"No. I'm with that Payback guy. He says his real name is Wayne."

Paul's pulse accelerated even faster; a chill passed through him. Alex sounded okay, but how long could that last? He remembered the gunman's face, contorted with rage as he pointed the gun at Paul and pulled the trigger.

"Is Wayne going to bring you home?"

"No, I don't want to go home. The police will make me live with April. I hate April. Wayne's gonna help me run away."

Oh Christ, oh Christ. He's only eight years old, you can't expect sense from a child. "Alex, if you run away, how are you going to see your mother?"

"Because I'll be dressed up like a girl so no one will know it's me, and I can meet her someplace."

Payback's gruff voice—Wayne's—spoke up in the background, "Get to the point, Alex. Don't stand there talking until midnight."

"Okay, Wayne, just hang on." Alex didn't sound very frightened. "Paul?"

"Yes, I'm still here, Alex."

"Wayne needs to get his regulator shot. We've got a deal, Wayne and me. If you'll give him his shot, he'll help me run away and hide."

"Give me the phone, Alex," the deep voice broke in. "Hey,

Dr. Gibson. I don't wanna say things that might upset the kid. Know what I mean? But between you and me, man to man, I think you can guess what might happen if I don't get that injection. I'm going to leave Alex with a friend of mine, okay? Then I'll meet you at the Theater Arts Building. Know it?"

"I can find it on a map."

"Can you get there in an hour with my dose?"

"Yeah. And you'll have Alex with you, or no deal."

"Hell, no, be reasonable. I'm leaving him with friends. I don't get safely back, they have their instructions. But don't you worry. If I get my shot, Alex will be fine, and I'll help him get to wherever he wants to go. He mentioned some ranch out in the country somewhere."

It was worth considering. His mind raced wildly. Should he insist that Alex be handed over to the police? No. If Alex were taken back to April and Keith, he'd forego the final auxosome regulation treatments, with God knows what consequences. Probably he'd die within months or even weeks, his poor brain bursting like a garden choked with weeds. Maybe Wayne's deal was not such a bad one. Roberta's ranch, he thought. Wouldn't hurt to ask. After all, she took in stray puppies and illegal mice.

"We'll talk about it when we meet. I'll see you at the Theater Arts Building in an hour."

110: THURSDAY, JULY 3

Wearing a paper hospital gown, Jill lay woozy and unhappy on a bed in the emergency room trying not to touch the dressing that covered half her forehead. A nurse pushed back the screen. "You have a phone call. You can take it here." The woman passed Jill a small handset.

"Jill! I'm so sorry. I should've been there with you." Paul's voice was shaky. "They told me you've had sutures in your forehead but you're going to be okay."

"I'm feeling worse from the sedative than from this little

bump on the head." Her mouth was gummy; she felt dazed. "I wanted to go straight back out and look for Alex, but they insist on keeping me here. Shit, Paul, you don't know, do you? Payback's got Alex."

"I know."

"You do?" Her heart leaped. "Did the police catch him?"

"No, he phoned me. I talked to Alex. He's okay, Jill."

Relief flooded through her. For the first time since she'd seen April's empty car, she dared to feel optimistic.

"Have you called the police? What are you going to do?"

"The nurse said I could come and pick you up tomorrow or the next day. They want to keep you for observation."

"Not a chance. Come get me right now."

"I'll be there in two hours. We can talk then, in person."

There was something he didn't want to discuss over the phone. "Okay, love. Maybe by then the sedative will be worn off enough that I can walk in a straight line and talk without chewing a hole in my tongue."

111: THURSDAY, JULY 3

Dirty, bruised, sticky with dried Coke, Alex sat on top of a bookcase in the office of Yvonne Reyes, PhD (it said on the door), and looked down at Wayne with a disapproving frown. "Why'd you tell Paul that stuff about leaving me with friends?"

"Sometimes you have to stretch the truth a little, to get people to see things your way."

"That wasn't stretching the truth. That was an outright fabrication."

"Ha! That's a big word for a kid your size. Well, anyway, it worked, didn't it? He's bringing the shot. C'mon down now. We need to get you cleaned up and find ourselves some better clothes."

Alex began to climb down, using the shelves as if they were the rungs of a ladder. "My mom would have a cow if she saw me doing this." He gave a barking laugh.

"Yeah, well, it does look a little dangerous. What if the book-case fell over on top of you?"

"Then I'd do this!" Alex dropped the last three feet, pushing himself away from the bookcase.

"Huh. Think you're pretty smart, don't you?" Wayne led the way out of the office into the hallway. "*Did* it make you smart? The shot, I mean."

"Yeah, I've been figuring stuff out. How about you? Did it make you smart?"

"At first, I guess." Wayne held open the door of the Men's room and motioned for Alex to go in. "Later on I started feeling weird. Getting headaches. They've eased off for now, but I still feel weird. Having spells, like, you know, feeling euphoric one minute and suicidal the next."

"Paul took me and my mom to a neurologist for a checkup. That's a brain specialist. Did you go to a doctor?"

"Nope. Hop up here, let me wash you off. Damn, boy! You got a couple of nasty bruises there. Hurts just to look at them." With Alex perched on the edge of the lavatory, Wayne wet a paper towel and roughly wiped the mess from Alex's face, head, and arms. "I'm sorry that happened. If I'd known we were gonna be chased, I'd have brought some pillows for padding."

"My mom's in the hospital."

"Yeah, they're taking good care of her. She'll be okay. She shouldn't have run that red light."

"You did. And she was trying to save me. You were pretty scary that day in the lab. You seem nicer now." Alex looked up at Wayne and smiled.

"Long as you do what I tell you." Wayne had to fight to keep his face serious. Despite his pale skin and patchy head, the kid was beginning to grow on him. "Did you have a booster shot already?"

"Sure. It's not exactly a booster, it's more like a slower-downer. Paul said we have to regulate the growth of our neurons. Otherwise, you might have problems."

Old pain surged up inside, made his chest ache. "*Problems.* My wife died 'cause of drugs that were supposed to make her well. But they caused *problems.* They shouldn't use drugs that are gonna cause *problems*, goddamned *scientists.*" The anger was building up, as it always did.

"Well, Wayne, I dunno. Paul didn't *want* to use his auxosomes on people without any clinical trials. You *made* him do it."

"He gave you a second shot. I didn't make the son of a bitch do that." Sensing Alex's alarm, Wayne turned away, caught a glimpse of himself in the mirror: his face was ugly with rage.

"Just calm down, mister." The boy reached out and grasped Wayne's shoulder, as if to steady him. Wayne was torn between two impulses: give the kid a fist in the face, or hug him. Robbie again. "You'll be okay after you get your regulator shots. It'll be all right. You'll see." The kid's face looked so earnest it made Wayne want to laugh and cry at the same time.

"Why should you care?" Wayne pulled another paper towel from the dispenser and blotted the wetness from Alex's skin.

"Because I need your help."

"You want to hide from that blonde gal, right? You could get Paul or your mom to hide you."

"No, then they'd be charged with kidnapping."

"Don't give me that crap. Your own mother can't kidnap you."

"Yes she can. My dad said so, and he's a lawyer. If the judge signs an order to make me stay with my dad, then my mom would be kidnapping me if she took me away."

"And I'm *not* kidnapping you? Here. Jump down, let's go find something to wear." Wayne glanced at his watch. They still had forty minutes.

"You already *did* kidnap me. Taking me to the ranch won't make it any worse."

"Kind of hard to take you there if we don't know where it is."

"Paul will tell you."

It occurred to Wayne that just being here with this kid was

one of his more serious crimes. "We're in this together, right?"

"Right."

"So if we do get caught, we should cover for each other. We should make up a story and stick to it. Something like, say, you wandered away from that April's car and got lost, and I found you and—"

"How about, you found me wandering around and picked me up to take me home, but before I could tell you my name or where I lived, you had to stop the car suddenly, and I hit my head and when I came to I couldn't remember who I was. Amnesia. Like in a movie."

"Hmm. Not bad. You even have a bump on your head to prove it. What about all those bruises, though? They'll think I beat you up. In here." Wayne held open a door for Alex.

"Where are we going?"

"There's this room back here where they keep all sorts of stuff they use when they put on plays. Wigs, dresses, glasses, fake beards, you name it."

"Cool!"

"So what are we gonna say about the bruises?"

"I borrowed some kid's skate board and fell off going down a hill. Wow! Look at this!" Alex held up a helmet that was part of a knight's armor.

"Yeah, yeah. Come on, we don't have time to play around. We need to find a little girl's clothing and...what do you think? Shall I go for the bearded look or find a woman's wig?"

"Depends on whether my mom reported you to the cops."

"Yeah. Let's assume she did and go for the beard."

"And you could wear stuffing under your shirt and be a fat guy."

"Not a bad idea. The skate board might work as good as anything for a story. Maybe that's how you got the bump on your head too. No point making me out to be a careless driver. Here, let's see if this fits you." It was a pink dress with a white pinafore, and the kid shuddered. You couldn't blame him.

"What happened to your fingers, Wayne?" Alex took the

dress but made no move to put it on.

"I was careless with a saw.... No, I wasn't, fuck it!" he cried angrily. "What it was, my goddamned father made me use a power saw without proper training."

"How come they look so weird on the ends? Your fingers, I mean."

"Must've hit them against something." Wayne held his right hand slightly behind him, getting angrier. He could feel Payback hovering over him, behind his shoulder, ready to swallow him up.

"Wayne?"

"Yeah." Little shit, if he mentions my damn hand again—

"There's a problem, saying you found me on the street. If my mom reported you, they'll know you were trying to get away from her."

"Maybe not. No way to prove that was us she followed. They probably won't find that car for weeks. Doesn't look like anyone ever goes over to that house. I wonder if Fern's reported me missing...."

"Who's Fern?"

"My wife."

"I thought you said your wife died from taking drugs."

"Hey! What do you say we shut up and look for clothes."

112: THURSDAY, JULY 3

The front doors of the Theater Arts Building were locked. The place appeared deserted. Following Wayne's instructions precisely, heart thudding, mouth dry, Paul made his way around the building's perimeter. A heavyset business man stood near an Exit Only door on the east side of the building. Damn it! Maybe the man's presence had scared Wayne away.

"Over here!" the man called in a voice something like Payback's as Paul walked past.

"Wayne?"

"No, it's Paris Hilton. Come on inside."

"Looks like the auxosome affected your appetite."

"Very funny. Listen, doc, I've been having headaches and episodes of short term memory loss, confusion, and like that. You know?"

"You really should let us do a complete check up on you, Wayne."

"Yeah, right. Like you're gonna do that for me."

"I don't feel comfortable giving you this injection without a medical. Especially since you've been experiencing problems. That's not altogether unexpected, since you weren't able to get the neuro-regulator shot on time. Still, the apoptotic enzymes should correct the problem. But...." Paul chose his words carefully to avoid offending Wayne, "I'm operating in the dark here. If we could get you to come in for—"

"I'm a kidnapper, remember? A wanted man. Just give me the shot."

Paul hesitated.

"The fucking shot," Wayne repeated. "If you want to see the kid alive again." He moved into the shadow of the door frame, took off his coat and held out his bared arm.

"Once I give you the shot, will you let Alex go?" At some stage Wayne would remember that he'd still require a third regulator dose, that holding Alex was his only get-free card.

"The boy wants me to take him to some ranch in the country. Said you'd tell me how to get there."

"Ranch? Cowboys and Indians, eh? Maybe that's just something Alex made up. He's an imaginative eight year old, Wayne." Paul tightened a tourniquet on the man's heavy upper arm. "I'm injecting this intravenously, so it should start working fast."

"Come on, doc, let's not play games. I screwed up big time, but when I give my word I keep it. You're gonna have to trust me this one time." Wayne pushed his bare arm under Paul's nose.

Paul inserted the needle, injected the suspension, released the tourniquet.

"Right, I've done what you wanted. Now please let me try to explain something to you. Do you know what chromosomes are?"

"Stop talking down to me like I'm stupid or something. Yes, I know what chromosomes are."

"Sorry, I'm just making sure we're talking the same language. You probably also know that human chromosomes are very similar to monkey chromosomes and dog chromosomes and mouse chromosomes." Paul paused to see how Wayne would take this statement; he merely nodded, and Paul continued. "A small change in the genetic material of an animal can cause a large change in the observable characteristics of the animal. What I injected into all four of us is a synthetic chromosome, a sort of box of tricks with extra genetic code."

"So you're changing my genes?"

"Adding to them. We still don't understand exactly how it works. The new chromosomes are designed to act as a switch that amplifies and regulates cell repair and growth, including the growth of neurons."

"Yeah, I know what neurons are. I finished high school, before—" Wayne broke off. "Neurons are brain cells, nerve cells."

"In that case you probably already know that the growth pattern of neurons varies at different stages in a human being's development."

"Yeah, you were talking about that in the lab, before I...."

"Right." Shit, was that guilt in the bastard's voice? "In a developing brain, the neurons grow rapidly and branch out in different directions."

"Axons and dendrites," said Wayne.

"Yes." The son of a bitch really had been reading about neurons. "As the brain matures, some of the branches die back, like being pruned."

"Yeah, you said that too. And then they stabilize. I read that, but I don't really understand it. What makes cells just stop growing?" Wayne leaned forward, clearly interested.

"There's a cascade of chemical switches that causes the neurons to shift from one stage to the next. Drew and I think the auxosomes—the new chromosomes, that is—that they regulate the switches themselves. We've pushed our neurons back into the rapid growth stage that normally ends in childhood."

"That explains why...I haven't felt this way since I was a kid. Interested in things, know what I mean?"

"Yes, I know exactly what you mean. Now, the reason I'd like you to get a medical checkup is that if the switches aren't regulated in exactly the right way—if they stay active for too long—your neurons may grow *too* rapidly."

"Fuck!" Wayne suddenly laughed coarsely, rolling down his sleeve and pulling his business suit coat back on. "So my head really *might* swell up and explode? Thought that shit only happened in Stephen King movies. I've been feeling that way for days."

"Well, not quite *explode*." Paul broke the hypo's needle, put the used set away in his pocket. "There are other control systems, they'd stop the overgrowth before it went that far. But yes, the symptoms you mentioned—headache, memory loss, confusion, violent emotional swings. Look, Wayne, the four of us are the only people this's ever been tried on. I was working on a way to insert the regulators along with the auxosomes so there's no need for follow-up injections. It's working well in the mouse trials. But obviously I didn't have that ready when you...." He tried to contain his anger, keep his voice level. "I just can't be sure *what* the unregulated auxosomes are doing to you."

"And you don't care, do you?" Wayne, too, was furious again. "You're the scourge of Gaia, you fucking scientists."

Paul backed away. "Fucking *scientists?* You pointed a fucking *gun* in my face. You threatened to kill us all, including a little sick boy, unless I—"

"Yeah, yeah." Without a break, the man had exhausted his fury. He slumped against the wall, rubbing his eyes.

Watching him carefully, Paul chose to stand his ground, breathing carefully, bringing his pulse down. He could smell the stench of his own sweat. His mind roared down half a dozen tracks at once. "Wayne, I'd like to run some skill tests. You'd improve your own chances."

"Yeah. And it'd be good for the textbooks, and your Nobel Prize." He sighed heavily. "You're not talking about doing some kind of test right now?"

"No, no," Paul told him hastily. "Let's get Alex safely back to his mother. You probably want to be out of town as soon as possible."

"Did she report me to the cops?"

"I don't know." Paul met the shadowed eyes candidly. "After the crash she was unconscious for a while. They might've interviewed her by now, but I doubt it. She was pretty groggy when I talked to her. Still, play it safe, wouldn't you think?"

"Yeah. Better safe than sorry. So let's get the show on the road, doc. Where's this ranch of yours?"

"It's not my ranch, Wayne, and I'm not free to tell you the exact location. I have to ask the owner if it's okay to go there. We need a meeting place. Neutral territory."

"That'll do."

"Do you have a car? How about the auxosome side effects? Can you drive safely?" Paul had a brief vision of Wayne, stoned or ill, driving off the road or crashing into another car. But the chances of a good outcome seemed much higher if he trusted Wayne than with any other alternative.

"I'll have a car. If I start to feel bad, I'll pull over and rest until I'm okay again."

"Right. Just west of Junction there's a place called the Lucky Star Motel." He could hardly miss it, because of its preposterous billboard—a Texas Longhorn cow jumping over a laughing quarter moon wearing a five-pointed star as a hat. "I'll get a room there and wait until you show up. Look for the black Humvee parked outside. That way you won't have to ask for my room number at the office."

"I'm not sure when we'll be there. I have to get some money together for the trip."

"Here." Paul took a money clip from his pocket, handed Wayne three fifty dollar bills. "I'll wait at the Lucky Star until you get there. Make it as soon as possible."

"Hey." Wayne was suddenly suspicious again. "You said.... Back in the lab you were talking about three shots, not just two. We gonna find some way for me to get the third shot?"

"Sure we are," Paul said, walking away. "Just so long as nothing happens to Alex. Or Jill." Or me, he thought, the flesh crawling over his exposed back.

113: THURSDAY, JULY 3

Wayne half expected the kid to be gone when he returned to the costume storage room, but Alex lay stretched out in a pile of clothes he'd pulled from a box, just as he had been when Wayne left, dressed as a girl.

"Alex?" The pale figure lay perfectly still. Shit, the kid had something bad wrong with him. Maybe he'd died. Frantically, Wayne grabbed at the boy's shoulders to shake him, suddenly remembered Fern talking about some babysitter that killed a kid by shaking it. Instead, he gave him a slap on the cheek.

"Hey!" Alex opened his eyes, scowled indignantly at Wayne. "Don't slap me."

"Just a little pat to wake you up. Time to hit the road. We gotta find a car."

"Okay."

Safest thing to borrow would be some ride ordinary enough to be inconspicuous and new enough to be reliable. They got lucky in the parking lot of Mr. Gatti's Pizza: a late model Ford Ranger with doors unlocked and keys in the ignition. He lifted Alex into the front, tossed the wagon into the bed, slid behind the wheel and took off. It was that easy.

"Even has a full tank of gas!" he told Alex jubilantly.

"Won't the cops be looking for these plates?" the boy asked.

"Yeah, soon as they finish chowing down, the owners of this

pickup'll report it stolen. So just to be on the safe side, we're gonna switch license plates with another vehicle."

"Cool," the kid said.

POST MORTAL

114: THURSDAY, JULY 3

In 1951, twenty-two days after Bruce Blick's ninth birthday, his classmate Edward Eichner had knocked him down and broken his glasses. Bruce sat on the sidewalk and screamed, "I hate you, Eddie! I wish you were dead!" The following day, red-eyed Mrs. Colin told the class that Ed Eichner would not be coming back to school anymore. On the way home from the grocery store, running an errand with his twin sister Isabel, a furniture delivery van had ploughed up over the sidewalk, wildly out of control, killing both children instantly.

Hearing the news from his distraught teacher, Bruce realized his power and his responsibility. It marked a turning point in his life. He never again wished anyone dead unless he really meant it.

When Bruce completed his schooling at the William Parsons Military Academy, his father gave him flying lessons as a graduation gift and bought him a Piper Cherokee. When he graduated with honors from Yale with a dual degree in physics and political science, his father gave him a summer-house in Portugal and a corner office on the executive floor of the Fitzgerald Hotel in New York. When he married Patricia Elaine Newfoundland, a former debutante and minor heiress, the wedding was among the events of the season. Two months after Bruce's 48th birthday, his father died, leaving him a financial empire that included a chain of hotels and a company that produced and sold generic pharmaceuticals. It was a license to print money.

Hundreds of millions of people would have given up their right eye to have Bruce's life, but his predominant emotions were fear and anxiety. Over the years, his concept of the power he wielded had matured from the limited understanding he possessed at nine years of age. Nevertheless he knew the power was real, and he spent most of his time pondering what was best for the world, worrying desperately that he would make a mistake.

The year Bruce turned fifty-four, Jesús Martínez of Phoenix, Arizona took a shot at him with a .22 caliber rifle and wounded him in the shoulder. The police investigation revealed that Bruce had attempted to buy the house and land Jesús had inherited from his grandmother. When Jesús would not sell, Bruce put financial pressure on the City Council to condemn the house so that the street could be widened. In fact, the street-widening project never materialized, and the city sold the land, along with ten adjoining lots, to Bruce's company North Star Limited. Through its wholly owned subsidiary, MorningStar Incorporated, Blick built a high-rise apartment building there, with shops and offices on the lower floors. The land that had been in the Martínez family was worth $3,285,995 on the day Jesús shot but failed to kill Bruce. The city had paid Jesús $12,000.

The shooting marked a second major turning point in Bruce's life. Although he was not seriously wounded, and his shoulder healed rapidly, he found himself growing excessively jumpy and seldom ventured outside his residential suite at the Fitzgerald. Unable to tolerate his paranoia, his wife Patricia left him. After six months, his psychotherapist, Dr. Rutherford, advised him to spend some time far away from the city. Bruce considered the house in Portugal, but too many people knew he owned it, and besides it was in an area with an unacceptably dense population. He sent his personal assistant Tom Gebhardt to locate a secluded place well off the beaten track. Tom flew to Monte Capanne and crossed the water to consider Amalfi, took a company Sikorski to fifteen hamlets in Bulgaria and Bosnia, startling the locals, tested the sentiment in Bangalore and the former Congo Republic but found both severely wanting, and finally pinning down a ruined seventeenth-century monastery near San Miguel Regla in the state of Hidalgo, México. Bruce approved the purchase and Tom hired architects and contractors from Mexico City to handle the restoration.

Isolated as he was, Bruce Blick had ample time to study the world and to ponder which course would be best for humankind. He realized that his power was far greater even than he had known, that in fact he could change the course of human evolution. What a pity that he could not carry out his plans single-handedly, that he must rely on idiots and madmen shaped to his purposes.

The moment he was satisfied that Gibson's experiments were not just another bogus bid for funding, that they appeared to be the real thing at last, he flew back by corporation jet to his empty palatial Manhattan apartment. There was a child, and the child was missing. Blick called Tom Gebhardt to him and within hours sent all his dogs baying after this infant whose tissues, perhaps, contained the elixir of eternity in its most uncorrupted form. He knew death was within his gift, had known it since his childhood. If he had to slaughter the lot of them, child and mother and scientist and vigilante alike, and strip them down to code and chemicals, he would do it easily and without qualm. He would find endless life, and make himself new, forever.

115: THURSDAY, JULY 3

A party was roaring at the Sigma Chi fraternity house, and cars lined the street for more than three blocks.

"Perfect." Wayne pulled up to the curb behind a sleek Italian sports car. "You wait here. I'm gonna take the plates off that sucker and put them onto our Ranger. Stay in the car." His Swiss Army knife had a fairly stout screw driver. It took only a moment to switch the plates. Luckily it wasn't a frat boy's vanity plates saying BIGUS DIKUS or something. "Nobody looks at their license plates when they get in their car." Wayne started up the Ranger. "Especially people as drunk as these kids'll be by the time their party's over."

"What if a cop stops us and looks up the plates on the computer and finds out they're on the wrong vehicle?"

"Well, could happen. But let's not look for trouble. Cross that bridge if we come to it. Shut up now, okay?"

Nearing the outskirts of town, Alex said, "Wayne, I need to pee." After the silence the kid's high-pitched voice was painfully loud.

"Shit! Why the hell didn't you do that while I was switching the plates?"

"You said to stay in the pickup."

Wayne pulled over to the curb. "Okay, get out and pee. Make it quick."

"There's no bathroom!"

"Just pee on the fucking ground! Come on, move it!" Wayne felt as though his nerves would snap if the kid didn't hurry.

"I think I may need to poop too."

"No time. Hold it in for now and do it later. Get back in the frigging car."

"It's not a car. It's a pickup truck."

"Get the fuck in and shut up. I mean it, you little shit. Sit still and be quiet."

"I'm hungry, Wayne." Alex closed the door, but not hard enough to latch it.

"God damn it." Wayne reached across and slammed the door.

They had gone another quarter mile when Alex piped up again, "I'm hungry. When can we eat?"

"You'll just have to wait. We don't have time to stop."

"But I get sick if I don't eat. I'm already getting a headache."

"Well, then, lie down and go to sleep. You won't know you're hungry if you're asleep."

"I can't go to sleep when I'm hungry," Alex whined.

"If you don't shut up and do what you're told," Wayne roared at the top of his voice, shaking the tree-shaped air freshener dangling from the rear-view mirror, "I'll fucking blow your head off and throw your body out on the highway."

For a minute there was blessed silence. He jabbed the radio, found a country station. The child's small voice reached him through his simmering rage and Emmy-Lou Harris's *White Line Fever*.

"Wayne, I'm sorry I upset you."

He grunted. "Just keep quiet and be good. Or I'll do what I'd said."

"Uh, you can't, you know."

Fury bubbled up again into his brain. He slammed on the brakes, pulled to the side of the highway and stopped. Grabbing at Alex's shoulder to shake him, he found himself looking into the boy's innocent, knowing eyes.

"Bullshit. I can do whatever I like."

The boy gazed back at him with terrifying quiet confidence. He should have been quaking in his shoes. He should have been shitting his pants with terror, like Wayne had done when his daddy threatened him with a knife.

"We're both—" Alex paused, seemed to shrink a little. "Wayne, promise you won't be angry if I say this?"

"Say what you like, small change." His anger had drained away. "Words can't hurt me."

"Look, I was thinking about this when you went to get your shot. If you kill me, they'll kill you."

"Hafta find me first. Hafta know I did it." He pulled back onto the highway.

"Mom and Paul both saw you. I mean, it's obvious."

"You want me to let you out at the next police station, is that it?" Wayne barked a laugh. "Well, no. You're my ticket to a check up and my final shot. If I let you go before Gibson's doc pal checks me out, my damned brain's gonna explode or something, right? I've got nothing to lose."

"Actually, I *don't* think you should let me go yet."

Astounded, Wayne looked at the kid again. He was perfectly serious.

"See, Wayne, think of it this way. It's like we're both hanging off opposite ends of this rope that's been slung over a high metal beam. Down in the pit under us there's these hungry lions and tigers waiting for us to fall."

Without wanting to, Wayne found the picture forming in his head. It didn't make that much sense, because he was so much heavier than Alex that his weight'd drag his side down in an instant. He put some gears and pulleys into the picture to even them up.

"Yeah, so?"

"This is the hard part. There's nets ready to spring out and catch us if we let go."

Wayne felt his irritation rising again. "That's a pretty stupid story. How can the wild animals hurt us if the nets are there?"

"There's a rule, Wayne. If you let go of your side of the rope before I do, you'll be saved by your net but I'll fall down and get eaten. Same for me, other way round."

"That's what I was just saying, you dumb kid. I can kill you any time I like. Why should I care if you get eaten by lions?"

"Because if you get caught by the net, Wayne, they've got you. They lock you up and throw away the key."

Wayne frowned, thinking it through. He felt somehow that his mind really was faster than it used to be, faster and clearer. Once, a puzzle like this would have thrown him into a shouting frenzy, or a cold narrow anger incapable of mapping the consequences. Since Rutherford. Since whatever that bastard had done to him. That much was clear to him, now that he thought about it. At best, he had been careful, diligent, and—blind. He'd acted out of trapped anger, and somehow never considered the nets and wild things. And the people he was hurting. Fern came into his mind, poor Fern. It made his eyes burn.

"We could both climb up our own end of the rope," Wayne said. "Hand over hand. Long as we balanced our weights so neither of us fell. When we got to the bar, we'd shimmy along it till we reach the end of the beam, and climb out."

"That's what I think we should do," Alex told him, head nodding. Wayne felt a burst of pride swell through him, and it was stupid, really stupid, here he was feeling so great because he'd solved a problem a goddam eight year old had set up. But it was a good problem, he saw that. It was a great problem, and a great solution.

His damned hand was aching again. He pulled off his glove to rub the pain away against his thigh, glanced back a moment later, astonished, at the two pink things jutting out against the steering wheel. God almighty. They had tiny nails growing at the end. He'd been lying to himself the past couple of weeks. He hadn't been hitting his stumps on anything; that was just something he told himself to keep from being afraid of what was happening.

The fucking fingers were *growing back*.

Creeped out, he shot a sidelong glance at the kid, then another. A real look, seeing what was actually there rather than what he expected to see because he'd seen it before. In fact the boy's face looked fuller; his color was pinker, healthier looking. It had to be Gibson's drug, this auxosome shit. It was fixing them up. Repairing the damage caused by disease and amputation. God damn.

He accelerated, heading west, out of town.

116: THURSDAY, JULY 3

Separated from Jill by only a thin curtain, some other human in pain moaned and moaned, a repetitive dismal complaint of suffering, a dreary litany. Too drowsy from painkillers and sedatives to get up, Jill lay on the narrow hospital bed and examined her own life carefully for the first time in years. It was brutally difficult to concentrate; her forehead throbbed, and she tried to suppress the terror that on top of everything else she might now be brain damaged from the shock of the collision.

Between trying to make a living and do a decent job of mothering Alex, she realized, she had raced from one urgent task to the next, seldom finding time just to sit and think.

She had been so sure the ideas propounded by Nature Forever were right, but now she saw that they had come predigested, in the form of flyers that presented only one narrow view of the world. Paul had shown her a completely different world. Because at first she mistrusted his ideas she had questioned them, tested them against reality. Until recently she had not tested her own beliefs. Her intolerable situation, she saw now, was a direct result of trying to reconcile two mutually exclusive views of reality.

Okay, so she had to choose: face the mistake she'd made, and pay the price by giving up her standing as a law-abiding citizen. That was the only way to save her son's life. Or she could keep her old friends (perhaps they would forgive her this one transgression), maintain her social position, get another job...and let her son die while she herself was still young.

I wish I'd thrown his damned *Mitochondria* book into the hospital cafeteria trash bin, she thought. Better yet, never laid eyes on him.

Horrified, then, she realized she had just wished for ignorance and, along with it, an early death for Alex. She told herself: That's exactly what would've happened if I'd never met Paul Gibson. I'd never have known there was any other choice for my son. She felt dizzy, closed her eyes, drifted into a dream.

§

"Jill." Someone held her hand. She opened her eyes. Paul stood by her bed.

With great effort, she focused her mind. "Where's Alex? Did they take him back to Keith's house?"

"He's still with Wayne. I'm going to get him now."

A fog of hopelessness and hatred.

"Still with Wayne? Paul, I don't want Alex to go back to

Keith's. I don't want him to die."

"There's a way, I think." He leaned across her, lowering his voice. On the other side of the curtain, the moans went on and on, like an animal panting in pain. "I'd like to take him to Roberta's ranch. We don't have time to talk about it now, but I have a plan."

"I'm coming with you." The fog began to lift. "Getting out of here. Right now." Jill sat up, grabbed at Paul's arm to steady herself.

"The doctor won't release you until she's had a chance to examine you again. I don't think that'll happen any time soon. They just brought in six or seven people from another car wreck."

"Paul, see if you can find my clothes. I don't care what the doctor said, I'm leaving."

"Can't see them. Maybe your clothing got cut off you when you were brought in."

"Improvise. See if you can find something, anything I could put on."

"Let me see your eyes." She saw his gaze go to the padded bandage covering most of her forehead. Frowning, he looked at her eyes. He cupped her face in his hands, then, and kissed her lips. "I don't see any abnormal pupil dilation. You're going to have a hell of a headache when the analgesics wear off, and you'll need to keep that wound clean. Okay, I'll get you some clothes. Be right back."

Minutes later he returned with a maternity dress, large orange, red, and pink flowers on white, and tartan slippers. "Some unlucky mother will have to call home for a change of clothes. She'll make the hospital buy her a new dress, but they'll never find another one this gorgeous."

"We can return it later. God, this is atrocious!" Jill pulled the thing over her head. "How do I look?"

"Like the 'Before' footage for an Extreme Makeover. Will you risk arrest for petty theft to own this dress?"

"Maybe we can find some rope to cinch it up around the

waist." She hitched at the vile fabric, struck a pose.

Paul smothered his laughter. "Let's worry about the finer points of style later. Come on, we'll sneak out while everyone's busy."

117: THURSDAY, JULY 3

The streets of Junction, Texas were deserted at 1:00 A.M. The kid had fallen asleep a couple of hours back, and Wayne had let himself coast, switching the radio back and forth between Country 101 and Oldies 103. Not a cop in sight the whole trip, and almost no traffic.

Okay now, according to Gibson the Lucky Star Motel was just on the other side of Junction. We've got it made, Wayne thought. Past the last yellow blinking traffic light and heading back out into the darkness of the countryside.

A red light flashed behind them.

His first impulse was to step on the accelerator, try to outrun the cop. No, that'd be futile. He'd had the bad luck to pick a vehicle in need of a tune-up. It was all he could manage to get the shit heap up to sixty miles per hour. With a deep sigh he slowed, pulled to the shoulder and tried to stop his hands from shaking.

The cop checked the license plate on the Ranger.

"Good evening, sir." That gave him a momentary shock; people didn't usually call him "sir." It's the business suit, he thought. The cop shone his flashlight in Wayne's face, moved it to get a view of the kid. With relief Wayne saw that the boy's wig had stayed on straight.

"Good evening, officer." Wayne tried to make his voice and diction as dignified as his suit.

"Are you aware that your brake lights are not working?"

"No, sir, I wasn't." Please don't ask to see my driver's license.

Alex stirred. Oh my God, please don't wake up. Please don't say anything.

"Are we there yet, Dad?" Alex yawned. In the flashlight beam, wearing the wig, you couldn't tell that he had some awful disease. If he even did, anymore.

"We're still on the road, Matilda," he said. "The officer stopped to let us know our brake lights are not working properly."

"Wait here, please. I'll be right back." The cop walked back to his car.

"What's he doing?" whispered Alex.

"Probably running a computer check." Wayne prepared himself for violence, struggling to retain his composure. In the rear view mirror he saw that the cop had stopped at the rear of the pickup. He turned and yelled to Wayne, "Hit your brakes, could you?"

"Okay," Wayne yelled back.

The cop approached the front of the truck again. "Right side's working, but not the left. I'm not going to ticket you on this, sir, but make sure you get that problem taken care of first thing in the morning." The cop smiled at the dear little girl in the passenger seat.

"I surely will! Thank you for letting me know."

"Y'all take care." The cop nodded and walked back to his car.

For a moment, Wayne's body shook so badly he couldn't move. As he started the car again, his hands were damp with sweat. "Good job, Alex. I was scared you'd say something to give us away. Wouldn't have been good for *any* of us."

"We're climbing the ropes together. Well done, my good man."

Wayne gave an incredulous laugh, but the kid wasn't mocking him in some smart ass way. He found himself relaxing. "Yep, pardner, I haven't forgotten."

118: THURSDAY, JULY 3

Room number 8 of the Lucky Star Motel was at the inner corner of the L-shaped red brick building. Carpet and bedspread were threadbare, walls dingy, but Jill, head reeling, was thankful for a stationary place to lie down. She truly felt vile. Was it her delayed period, on top of everything else? God, I hope not, she thought. Something nagged at the corner of her attention: *It's been two months now.* Then the thought was swamped by a bout of nausea. Paul sat at the dusty motel window watching for Wayne and Alex; she allowed herself to rest, give way to the exhaustion of the trip from Austin. Half hysterical with fear for her son, she'd vomited twice by the side of the road.

Not allowing herself to contemplate the worst possibilities, she snuggled into the pillow, marveled that a lumpy bed in a sleazy motel could feel so comforting. The door, voices. Incredibly, then, Alex's arms were around her.

"Mom! Wake up. I was so worried about you. Wayne said you had a wreck. Oh, your poor head!"

It was a little girl, herself at eight in old photographs. "What in the world?" Her son's face was framed by long golden curls. For a moment Jill wondered if the concussion had brought on hallucinations.

"It's a disguise, Mom. Wayne took me to this really cool place with all kinds of costumes. Knights and cowboys. They even had part of an old car there."

"I'm so glad to see you, honey." In real life and in movies, Jill had always felt slightly contemptuous of people who cried from happiness, but she found herself weeping now, overcome with joy and relief. She hugged Alex until he squirmed to get loose.

"I'm *starving*, Mom. Wayne—that's Payback's real name— he said there wasn't enough time to stop and eat."

She lowered her voice. "Where is he now?" Paul was sitting in the room's one chair, watching them tensely. He came over, sat on the squeaking bed.

"Wayne wanted to wait in the car. Said he didn't want to upset you." Paul tousled the boy's wig, grinning, and placed his open hand above the bandage on Jill's forehead. "How yuh feeling?"

"Wimpy, but a little better. Get the son of a bitch in here, Paul."

"You sure?" Paul looked doubtful. "He didn't have to bring Alex to us, but he did."

She was shaking. "I want to kill him."

"Mom, he *helped* me."

"Hush, sweetie," Jill said. Her muscles remained locked with fury, and her head was pounding again. "This is big people business."

"I called Roberta," Paul said, "and I explained what's going on. Told her we're on the way. I hate to ask you to get up again so soon, Jill, but I think it'll be best to go on tonight. Sooner we get Alex safely hidden away, the better."

"You're right, of course. Don't worry, I don't have a weapon. I won't shoot the bastard in the back.""

Alex looked anxiously from Jill to Paul. "You won't send me back to Dad's, will you?"

"No way, sweetheart." Jill hugged him again. "We're going to that ranch first, then we may go on to Mexico." She pushed herself up from the bed, sick and angry and somehow at the same time filled with waves of relief. It surprised her that a single human could contain such conflicted emotions. But the anger was ebbing, she could feel it falling away from her in a continued rush of gratitude for her child's return. Was it God she had to thank? Paul? God forgive her, did she owe the monster Wayne Elliot a debt? Tears flooding down her face, she walked with Alex and Paul to the door, and stepped into the night.

119: THURSDAY, JULY 3

Now that he was back with Mom and Paul, Alex found he wasn't frightened anymore. This was high adventure, the most thrilling experience of his life. He was relieved Mom and Paul had decided to let Wayne come with them, and a little sorry Wayne had fallen asleep across the back seat almost the second he climbed in. Poor old Wayne! He was entertaining to talk to when he wasn't having one of his crazy anger spells.

Facing backwards in the rear of the Humvee, Alex looked up at the stars, expecting his mother to go frantic at any moment and order him into the front. She must be sleeping too, he thought. Paul said they'd given her some sort of medicine at the hospital to relax her. Funny, Alex himself didn't feel tired at all. Far overhead he saw the lights of some sort of aircraft. Maybe it was a spaceship, he thought. It wouldn't surprise him all that much if a spaceship landed directly in the Humvee's path. It had been that kind of day.

Paul called to him quietly. "You all right back there, kiddo?"

"Uh huh."

The lights were still there, high in the air. Whatever it was seemed to be moving in a circle, roughly centered on the Humvee.

"Paul." He crawled toward the front on his hands and knees. "Someone's following us up in the sky."

"Really? What do you think it is?"

"I don't know. Maybe a spaceship? A UFO? They abduct people, you know."

"Well, keep an eye on it for us, will you?"

"Okay." Paul was just playing along, not really taking him seriously. Alex loved Mom and Paul, but they still seemed to think he was dumb just because he was a kid. Wayne was the only one who took him seriously. Wayne had said, "You're a genius, you know that? They rewired you into a genius, just like they said. Pity it didn't work with me." He'd given a gritty, bitter laugh. "Awakened the goddamned serial killer within." Whatever that meant. Alex hoped it wasn't something to do with Wayne's dead brother Robbie, who he'd said had drowned when they were both just kids. Maybe Wayne felt guilty about that; maybe he felt responsible for the death of his own brother. Maybe that was why he'd helped Alex, despite threatening to kill all of them. It was the only thing that made sense, really.

It was a long time before the Humvee turned off the highway onto a narrow, bumpy road. Alex passed the time by memorizing the patterns of the brighter stars, giving certain groups of stars names based on objects they reminded him of: The Eyeglasses, The Motorcycle, The Dog Turd. He laughed quietly at that. Their airborne escort stayed with them, but Alex didn't bother to mention it again to Paul. He tried to tune in to their crackly discussion with his little home-made radio, and what he seemed to hear the voices saying scared him badly but he knew there was no point telling the adults, not even Wayne. The spaceship people couldn't really have spoken his name. He found a trap door in the floor and played with it, snicking it up and shutting it quietly. It didn't seem to have much in it except a few tools.

The darkness on either side of the car was thicker and blacker than he had ever seen before. Nothing existed except the sky, the Humvee, and the short section of road illuminated by the Humvee's lights. It was mysterious and exciting; he liked it. He pulled something small and heavy out of his backpack, a small sphere about two inches in diameter, and switched it on with the GameBoy console. Slowly it rose and hovered just below the roof of the Humvee, emitting a soft green glow. Chuckling, Alex plucked it from the air and tossed it in his hand. He really liked making these toys. Sherry would love this one. He wondered when he'd see his sisters again. He heard a hiss of indrawn breath. Wayne was watching him from the back seat, eyes glimmering in the pale green light. Alex quickly put the flying machine back in his bag.

At last they turned onto an even narrower road and stopped

in front of a sprawling multi-level building with huge windows and a wide porch with columns like carved tree trunks. Paul got out and walked over stiffly to a tall blonde older woman who came out the door.

"We're going to have to help Jill," he said. They came back to the vehicle.

"Lean on me, dear," the woman said kindly to Mom. "Come on, let's get you into bed."

The lights in the sky were bigger now and farther apart. Whatever had been following them was getting closer. Far back down the road, he could see headlights. Farther away, more lights. Cars coming. Not just one car. Alex didn't like it. What if they were looking for him? The blonde woman had her arm around Mom, walking with her into the house.

"Hey, where've you got to, kiddo?" Paul turned back to the Humvee. Moving as quickly as he could, Alex pulled open the trap door, exposing its rectangular opening. Wayne was gone, scooted out the back the moment they'd stopped.

"Alex, come on in and get something to eat." As Paul reached to open the passenger side door, Alex lowered himself silently into the hiding place. It was a tight, uncomfortable fit, but he was able to lower the top as Paul opened the door of the Humvee.

"Alex?" After a moment the door slammed, and he heard Paul walking away toward the house. A few minutes later there were footsteps again. Paul and the blonde woman talking.

"She was asleep the minute her head touched the pillow. Where's the boy?"

"He seems to have disappeared. Along with the man I told you about." Paul sounded worried, but it was probably better to stay hidden in here.

"Maybe the boy's asleep in the back," she said.

"I checked, but it won't hurt to look again. Alex!" Paul sounded really upset this time.

"What's that?"

Alex recognized a new sound, the throb of a helicopter. Oh. Not a spaceship after all. That's what those sky lights were, and they really had been talking about him.

"Oh my god, Paul, looks like they've got the police forces of four counties coming up the road."

"Roberta, don't say anything about Alex, okay? I have a feeling he saw this coming and hid."

Yes! Old Paul was a little slow, but at least he'd finally figured out what was going on.

120: FRIDAY, JULY 4

Each time her eyes closed, Jill felt nauseated, as if she were still in the jolting Humvee. Taking care not to move her head, she kept her gaze fixed on the strip of light at the bottom of the closed door.

She didn't regret leaving the hospital; it was worth dealing with the nausea to know that Alex was safe. She listened for his voice, the sounds of his sneakers on the tile floor. He must have fallen asleep in the back of the Humvee. Paul would carry him in.

So lucky to know Paul. So good, being able to trust someone. Drifting into sleep, she imagined she heard a dog barking.

A man's shout. A gunshot, the dog howling in pain. A woman screaming. Oh my god! Alex!

Head reeling, Jill tore open the bedroom door, ran down the hallway toward the front door.

Alex!

The front door burst open as Jill stepped into the darkness of Roberta's living room. Two men dressed in black jumpsuits stood there, one pointing a rifle, the other shining a flashlight around the room.

"Get over here right now!" the gunman yelled.

"Ninety degrees!" The flashlight had discovered Jill.

The gunman, shockingly young, no more than twenty-two or three, was obviously jittery. I've had practice with a killer, Jill thought, drenched in traumatic memories of Wayne, the lab, the terror. "There's no need to point the gun at me." Keeping her voice as calm as possible. "I'm not armed or violent."

"Get outside with the others." He spoke very loudly, kept the gun pointed at her.

Roberta was weeping and cursing outside. Was Alex still asleep in the car? Carefully, Jill shuffled toward the front door.

Roberta knelt on the porch beside the body of a golden retriever. Two men in brown uniforms held their rifles on Paul, who stood between the Humvee and the house.

"Over there." The flashlight directed Jill to stand next to Paul.

"She's been in a traffic accident," he told them. "She needs to sit down," Paul put an arm around Jill's shoulders.

"Shut up."

"Who *are* you?" Jill's head was throbbing again. I will not let myself pass out. I will concentrate all my effort on standing here and talking to these people.

"Police."

"Do you have a warrant?"

"We don't need one. We have probable cause to believe that a missing child is in the vehicle or on the premises." The man with the flashlight shined the light on Roberta. "Ma'am, is this your house?"

She looked up from her dead pet, grieving and furious. "Yes. It belonged to my natural father, George Milton, and so did Sitka. Dad died last month. Now you've killed his poor old dog, you bastards."

"If you have nothing to hide, I'm sure you won't mind if we look around."

"You're not from our local sheriff's department. Who are you? Where are you from?"

"I'm from Johnson City."

"But that's sixty miles away. It's a different *county*. What are you doing here?"

"We're cooperating with the FBI. We just want to have a look around."

"You don't have to let him search your property, Roberta."

Jill's voice was strong, but she was not sure she could have remained standing without the support of Paul's arm. "Not without a warrant."

"If you have nothing to hide, why should you mind if we look around?"

"Because this is private property, it's the middle of the night, and I've been ill and need to go back to bed."

"Are you Jill Shannon?"

"Yes, I am. I'm an attorney."

"Is your son Alex Hindley with you?"

"Alex Shannon. No."

"Did you know your son has been reported missing?"

Jill was relieved to see the guns being lowered, but the officer was studying her face closely, gauging her emotional reaction to his statement. "If you know who I am, you already knew I'm an attorney. We don't have to answer your questions now." Simply speaking made her feel ill. She forced herself to meet his eyes. "If you want to search this property, you people need to get back into your cars, drive back to wherever you came from, and obtain a proper warrant." The man with the flashlight stepped toward the Humvee. Jill fought to keep her voice calm. "Did you have Ms. Treadwell's permission to enter her house earlier?"

"They certainly did not." Roberta stood. "Nor did I give them permission to kill my father's dog." Her voice broke, and tears ran down her face.

The man turned away from the Humvee. "The animal attacked us."

"The dog was doing her job, trying to protect me. Whoever told you there was a missing child on this property?"

"I'm not at liberty to give you that information, Ma'am."

"Please leave now." Roberta's voice and manner had regained their usual authority.

Somewhat to Jill's surprise, the flashlight man walked away, motioning to the others to follow. The four men climbed into two unmarked cars, and pulled away, radio crackling faintly. Jill whispered urgently, "Paul, where's Alex?" The other six cars had stayed back on the road, blocking access to the property; now they began to move away. Jill sank to the porch steps, thankful to be sitting down.

"Hiding somewhere. I don't know where. Smart, smart kid. He knew what was happening before I did. They followed us here in a helicopter. Be a good idea to let Alex lie low until those guys have gone on down the road."

"They really were looking for Alex?" It seemed an extraordinary over-reaction, even to a possible kidnapping. "Where's that prick Wayne?"

Paul shrugged, shook his head "Probably took off when he saw the cops coming."

"I felt like running away myself," said Roberta. Her cheeks with wet with tears. "Poor old Sitka, trying her best to protect us. I was afraid one of us would be their next target."

Jill stood, swayed and almost fell. "I'm going to look for Alex," she said, and sat back down with a thump.

"I have a pretty good idea where Alex is." Paul crossed to the Humvee, opened the door.

"But that cop was shining his flashlight in there."

There was a bang and a muffled voice. Paul opened the trapdoor.

"Oh man!" the young voice muttered from the darkness. "I thought I was gonna suffocate in there."

Paul patted him on the back. "Well done, my good man."

"Alex?" Jill stood carefully, took a step toward the Humvee. "Alex! You little genius! Have you been there all along?"

"I was pretending to be an illegal weapon." Grinning, Alex staggered out. "My legs don't feel all the way unfolded yet."

She was astonished. "How'd you know you should hide?"

"I saw 'em following us, then I heard them talking. I told you." The boy threw his arms around Jill.

Heard them talking?

"Mom, where's Wayne?"

"I don't know, son. Lots of things I don't know right now." Jill walked unsteadily to the porch, sat on concrete edge. To

Paul she said: "We can't stay here. I am not going to let them take Alex back to Keith's."

"We won't!" He put an arm about both of them. "Happy Independence Day!"

121: FRIDAY, JULY 4

Drew lay comatose, as he had for days, brainwaves close to flat.

"Alyssa, he'd want us to remember him the way he was, not like this." After that first ghastly time, Maureen had not wanted to come back ever again to the hospital. What was the point? Drew was not here. *That* thing was not *Drew*. But here she was anyway, day after day. "There has to be an end to it. Alyssa, please, we must let your son die with peace and dignity."

"Don't speak of this, young woman. He is my son, and he will return to us."

Maureen had to make the woman understand. It was a matter of dignity. More than that, it was a matter of her own psychic survival. She could not countenance this shell of the man she'd loved being *breathed* by machines. "He and I talked about it, don't you see? Drew absolutely did not want to be kept alive this way. I think we should honor his wishes and take him off the machines."

"What sort of person spoke of such things with their loved ones? He may have *said* that," Mrs. Chang told her coldly, "but Drew did not always act in his own best interests."

Her glance up and down Maureen's rumpled sweatshirt and jeans, uncombed hair and running shoes, made that clear enough. The woman added caustically, "I've known him a little longer than you have, dear."

Count to ten, Maureen. Don't say a word you'll regret later. We will share his beloved memory all the days of our lives. Taking a deep breath, she said, "I'm sure that's true, Alyssa. But no good, godly purpose can be served in this gruesome...

this...." Her eyes flooded with bitter tears. "In keeping Drew's body alive when it's only a shell."

"Shh!" Mrs. Chang was sharp in her rebuke. "He hears us. His spirit knows what we say."

"Oh, please, Alyssa, if we're reduced to *feng shui* superstition—"

"Young woman, show respect!"

"I'm sorry, I'm so—" Maureen collapsed in tears. She was so tired. She was tired to death. After a moment, she felt Mrs. Chang's arm around her, smelled the perfume.

"Maureen, we both love him very much. I'm certain I saw his eyes moving this morning when I was reading to him. His father brought all his favorite stories from when he was a little boy."

Maureen nodded, withdrew from the conciliatory, manipulative embrace, went out into the corridor. She ran a comb through her messy hair. Who the hell could she call upon for help? Roberta Treadwell had been at that party where they were talking about personal identity. Roberta had heard Drew say he'd never wish to be kept on life support indefinitely. And it had been Roberta, after all, who had identified him when they brought him in to the hospital from that madman's shed.

She pulled her cell phone from her pocket.

122: FRIDAY, JULY 4

Thirty thousand feet above sea level, Tom Gebhardt pushed aside a barely touched plate of fresh Gulf crab *au gratin*, picked up his cell phone.

"Call Bruce Blick, private line." Automatically, the phone activated its encryption program. Blick answered within seconds.

"Tom. Are you in Austin?"

"Just left thirty minutes ago."

"I want you to talk to them in person." Soothing electronic

music played in the background; Bruce must be enjoying a therapeutic massage.

"They weren't taken into custody, damn it. The local sheriff backed down and ordered his men to leave before they found anything. Shannon and Gibson were there, no sign of the kid, no evidence of any research facilities."

"What about Wayne Elliot? It's possible he's had the Gibson treatment too. I'm informed his fingerprints were found on an abandoned stolen car."

Tom gritted his teeth. "Yes. A cop had pulled them over earlier for a broken rear light. Computers were down when he called in the license number, which turned out to be for a different car—he'd switched plates. The cop let Elliot go."

"Shit. Listen, Tom, have Steve send out the UAVs."

"To find Elliot? Is he really that important to us if—"

"After the mistakes you've made this past month, Tom, I'd say you've lost the right to question any decision I make. Just do it."

Asshole. I should just walk out on him. See how he likes that. It was not the first time Tom had thought about leaving his job, his life with BlickPharm. But there was nothing else for him. As ever, uneasy, he dismissed the temptation as absurd.

"Put the UAVs on standby in case we need them," Blick was telling him. "I want Elliot brought in, but my concern at the moment is with the other three. I want the kid in one of our labs. I want his biochemistry peeled like a fucking onion."

Easier said than done, Tom thought, if the child's with Wayne the Insane. He suspected Bruce would have Paul Gibson killed or permanently brain damaged to halt any further work on auxosomes. Possibly Roberta Treadwell as well. It'd need to be done soon, before they could release their results to date. If MJT got frightened enough to make the information public before applying for a patent, virtual publication could happen literally at any minute. Twitter, email and the World Wide Web could splash the information around the planet in moments.

"What do you want me to do?" Tom had never been directly

involved in anyone's death, unless you counted the Rutherford program. But too many of Bruce's enemies died or disappeared conveniently; it could not be chance coincidence.

"Get Alex Shannnon. Get Gibson into custody. You've already arranged a thorough search of his Austin lab?"

I'm not incompetent, you damned— "Of course, Bruce."

"Gibson's violated PAHGE. If that won't stick, get him for child kidnapping. And I want Treadwell and Jill Shannon closely monitored. Know where they are at all times. This is important! I want you to stay in Texas and make sure nothing else goes wrong."

"Right, Bruce." Tom silently ground his capped teeth. Arrogant prick. "I'll give the order to turn the plane around."

123: FRIDAY, JULY 4

Disturbed by a yapping dog, Alex sat up, not sure how long he had been asleep. He was still on the porch, head in his mother's lap.

"Mom?"

Paul was saying: "But you might be able to win at the final hearing."

"I've already lost! Can't you see? There's no way.... Remember the case Carol and I talked about?"

"Where the bloke gave his son the veterinary medication, yeah."

"Mom?" Would they ever shut up and listen to him?

"Yes, but —"

"What's the matter with that puppy? Maybe he's upset about Sitka being killed. What is it, Basil?" Roberta was calling to the puppy.

"Mom!" Alex tugged at Jill's flowered skirt. "They don't want to take me back to Dad's house. The guy in the plane said they're going to take me to some kind of lab. Like Paul's."

"We'll talk later, sweetie." Jill turned back to Paul, but Paul was staring hard at Alex, forehead creased.

"Hang on. How do you know they want to take you to a lab, Alex?" Paul asked slowly.

Alex dug around in his bag and pulled out the radio he'd made from the pieces of old equipment dad had given him. "I heard them talking. I thought they were space aliens in a UFO. But it was the men in the helicopter. They want all three of us, but especially me."

Mom looked like she was really seeing him for the first time. "Oh my goodness! You *built* that?"

"Did you hear anything else, Alex?" Paul crouched in front of him, very serious, looking from the radio to his face and back again.

Alex thought hard, recalling the scratchy, broken words. "Mostly they were just talking about where we were and complaining about missing a Fourth of July party. There were some other men, they must have been in a different helicopter. Or an airplane. They said to be careful not to damage me because some guy needed me in the lab."

"Dear Lord. They know about the auxosomes," said Mom. "Somehow they know."

"A spy at MJT?" Roberta looked appalled.

"Or the university." Mom buried her face in her hands, then straightened up. She had that look on her face she'd been getting more often lately; it meant she wasn't going to let anyone push her or Alex around. "We'll go straight to Mexico," she said after a moment. "Should be able to disappear. But obviously we can't use the Humvee, damn it, way too visible."

"And too thirsty—they'd get the MJT credit card next time we fill up the tank," Paul said. "But they'll have our names on the computers at every border crossing."

Roberta broke in, her voice soothing and confident in the dark shadows. "I think I know someone who can help. My housekeeper has family in Mexico. Various members come up here from time to time to work. She knows someone, a local woman, who...arranges papers for people."

"Fake passports?"

The shadow nodded. "From what Maisie tells me, this woman is a real artist. She can come up with anything you need." The puppy's yapping started up again. Roberta stood suddenly. "I think there's someone under the porch."

"Be careful." A decorative iron door was slightly ajar. The dog's barking grew frantic. Roberta leaned down, pulled open the door. Alex found a penlight in his backpack and handed it to Paul, who was peering into the dark opening, then glanced at Mom to make sure she was observing Paul's bravery as he shone the light under the porch.

"Wayne? That you under there? It's okay, man. The police have gone."

A commotion under the porch; Wayne squeezed himself out through an opening so small it looked to Alex like it would've been a tight fit even for him.

"'Bout scared the shit outta me." Wayne leaned against the stone wall, looking pretty sick. "Can you believe it? I got under there and fell right back to sleep. Haven't slept in three or four days."

"That's the regulator kicking in. Think you feel up to staying awake just a little longer? Roberta has contacts that can get us some passports."

"Is there time for all that bullshit?"

Alex said urgently, "I think I see them coming back." He squinted at moving lights close to the eastern horizon. "More of them this time.

"Is there someplace we could keep a low profile?"

"They'll probably bring dogs to track us." Mom shook her head despairingly. "If there's any way to get Alex to safety...." She stood up shakily. "Maybe I can distract them."

Roberta said, "Pipe down. Listen." Everyone stared at her in surprise. "When my grandfather had the original house built during the Prohibition era, he chose the location for a...." She cleared her throat. "A certain convenient reason."

"The bootlegger fortune," Mom said, then looked away,

embarrassed. A bootlegger must be some kind of crook.

Smiling slightly, Roberta told them, "We're standing on top of the entrance to a series of caves. Follow me. If the boy is right about the police coming back, there's not a minute to spare." She led them into the house. Alex glimpsed shiny tile floors, brightly colored rugs, and a huge white wall hung with large paintings. A heavy glass door took them into an open area with an irregularly shaped swimming pool in the center, shockingly blue, illuminated by underwater lamps.

"Under the water," Roberta said, "you'll find a grate on the northern wall of the pool." She pointed. "Pull the grate off, swim through. Go up the steps you'll find there. You'll be in a small room you can stand up in. The water's only about a foot and a half deep in there. At the end of the room are some more steps. Go up the steps, and you come to a large pump. It looks too heavy to move, but the pump housing will slide forward, enough so you can squeeze through into the cave entrance."

"If they bring dogs," Jill said, "they'll follow our scent to the pool."

"Let me worry about that. Maisie and I have been house-training the puppy, we've got about ten different cans of spray stuff guaranteed to clean up odors. Just get out of here. But please, be careful." Roberta walked quickly back into the house, obviously taking it for granted that they'd follow her instructions. She'd left a couple of things out, though.

"Mute your cell phone, Mom," Alex said.

"What?"

"The phone. If it rings, it'll give us away."

She gave him a respectful look; it warmed him. "Here, hide it in your pack. Got a ziplock bag in there?"

"The pack's water-tight."

Swiftly, she delved into his pack, stowed the muted phone. "Okay, troops, I'll go first," she said.

Paul immediately rose. "No, Jill, I—"

"Let her go," Alex said, tugging on Paul's sleeve. He was still learning this new, tough side of Mom, but he already knew enough to tell that when she got that hard look on her face, it was *not* a good idea to mess with her.

124: FRIDAY, JULY 4

Cutting through the cold water, soaked clothes clinging to her skin, Jill was filled with an old confidence, the way she'd always felt when she was a kid. She found the grate, pulled at it. It failed to budge. I won't panic, she told herself. Resolutely, holding her breath, she found hinges at the top, slipped her fingers through the grate, lifted up, pulled. The grate swung out and up at the same moment she knew her lungs were out of air. Fighting panic, she pushed herself through the small opening. Blackness ahead. Pressure squeezed at her chest.

125: FRIDAY, JULY 4

"I can't see her anymore." Alex lay on his stomach, his head almost touching the water. "She's been down there too long. She's drowning!"

Paul realized he was holding his breath, exhaled, forced himself to breathe in slowly, calmly. "Don't worry, Al, she's an expert swimmer, remember? It's our turn now. Let's go, quick." He glanced at Wayne.

"You and Alex go first, then me." Wayne took a step back, away from the pool.

Alex jumped in with a splash, was gone. Paul followed without a pause. Chemical-tainted water stung his nostrils and eyes. By the pale green-blue pool light, he found Alex stuck in the opening and flailing; the bulky pack he still wore on his back had wedged against the grate. Clearly, he'd have to shed the pack. Paul reached for the straps and the boy kicked frantically. His shoe struck Paul's nose. Through blinding pain, Paul could see Jill's hands, trying to pull her son in.

"No!" he tried to shout, but the sound was unintelligible,

even to himself. Lungs burned. He grasped one of Jill's hands, moved it roughly to the backpack. She stopped pulling on Alex, pushed him away. Thank God! She had understood instantly. Holding the struggling boy close to his own body, Paul kicked back to the surface. They broke free, frantically gulping air. As soon as his head was above water, Alex stopped kicking. He coughed convulsively, but Paul was relieved to see that his face was a healthy shade of pink.

"Alex, listen to me," he said when the coughing and sputtering stopped. "You're going to have to take off your backpack and let me pass it through to you."

Had he understood? The boy trod water while Paul slipped the straps from his shoulders. "Okay," Paul told him. "You go in first, then I'll hand your pack through and then come through myself." Alex dove, disappeared through the wall. "Come on, Wayne." Without waiting for an answer, Paul let himself sink, speeding his downward motion with his hands. He pushed the bulky pack through the opening, then squeezed himself through.

He searched with his feet, found a floor not more than eighteen inches below the bottom of the opening, pushed, burst up into air. Jill and Alex bobbed close by in the water, illuminated by a small electric light that shone from a ceiling barely six feet above.

"Automatic," Jill said. "It came on when I arrived on this side."

"We need to switch it off," Paul said. "Or the cops'll see it from over there."

"There are steps going up." Alex pointed to the side of the room opposite the opening they had come through.

"Let's go," said Paul. Jill was already kicking toward the steps. She found the switch with uncanny speed, flipped it off. Paul blinked in the dark, waited for his eyes to adapt. The room was not entirely lightless, washed by an eerie green glow from the pool.

"Where's Wayne?" Alex asked, anxious. He was pulling on his pack over his dripping clothes.

"I suppose we have to wait until the bastard gets here," said Jill. "We have to make sure the grate's closed. Where the hell *is* he? Maybe he's drowned."

"He's afraid of water," Alex told them matter-of-factly. "His little brother Robbie drowned. He's probably too scared to jump in."

"Shit. If the cops find him here—"

Paul said, "I'll go up." He turned back, but the boy grabbed his arm.

"Me. I'll go," said Alex. "He'll come with me. We're partners." He shucked his pack.

"Alex, no!" cried Jill, reaching for him; he thrust the pack into her arms. He was already underwater again, halfway to the opening. She took a breath, clearly preparing to follow him; Paul put a hand on her shoulder.

"If necessary, I can knock our gun-happy friend out and bring him down the hard way."

"Oh shit, Paul. Oh shit." Jill sounded as though she had lost all hope, but she made no move to stop him as he dove toward the opening.

126: FRIDAY, JULY 4

It could've been kind of funny, Alex thought, a grown man cowering away from the water like a scared little kid. But obviously it was not at all funny to Wayne. Thinking about his dead brother, for sure. Alex wished he could figure out some way to make Wayne feel better. No time to think complicated stuff right now, the important thing was to get Wayne down here into the water. He could hear the sounds of car engines. The police arriving. No time to waste. Might be too late already.

"Look, it's not a big deal, pardner," Alex called to Wayne, using all his will power to stay calm. "You don't have to know how to swim. All you do is go down and then back up. Nothing to it."

As Wayne took a tentative step toward the water, Paul surfaced with a giant splash. Wayne cringed back from the edge of the pool. Behind the noise of the splash, Alex heard the faint throb of a helicopter.

"Wayne." Paul shouted. "You've got to come down with us. We're all dead if they catch you up there."

The sound of the chopper grew louder. A car door slammed. Alex heaved himself up from the water, onto the concrete deck. Wow! My arms are getting strong. Gotta get Wayne into the water now. Wish Paul had stayed down below.

He caught Paul's eye. "Stay back!" Turned to Wayne again. "Hey, come on, Wayne. We're partners. I won't let anything happen to you. You can go in ahead of me."

Roberta came running toward the pool, brandishing a spray bottle like someone in a cartoon advertisement. It should have looked hilarious, but the reality was frightening, nightmarish. "Hurry it up!" she shouted. "They're coming to the door."

Alex controlled his own fear. "Wayne, remember what we were talking about when we borrowed that truck? Ya gotta stay cool. Concentrate on your work, man!" The man's terrified eyes locked onto Alex's. "Come on, pardner, you can do it." Eyes tight shut, squeezing up his face, Wayne leaped into the pool. Alex was right behind him.

127: FRIDAY, JULY 4

I'm going to be okay. Concentrate on your work, Wayne said to himself. Concentrate. Concentrate. But then he had to open his eyes, find the underwater opening, and the cold pressure of the water against his retinas almost caused him to gasp. With the last remnant of his self control, he forced himself not to take a breath. I can't do this. I've gotta go back up. I don't care how they punish me. I deserve it. I'd rather die on dry land than down here. He kicked frantically, and his faced scraped something hard. The edge of the pool. Or the bottom? A small hand closed over his wrist. Robbie. He had to control himself for the kid's sake. With the greatest effort of his life, he forced himself to be still and allow Robbie to pull him through the water. Before he quite realized it, the boy had vanished into a narrow slit in the wall, and he himself was halfway through.

The green pool lights went off.

He wanted to scream in the darkness. Too late to go backwards. No choice left but to kick himself gently forward. The kid would keep him safe. Then his head was above water again, and he heard the mother's voice, half hysterical.

"Come on!" she said softly but urgently. "Where the hell is Paul? Damn it, Roberta must have switched the pool lights off."

"He's closing the grate," said Alex in a calm tone. "So they won't find us in case they look in the pool. Are you okay, Wayne?"

The kid really *cares* about me, Wayne thought in disbelief.

"I'm fine," he said gruffly. Like hell I'm fine. If he didn't get out of the water soon, he'd start to panic again.

"This way, Wayne. Follow my voice. There are steps. How about you scout ahead and see what's in here? Mom and me can wait for Paul." The kid understood. And he cared. It made Wayne want to cry. He paddled awkwardly toward the unseen steps.

The water began to thrum and vibrate.

"Must be the helicopter landing." Paul's voice. "Or helicopters. Sounds like more than one. Everybody stay calm. We'll be fine down here."

Wayne had never felt anything as comforting as those solid steps, slightly slippery, under his feet in the shallow water. A few steps and he was on dry concrete. He stepped forward cautiously, cursed as he struck heavy steel. Probing with his outstretched fingers, he decided he'd run into the big pump. Huge, solid. Wayne pushed against it in the blackness. It stayed put. It stank of dust and he felt spider webs on his hands. Fuck. Maybe the Treadwell bitch had been lying to them.

128: FRIDAY, JULY 4

More cars pulled up in front of Roberta's house. Place looked like the parking lot of a shopping mall the day before Christmas. She glanced at her watch. Unbelievable: not even a minute since Wayne finally vanished into the water. It felt excruciatingly longer, yet not nearly long enough. Had they found their way in? Been able to move the pump? It was decades, probably, since that bootlegger's concealed entrance had been opened. Oh Christ, the automatic lamp would have turned itself on. All she could do was hope that one of them would have the presence of mind to douse it.

She went to the front door.

"I'm sorry, Dr. Treadwell. I have to follow my orders." Joe Waltrip of the Sutton County Sheriff's Department thrust a paper into Roberta's hand and stepped back. She knew Joe, but didn't recognize any of the other men and women spreading out from the vehicles. She scanned the first few lines of the document.

Search Warrant
United States District Court Western District of Texas
SEARCH WARRANT W03-19Y

In the Matter of the Search of residence of Roberta Treadwell, 432 Treadwell Road, Sutton County, TX, its appurtenances, vehicles, underground structures located on entire premises of the 5000 acre tract. See attached photos property description Attachments A, B and C.

She wished Jill were here to read the thing, or that lawyer friend of hers, Carol Glassman. When she looked up to ask what the police planned to search, half a dozen rifles were pointed at her. Roberta moved back away from the door. Didn't look as though she had a great deal of choice.

A tall, heavy man seemed in charge of the operation. "You'd have been better off if you'd kept things on a friendly level and let us look around the first time." He glared at Roberta, began dividing the men and women behind him into groups of three to search specific areas of the house and outbuildings. One of the men had a German Shepherd dog on a leash and carried a child's red slipper. They must have gotten it from Alex's father, she realized. From inside the house, the puppy began barking piteously.

"Are you going to shoot poor little Basil too, same way you murdered Sitka?"

"Ma'am, if you'd please step outside on the porch here, Officer Trejo will stay with you. We'll take good care of your animal. I'm sure I don't need to warn you to remain here quietly, Miz Treadwell. Okay, men, let's get this done." The leader led his own group into the living room.

From the front porch Roberta could hear the scraping sounds of furniture being moved. A crash, a sound of breaking glass. Shaking her head in angry resignation, she looked away from the house, across miles of rocky, mesquite studded land, empty of any sign of human life. Trejo followed her gaze.

"Not much to look at out there," Roberta told him. "They say when the Spanish first explored the region northwest of here, the land was so featureless they had to drive stakes into the ground at intervals so they'd be able to find their way back. In fact the region's known as the Llano Estacado, the Staked Plains."

Trejo was still looking off into the distance. "I never knew that."

Roberta's cell phone chimed. She wished desperately that she could have a moment of privacy, tried walking to the other end of the porch. Of course Trejo followed her.

"Dr. Roberta, it's Maisie. I got your message—"

"We're having a little excitement," Roberta said, using all her willpower to speak slowly and calmly. "The police are here looking for someone. I don't know anything about it or even who the fugitives are. It reminds me of Humberto and Lupe." Roberta felt Trejo watching her. I hope to goodness Maisie gets my drift, she thought. "I've been thinking of my grand-dad, too, and how he was always in trouble...."

129: FRIDAY, JULY 4

Standing in the musty darkness, they heard a clatter of distant footsteps. Suddenly, then, it was as if an invisible police force searched the very corridor they stood in.

"Look at this. It must've cost thousands." A female voice, directly above them. "Can you believe—"

"They say she's worth billions." A male voice with a heavy Texas accent.

Crackling of the radio, and an indistinct male voice saying something about checking in the barn.

We must be directly under the lower level of the house, Jill realized. She hoped the police would not think to search the pool, because it looked like they were stuck here for the duration. They had inspected every inch of the huge pump, heaving at it, prodding in the dark with their fingertips, but the thing refused to budge. She fished out her phone from Alex's backpack, keyed in Roberta's private number.

"Hello?"

"The damn pump's stuck," she whispered.

A pause. In a brisk tone, Roberta said, "I'm busy at the moment, Gerald. I'll arrange for somebody to look into that matter." She disconnected.

Wayne sneezed. Jill jumped, startled, nearly dropped the phone. Damn! Couldn't the idiot at least have tried to muffle it? If she could hear everything happening upstairs, odds were the police upstairs could hear them as well.

Something wet and soft flopped into her left eye. Jill stifled a shriek, slapped at it. Wet gauze fluttered to the floor of the tunnel. Damn. Her bandage had soaked through and peeled away.

130: FRIDAY, JULY 4

Tom Gebhardt had not enjoyed the ride to Roberta Treadwell's ranch, nor bothered to be polite to the garrulous driver. "One of my mother's ancestors was a Spanish explorer," the fool had babbled. "My grandmother used to tell stories of how they found a city of gold. They went to get horses and wagons to carry it to the coast so they could ship it back to Spain. But they could never find the place again. It had been swallowed up by the earth. You know, like from an earthquake or something." Finally, to Tom's relief, the idiot had shut up.

Standing to one side of the huge house, feeling completely useless as the search progressed, Tom wondered what the hell Bruce had expected him to accomplish here. He'd come on this wild goose chase for no better reason than that Bruce Blick had felt like ordering him about. It seemed clear, abruptly, that Bruce was slipping into senility or paranoia, a little more each day. Meanwhile, Tom kept on like a faithful dog. Or maybe, he thought bitterly, a whipped one.

Oh, he was well paid. Tom Gebhardt acknowledged to himself that he'd been a friendless geek in high school, little better at the Georgetown University McDonough School of Business. During his rise through the ranks of Blick's empire, Tom had learned to dress impeccably, to manipulate human nature without qualm or regret. He called hundreds of people friend, was feared and envied by many. But he was intimate with no one. Seldom had the time for women, and his sexual relationships were at best two-dimensional. I'm worse off now than when I was in high school, he thought in chagrin. At least back then I never would've dreamed of hurting a little kid. What was it Bruce had said? *Peel his biochemistry like an onion.* Jesus!

Tom shuddered. I have to get away from all this for a little while. Just for a few minutes. He turned and walked away into the darkness.

The amount of starlight reflected by the pale stones crunching under his feet surprised him. Once his eyes adjusted, away from the lights of the house, Tom could easily see well enough to follow the double tracks marking the road that wound through the pasture behind Roberta Treadwell's house. Still, the world seemed filled with threats. The dark shapes on either side of the road were trees and bushes, nothing more; he was able to believe it as long as he could look over his shoulder and see the glimmer of the ranch house. He stopped; the lights were gone, obscured by trees. Now he was part of the wild landscape, no better than an animal, waiting to be caught and eaten by other animals. It was not impossible, way out here; the dark shapes seemed to move and take on the form of mountain lions or wolves or packs of javelinas. Wild native pigs, they prowled in Texas, didn't they? Oh Christ. They could pull him down and peel his own *flesh* like an onion.

Somewhere to his right, perhaps not more than a few yards away, a stone fell against another: some feral thing stalking him? He began to run blindly. One foot slipped; he found himself on the ground, the palms of his hands burning, sharp pain shooting through his right knee. He managed to stand, saw that he had lost the road he'd been following. He strained his eyes, searching for the predatory animal that even now might be ready to spring on him. A mound of white stone stood somewhat higher than his head. Instinctively, he stumbled toward it, seeking shelter among the boulders. He pressed himself into a shallow depression and held his breath, listening. Only the sound of wind blowing across the rocks, the drone of some sort of insect.

Squatting tensely among the rocks, he considered his future. Yes, he could continue his life as Bruce Blick's protégé and never look back at this night; edit it out of his life and his memory. He uttered a sharp bark of self-mockery. The fabled

Dr. Rutherford...*he* could have done that for him. But such psychologists' games with the mind were child's play compared to this new genetic discovery of Gibson's.

It made Tom's head reel. If what he'd been told about the auxosome treatment were true, if it genuinely held the key to unlimited youth and lifespan, it might be on the high-end market within a few years. At an enormous premium, naturally. Working for Blick, he'd have the income to purchase his own supply. But Blick would be relentless now that he knew what sort of research Roberta's lab was doing. The old bastard would block all research that posed any threat to his established power. Already he was unimaginably wealthy and powerful; he'd cauterize Roberta's continued research if he had to kill them all. As Blick's right-hand man, Tom knew he would be expected to participate in destroying the possibility of eternal youth for all but a few. Perhaps himself included.

It was insane.

Walk away from it now, he told himself. He really could walk away from his poisoned future. Probably, that'd have little effect on Roberta's fate, and certainly it would ruin his own life. Ruin his life? No, he'd be regaining his life. Blick was powerful enough to prevent Tom ever again working in any but the most menial job. The best he might hope for would be a low-paying middle management job, the sort of work he had done years ago as a stepping stone to greater things. He had no money saved; he'd always anticipated plenty of time for that in the future. His new future would be one of low rent apartments, cheap clothes, domestic beer.

Blick might even have him killed. But at least, before he died, he'd be able to see his face in the mirror without feeling revulsion. He'd be able to feel pride. In himself, finally, for making his own decision and acting accordingly.

His cell phone sounded its musical tone. Reflexively he pulled it from his pocket. His injured hand stung; that was reality, here and now. He glanced at the illuminated caller ID, held the phone to his ear, found it impossible to speak.

"Tom?" It was Blick. "Hello? Shit. Tom, are you there?"

Without a word, without disconnecting, he set the cell phone on the ground next to his foot, found a stone small enough to fit in his hand, heavy enough to do the job. He raised his arm and brought the stone down hard, shattering the phone. From his pocket he took a small penknife. Gritting his teeth, he cut deep into the flesh of his left forearm. His arm jerked; he sobbed at the pain. Something small and wet glistened, his GPS tracker chip, and fell among the stones. He smashed that as well, blood trickling down into his hand.

Too late for all that. Too late for anything, really. He had sold himself long ago, and the price was not just his own eventual death, this time, if they tracked him down. Really, that was no more than the price of every man's life, had been since humans first walked the world. *He* would have to live with the knowledge that he had helped kill the possibility of extended life for himself—youth and joy for a thousand years, or who knew how much longer than that—and for the whole of mankind as well. His penalty was far worse than death: from this day, he was doomed to live out another forty or fifty years knowing, in guilt and self-loathing, what had been possible. But at least he would no longer be a part of Blick's apparatus of death.

Shadows closed in around him; he walked away through them.

131: FRIDAY, JULY 4

Leaning against the pump, Wayne detected a faint odor of motor oil. That smell, in the dark, took him back to his dad's workshop.

§

Standing in the doorway, his little brother eager behind him, Wayne raises his voice so Dad can hear him over the noise from the baseball game on the radio.

"Hey Dad, can Rob and me go swimming?"

"Have you finished mowing the yard?"

"Yes, sir."

"Well, I don't know." Wayne knows Dad is trying to think if there's any other chores he can make Wayne do.

"Please Daddy?" says Rob in a babyish little voice

"Well, okay then." Dad has a soft spot for Rob. Pretty much lets him do anything he wants. Usually Wayne hates it that Dad likes Rob better than he likes Wayne, but this time he's glad, because it means they can get away from here for a while, have some fun.

At first it's great fun wading in the river, sinking their feet into the sandy bottom, laughing as minnows nibble their legs. But then Billy-Joe Taylor and Kenny Bingham and a tall guy with blond hair show up.

"Hey, Wayne, stuck with baby-sitting, huh?" Billy-Joe taunts him. "Can't find anybody else to be friends with? Have to hang around with babies?" The other guys laugh.

Wayne acts like he hasn't heard. "C'mon Rob, let's go home," he says, taking his brother's hand.

"Aww, you can't leave now. You haven't even had any fun yet." The tall blond boy shoves Wayne so hard he loses his grip on Rob's hand. "Hey, little guy, you look like you need a good bath." He picks Rob up and tosses him into the river, at a place where it's too deep for the little boy to stand up.

"No! He can't swim!" Wayne makes a mad dash into the water and reaches Rob, who clings to him. "It's okay, Robbie. I won't let them hurt you," he says.

Billy-Joe and Kenny begin throwing rocks at Wayne. A small stone thrown hard catches Wayne on the cheek. He touches the pain and finds his fingers smeared with blood. Water enters his nostrils and his mouth. Then he's on the shore, by himself. Billy-Joe and Kenny are gone. Oh no. No! Rob is gone, too.

§

When the search party found Rob's body almost a quarter of a mile downstream, Dad blamed Wayne for not taking care of his brother. Wayne never knew what really happened. Payback, he thought, and felt again as if he were drowning. Moaning, slipped into fugue.

§

"You dirty fuckin' creeps!" Payback begins screaming his rage the moment he gets control. Billy-Joe wades toward him, shoves him. Payback loses his footing. The current catches them both, pulls him and Rob into deeper water. Payback struggles to get back toward the bank, but he's not a strong swimmer, and the current is too swift. His brother goes under and he comes up coughing and gasping for air. The current tears him away just as Payback gets a mouthful of water himself. I'm drowning! All he can think of now is getting back to the bank. He kicks as hard as he can, paddles with his arms. Without quite knowing how he did it, he finds himself lying face down on the sandy river bank. A moment of pure relief. Then he understands that he is no longer holding Robbie's hand.

§

Wayne pressed his head against his knees, shedding tears held in all those years ago. "You killed your little brother." His father's voice, but also the slow, droning voice of Dr. Rutherford.

I didn't do it, he thought. I didn't kill my brother, maybe I didn't kill the woman in the trailer. But he'd killed Rutherford and Pritchett, for sure, and he was almost certain that the young man Payback had left to die in his dad's workshop, Drew Chang, was real. I've got to get back to Delmar. Whatever it costs me, I've got to get back there.

132: FRIDAY, JULY 4

At last Paul dared to hope they might get away. It had been quiet again upstairs for almost an hour, according to Alex's watch, which had stayed dry inside the backpack. Jill and her son had actually managed to fall asleep, the boy cradled in his mother's arms. Paul felt a tender urge to embrace both of them but held back, not wanting to risk waking them.

He sat slumped against the base of the great pump staring at the empty black, and jerked his head up at the sound of footsteps coming from the far side of the machine. He jumped instinctively to his feet, but there was nowhere to retreat except back to Roberta's lightless swimming pool.

"Goddamned thing's moving," said Wayne softly, near his ear. He felt the man's warm breath. "Maybe if we all push against it we can keep them from getting in."

"Could be someone Roberta's sent."

Or not. Paul threw his weight against the pump. It stopped moving. But it was only a matter of time before the police called in reinforcements. They could bring twenty men if they had to. Hell, they could blast the thing away with explosives if they felt like it.

Softly but distinctly, someone called his name.

"Paul. Hey, Paul. It's Ambrosio. Maisie's son. Roberta sent me to help you. Let me in, man."

"A trap," said Wayne, his voice wild with terror.

"If it's the cops, they'll get us eventually anyway," Paul told him. "Maybe Roberta really has sent help." Still he stood with his shoulder against the body of the pump. Wayne shrugged, stepped back. Paul moved aside as well, and the huge machine slowly swung inward toward them. Pale light entered. Jill, waking, stared dubiously, as though unsure if she were dreaming.

A tall thin youth stood in the opening. "My mother says we have to hurry," he said. "The cops are thick as mosquitoes after a rain and they'll be putting up road blocks. I need to get pictures of everybody." He took a small camera from his shirt pocket. "My mother's going to get passports so you'll have a chance to get away, cross the border into Mexico. Her friend says you don't want to try to swim the river, because they'll probably be flying the whole area looking for you."

"I have this damned scar on my forehead," Jill said. She touched the accident wound. With the bandage gone, the sutured cut was pale yellow with some sort of antiseptic swab. We'll have to cover that, Paul thought, or scrub it off. "They'll know—"

"Digital camera. We can clean you up." Light blossomed, made them all flinch. "Hold still, lady."

It was surreal, Paul thought, this kid taking flash pictures in a cave. Like holiday snap shots. Should he trust this kid? Really there was no alternative.

"What about Alex?" said Jill. Hearing his name, the boy stirred. "You can't put a picture of a half-bald kid on the passport. That's exactly what they'll be looking for."

"The boy? My mother said not to worry. We'll use a picture of a kid with blond hair."

Jill nodded, shrugged.

"I'm bringing a car for you to take. Roberta said you shouldn't use one of hers, because they might be looking for anything registered to her. So she bought a car from a friend of mine, and see, my friend and me go to pick it up after I take your pictures to my mother, and we leave it at this place where there's a road nobody knows about."

"How are we supposed to find this road?" said Paul.

"You go back with me the way I came in. My friend dropped me off and drove around for a while so there wouldn't be no car parked there, just in case. There's still helicopters flying around out there." He ducked away through a low opening, stood waiting on the other side. The cone of illumination from his flashlight seemed pitifully insignificant in the darkness of the cave, but even so wonderfully welcome after the dark.

"You can wait up at the top for my friend and me to come

back. My mother says it'll take about an hour to get the passports ready." Ambrosio was already moving off down through the dark cave. "Hurry," he said over his shoulder.

Trying to keep up, stumbling on the uneven floor, they followed him into the light-flickering blackness.

133: FRIDAY, JULY 4

It was cool in the open night. Road was too grand a name for the rocky tracks meandering past the hillside where the cave made its unspectacular exit. Jill, Paul and Alex curled up on the blankets Maisie had sent for them and fell asleep. But Wayne doubted he would ever sleep again.

Something flashed in the corner of his eye. Two small glowing objects hovering just above Alex's head. They hummed, barely audible. Wayne wanted to ask the boy what the things were, but he knew he must be dreaming again, or trapped inside one of Dr. Rutherford's nightmares. He opened his mouth to cry aloud, but could not get his voice to work.

Listen to me, young man.

No! Wayne screamed in his mind, but his voice remained silent. He sank again, terror rising around him like drowning water.

The subject is a twenty-five-year-old male....

134: FRIDAY, JULY 4

Long before he saw their headlights Alex heard the cars coming. He had to tell the adults; their ears didn't seem nearly as sharp as his, nor their eyes. In fact, they seemed to be duller than him all the way around. Paul had said something about the auxosomes working faster on younger people.

"Hey Mom! Hey, everybody, someone's coming," he whispered.

"Stay back until they get here," Jill said.

"Yeah," Alex agreed. "Could be the cops." He thought of sending out one of his little toys, but he didn't know their range for sure and was reluctant to risk losing one of them. He could feel Mom's tension, hear her rapid breathing as the headlights brightened.

The car pulled up to the mouth of the cave, light splashing back on it, a bright red Mustang. Ambrosio opened the driver's door.

"You want to keep going straight ahead," he told them, without a greeting. "About a mile down this lane you'll come to the county road. If you turn right, it'll take you to FM 415. Go right again when you get to the highway. It'll take you to Sonora and from there you can get to Del Rio and go across into Mexico. My mother says you'll be safer over there."

"Thank you so much, Ambrosio," Mom said, but he was already walking away toward the pickup.

"I'll take the first shift driving," Paul offered. For once, Mom seemed glad to be just a passenger.

"C'mon, Wayne. You and me can sit in back and keep a lookout behind," said Alex, climbing in.

"Which way you going?" Wayne called to Ambrosio.

"Back the way we came. To Villa Mirasol."

"Mind if I catch a ride with you in the pickup?"

"But—" Alex couldn't believe Wayne would just take off like this. "We're partners, remember?"

"You're right, young fella. Pardners forever. But there's a few things I have to do. I'll catch up with you later."

"No, Wayne! Come with us!"

Wayne got a weird expression on his face, thrust a folded piece of paper into Alex's hand. "These are some bad people, Alex. Maybe someday you and me can do something about them." He turned abruptly and climbed into the back of the pickup truck.

"Hey man," Ambrosio called to Paul as the truck backed up to turn around. "Take good care of my Mustang, okay? Dr. Roberta is giving him to me after you don't need him anymore."

135: FRIDAY, JULY 4

They had been driving on the county road for about ten minutes when Alex yelled out sharply from the back seat, "Enemy chopper on our tail."

Jill sagged. For the first time since Judge Patterson's office she'd begun to feel hope, but now realized how foolish that had been. Two adults and a child in a ten year old car, escaping the police in a helicopter with their sophisticated equipment? Not to mention Bruce Blick or whoever the heck else was after them.

They made it almost to the highway, were just passing the sign that read *U.S. 277 1 mile*. Alex yelled, "Here they come. Hey Paul, stop the car please? I have a plan." The boy was pulling something out of his backpack.

"Might as well stop," said Paul. "No point trying to outrun them."

"Don't turn off the engine," said Alex.

They sat silently in the growing roar of the chopper overhead. Bent over a GameBoy console he held in his lap, Alex seemed oblivious to the howling in the air.

"No crew," he said, looking up.

"What? Alex, honey, I don't—"

"It's a UAV. An unmanned aerial vehicle. Remote controlled." The helicopter pulled in front of them, hovered a few feet above the ground, dirt flung up from the country road. The machine was smaller than a standard chopper, yet in the night, this close, it looked gigantic, a baleful insect.

"Darn," said Alex. "I hope they don't block the road when they go down. Be ready to hit the gas."

Jill saw Paul frown at her son, turn a questioning glance to her. She shrugged, shook her head. The noise was awful; it got worse as Alex rolled down his window, leaning far out. "Be careful!" she screamed, but couldn't be heard above the rotors. He threw something into the air, then again. To her disbelief, Jill saw two small glowing machines lift away on a trajectory toward the chopper. Alex wasn't watching any longer. With rapt, child-intense attention, he manipulated the keys on the GameBoy console in his hands.

"Main rotor pitch links," he was muttering, "that should do it."

She heard a high metallic shriek, like iron tearing. The roar from the UAV changed pitch.

"And if I can just get the other one into the tail rotor, come on, come on—"

Hanging in front of them like doom, the machine veered sharply to their left, lurched. The main rotor struck the ground. The UAV spun, flipped over. Thunder shook the air; a fireball exploded toward them.

"Go, Paul, go!" screamed Alex.

Paul hit the accelerator and they screeched away. Jill looked back at her son, his face illuminated by the flames of what had been a multi-million dollar technological marvel.

"It's okay, Mom." Alex seemed to be reading her mind. "No crew in the helicopter. It was a UAV, like I told you, like in Afghanistan."

"You made it crash, right?"

"Yep." He grinned, still so much her little boy: *Watch me, Mom!*

"What the *hell* were those things, Alex? Don't tell me they were some battery-powered toy from K-Mart. You built them, didn't you?"

"Yes. It borrows its juice from...well, it's hard putting it into words, and I don't have the right math yet. The space between things. I think the auxosomes do that too."

The adult glanced back at him with an expression of thunderstruck respect. Alex preened a little. It felt good to be taken seriously, especially by someone you admire. Someone you love, actually, like a father.

"Zero point energy," Paul said very quietly.

"Maybe, I don't know what it's called."

Nobody said anything for a moment. "We'll have to ditch the

car before too much longer," Paul said tensely, then. "They were close enough for their cameras to read our plates."

"We can't just leave the car on the highway. They'll know exactly which way we've gone."

"I know, we'll pull off the road someplace we can hide it." Paul sighed, and turned quickly with a grin. "Alex, thank you."

"My pleasure," the eight-year-old said, gravely polite.

136: SATURDAY, JULY 5

They had been walking for so long Jill's entire body was numb. She felt certain that if she glanced down she'd find her feet worn away to bloody stumps. Paul hadn't said anything for some time now. From his soft, groaning grunts she could tell he was running on sheer will power. He'd been carrying Alex on his back ever since the boy had hurt his ankle when he stumbled into a hole outside the old barn where they'd left the car.

She swung her bandana'd head at the sound growing louder at her back. Lights brightened, shone in her eyes. Paul said, in a voice stupid with exhaustion, "It's a truck."

No place to hide on this barren stretch of road. Jill steeled herself as the pickup truck pulled even with them, stopped.

"You folks need a ride?" Thick Spanish accent, speaking softly. The driver was a clean-cut man with dark skin. Jill noticed the pockmarks on his cheeks, as bad as her own. Beside him were two children and a woman, all asleep. "Climb in the back if you want. I'm going almost all the way to Del Rio."

Paul and Jill looked at each other. "Let's do it," she said.

"I was hoping you'd say that." Paul set Alex down in the truck's bed, helped Jill up, then climbed in himself. It was already filled nearly to the top with burlap bags weighted down by large stones.

"Nice and soft," said Paul. "I can think of worse ways to travel."

Jill loved him for remaining calm and upbeat even now. I can think of worse companions to travel with, she thought.

§

The sun was shining in her eyes. The truck driver was leaning over her, a worried expression on his scarred face.

"I heard on the CB radio, there's a checkpoint up ahead. Your business is none of my business, but I thought.... Well, maybe you don't want to be in the truck when they search it."

"Thank you," said Jill gratefully. She should have been stiff and sore after sleeping on a lumpy bed of burlap bags, but to her surprise she felt fine. Paul, too, seemed to be suffering no ill consequences from the recent hike.

"Want to climb on, sport?" he said to Alex.

"Nope. I'm fine now." The boy proved his words by hopping down from the truck.

Jill and Paul looked at each other. "Auxosomes," she said, and simultaneously Paul said with a grin, "The Modern Miracle!"

"We're four or five miles from Del Rio," said the driver, glancing in puzzlement between them. "I know it's a long way to walk, but.... You want to get off the highway out of sight whenever you hear a car coming. I heard on the radio the police are looking for a woman and man with a boy."

"Thank you." Jill took his hand, wishing there were something she could do to repay his kindness.

"It's nothing," he said, looking toward the cab of his truck. "I know how it is. I have a wife and kids."

§

They reached Del Rio around noon, went straight into the Fargo Grill and ordered the Saturday lunch, chicken fried steak and French fries. Jill and Paul cleaned up together in the bathroom. He scrubbed her forehead clean with wadded toilet paper and cheap soap.

"The wound's closed right up," he muttered, astonished. "In

fact, it's almost healed. Do you have any nail scissors in your purse?"

"Of course." Gritting her teeth, she kept her eyes averted as always from the mirror as he snipped and pulled out the stitches. "Okay, buster, you can go now." To her relief, no one seemed to have taken any special notice of them. In the stall, she opened the envelope Ambrosio had given Paul and for the first time examined the contents. Three passports rubber banded together and a smaller envelope.

While Paul and Alex took their turns in the bathroom, she examined the passports under the edge of the table.

Benjamin K. Peters and Joyce Eileen Peters were traveling with Richard John Peters, whose baby picture bore a remarkable resemblance to Jill's memory of Alex at the age of nine or ten months. She noted with surprise that they had airbrushed her photo, smoothing away the acne scars as well as the wound on her forehead. In the envelope she found $10,000 in hundred dollar bills.

"Bless Roberta Treadwell," said Paul, when she passed him the envelope and his passport.

"We can buy a car."

"No, Mom. We *shouldn't* buy a car." Alex spoke slowly, as if explaining things to a not-very-bright five year old. "They'll be looking for us to be in a car. Our best chance of getting away is to go on foot. Besides, we need to save our money. We don't know how long we'll have to live on it."

"He's right." Paul nodded thoughtfully. "We'll be better off traveling light."

"They're looking for a man and woman traveling with a boy," added Alex unsentimentally. "We might have a better chance if we split up."

"Good idea," said Jill. "You and I can go together, Alex, and—"

"No, Mom. I think each of us should cross the river separately."

She blinked, throttled back her automatic refusal. "Don't you think that would look weird, Alex, an eight year old boy all by himself?"

He shot her a look. "See, I'll find somebody to go across with."

It could work. "What if we can't find each other? You've never been in Mexico."

"Me neither," Paul said.

"We'll choose some place to meet. Look." Alex picked up a card wedged between the sugar bowl and the salt and pepper shakers: *What to see in Piedras Negras.* "See this?" He pointed at a bright pink bandstand in the middle of a park. "It says this is in the center of town. We can meet right there."

Jill shrugged her agreement, looked down at the table so Alex wouldn't see her tears. I'll never make it across, she thought. Not with the border patrol checking IDs of people going into Mexico. They'd be looking especially carefully for a woman my age with a face ruined by acne scars. She tried to comfort herself with the thought that Paul would take good care of Alex, but the pain of it swelled in her breast and flooded her eyes despite her best intentions.

137: SATURDAY, JULY 5

It was not difficult to fall in with the group of boys who raucously told him they represented the youth choir of the First Baptist Church of Karnes City.

"Kansas City? Wow, that's a long way to come."

"No, man, *Karnes*," a kid his own age said boastfully. "Here in Texas. Home of the fighting Badgers!"

"Wow! Cool!"

As they approached the border, Alex doubted there had really been any need for such an elaborate charade. A line of cars stretched two blocks, and he could see the customs officials checking each one. Pedestrians, though, seemed to flow freely into Mexico. Would it be this easy for Mom and Paul? Hope so, he thought. He worried about them, on their own without him to keep them out of trouble.

138: SATURDAY, JULY 5

Fern sang along with the Dixie Chicks as she ironed open the seams of the new skirt she was making to wear to the weekend dance at the Boot Scootin' Dance Hall in Houston. She ran to answer the phone. It'd be Ray, calling to let her know when he'd be by to pick her up. Or maybe Linda, eager for the latest update on Fern's romance with the boss.

The scratchy voice said, "Hello, Fern, honey."

Her heart lurched with dread.

"What do you want, Wayne? Where are you?" she said sharply. That poor brutalized man, that Dr. Chang. Wayne had done that. And maybe Dr. Nathan as well. It made her sick to her stomach.

"On my way home. I'm not sure what I'll do next. Just wanted to see you one more time, Fern and to...take care of some business."

With a spurt of anxiety, Fern glanced around the bright, cheerful room. She had gotten rid of the awful green sofa, painted the walls a soft yellow, hung curtains with a peach and white floral print at the window. She'd brought out her sewing machine which had sat uselessly in the bedroom for the years of her marriage, wedged between the bed and the wall. He'll kill me if he comes home and sees this, she thought.

"Uh, I don't think that would be a good idea, Wayne. The police have been here looking for you."

"I won't stay long." He didn't seem surprised about the police. "Just want to be with you for a little while. Wanted to make sure you'd be there when I got home."

"Where are you?"

"I don't know. Kerrville. I'll be home late this afternoon."

Fern couldn't think straight. First she'd betrayed Wayne by

letting Linda talk her into searching the workshop and calling the police, and thank God she had, but then she'd compounded the betrayal by going out with Ray. It was frightening to consider what Wayne might do when he found out, but there was no way she could order him to stay away. The land and mobile home were his. Well, half was hers, she thought, under Texas divorce law. She could just up and leave, but damn it, this was her home too. She recalled what the policeman had told her. It would be in Wayne's best interest to stop him before he got into even more trouble.

She walked into the kitchen, found Deputy Murphy's card stuck to the fridge with a magnetized miniature toaster.

139: SATURDAY, JULY 5

Roberta keyed in Maureen Baumgarten's cell phone as she exited Loop 410.

"Yes?" Maureen spoke so softly Roberta could hardly hear her.

"Maureen, it's Roberta. I'll be at the hospital in about ten minutes. Less if there's no hassle with parking."

"I'll meet you at the nurse's station. Do you need directions?"

"No. I called the hospital before I left."

§

The third floor, where they had moved Drew two days earlier, bustled with visitors, several of them crowded around the nurse's station. Roberta had a hard time picking Maureen out of the crowd. She remembered an attractive woman in her early thirties, but today the poor creature looked ten years older. Little wonder, considering what she was going through.

"Roberta?" Maureen asked uncertainly.

I probably look a little worse for wear myself. "Maureen! I'm so sorry I couldn't come sooner. Had one crisis after another, and then it seemed I might be coming down with the flu and I didn't want to risk infecting Drew." The crease between Maureen's eyes deepened. "Don't worry. I'm feeling better now. Just stress." She laughed. "Playing with Paul's mice has helped relax me."

Maureen relaxed a little, too. "Thank you so much for coming. Drew would surely appreciate it. The flowers you sent are beautiful." She swayed slightly; Roberta put a hand on her arm to steady her.

"How is Mrs. Chang today?"

"She's—" Maureen scrunched up her face. "Roberta, I think she's totally losing it. She imagines he's trying to communicate with her. She insists he smiled at her."

"Oh, dear. I don't know if I'll be able to do any good, Maureen. But I'm willing to try."

"Go in without me, that'd be best. I told Alyssa I'd visit the cafeteria and get lunch. Room 314." She pointed. "Right side of the hall."

Roberta dodged a small girl being chased down the hall by a larger boy. One of the rooms she passed was a riot of flowers and balloons. Drew's was bare, save for the large floral arrangement from MJT Labs and a couple of smaller ones from co-workers. He had never been a sociable person, had few friends outside of work. A small Chinese woman with red hair sat beside the bed, eyes closed, dozing.

Roberta forced herself to look down at the bed. On the phone Maureen had said Drew looked like an ice carving; today, at least, his face showed a little color, almost as though he were merely asleep. She felt an odd impulse to call his name, try to awaken him. She glanced at Mrs. Chang. Could she advise this woman to let her only son die?

What did she know of the agonies of bereaved motherhood? She'd never married, had no children of her own. Yes, her lab staff was like an extended family, and in some ways Drew had been like a son. To her he confided things he surely told no one else. His mother, he had once smilingly said, was an enigma.

She adopted a Western name and colored her hair, but she wept and threatened to disown him when he brought home his Jewish girlfriend Maureen. "My mother is a tiny, frail little thing. But you don't mess with her. A will of iron!" There was nothing she could possibly say to change this woman's mind. *He's my son too!* No, that would hardly be appropriate.

Until this moment, she realized, she'd been numb all the way through, numbness slashed open by bursts of rage at this Wayne Elliot lunatic. Standing over her surrogate son, bright green instrument displays pulsing at the edge of vision that represented whatever last life force was left in him, helpless sorrow overcame her like a seizure. Roberta Treadwell stood over a hospital bed sobbing uncontrollably. Her tears fell unnoticed on Drew's pale cheeks, ran toward the corners of his motionless mouth.

A hand touched hers; she shuddered, opened her wet eyes. The little red-haired woman gazed at her in sympathy.

"You are Dr. Treadwell, are you not?"

Roberta nodded, turned her face aside, tried to control her weeping. To her dismay, she began to hiccough.

"Here, sit down, drink some water. Drew has spoken often of you. He will be glad you came to see him."

"I—think very highly of your son. He was—is—one of the brightest scientists we have."

"It helps to have a good cry." Alyssa Chang nodded wisely. "It helps. But don't you cry anymore, Dr. Treadwell. Drew will wake up and be fine. You'll see. He's going to get well. A mother knows these things." Mrs. Chang took a hand towel from the bedside table and patted away the last of Roberta's tears from her son's immobile face.

140: SATURDAY, JULY 5

Since he was a child, Wayne had found comfort in the woods, alone. He remembered leaning against a tree trunk, watching a pair of warblers carrying food to their young; he had felt more closely related to the birds than to his mother and father, more at ease with a distant pack of wild pigs than with the friends who were constantly judging him so that he could never for a moment relax. But if he had always loved the woods, never until now had he so keenly appreciated the beauty of the shapes and colors of the leaves, the endless bifurcation of branches growing up, roots growing down.

A little to his surprise, he was overwhelmed by feelings for Fern, which seemed to grow from his joy in being back home again. It was a side-effect of the auxosome treatment, he knew that, but it did not diminish his feelings or their truth and urgency. He quickened his pace, eager to hold her in his arms, beg her to forgive him for not being a better husband. That moment of seeing Fern again was as far as he dared look into his future; from her he would get the courage to take care of whatever he found in the workshop. He would begin the remainder of his life from the safety of Fern's embrace.

Here was the fence he had built with his own hands; he was almost home. He heard a bark. Gretchen.

141: SATURDAY, JULY 5

Alex was nowhere to be seen. Ahead of her in line, Paul moved with an easy saunter. Not brashly confident, nor at all nervous. Two uniformed men stood checking IDs at the entrance to the pedestrian lane of the bridge spanning the Rio Grande River. On this side, Del Rio, Texas, and the ferocious people in pursuit of them. On the other, Piedras Negras, Coahuila, and the unknown. She saw Paul flash his fake passport, engage in cheerful conversation with the guards. They waved him on. Thank God.

The line moved forward. Jill tried to step back from herself, take inventory. Heart racing, breathing rapid and shallow; she found that she was actually wringing her hands. I'm an intelligent woman, she told herself sternly. With the auxosomes at work inside my little gray brain cells, I'm probably smarter than I've ever been. Calm down. Deep breath. In.... Out.... You are a tourist visiting your neighbor nation for the first time, filled with interested enthusiasm for the adventure. Maybe you'll pick up some items cheap, something pretty or even gaudy to remember the holiday with and show the family back home.

There. That's better. She recalled a psych prof once telling her class that *how* you say something is more important than *what* you say. Okay. Generalize that: how you *behave* has more impact than how you *look*. For years, she knew, she had cringed away from the world, had hidden her brutalized face. Not anymore. Alex loved her, Paul loved her. She was a lovable person, thinking happy, carefree thoughts. Swimming. A leisurely backstroke. Walking in the woods with Dad.

"Your ID, please." The guard glanced at her face, took the passport she offered him. "Name?"

"Joyce Peters." She smiled effortlessly.

"What takes you to Mexico today?"

"I'm looking for one of those carved marble chess sets. A friend of mine got one down here for a very good price, and—"

"Okay, you can go on." He waved her through.

§

Paul waited in an open-air tourist cantina on the Mexican side of the bridge, not looking around for her, swinging one foot. Jill wanted desperately to give him a good, long hug, but she was not completely sure they were safe, even now. She passed him by, and a moment later he ambled up alongside. Sweat began to run into her armpits; she trembled with aftershock nerves.

"Oh my God, Paul, oh my God."

"You're here, we're through, take it easy, dear heart. You were brilliant."

Ready to faint, she held his arm. "I was sure I wouldn't make it across, Paul. My acne scars! But I *behaved* as if there were nothing to see, and it worked!'"

"Scars! Perhaps the auxosome has bestowed marvelous acting talent upon you!"

She glanced at him doubtfully. "Do you think?"

He laughed out loud. "Actually, no, sweetheart, I'm sorry, the stage will not be your new career. Have you looked in a mirror lately?"

Nettled, Jill released his arm.

"I didn't mean— Here." He cast about, picked up a heavily ornamented mirror from a sidewalk display of goods for sale, mostly tourist items. "Take a peek at your face."

What? She took a quick, averted glance.

"No, damn it, you always do that." Paul sounded cross. Perhaps it was the tension of the border crossing. But he was brandishing the accursed mirror in her face. "Go on, have a bloody good *stare.*"

Jill forced herself to have a long, hard look, pulling her bandana and hair back.

Good God in Heaven.

If you knew where to look, and looked very closely, ignoring the healing impact injury in her forehead, the acne scarring was still there. Just. The faintest shadow.

She was dumbfounded.

And her features were...leaner, somehow. More chiseled, the way things had been when she and Keith were first married.

Then Jill caught herself doing the silliest thing she'd ever done in her life—she turned the mirror around and looked at the back of it, as if some disbelieving part of her suspected a cruel conjuring trick. Paul doubled over, screeched with laughter, then caught her up and kissed her mouth. When she happily disentangled herself, she said, "I guess I should've known it would happen once your dick started to—"

Paul shook his head, grinning, and paid for the mirror. "Ugly bloody brute of a thing, this, but it'll be a memento. Jill, to tell the truth, I hadn't consciously noticed either." He paused as she tucked the mirror in her bag, placed his hands on her shoulders, subjected her to a comically critical appraisal, frowning, shifting his head from side to side. He nodded judiciously. "You know, Jill, you're bloody *gorgeous!* Better dump your Botox and Revlon shares, sweetheart—this is going to put a *real* crimp in cosmetics stock!"

142: SATURDAY, JULY 5

When the federal agent arrived at Fern's home, dressed in jeans and a blue and red sports shirt, he and three local sheriff's deputies had tried to ease the tension by making small talk. They mentioned the heat, the possibility of rain, asked Fern about her peach trees, talked about the latest episode of *Hog Heaven* on TV. By the time they'd waited and watched for three and a half hours, they'd long since left Fern out of their conversation.

For almost another hour she sat at the kitchen table, expecting Wayne to come walking in at any moment. She got up, pulled her memory album from the shelf next to the entertainment center. In several wedding photos, she and Wayne looked fondly at each other. On the following page was the birthday card he had given her five months after they got married. "The day I met you was the luckiest day of my life, darling," he'd written.

Had she done the right thing, calling the police again? Maybe it would have been better to warn Wayne to stay away. He sounded so different on the phone, so...sweet and loving...she could almost believe he'd gone back to being the same man she married.

She went to the bathroom, sat on the toilet seat and put her face in her hands, blank with confusion. When she came back out, alerted by some rustle or whispering, two of the deputies and the federal stood at the windows, peering out over the back pasture. One had unholstered his pistol, clicked the safety off. Outside, someone yelled, "Stay where you are and put your hands over your head."

"Fern!" Wayne's voice, roaring from farther away. "What

have you done to Fern?"

She got up to look out, but one of the deputies yelled at her, "Stay back!"

Through the half opened door, she caught a glimpse of Wayne walking steadily toward her, his dog Gretchen at his heel. Maybe it was because she had been looking at the old pictures but he looked younger than she remembered, more alert.

"Police! Stop or I'll shoot."

After a moment, a deafening blast.

"Wayne! No!" Before anyone could stop her, Fern flung the front door wide and raced down the steps.

He lay on his back, a red stain spreading on the front of his shirt. When she knelt beside him, shrieking in fright, he looked up at her. And it wasn't him after all. Did Wayne have a younger brother? Robbie. No, he'd drowned years ago, when Wayne was a boy. Oh my god, he's dying, she thought. Maybe the wound isn't so bad after all. Her thoughts were making no sense to her. Maybe Wayne would be okay, wherever he was.

"Fern, darling." It was still his voice. "It's so good to see you." He reached up and touched her face. "They haven't hurt you?" His head lifted head slightly, fell back with a groan.

"Wayne, oh honey, I'm sorry." She took his hand and raised it to her lips. "I'm so —" She stared at the fingers with their clean new skin and dropped the hand as though it were a poisonous snake, jumped to her feet, backed away, screaming, "Who are you?"

"Fern, don't look at me that way." The wounded man coughed, and red froth came from the side of his mouth. "Fern. You have to do something for me. I think...." A shudder ran through his body. "A man...in the workshop...."

The FBI agent touched her shoulder. "Mrs. Elliot, go back to the house, right now." Others cops stood back in the pasture, guns still warily drawn.

Fern turned to face the agent, stood where she was, shaking with fright. "This is not Wayne Elliot. My Wayne lost the last two fingers of his right hand when he was a boy."

"It *is* me, Fern...." His breath was fading, words coming in broken gasps. "New fingers...they, they rewired...." The face was Wayne's, but the gaze seemed different somehow, more—focused. "Workshop...old farmhouse."

Ignoring the FBI agent, Fern knelt again by her husband's side.

"They came and got him, Wayne. Took him to the hospital." She couldn't stop the words; she had to know. "Did you do that to him?"

Wayne's face relaxed. "Made a lot of mistakes, darling. Wasn't quite myself...." He coughed. Drops of his blood fell on Fern's arm. "You'll be glad to learn I'm a new man." He said it with a ghastly, white faced grin. "Gonna try to make things right, but firs—" Through his coughs, she heard a ominous rattle in his chest. "First I want to tell you how much I love you, you and my sweet lost Melody, and—"

The agent took Fern's arm. "You need to come away now, Ms. Elliot."

"Wayne! No, don't leave!" Furiously, in great distress, she jerked her arm free and put a hand on Wayne's chest. It was still; she could feel no sign of breath or heartbeat, but he continued to look at her.

Intelligence and life faded from the brown eyes.

143: SUNDAY, JULY 6

Mrs. Delia Clarke Munson especially requested Bruce Blick's presence as a guest of honor at the $400 per plate Nature Forever dinner party, to take place in her own antebellum Greek Revival mansion in Charlotte, North Carolina. Bruce regretfully declined but sent James Branigan in his stead, with instructions to pay particular attention to Randy Hartnet, CEO of Terralink Computers, a company that had previously used the Green theme in their advertising strategy.

During pre-dinner cocktails James Branigan dutifully

sought out Hartnet. They had met once before, when Randy himself visited BlickPharm's executive offices to coordinate the delivery and installation of eight hundred Terralink PCs. James had re-read Hartnet's profile before coming to the party:

42 years old
wife, Nicole, 34
2 children, Tracey, 12, Randall, Jr, 10 years old
enjoyed college football
invented the slogan "Save a tree, use the net"

The file included a photograph of a youthful man, well-tanned, apparently thirty-something, with longish, sun bleached hair, relaxing on the deck of his Maui beach house, a cascade of green leaves in the background. James waited until Hartnet walked across the room alone, and crossed his path as if by chance. "Hi! How's the computer business?"

"Great! Wonderful!" It was clear Randy had no idea who James was. Probably expecting Tom Gebhardt.

"Glad to hear it," James said enthusiastically. " BlickPharm couldn't be happier with the job your people have done."

Light dawned. "What I love to hear from customers. Is Bruce here tonight?"

"He couldn't make it, regretfully. We're quite impressed," James said crisply, as Randy's gaze wandered across the room, "with your latest advertising campaign."

"Green's a popular color this year."

"Right, we've bet big that the environment will continue as a hot topic. We're about to launch a major ad campaign against genomic research."

Randy looked at him. "Can't agree, man. We're selling a lot of crunch to the genomics people."

"Well, of course," James told him blithely, "*every* kind of business will suffer if two thirds of the population gets wiped out by a super-bug plague."

The other man recoiled slightly. "That's just conspiracy

bullshit for stone truckers listening to crazies at 3 A.M."

"Bruce doesn't think so." James shrugged. "By the way, we've been thinking of upgrading the PCs we haven't already replaced with Terralinks."

"Randy!" A breathless young woman with a Barbie-doll figure appeared from somewhere behind James and grabbed Randy's hand. "I didn't know where you'd gone. You have to come and pose. The *Time* Magazine photographers are here."

"Duty calls." Randy did his patented Maui-tan grin. "Hey, pal, call you Monday."

James Branigan relaxed; half the evening's business accomplished. He was moving around the room, engaging here and there in meaningless conversation, when Patricia Newfoundland Blick made her entrance, unescorted. She noticed him at once but made a point of greeting her hostess and talking to several other guests before she casually approached him.

"James!" Pretended surprise. "How nice to see you again." An extremely attractive woman, even at the age of sixty-three, she wore a tightly fitting black dress cut low to reveal firm breasts. Her shoulder length blonde hair shone, her smooth face glowed with good health. Rumor said that as well as the fashionable rounds of cosmetic surgery, she had undergone treatments with genetically engineered growth hormones.

"Mrs. Blick." He took the hand she offered. "Where's the Senator?" Patricia Blick and Senator Burcham Huber had been seen together in public so often, for so many months, that it was no longer worthy of gossip.

"He wasn't able to come tonight. Too much work. How is Bruce?" Patricia drifted toward an empty corner of the room, and James followed her.

"As well as could be expected."

"Does he ever mention me?" When she smiled, her lips trembled slightly.

James shook his head regretfully. "With me, he never speaks about his personal life. Only business. Perhaps it was different with Tom."

"I was talking with...someone last week who mentioned that Bruce is enthusiastic about our campaign against genetic research." Patricia had been instrumental in the creation of Nature Forever, and it was no secret that her views on environmental issues had lately influenced Senator Huber, who had surprisingly adopted a new position in the debate.

"Of course," James told her. "Bruce is very concerned about the danger such research poses to all of us."

"Yes, it's terribly serious. As I was telling Burch yesterday, if it isn't stopped now, we'll be looking at pandemics that make AIDS look like a picnic. Not to mention the possible allergy problems associated with genetically engineered food." She shook her head in pained disbelief, and her lustrous hair swung. "And if those Frankenscientists actually manage to extend the human lifespan the way they claim—imagine the drain on resources!"

For a sardonic moment James considered asking how much guilt she suffered over the resources she had drained during the course of her life, but kept his face politely attentive.

"Indeed," he said. "It's completely immoral that some people want to live past 80 or 85 when so many people in the world starve to death before they're half that age."

"We ran a petition in support of the law that will strictly control that sort of thing." Mrs. Blick paused, waiting for approval.

"Yes, Bruce is very pleased about that," James assured her.

"So he's been keeping track of what we're doing?" For a moment her smile looked sincere. No doubt it was. Clearly the Senator kept his contacts with Blick close to his manly chest.

"Oh, absolutely. He thinks what Nature Forever is doing is very important. Weren't you aware that he donated $150,000 last month?"

"I didn't know! It's so like Bruce to do it anonymously. He's always been modest."

"I'm sure he pays close attention to what you're doing. Keep up the good work, Mrs. Blick."

"We will, we certainly will." Her perfume's slightly metallic scent made James want to back away as she leaned close. "I've tried to phone him, James, but he never returns my calls. I don't know—maybe he hasn't gotten the messages I've left. Could you tell him you saw me and that I'd like to talk to him?"

"Surely, Mrs. Blick. Please don't take it personally if he doesn't get in touch with you. He's just not seeing anyone. I take care of almost all North American business for him, but even I mostly communicate with him by email."

Sadly, she nodded, shrugging her beautifully preserved shoulders. "I can't help but wonder. If I'd been there for him, maybe—"

"Mrs. Blick, Bruce used to tell me not to waste time regretting this, or wishing I'd done that. We have to take the world as it is."

144: MONDAY, JULY 7

The computer store had a sign in the window that read "Internet 24/7." Paul's back and neck ached a bit from his uncomfortable sleep on the train. Still, all things considered, he was feeling fine. More benefits of the auxosomes. Guilt pinched at him. Wayne was presumably on the run somewhere, and he still hadn't had his final regulator shot. Paul could think of no way to get it to the man in time. Roberta might provide the transfection proteins, but neither of them had any idea where Wayne might be, by the man's own design. He shook his head, went inside the store with the others.

In newly purchased skirt and blouse, her hair held back loosely from her face with barrettes, Jill looked lovely. Enviably energetic, Alex had run in ahead of them, eager to find out what sort of computer games people played in Mexico. As Jill and Paul gazed about them, he was already conversing in broken Spanish with one of the clerks.

"You'll have to help me with this, buddy," Paul called to him.

"'Course." Obliging as usual, Alex got him set up on an internet computer and went back to his games. Genius or not, *super*genius maybe, the kid was still an eight year old. Jill sat on an empty table top, reading through a book of Spanish phrases.

"Jill, look at this," Paul said after a moment, glancing up from his Gmail. "From Rachel. You know, my office mate."

> hey Paul, hope everything's okay with you. you'll never guess who called looking for you. Drew Chang. he has some adventures to tell you about, but he's out of the hospital now and doing fine. have something strange to report about the mice. you'll recall I brought 3 of yrs home w/ me. my kidz have a couple pet mice, were in the same room with yrs but not in the same pen. few days ago kidz mouses got a little sick. seem to be over the illness today but acting a tad like yours. seem more alert than before. is it possible yr intelligence transposon is transmissible across species barrier? are we all gonna catch smartness or somethun?

Jill read the email over his shoulder. "Oh my god, Paul. Last time I talked to her on the phone, Roberta thought she was coming down with a cold. But in fact—"

"Yep." He thought fervently: Thank God I got the regulator codes inserted into the auxosome. *Immortality's catching!* "Gotta get in touch with her. Before she gets any younger." Paul looked over at Alex, who had already made friends with another boy. The two sat close together, absorbed in a computer game. "So much for our concern that Alex'll be lonely."

"Without anyone else smart enough to talk to?"

"Yeah. At least one problem we won't have to worry about anymore."

Jill looked unhappy.

"Paul, I'm late. I haven't had a period since the shots." Breath caught in her throat. "How I'd have loved to give Alex a brother or sister."

He knew without another word spoken that she'd followed the unnerving logic: the repaired, modified auxosome contained its own regulator operons, but also the Terminator code. People might be catching immortality in a wave spread from the infected, like Roberta, but they'd be contracting sterility at the same time. In the same instant, he saw the flaw in her personal reasoning.

"I think your period is just delayed by this non-stop stress. We're not sterile," he said. "Neither will Alex be, or Wayne for that matter. The auxosome *we* injected doesn't have the Terminator code. I'm pretty sure AUX-1's not infectious, either, or everyone else we've been in contact with would have come down with it by now."

He watched Jill gaze across at her son, chattering away in Spanish. "All right," she said. "I'm glad of that, on a selfish level. But the fact remains: You've changed the world forever, without asking anyone's permission. No more death from illness or age, yes, but also no more children, if this thing does become an epidemic." She shook her head, face creased by sudden misery. After a moment she went back to her book, but looked up again. "What was the phrase you once used? *Post mortal syndrome*? I think I've got it, love. Severe moral cramps."

Distressed, Paul began keying an encrypted message.

Hi Roberta

We're in Guadalajara, Jalisco, doing fine. Have received the money you wired. Lots more than we need, on top of the cash you sent with Ambrosio. But thanks much. Hope he found the car. Have appointment to talk to W. Gruene at the Universidad de Guadalajara tomorrow. Jill and Alex are well. Once enough time has passed, she'll see about letting Alex's dad know what's going on. Meanwhile, Jill's planning to enroll in law school here, after she learns Spanish. Shouldn't take long. Jill and I aren't as fast as Alex, but we're picking it up as we go.

Wayne Elliot left an interesting legacy for Alex. In the early 1980s, if his note is to be trusted, he was a subject in an experiment run by Blick Pharmaceuticals testing a psychoactive drug to enhance suggestibility and military prowess. Claims they tried to build on an existing personality disorder to turn him into an assassin. Manchurian Candidate sort of thing. Pretty far-fetched story, but hey.

Blick Co. could still cause problems for us, even down here. But I'm sure we'll be able to (coff coff) outsmart them.

I hope you're feeling better, Roberta. There's extremely important news. I'll tell you in detail when you get down to set up the new MJT labs, but see the attached preliminary report. The mice are contagious! We might have a containment problem after all, though probably only with AUX-2. Our friend Carol Glassman was in close contact with Alex and Jill but tells us she hasn't contracted it.

Later, Paul

He hit Send, and saw that Jill was weeping silently. Uncannily, Alex had noticed already, was crossing the room with his arms outstretched. Wretchedly, Paul took her left hand.

"Roberta has caught it," Paul told the child.

"Right," the boy said with dazzling insight. "Cross-species infection. The Terminator gene?" After a comforting moment of embrace, he drew back, looked from one to the other with his clear, penetrating gaze. "Don't worry," he said. "If you can do something, you can find a way to undo it. That's what Carl Clueless always says, and he's the man with all the frangimuffles." He grinned, and one of his adult front teeth was growing in, charmingly. "Trial and error and improvement, right, doctor?"

"I hope so," Paul said. He was not entirely convinced. Sometimes you really can't get the toothpaste back into the tube, no matter how much effort you expend. And nobody had yet learned to unscramble eggs. Especially human eggs. "I will surely do my best." He looked at the two people in the world that he loved best, loved fiercely, and swore that dedication to himself.

145: MONDAY, JULY 7

They rolled the body from the refrigerator room to the examining table on a gurney with one squeaking wheel, which set Graham Shelby's teeth on edge. He pulled on his long rubber gloves, one pair over the top of another, and adjusted his face shield while the diener checked out the documentation.

"Elliot, Wayne. Funny. Why's it taken this long to authorize the examination?"

"Damned if I know, Bill." Shelby glanced at the flimsies. "Paperwork's from Harris County Sheriff's Department. I guess they must have asked for the body to be held for positive identification."

"I dunno, the decedent's wife okayed it at the scene. It's been here in the cooler since Saturday."

"Hmm. Turf wars higher up the chain, Bill, that's my guess. See there at the end, the FBI was involved. Give it here." He flipped the sheets, frowned, flipped back to the top.

"How come they didn't ship him to Bethesda or Walter Reed, then, doc?"

"Looks like...hmm...BlickPharm was trying to get them to waive the autopsy. We're to ship him to their facility in San Marcos after we finish. They're not likely to enlighten us. 'Some things man is not meant to know.' Hoist him over here on the slab."

His assistant unzipped the heavy mortuary bag, heaved the cold flesh on the aluminum autopsy table. The cadaver was a young man in good condition, skin pallid but without lividity, rigor long since gone off, no visible signs of damage. He matched ID against the name on the toe tag.

"I thought he'd been shot to death during a stakeout?"

"One of their crack shooters. Died within minutes."

"I find no penetration site. Bill, we've got the wrong body. God *damn* it, can't those thumb-fingered dolts get the *slightest* thing right! We'll be here for hours setting this straight. I have a Rotary meeting at seven."

"Don't look at me, Dr. Shelby, I just haul 'em in and haul 'em back after you've hacked 'em up."

"Come with me to the office. I want the Harris County office on the line."

"Do I put him back in the freezer?"

"Just throw a bag over it."

They walked with echoing tread across the hard tiles. The heavy rubber-edged doors slapped shut.

On the mortuary table, with its raised edges on either side of the hip-high aluminum platform and the cold fluorescent lamps casting their shadowless light from above, Wayne's unmarked body warmed in the cool air. Inside his tissues, auxosome pairs in their trillions continued the function for which they had been designed, and in ways that their configuration exceeded the limits of design. Assembled as their coding directed, amino acids moved in cells where the ancient rituals of decay and decomposition had been forestalled, rebuilding proteins, accelerating repair routines that in a child quickly healed a skinned knee or scratched hand. The optimized proteins reached into the vaults of zero point energy that filled the vacuum and drew out power to rebuild tissues cooled by the chill of the mortuary refrigerator.

Faintly, from the office. Dr. Shelby's voice rang out in wrath.

On the autopsy table, Wayne's ten fingers twitched.

146: MONDAY, JULY 7

Starvingly hungry, he eased out of the mortuary, dressed in mismatched stolen items, creeping from a side door that creaked noisily. As he'd hoped, though, no alarm burst into shrieking life; the system was set to alert against intrusion, but nobody expected the dead to escape.

Wayne found each step excruciating. His body still held its slug of lethal metal. Cells strained to reconstruct their original order and improve upon it. To add to his misery, he had to stop twice and throw up. He remembered what Paul Gibson had said about the possible side effects of the drug without the completed regulator dose, and wondered sourly if he were going to die a second time.

In his misery Wayne Elliot almost longed for the cessation of all pain that death would bring, that it had brought him once, if only for a timeless interval that was now done. Perhaps religious teachings about death were true, and he'd get to see Melody again. He tried to remember being dead. He had not seen her on the far side, he felt sure. No, he had a mission to complete, a reason to stay alive. Blick, he thought, and the name was a curse and an anathema. Rutherford and Blick. But Rutherford was dead.

He found a half-empty dumpster full of rags behind an upholstery store and lay nearly torpid until morning. His thinking was too muddled for long-range planning; he hoped only to scrounge something to eat and drink and find a safe place to spend the next few days. He had no idea where he was, where he'd awakened. Houston, probably. The county morgue, maybe.

A pushcart vendor ringing an annoying bell woke him, gave him an aging tuna sandwich for free, and told him about The Edge.

§

Like a scab on the edge of San Antonio's central business district, The Edge Community was started by a homeless woman who built a rough shelter out of scrap sheet metal on a vacant tract of land at the intersection of three huge freeway overpasses. The city had left the unattractive zone to use eventually as parking but never developed it. While the Edge's founding mother had long since moved on, people kept coming. It was one of the few places in the city you could camp without being hassled by the cops, with the added benefit that the river ran past and provided enough water for drinking and cooking, after boiling, and for bathing if you weren't fastidious. The inhabitants of the Edge had never been known for their cleanliness.

As knowledge of The Edge spread and its mostly transient population grew, the level of violence increased, and its frequency. Police took sporadic action, but found life easier if the vagrants gathered themselves together. But after the rape of a young woman and her eleven-year-old daughter, one of the longer-time residents decided to do something to improve living conditions. A large, handsome man known only as Curt, he posted a set of rules and enlisted the help of several other residents to enforce them. Within a month, The Edge was transformed into a safe, comparatively clean place to stay. Within six months, Curt was undisputed leader. People began calling him King Curt.

§

"Sounds like the place for me to hide out," Wayne told the vendor.

"Hey, you go see my buddy when you get there. Yusuf. I teach him how to make a living. Poor bastard, they lock him up in prison eight months. Why? Because he Iraqi *refugee* but follow Islam. Here for *years*, they lock him up. Bastards!"

147: MONDAY, JULY 7

James Branigan settled back for the flight, a china plate of *hors d'oeuvres* by his side. He had expected the reading material to deal with current genetic engineering; but instead it was political theory in date order of publication, beginning with *The Prince* by Niccolo Machiavelli and ending with an article titled "A New Definition of Negotiating Power," apparently copied from an academic journal. He sank into his assigned reading, scarcely surfaced until the airport limousine dropped him off in San Miguel.

When Franz the butler ushered James into Blick's underground office, with its ancient Persian carpet that could properly have hung in a museum, Blick was already at his antique mahogany desk. Without rising, he waved James to a nearby chair.

"You read the material I sent you." Blick was not one for elaborate greetings.

"Naturally."

"Tell me, then, what do you think of the notion of using fear as a uniting force?"

James frowned. "Those psychological studies do indicate fear as a primary motivator. People are more likely to avoid what they dread," he said, "more than to seek whatever it is they believe they want."

"And what do you think people fear the most?"

James mentally searched through the huge mass of new information he had just absorbed. "Machiavelli mentions swift and severe punishment. Actually one of the psychology papers claimed that people fear public speaking even more than death." He allowed himself to smile.

Bruce, though, did not find the comparison amusing. "And well they might. To make oneself ridiculous in front of the tribe could result in expulsion and awful suffering, before subsequent death. To be different. To stand out. Wouldn't you think?"

"I don't know about that. I should think most people would be more afraid of ten lashes with a whip than being sniggered at."

A small dark skinned girl of sixteen or seventeen appeared at the open doorway. "Mr. Blick, your lunch is ready," she said timidly.

"Thank you, Almaz. James, the reason I asked you to come all the way down here today is that I want you to put together a public relations campaign of fear. I want people to be so afraid of genetic engineering they'd jump off a hundred and ten story building to get away from it."

James clamped his teeth tight. It was typical of Blick that to make his point he could draw without a qualm upon so frightful a memory as the September 11 terrorist attacks on New York. He forced his expression into neutrality, nodded, rose and took his leave. There had never been the least chance that Blick would invite him to share luncheon.

148: MONDAY, JULY 7

A noisy bunch of small children were playing outside at Li'l Tykes Daycare when Wayne passed, and he stopped for a moment to watch them. He and Melody might have had grandchildren this age by now, if she'd lived. *I hope you don't hold it against me, Baby, what I'm fixing to do now. I hope you understand.*

But Melody was dead and buried, and it was time to bid her farewell at last. And Fern, too, was now part of his past. She had seen him die; kinder to let her go her own way without troubling her dreams. That decision grieved him terribly, he found.

He remembered the days when he and Fern were first going out together, how his heart would lift when he saw her little blue car coming to pick him up from work. Fern had been nothing but sweet to him all these years, and he'd paid her back cruelly. Surely he'd do things differently if he had them to do over again, but there could be no turning back now. He had burned those bridges. To Fern he was dead, and he must remain dead.

He stole a black Ford Focus two blocks from the mortuary, drove carefully, stopped after an hour to buy gas on the outskirts of Sealy. The girl at the cash register glanced at his ill-fitting medical scrubs and rubber boots, and he diverted her with a charming smile as he leaned across the counter. His right hand with its sweet new fingers flashed into the register and seized a handful of notes with blinding speed. He cursed his luck in sleeping in an upholstery store dumpster, and swore to find a Goodwill store. No need to pay them for less conspicuous clothing, either, if he was quick enough.

At the edge of the parking area a man wearing cowboy boots and hat had set up a display of purses, silver buckled belts, rugs, brightly colored blouses and scarves under a red-stenciled banner: "BARGAIN SALES." Fern liked to wear a scarf around her neck to add a touch of color. Wayne picked one out in char-treuse with bright orange tropical flowers, and paid the cowboy $3.50. If he mailed it today, anonymously, she should get it before the end of the week. Yes, she thought he was dead and he would stay dead, no need to screw up her life any further. But she'd be touched, he sensed, by a gift arriving from nowhere. Maybe she'd assume he mailed it before the cops had cut him down.

He stopped at the post office in Luling, and marveled at how alive he felt, waiting in line with six other people. Oddly, nobody gave him a second glance; no one had the slightest suspicion of what he had done in the past, or what he planned to do now. Still, he worried. People might remember seeing a brown haired man of medium height. Maybe he should try a disguise, dye his hair, wear a fake beard and glasses. Or something more drastic.

FBI Wanted posters were pinned on the bulletin board. Christ, his own name and photograph might be there, if he was unlucky. His gaze passed with lightning speed across the board. Some of the fugitives were shown in several different views—long haired, short haired, bearded and clean shaven.

His own face was not on display. Wayne smiled to himself at the antics some of these clowns got up to. One guy, he saw, a Horace Cleburg, sometimes posed as a meek little gray haired woman; looked like someone's kindly grandmother. Well, he'd done it himself and gotten away with it. He mailed his package, checked his wallet. Just enough stolen cash to replenish the nearly empty gas tank.

A somewhat dubious Hispanic woman with an alert pit-bull paused for a moment on the sidewalk at his enquiry and advised him to try Seguin for inexpensive clothing. It was on the way to San Antonio, she told him, pretending not to see her dog take a shit in someone's front lawn.

In the Plaza del Rey Shopping Center in Seguin, he found two large dumpsters to one side of the Goodwill store, emblazoned with warnings against placing perishable foodstuffs or explosive devices inside, nor to sleep therein. He foraged out a shirt, trousers and, luckily, a pair of worn-down shoes only one size too large. He pulled on an extra pair of hideous socks, despite the prickly heat. A passerby or two looked away, embarrassed for him.

Back on Interstate Highway 10, Wayne mused on his plans. Stay in hiding, he thought. Get in touch with Roberta Treadwell. They owed him, he told himself. He'd looked after the kid, hadn't he? It would work, he thought, as long as they didn't turn him in to the cops. Just long enough to get another shot. Long enough, after that, to hunt down the motherfucker Blick.

149: MONDAY, JULY 7

Drew leaned across his girlfriend's plate of chicken-fried steak and grinned shyly. "I ran blood tests on me and Maureen, Roberta. I have you to thank for my life."

She stared, then smiled back. "Not at all. You're an ornament to your profession and our labs, Dr. Chang. Why, without you—"

"No, he means it literally," Maureen Baumgarten told her.

"AUX-2," Drew said. "We're both carrying it. You too, I assume. I'll need a cell sample from you tomorrow, bucal smear should do, we'll look at it under the mike and put it through the scanner if you're showing 48 chromosomes."

"How could you possibly—"

"You infected him with the auxosome."

"From the mice," Drew said. He picked up his knife and fork once more.

Maureen grinned. "You didn't think he came back from the edge of the grave because Alyssa *prayed* for him, I hope?"

"I—What?" But the image presented it to her as if she were standing back and watching: Drew, nine parts dead, his breathing in the charge of brute machine. Herself leaning across his still face, tears dripping from her eyes and welling on his cheek.

"Oh my god," she said. "I did. I gave it to you."

"And nobody's ever been happier to catch a strange disease," Drew said, holding out his hand and taking hers, squeezing it tightly. After a moment, Maureen joined her hand to theirs.

"You're very welcome," Roberta told them both. She was weeping again, she found.

150: MONDAY, JULY 7

Wayne dumped his stolen car just south of the city, picked up a lift into the center of town, and walked north through teeming rain along the Riverwalk and beyond, for miles, to the Edge, where Olmos Creek ran beside the McAllister Freeway. For Wayne, despite the rudimentary living conditions, the community offered his best chance to stay in one place, secure, out of the direct sight of authorities and do-gooders, certainly out of Blick's purview, long enough to obtain the remaining regulator doses of the auxosome from Roberta or Paul.

He walked into the drafty space out of warm, drumming

rain. Despite the day's heat, fires burned in blackened steel bins. People stood about muttering lethargically to one another or themselves. Some sat by small tents pitched in the dirt. Wayne wandered cautiously until he found the rusted old car used by the friend of the Harris County food vendor. The Iraqi Muslim immigrant Yusuf gave him a cautious welcome. In exchange for help making sandwiches and other small food items, the newcomer got enough to eat for free. To his surprise, Yusuf offered him a cut of the small profits after Wayne showed him ways to speed up his food preparation and keep it fresh longer using several layers of plastic sheeting and crushed ice liberated, using a small trick he knew, from a gas station ice dispenser.

He settled finally under the drumming freeway's colossal burden of concrete, watching lightning snap in the sky, dust in his nostrils. Yusuf's laden pedal-cart stood next to the rusting wreck. Nobody touched it or its contents, and nobody would. The black man was curled in the back seat, taking a snoring nap while the rain made his profession unprofitable. Wayne wrapped himself uncomfortably around the shift stick, across both front seats, worrying obsessively about the neural regulator. In minutes, he fell asleep anyway.

§

In the cool late afternoon beside the insect-buzzing trickle of the creek, King Curt sat on his throne, the stump of a live oak tree that Ilya Santana, using only a chainsaw and chisel, had carved into the form of a Celtic knot years before he became a famous artist. The City Fathers had shoveled all these unwanted people away to make room for the long-promised final expansion of the Riverwalk. Dumpsters behind the city's many overpriced eateries, miles to the south, provided indifferent day-old food for the workshy, the luckless, the addicted and the half-deranged who made up the population of The Edge. King Curt had arranged food runs from the dumpsters that barely coped with the needs of his subjects, but kept them out of the hair of business and law alike. And dispensed justice.

Curt was maybe forty years old, with dark brown skin and dreadlocks. Wayne sat across the small camp fire on a folding metal chair, sipping coffee from a cracked china cup. This was surely the most delicious coffee he'd ever drunk, a complex tapestry of flavor. It seemed that he was distinctly tasting each chemical component of the coffee and simultaneously savoring its relationship to the whole. Must be the rain-freshened air and camp fire, he decided. He yearned for the woods.

"I like to meet each new person, get to know them a little, go over the rules." King Curt set his coffee cup down on a highly polished slab of redwood, his worktable, set atop a base made of galvanized plumbing pipe. The big man took a bite of a muffin one of the women had brought for him, washed it down with another swig of coffee. "Where you from?"

"Grew up in Memphis." Somehow, Wayne found it uncomfortable to lie to this fellow. He had given his name as Elliot, nothing more, which was enough with everyone. It was not uncommon here for people to use only given or nicknames.

Curt looked hard into his eyes without blinking. "Planning on staying long?"

"Don't know for sure. Not too long."

"We encourage people to look for work. There's a place just a few blocks west, beside the freeway exit, where you can wait in the mornings. People who need day help come by and pick up workers."

"I'm a little poorly right now, you understand," Wayne told him, almost apologetically. "Need to rest up for a week or so until I feel better." And until I can grow out this beard so people are less likely to recognize me, he thought.

"Okay. Long as you keep your space clean, don't cause any trouble, and pitch in a little with the work here."

"Yusuf told me you have a library."

Curt looked at him with new interest. "Over there." An ancient orange Volkswagen camper under the curving concrete roof of the freeway, no wheels, up on blocks. "I've run out of shelf space. I'm trying to come up with enough money to buy one of those Sea Train containers. I'm happy to let people read my books if they look after 'em. Just sign the list so I know you have the book, and don't take it away from here." He shook his head. "Not so many people interested in reading these days. People spend more time just finding food, scraping up enough money for soap and toothpaste." Curt's personal presence was remarkable, as was his beautiful preacher's voice. "I don't like trouble, Elliot. I find it works best to handle minor disputes as soon as possible, before they escalate."

Wayne kept his own voice gruff. "What about someone breaks stuff, or steals it?"

"We try to find a form of restitution both parties will agree to. If we can't work something out, we have a trial by jury. Anyone doesn't want to abide by the jury's decision, they can always take their dispute into the regular court system." His laughter barked. "That's only happened once." Without his standing or moving a muscle, it was plain that the interview was about over. "We've had a few troublemakers through here never had no intention of getting along peacefully. Those types we throw out."

It was not a threat. It *was* a clear warning. Wayne nodded, stood, went back to Yusuf's car. He stretched out next to it on a six foot strip of foam rubber he'd bought for $3 from an Edge resident who had found a job and was departing to rent an apartment in a four-plex on Dewey Street. He was utterly exhausted, and the auxosomes worked ceaselessly inside his tissues like a fever.

151: WEDNESDAY, JULY 16

Blick's evident connections with law enforcement might extend to federal aviation authorities. That risk made their trip more circuitous and far more time-consuming than Roberta was used to. They took a Greyhound bus to the border, a tedious and slightly unnerving experience, but crossed readily enough. Drew and Maureen went through immigration and customs together, Roberta following. The MJT corporate jet awaited them at the Laredo airport on the Mexican side. The flight across Mexico, east to west and north to south, they devoted to snoozing; all three had gotten up far too early in the day. They landed without incident and took a cab Drew hailed at random.

Squeezed in the back seat against the side of the bumpy old Volkswagen Beetle by Maureen and Drew, Roberta made the best of her discomfort by watching the Mexican streetscape. She had spent holiday weekends in Isla de Mujer, Tepotzlán, Mexico City itself, but Guadalajara was new to her. Exotic and beautiful and, refreshingly, not as hot as summer in Texas. It might be the nation's second largest city, but compared to the smoggy horror of Mexico's capital, where the air breathed daily by twenty million people literally contained a suspended haze of human fecal matter, it was paradise. A suitable site, perhaps, for the revived and transplanted MJT research center.

§

Paul's associate had arranged a small meeting room in the Universidad's central library. As they entered, a visiting troupe of mostly blond, tanned Californian fundamentalist missionaries in gaudy straw hats and vests, announced with a banner in blue and gold, were setting up outside in the grassy courtyard, to the bemusement of the locals. The meeting room was a cramped space with teak table, plain water jug and sturdy glasses, and a dozen padded chairs, but with state of the art display facilities. Paul closed curtains patterned gaily with tropical blooms, plugged in his laptop, ran them through a PowerPoint presentation of his latest results.

"Undeniable murine-human transposition, very rapidly, of the key auxosome elements," he said finally. His face in the colored LED light of the screen images was grave. "Drew, I believe you have something to show us?"

Drew Chang switched seats, plugged his own thumb-drive into a USB port of Paul's laptop, found a directory. The screen showed a microscope slide with blotchy shapes and blurred lines against a mostly empty white field. Roberta had seen it the day before and sat mutely, but Paul and Jill had an audible reaction.

"My seminal fluid, three days ago," Drew said blandly.

"No wrigglers," Jill said.

"Not a one," Drew told her. He bared his teeth. "I'm as sterile as a mule."

"I'm so sorry," Paul said, voice tight.

"Luckily it only impairs outcome, not performance. A sort of built-in permanent condom."

"Be sorry, but don't be *so* sorry," Maureen added. She rose from her seat, patted her loosely covered belly, bowed. "Regard the happy parents-to-be."

"Wonderful!" Jill cried, and went immediately to hug the woman. Roberta watched with a fond smile. She herself had passed through menopause five years earlier; there was no dread for her in this engineered Termination of her genetic line. Besides, she told herself, she fully intended to be her own offspring, to live as long and as fully and as goddam responsibly as she could, for a thousand years or a million. Or to raise a clone, if it came to that, once the technology was perfected and legalized. The men were shaking hands rowdily. Alex swung his eyes about in a paroxysm of embarrassment. He might be a genius, but he was still an eight year old kid.

"I've been pregnant for two months," Maureen was saying. "I hadn't even told the daddy. First he was nearly dead," and her voice choked, "then he was recovering, then I had to pry him from the grip of his attentive mother...." Everyone laughed except Alex, who was still in bashful mode. "And then I wanted to make completely sure. Now I'm sure, I had a Clearblue test and vaginal echography yesterday and all's proceeding very nicely."

Roberta led a round of applause, and poured glasses of iced water. Light from the screen sparkled as she raised a toast.

"Well, that happy news does take us rather abruptly back to Drew's results," she said at length. "I'm afraid we have to do some major and last-minute ethics assessment on this entire project. Dr. Chang and Dr. Gibson have created a profoundly Promethean moment in history, a crux, a watershed between past and future like no other, greater in significance, I think, even that the taming of fire and the emergence of language."

"The end of dying," Jill said.

"The end of conception," said Maureen, mouth twisting.

"Only for the moment," Paul said. "I think we can regard this as a lucky circuit-breaker. The world has been standing for twenty years on the verge of a major population crisis, getting closer and closer to the edge of unsustainability—"

"Sorry, Paul," Maureen said, face flushed. "That's Deep Green bullshit."

"I'm not saying anything about your baby, Maureen," Paul said placatingly. "This is a larger, global—"

"We can feed and house and clothe a hundred billion if we have to," she told him angrily. "In twenty years time we'll have nanotechnology to take care of food and everything else we need to get by. The analysis is on the web, it's not hard to—"

"From the Papal College of Celibate Gynecologists, I imagine," Paul muttered. He held up his hand immediately, shaking his head. "Sorry, that was a cheap shot."

"Paul, people do have a right to their own children," Jill said. "A powerful need, anyway. It's basic biology, seems to me. I know I'm no expert, but isn't it evolution? It's the deepest drive we have."

"I think Jill's right," Roberta found herself saying. "Without children, we have no hope for the future. That way lies madness and grief and social ruin." She shuddered, "God, a world without *children?*"

"No, no, *no!*" Paul said loudly. He slapped his hand on the table, leaning forward. "That's *history* speaking, making its last claims on us. But we are in the *future*. Roberta, you called this a Promethean moment. That's absolutely correct. The

Terminator-variant auxosome is the catalyst that will change us from, from...larvae to adults. From caterpillars to butterflies."

"I'm already an adult, love," Jill said. "Besides, butterflies die."

"And we *won't!* This is *so* hard to grasp intuitively, I know, I know, I've struggled with it for months now. Nanotechnology or not, we can't afford to let populations go haywire. I know it seems ruthless and inhuman. Our poor human minds find it impossible to take hold of the idea that we might live without aging, without deteriorating, without illness or automatic death."

"Well, Blick might have us killed at any moment," Chang said. "Or some fucking madman like your pal Wayne." He caught himself, glanced at the child. "Sorry, Alex."

"'Sorright, you should hear Mom, sometimes, she's swears like a...a myrmidon!"

"A *what?*" Jill laughed explosively, and her amusement broke the angry mood like a heavy cloud clearing.

Alex looked bashful. "A soldier, you know, in Homer?"

My God, Roberta thought. He did that deliberately. The child intervened. He really has become a genius. I hope, she thought, that we all can gain something of his wonderful intelligence and grace.

From outside the library, festive *mariachi* music broke out, diminished by the thick stucco walls but clearly audible, an epic of cultural insensitivity: guitars, a trumpet or two blaring, voices raised in song and laughter, not all of it derisory.

"Very well," she said, taking control again. "I'd like to open the next tranche of our meeting, a consideration of the known epidemiology and likely spread of this unexpected effect. It seems to me that we have an obligation to alert the Centers for Disease Control in Atlanta."

"But it's not a disease," Alex said firmly. Everyone looked at him in surprise. "It's a *pro*-ease." He glanced around the table, his head at shoulder height to everyone else. "It's a life-saver."

The adults regarded him once more in open-mouthed silence.

He added: "I'd like to go out and explore the library now, if that's all right with everyone? You know, play?" He grinned happily.

152: FRIDAY, JULY 18

Bruce Edward Blick strolled under the shade of an arbor from which hung fragrant clusters of purple Wisteria blooms. Although this room was more than sixty feet underground, it was a garden filled with sunlight delivered by a vertical series of mirrors that continuously shifted their alignment to track the hot Mexican sun throughout the day. A muted image of the true sky as seen from the surface was projected onto the ceiling of the underground chamber, thirty feet above Blick's head. Birds, insects, and microbes native to fifteen separate regions of the world shared the underground paradise, pollinating flowers, recycling organic materials and creating beauty for the few humans who were allowed access.

Blick leaned forward to breathe the fragrance of a Madame Hardy rose, sat down on a stone bench where the day's email had been downloading to his laptop as he walked. He sighed. It seemed harder each day to keep his mind focused. I'm getting old, he thought. I can almost feel my brain cells dying, a hundred here, a hundred there.

Lately he had been grooming a new protégé to take Gebhardt's place, allowing the younger man to make many of the top level decisions, but he always kept one task strictly for himself: strategic preventive maintenance. Each day he spent at least two hours reviewing national and world news digests prepared by his regular staff, and closely reading weekly reports from his special staff, a world-wide network of people, from corporate CEOs to unemployed laborers. Most of them did not know each other, and none knew that their specialized insights were being channeled to Bruce Blick.

Scrolling through his correspondence he read:

To: johansen@yahoo.com
From:henry engelke
Subject:antique amish quilts

i found some of the kind of papers you wanted me to
look for in the trash. let me know where i should take
them. i assume the price is still $10 each.

Blick thought for a moment, selected a name from his mail-
ing list and typed:

To: Rodney Baker
From: Webgambler
Subject:Retire in 5 Years!

Rodney, call the number I sent you for H.E. I will
wire money to your account. Send papers to address
in Ithaca.

He read the next five emails quickly and deleted them without response. The sixth one read:

To: Eric Johansen
From: Beryl Clarke
Subject:Fried Milk Recipes

Dear Eric,

I heard you seek Paul Gibson, formerly postdoc in
the pharmacy department at UT, Austin, TX. I believe
he is living in Guadalajara, Jalisco under assumed
name Ben Peters. He lives with beautiful young woman
claiming to be his wife, Joyce, not same as lawyer in
your document images. There is boy living with them,
Ricky, but he does not match the description provided.
Dr. Peters met with two visiting scientists from MJT

labs in San Antonio, TX, at Universidad. They were Dr. Roberta Treadwell and Dr. Drew Chang. That is only thing of significance I have observed this week.

Regards, Beryl

Without missing a beat, Blick began typing:

To:guardian
From:Monkeyman
Subject:bad teeth

Please provide all possible details, including photos and fingerprints if possible. Extreme urgency!

Blick's replies went to a server in Saltillo, Mexico, which forwarded them to a second server in Dar Es Salaam. From there they would go, in encrypted form, to their final recipients. The encryption program Blick used was flagrantly illegal; if by some remote chance the encryption was discovered, Blick would suffer at most a slap on the wrist in the form of a fine. He had learned early in life that he was not subject to the same rules as ordinary mortals.

153: FRIDAY, JULY 18

Alex sought out "Dr. Ben Peters" at his lab bench. They had found a school class for him to slot into, and it was driving him nuts although his Spanish was improving fast. He was far too advanced for his own age group, but Jill insisted that he needed the socialization of his peers. After classes, he was allowed to roam the library, drinking in a universe of knowledge and art. These days, though, he spent half his free time hanging about the electrical engineering labs, borrowing test equipment, tinkering with castoffs. He toted a bag of these toys over his shoulder, aware that Paul and his Mom could have no real understanding of what he was doing.

"Hi, tyke! How's it going?"

He started to speak, and the words caught in his throat like phlegm. "Wayne's still alive," he said, unbroken voice husky.

"I'm sure he is," Paul said, gaze still fixed on the screen of his atomic force microscope. He tweaked an atom closer to its target. "Got it! Sorry, you were saying?"

"I thought he was dead."

"Just a nightmare, Alex." Reaching down from his stool, Paul ruffled the boy's hair fondly. Alex pulled away.

"No, it's more than that, Paul. You don't—Well, the point is, he *isn't* dead. I think the auxosomes saved him."

He saw Paul start to roll his eyes then block the unconscious reaction. Pointless trying to explain.

"The thing is, he needs the second regulator dose real bad, and then the final one. We've gotta get them to him."

Paul shrugged, face sad. "I'd like to help him out, but we don't know where he is. I mean, son, he's in another country, hundreds of miles away, probably hiding out from the cops."

"That's not the problem," Alex said tersely. "I can find him. But I can't make the protein." He reached into his backpack, drew the transporter out.

"You can *find*—Oh. Oh, my. The things you used on the chopper."

A glowing sphere hung in the air between them, spinning, it seemed, on two axes at once.

Paul was smarter these days, Alex noticed. He didn't need any explanation. Just the facts.

"That will reach him?"

"Range is unlimited, but it might take a little while to track him through...you know, the space between things."

"The zero point energy field," Paul said.

"I guess."

"And this gadget gives you some sort of link to Wayne?"

"Not this one." He reached out, plucked the transporter from the air, placed it on the bench. Its glow diminished but was not extinguished. He popped a lid on its cargo compartment. "Something else." He smiled. "I think it uses the midichlorians."

"That's 'mitochondria,' Alex. Okay, those are the body's cellular power units. But how—"

"Not mitochondria. Sorry, *Star Wars* joke." The grown-up stared at him uncomprehendingly. "Never mind. It's the auxosomes, Paul. Their resonant frequency, I think you'd call it."

"But that's...that's...absurdly low-energy. You couldn't possibly sense—"

"Not by myself." Alex shrugged, nudged the transporter back into the air where it glowed like a tiny green moon. "Something else I built."

"And it tells you where Wayne is?"

"Where all of you are. Sort of. I mean, Mom's over *that* way," he pointed left, through the wall, toward the language labs, "and Aunt Carol and Dad and my sisters are in Austin *that* way, and Roberta and Drew and Maureen are...well, you know, back in San Antonio."

"Where's Wayne?" Paul was hardly breathing.

"Not sure. San Antonio somewhere, but there's all kinds of noise of cars, and people everywhere, it's all blurry, lots of them are sick. I think they're catching the auxosome proease from him. And he feels sick all the time in his head. We gotta get the regulator to him, Paul."

"Okay, son." The adult crossed the room, opened a locked cabinet. Glass vials stood racked inside the containment space. "No harm in trying."

154: FRIDAY, JULY 18

Wayne was careful to keep his space tidy and to do what he could in the way of community services. A scavenger had scored some photovoltaic panels and deep cycle batteries left over, unsold, from an auction of marine equipment, so Wayne put his electrician skills to work. It kept him close to the library van.

"Okay, Elliot, plug it in!" On the roof of the van, where he had just hung an improvised light fixture made from a car headlight backed by a metal garbage can lid, King Curt whooped. "Woo hoo! It works! Look at that, will ya? It works!" Curt grinned. "You're my man, Elliot!"

"We should increase the albedo of the reflector," Wayne mused. "Let's put out the word for everyone to be on the lookout for some white paint."

Curt climbed to the ground. "This calls for a celebration. Care to join me and a few friends for dinner this evening, Elliot? Maggie brought back some lobster and shrimp from the Quarry dumpster, and a couple of the girls have gone fishing down along a tad. We'll have a seafood feast."

"Sure." Wayne cleaned up his tools. "In fact, I saw an interesting recipe for ceviche in one of your cookbooks, and I think we have all the ingredients we need in the garden 'cept for the lime juice. I bet somebody around here will have some limes they can spare."

"That's what you've been reading? Cook books?"

"Cook books, medical books, art books, whatever." He shrugged, a little embarrassed. "It's all interesting, know what I mean?" I'm still changing, Wayne realized. As he made his way to the garden to pick tomatoes for the ceviche, he thought: Half the time I get so wrapped up in what I'm reading I forget about my mission. I have to be careful not to lose sight of the reason I'm here. But he had to wait until his body healed completely and his beard grew out a little more. I can't go anywhere that Blick might track me down, he thought, persuading himself. So it won't hurt to spend some time reading books. Besides, all this reading will be good exercise for my brain, help my planning. He wished the kid was here. Him and his partner.

He'd found in an old neurology text that the individual components of a human brain were almost identical to those of a mouse. The key difference appeared to derive mostly from the comparative number of brain cells and the number of different ways they could be connected with each other. Dendrites. Synapses. That had been Paul Gibson's claim, too. The auxosome treatment caused extra neurons to grow. Or maybe just forced them to build new connections, like him wiring up the lights on the van. He'd read that the brain produces intense electrical activity. Right! Rewiring brains!

It was scary and rather exhilarating, like he was, was...*interpreting* the world with newborn neurons. Like the sweet taste of fresh-grilled catfish caught on his own hook. It came to him that he'd felt this way as a kid, a small fry, when him and his friends went exploring, climbing on the roofs of houses under construction, poking around in Old Man McNutt's junkyard, watching tadpoles grow into frogs a little each day. Tomorrow I'll figure out how to get the final dose of the drug. Need to get on-line and reach out to that Roberta gal. If she's forgiven me yet for nearly killing her boy Drew. He was torn again by unaccustomed emotions: guilt and misery, for his past crimes, elation at what the treatment was doing to him. Back from the dead! He almost laughed aloud with delight at the thought of how those extra stem cells were growing, but caught himself. This was serious business. He had no right laughing when Gaia was in danger from that murderous son of a bitch Blick. And those burgeoning stem cells might be about to choke him into sickness and terrifying stupidity.

§

He woke in the depths of the night. A dim green light buzzed his eyes. He reached out sleepily, tried to swat it away. It swung around behind him, dimmed further, hovered at his left ear. For a moment it spooked the hell out of him, until he recalled the toys Alex had been playing with in the back of the Humvee. Some fancy Mattel gadget probably. A tiny insect voice spoke.

"Hey, partner."

"Alex!" His joy and relief were overwhelming. "Where are

you, little buddy?" But it had to be a dream, didn't it?

"A long ways off, Wayne."

He came wider awake. No toy, then. Some product of the kid's genius.

"I want you to do something really carefully," the kid's voice told him. "I'm going to pop open this transporter, and you'll find a micro-syringe inside. It's loaded with the next regulator protein. You know how to make a tourniquet?"

Yusuf poked his head out the rusty old car, stared at Wayne and his ghostly djinn visitor, shuddered, withdrew.

"Yeah, I know how to do that." Wayne closed his eyes, felt the flood of relief washing through his muscles, imagined that he felt the tightness inside his skull easing already. "I can do that."

155: TUESDAY, JULY 23

James Branigan gathered together on screen the package of intelligence he'd compiled on the movements of Dr. Roberta Treadwell and her staff. They had vanished from the face of the earth for several days, and it had taken a considerable amount of legwork to trace them. Greyhound to the Mexican border, private jet to Jalisco State. That much confirmed the anonymous report from Blick's local asset. Conference with "Peters," Gibson to a high probability according to the Bayesian filters, then back to San Antonio by the reverse route. Pointless spy vs. spy shenanigans, he thought, curling his lip. Do they take us for amateurs? He emailed the package and his crisp top summary report to Bruce Blick, faintly amused by the thought that his employer, in the fastnesses of Mexico's Hidalgo state, was physically nearer to "Peters" than James himself was.

Branigan was wrong about that. Blick was already in central Texas, flown in by BlickPharm chopper, beside himself with frustration. If you want something done right, he told himself savagely, you God-damned do it yourself.

"Get me a rental car," he told a flunky before settling down for an afternoon nap. "Some piece of crap nobody will notice. Not such a piece of crap that it will crap out on me on the highway. And a tranquilizer handgun. Something that will take down an elephant."

I'm not leaving anything to chance, he thought. Nobody will see me until I have the bitch laid out like a side of beef, and then those who do will be restricted to my own staff and nobody else.

He once more opened the emailed package of covertly gathered information and confirmed his itinerary.

He rang for his butler. "Franz, bring me my tailor."

157: WEDNESDAY, JULY 24

Sonora, Texas, was quiet most of the year. During dove and deer seasons the place came to life as hunters and their tourist dollars showed up from all over the country. This was one of the quiet months, the time she loved to come to her late father's ranch for a day or two.

By the time Roberta Treadwell got to the western boundary of her ranch, she was certain the brown Chevy was following her. She turned down the gravel road that went to the bat cave; the brown car turned in after her. Football sized rocks in the road must be tearing up the underside of the city car; he must want something awfully bad to keep on coming like that. Somebody from Blick's organization, she told herself. He is just never going to give up.

When she got to the old Comanche camp site Roberta slowed to a stop, got out carefully. She was bent down, reaching in to take her rifle from the gun rack, when the brown Chevy pulled up just behind. She left the rifle where it was and straightened.

"Hey there, I think you must have lost your way."

A man got out, a decade older than Roberta, wearing a ten gallon hat. "I just want to talk to you," he called respectfully, in a hoarse voice that was trying to disguise its origins. "I apologize for coming onto your land without asking permission first."

"Who are you?" Roberta felt no pressing need to introduce herself.

"My name's...Bruce Gage. I'm in television, nature documentaries, you know."

"Yeah, and?" Good Christ, could it really be Blick in person? She had never managed to find a photograph of the billionaire more current than twenty years ago. Like the fabled Howard Hughes, he was a notable recluse and eccentric. If this were really Blick in the flesh, could he be so contemptuous of her that he'd use his own given name? He must have a concealed weapon. Her hand went again to the rifle, and the man's gaze followed it.

"Hunting, eh?" he said. "Good! I'm interested in coming out here for some hunting next fall, maybe make a show out of it. Unusual landscape, you see."

"Hunting, right." Blick or not, this man was neither a hunter nor a television executive. "You one of those PETA pests," she asked, "aiming to stir up trouble against law-abiding hunters?"

"Hell no, Roberta," he said, in his odd accent. "My father used to take me hunting when I was a kid. Gave me my first rifle when I was eight. Attractive land you have here." The man looked out across the pasture toward the creek, and Roberta could tell by his eyes, disconcertingly, that he really meant it. "Would you mind if I walk around a little? Just to get a feel for it?"

"I'll walk with you. How did you know my name?"

The man paused a fraction of a second, recovered almost instantly. "Sorry, I guessed you must be George Milton's daughter. My program researchers tell me he owned this land before he passed away." Well, that was widely known.

"Yeah, well, Daddy loved this place. It's pretty out here, all right. He spent almost forty years in the Alaskan bush, and he loved it there, too. Told me land up north has its own kind of beauty. But he never did completely get over being homesick for Texas. Guess that's why he came back after they took his land."

A sudden gust of wind whooshed around them, and Bruce clutched his absurd hat with both hands. Roberta frowned. Anxiety began to curdle in her.

"They *took* his land?" Bruce shook his head.

"Yeah. City of Fairbanks just kept growing, and after a while it swallowed up my daddy's place. Then they raised the taxes so there was no way he could pay them."

"Swine." That sounded sincere. "What happened to his property after they ran him off? Sorry, hope you don't mind my prying, but this is—"

"George didn't like to talk about that." Roberta took out the rifle, shut the door to her pickup, and turned away from the road. Every time she thought too hard about what had happened with her father's land up in Alaska, and what it had done to his soul, she ran the risk of weeping, and she couldn't stand for people to see her get emotional. Doubly so, if this were Blick

" Look here, Bruce." She stooped, picked up what looked like a loose flat stone from the ground. "See this? It's a flint spear head. Used to be Indians all over this land. Comanches mostly towards the end, but before that they say there were other people." She handed the flint to Bruce. His hands were soft, the pale fingers of a recluse who had others do everything for him. They didn't go with his being out here alone with her. But then people are complex, she thought. Nobody is just one simple thing. Certainly not a devious prick like Bruce Blick.

"I'd like to have lived back then." Bruce rubbed the spear head between his fingers and thumb.

"Me too. Most women prefer civilization, I know, and most men. Watch your step there, sir. Don't get in that cactus." Roberta took Bruce's arm. The man pulled away from her, then relaxed, allowed her to steer him around a large prickly pear.

158: WEDNESDAY, JULY 24

Bruce sat himself down carefully at the top of a low hill, still holding the flint scraping tool some savage had abandoned hundreds of years earlier. It fit comfortably in his hand, as though made for him. Perhaps it had been. Looking out at the creek winding past the foot of the hill, Bruce imagined the smell of cooking fires and the sounds of tribal life. So the nomadic Comanche people used to return year after year to set up their tent village on this site. This exposed country could hardly be more different from the lushness of Mexico, but it conveyed a curious sense of freedom. Sometimes he resented his self-imposed isolation and exile, resented it bitterly. It was his obligation.

"I wish we could go back to the way things were then," he said to Roberta. "Wipe out all the years of civilization, like erasing a mistake."

"Well now, my daddy was happy in Alaska where he could step outside his front door and bag a moose for his yearly supply of meat, but it's not for me. Bruce, I'd be dead now if it were not for antibiotics and tetanus shots. And I guess you would be too. We couldn't survive without pharmaceuticals, not any longer."

Was she baiting him? Had she realized his identity? He had over-reached in mockingly using his own given name. Roberta Treadwell was no fool. And now, in his pleasure at these untainted surroundings, Bruce had almost forgotten his motive for being here. "Well, you're right, Roberta. I'm glad there are people like you working on new ways to fight disease."

"You're an astute man, Mr.... What was the surname again?"

Yes, certainly baiting him. Blick's nerves thrilled. Her body, her tissues, surely swarmed with whatever Gibson had introduced in his extreme treatment. Rutherford's rogue asset had vanished from the morgue in Houston after being shot dead by police, the damned scientist and the lawyer woman and her kid had eluded his UAV and police alike, and now MJT labs were locked down as tight as a goddam nun's twat. This woman in retreat on her own land was his last best hope, and this the last available opportunity to reach her. Fell her, out here away from prying eyes, and haul her carcass in for the most thorough biological investigation of all time. He bared his teeth unconsciously. He saw that she held the rifle loosely in her right hand, crouched nearby gazing down the small rise.

"Just Bruce," he said. "No call to be formal on a day like this. It sounds like you're doing some really important research down there in San Antonio, Dr. Treadwell."

"You bet, Mr. Blick." She rose, stood over him, all pretence at an end. "Why, just the other month my researchers came up with a drug that makes animals smarter. Maybe people, eventually. Isn't that something? That was before the bomb destroyed a quarter of our lab, of course."

"I saw that on our news program, Roberta. Terrible. A tragedy." Bruce shook his head.

"Yep, but that's not going to stop us mad Frankenscientists, is it? We have a new project on the boil now, Bruce, we're going to end up with a whole world full of deathless Einsteins. Or smart mice at least." Roberta Treadwell laughed, started back along the track. "Enough of this nonsense, Mr. Blick. You're going to climb in your car and drive the hell away now and leave me in peace. If I ever see you on my land again, I'll have no hesitation in shooting you. That goes for your damned flunkies as well." She turned on him, face blotchy with sudden fury. "*They killed my father's dog*, you God-cursed bastard!"

Bruce's spirits soared. He would put a stop to this abomination. Kill the bitch before she could do anything worse to pervert the human race. He leaped at her without warning, slammed the rifle aside, thrust his big stupid western hat in her face. It confused her, put her off-balance. She was a big woman, though, and at least ten years his junior, and she slammed him back painfully. No time for the tranquilizer. With the ancient flint scraper stone, its edge still sharp after centuries, he slashed

Treadwell's throat along the heavy carotid artery and saw her blood spray, then pulse and dribble, over the dry soil and stony ground. Bright red splattered the sparse desert flowers and his own hands and face. He let the warm blood drip down his fingers. Blick was in a furious, exultant rage. When the woman stopped jerking, he shoved her fallen body aside and took out the phone. Its GPS locator told them precisely where he stood in the stark open ground.

"I need to be picked up, James," he said. "Get a transfer vehicle here right now. And ready the San Marcos pathology unit to prep a body for autopsy and immediate lab work. Moderate containment."

159: WEDNESDAY, JULY 24

The new *nordamericano* student with the special advanced syllabus jerked at his desk, fell forward moaning. His teacher rushed to his side. Oh no, not another attack for that poor boy! Pushed too hard! His mother, Mrs. Peters, had explained about his terrible brain tumor, and its miraculous remission, may the saints be praised for their kindness! He'd been doing so well at his Spanish!

"Look at me, Ricky." The child was breathing in gasps, muttering, eyes rolled up. She spoke in English. "What is it, son?"

Lourdes Martínez couldn't make out the mumbling. "Quick, Jesus, the nurse. Get a nurse. Right now! And you, Yvette, tell the Principal's office. Get them to call Ricky Peters' Mom. Hurry!"

"Roberta," Ricky seemed to be mumbling. He was shivering and shaking. "He killed her," he said in English. "It's Roberta this time."

"There, there, son." Mrs. Martínez tightened her arm about his shoulders. "Nobody's hurt. It's...it's a bad dream, that's all."

Richard Peters sobbed.

160: WEDNESDAY, JULY 24

In the steamy Texas afternoon, Wayne heard the news from a floating ball of light. His teeth bared to the heavens, he uttered a scream of such wrathful rage that the few derelicts not already terrified by his uncanny familiar scrambled into the shadows and huddled there. He stood panting.

"Blick! Rutherford! Bastard, I kill you filthy!"

The machine spoke in his ear.

"Find him for me, partner. Tell me where he's hiding. He *owes* me."

A small woman crept closer. "Mr. Elliot, the King says that you should try to—"

He raised his hand to her, caught himself in time, face contorted, lowered it. "Sorry, Betsy-Anne." He shook his head like a confused animal. "I'm sorry, I've been making a fuss. Tell Curt I'm heading off for a while."

The ball of light hung above him like a halo of wrath.

161: WEDNESDAY, JULY 24

Jill sat beside her son's bed, drained of emotion. He lay there before her, yet he seemed in another world. His temperature was normal, his muscle tone relaxed. He spoke to her and Paul when they addressed him, then shushed them and went back to muttering into the machine at his throat. It looked like something from a very cheap and cheesy sci-fi show from half a century earlier—*Captain Video,* maybe, according to Paul, whose aging father in distant Australia was an aficionado. Just another of Alex's contraptions, and not as disturbing, in fact, as the globes that spun in two directions at once as they flew across the room like tiny balloons entrapping a firefly. The thing was palpably a communicator of some sort, that much was clear. And Alex was striving with all his appalling immature genius to prevent a murder.

To save a human soul, she thought, and felt her eyes bead with hot tears.

"It's just revenge, Wayne," he was saying in his half-hypnotic drone. "It'd be murder. I know they killed her, but if you kill Blick you'll be no better than he is. This isn't why Paul created the auxosome, partner. It's to help us stay alive, not help us kill. Mom, can I have some Pepsi, my throat's awful dry."

"I'll get it," Paul said, and his clear voice seemed shockingly loud in the bedroom.

"I'm pretty sure she's dead," Alex said to his throat machine. "But then you were dead, for a while. Maybe she'll come back."

Tears ran in a fresh flood down Jill's cheeks, and she held his hand very tightly. It was impossible to believe that he was in communication with the beast who had tried to kill them, who had blown an innocent guard to death and done his best to slay Drew Chang. It was impossible to credit that Wayne Elliot had truly died and returned to life, despite Alex's muffled testimony. On-line in Paul's borrowed lab, belatedly, they had read the Houston newspaper reports. Shot at point-blank range by police. Body identified by fingerprints (no mention, it's true, of the *extra* fingers and their anomalous prints) and by the murderer's widow. An odd spot a couple of days later about a body vanishing from the morgue where, reading between the lines, Elliot had been taken for autopsy. She and Paul had decided they saw Blick's hand at work here. It was a chilling thought. With Wayne's corpse, Blick's biochemists could surely recover the auxosome—and not the new, improved version, but the incomplete genome with its need for protein regulation.

And Alex had set them back on their heels a second time with his claim that Wayne was alive, after all, and in urgent need of his final regulator shot.

It was entirely typical of a child's mind, she told herself, that Alex would make the desperate, wishful leap from Wayne's post-mortem recovery to a conviction that his beloved Roberta might also return from the dead. Assuming she *was* dead, and that all this was not a fevered fantasy of a mind disordered by a genetically engineered intrusion nobody had ever trialed in clinical tests.

"Here's your soda, chief," Paul said, and placed the frothing can in Alex's slack hand. The finger tightened and the can went up to his lips. He drank, and brown foam trickled from the corners of his speaking mouth. Jill mopped the Pepsi before it stained the pillow, and tried to stop weeping.

"Hey, Mom, come on, it's not the end of the world!"

The scamp was sitting up, looking at her with teasing eyes.

"Oh, Alex!"

"Hey, don't get mooshy on me. Listen, we have to get the laptop fired up, I think I can find Roberta. What you always say, Mom: Enquiring minds want to know." He grinned, afire. "Wayne and mine, that is."

"You think she's—"

"She's got the auxosome, same as Wayne." The child lifted his gaze and clawed his hands. "Remember this, Mom?" Alex uttered a classic Dr. Frankenstein laugh which didn't quite work with his treble voice. "*'She's alive! Ha ha ha ha! She's alive!'*"

Jill burst out laughing, despite herself. "You're so bad! This is our friend we're mocking!"

He shrugged, lowered his eyebrows, grew serious. "She's in trouble if that bad man has her. I have to lead Wayne there as fast as possible. Then try to keep him from going Rambo on their asses."

"Alex!" Paul said, and stifled a snort. "Where *do* you hear such language?"

"Guess you don't listen to MTV anymore, doc. Come on, folks, it's Googlin' time!"

162: WEDNESDAY, JULY 24

The body was stretched on a surgically aseptic sheet of linen, atop a sheet of rubber and heavy duty steel beneath that. It was not a mortuary autopsy table, nor was it an operating theater table. No anesthetic apparatus cluttered the site, but bright racks of lamps shone down on the naked, supine body of a middle-aged woman with a fatal external lesion across the left side of her throat, slashing her carotid artery. From her pallor it was evident that she had bled out quickly, lost pints of blood before the wound site closed with unusually rapid clotting. Incredibly, by simple inspection it was apparent that this corpse was...well, *repairing* the trauma site. Cleaned of dirt and grit and lightly sutured after arrival at the covert medical technology facility two blocks from Southwest Texas State University, the wound was almost visibly closing, like a digital recording of the healing process run at exaggerated speed.

"It's not unusual for fundamental metabolic activity to continue for minutes, hours or even days after cessation of brain activity," said the military pathologist in green scrubs and plastic face mask. He held a gleaming scalpel, poised in the air as if he were considering a subtle argument during dinner. "This case, though, is thoroughly anomalous. I don't suppose you'd care to let me in on the background. Mr. Blick?"

"She had a...call it a *syndrome*." Blick was pleased with the coinage. "A man suffering the same condition was shot at least once, fatally. He died instantly."

"That can happen," the pathologist said dryly.

"Quite. My staff arranged for the remains to be transported to this lab but the damned incompetent medical examiner in Houston—" His savage tone rang in his own ears, in this confined space; he paused, drew a deep breath. "The body was shipped to the crematorium in error. Or so they claim. Covering their damned asses, more likely."

"Oh? Well, one thing I can assure you of, sir. It didn't get up and walk away."

Blick snarled, seized up a scalpel from the tray beside the table, slashed once deeply across the abdomen of the dead woman. Flesh parted; only a thin seepage of plasma exited the new wound. The pathologist stiffened. His temporary employer said, "In fact, doctor, I believe that's *precisely* what happened. I think the fucking corpse got up and ran away. And now I have no idea where the psycho prick is."

163: WEDNESDAY, JULY 24

Wayne stood at the feeder entrance to Interstate 35, at the lights. A big eighteen wheeler squealed air-brakes, idled at the red behind a Korean sports car the same color as the light. He walked back, reached up, slapped his hand three times, brutally hard, on the door. The guy in his high seat stared in disbelieving wrath, snapped off his seat belt, hit the lock release. The light switched to green and the speedster zoomed off. Wayne flung the door open and dragged the trucker out. The man could not believe what was happening. He was half again as big as his assailant and he fell like a sack of shit. He bounced on his but-tocks, swarmed furiously to his feet, grabbed up at Wayne. A floating pale bulb of light dashed itself in his eyes. He swiped at it and Wayne was in the truck seat in a vaulting leap, one hand on the wheel, the other on the gear shift. His feet went to clutch and accelerator as if the truck had been designed for him. The eighteen wheeler jerked once, flung itself at the feeder ramp. In the big mirror he saw the outraged trucker running after him up the ramp, arms waving, falling behind. Wayne's eyes flicked to the big dashboard, found the radio. He clicked through the stations, pushed up the volume. Roy Orbison, "Ride Away." He sang along with violent intensity, gunning his way north toward San Marcos. "Big motor wind up, ride away from here."

Roy, my man. Big bad bike, he thought, banging his hand on the wheel. This is too damn slow. Forty five minutes. Shit. Need a chopper, he told himself, tearing along the freeway. I wonder if the kid can arrange that for me.

164: WEDNESDAY, JULY 24

"Our instruments confirm your brilliant guess, Mr. Blick. This woman is in an unprecedented state of biostatic arrest. From your testimony I accept that she received the fatal wound five hours ago; from my study, I find that she is poised in a kind of...how shall I put it...no man's land."

"She's undead."

The pathologist allowed himself a smile. "A fortuitous turn of phrase, sir. One might indeed—"

"There was nothing accidental about my phrasing."

"I'm sorry?"

"'Fortuitous' doesn't mean 'fortunate,' you pompous jackass. It means 'by chance'."

The pathologist stared, face white with anger above his mask. "I see. How interesting. I am indebted to you once more, Mr. Blick. May we turn now from the niceties of grammar to the business at hand?"

"Lexicon, not grammar, you insufferable—" Blick broke off. He felt disoriented, as sick as a dog. "I'm sorry, this situation has me on edge. Beyond the edge, to tell the truth." He had never killed before, not by his own hand; it was intensely galling to think that he might not be a murderer after all. "You're telling me she can be revived?"

"The woman is badly dehydrated. She lost a lot of blood."

"I know," Blick said. "Quite a lot of it soaked through the suit I was wearing." He glanced at his hands. The pathologist stared in fresh distress, unable to believe what his reason told him he'd just heard. Let the bastard think what he likes, Blick told himself. I pay him enough. "I'm not Jack the Ripper," he said. "An unfortunate accident. You think you can get her back?"

The pathologist pressed a button. "Get me four liters of AB, stat. And have another eight ready." He moved with deft competence to the head of the table, found a cannula, inserted it into the limp arm of the corpse, taped it. "Let's see, shall we? This would be worth a Nobel Prize."

"Only if anyone learned of it," Blick said sedately. "And nobody shall."

"Of course, sir." The door banged open, and two scrub nurses rushed to the table with bags of whole blood and a portable stand. The line of red flowed downward, entered the corpse's arm, slowly flushed the nearly dormant tissues.

A phone buzzed discreetly. One of the nurses answered in a mutter, passed the handset to Blick with a gloved hand. "The lab, sir."

"There seems to be some mistake, Mr. Blick," the genetics specialist told him. "The human from whom this tissue sample was drawn is a polyploidy syndrome of a kind I've never seen before. He or she should be badly deformed, almost certainly retarded."

Blick shook his head. "'He?' She's a brilliant business woman in excellent physical condition."

"That's why I suggest that a mistake's been made, sir. Are you sure the tissue sample—"

"I'm quite certain. You're telling me she has an extra chromosome?"

"These cells are anomalous, and they seem to display a detached 47th and 48th chromosome pair, that's right, sir. In size they're somewhat larger than a Y, which would make this subject a variant on XXY Klinefelter male with hypogonadism—"

"She's a woman, trust me." Blick's detached gaze traveled down the naked white body.

"Alternatively, there might be a duplicate chromosome 22 pair, which codes principally for structural ribosomal RNAs and—"

"No. Shut up." In a taut voice, Blick said, "I see what he's done. It's an artificial chromosome!"

He understood now the immensity of what he held. The logic of it burst with clarity across his mind like a blazoned set of headlines for the end of the world. "Gibson transfects his subjects somatically with a tailored cocktail of maintenance enzyme code. Christ! The audacity!"

The geneticist remained silent for a moment. Then she said, "We're running a polymerase chain reaction right now. We'll have sufficient PCR copies of the anomalous strand within hours, and you'll receive a complete sequence display and print-out by—"

"Do it. Thank you, Lois, good work."

He placed the handset back in its cradle. The tips of his fingers tingled, as if his body had been anesthetized. He felt ill. It could not be remorse, surely?

The white flesh on the table grew pink. After twenty minutes the pathologist applied cardiac paddles. Roberta Treadwell gasped, coughed, sat up convulsively, clutched at her damaged throat. The scalpel slash across her belly started to bleed in earnest.

165: WEDNESDAY, JULY 24

"She's back!" Alex squealed. "Oh, oh, she's back." He hunched over his gadgets and started to cry with relief, like a child.

166: WEDNESDAY, JULY 24

Treadwell looked about her in momentary confusion, clutched for an instant at her nakedness, flung herself without warning at Blick. The IV line pulled its stand across the examination table, upsetting its sterile fluid bag and squirting blood in a red splash across the white linen. Her right fist struck his face mask, sent it clattering across the tile floor. Blick recoiled. Voices shouted. The pathologist was on the far side of the table; he watched dumbfounded as one of the scrub nurses, a sinewy Filipino, caught the dead woman's arm and twisted it behind her back.

"What the *devil—*"

"Hold her down, damn it!"

The second nurse took Treadwell's other arm, and they wrestled her back to the table. Her strong legs slammed up and sideways, catching Blick in the belly. He stumbled, staggered back against the wall, watched with his white capped teeth bared.

"Tie her down."

"We don't have any—"

Blick found a heavy-duty electric drill, hefted it in his gloved hand, and cold-cocked her, striking her brutally across the roof of the skull. She sagged and did not move.

"Good god, man, that wasn't necessary!"

He stepped back, holding his weapon, looked from one to the next.

"Now we're going to kill her again," he said savagely.

"What!"

"We're going to keep killing her until we find the limits of this thing. If there are any limits. And if there are none, we'll take her to pieces, limb by organ, and watch what happens." He was exultant, as he had been when he slew her as she threatened him with her rifle. "We've moved from medicine into the territory of myth, gentlemen. Put aside your scruples. This is the dawn of a new age."

167: WEDNESDAY, JULY 24

Alex screamed in agony. Jill hugged him tighter, heart pounding, shushing him. To Paul she whispered, "This is too much for a child. We need to get him a sedative. Does your lab—"

Her son pulled away, pressed his back to the wall, eyes swollen and red. *"No!"* he shouted. He was desperate, shivering. "They cut her again. I have to tell Wayne where to find her. No medicine! No medicine, Mommy, please!"

Outside the window with its closed venetian blinds, dusk was falling. Perhaps their new neighbors looked up from their

TV dinners in suspicion or concern at the wailing and bursts of sympathetic pain. But no one came knocking at their door.

"I need to compile a bigger transporter," the boy said, struggling from the bed. He threw off his mother's restraining hands. "I have to get help to Wayne. They're killing her all over again."

168: WEDNESDAY, JULY 24

Air brakes shrieking, Wayne Elliot veered off the freeway at the Live Oak four-leaf clover loop. The cop channel on the trucker's scanner told him that he'd been made three miles back and the pigs were on his tail. Time to drop this white elephant and grab something less conspicuous and more agile.

He thundered into the small shopping center and slammed on the brakes with the eighteen-wheeler jack-knifing across the street, blocking pursuit. He left the cabin from the right-hand door, slipped along the trailer and strolled in an unconcerned fashion toward a strip mall of cheesy shops. People were standing in amazement, staring at the stalled truck. A few followed him with their eyes in the late afternoon light. Nobody moved to block his path. He entered a women's clothing bazaar, sniggering for a moment at the notion that he might once more dress up in drag and make his escape. A stout woman with a tape measure approached him. He veered to the side of the store, looking for a back exit. Two jaded shop girls at the front ignored him. He pretended to forage in bolts of gaudy cloth, then sidled toward the rear of the store.

"Sir, you can't go in—"

The glowing globe lifted out of his shirt pocket, buzzed his left ear. The store attendant closed her mouth in shock, tottered. She crossed herself.

"Angels unawares," she muttered.

Yeah, right, Wayne thought, and dashed through the unlit rear room for the back door. It was a deadbolt, with a key in it. He pulled out the key, clicked the door behind him, shot into an alley. A man unloading a truck frowned at him.

A tiny voice told him, *Get out into the open. Wait.*

He was beyond questioning. Sirens were hooting in the street on the shop-front side of the mall, voices raised. He ran full pelt for the end of the alley, rounded it, found a grassy lot with a square of stained concrete poured as foundations for a house that had never been built. He stood on it looking around, starting to shake with unused adrenaline.

A faint light in the south caught his eye. It approached with surprising speed. Not a police chopper. Light brightened above his head. Open-mouthed, Wayne stared upward. A spiral of electric blue light dropped, hung ten feet from his face. Not a spiral, a *helix*. It came down like a cloak of light and closed about his shoulders and arms.

"Hey! What the fu—"

Like a fun fair ride, or the very fast elevator that took him down in a daze to the street from an appointment in Dr. Rutherford's office, it left him weightless and momentarily dizzy. This time, though, he was going up. The light plunged down the spectrum to cobalt, then to black. He could see nothing, felt wind blowing hard in his face and against his hands. His shirt loosened at back and front and made a drumming sound like a flag in a gale.

That made him grin. "You goddam little scamp," he said. "Hey, this is way better than a chopper any day." The darkness cleared, like a cloth scrubbing dust from a TV screen, and he was looking down thirty or forty feet. The concrete clover loop was at his back, the last of the rooftops of Live Oak below; he was moving faster than he'd ever pushed a car, maybe a hundred twenty, still accelerating across the fields.

He dropped ten feet, spun, steadied.

"Jesus! What are you *doing* to me?"

"Sorry, I'm still learning to drive this thing. I've only just invented it, after all."

"Great! And you're eight years old and way too young to be flying a plane, let alone a freakin' fluorescent lamp."

"Tell me if we're going to run into a plane or anything, okay?"

"Hey!"

"Just kidding."

The thing flung him through the dimming light and increasing chill. Something puzzling struck him.

"Why are you fooling with *me*, partner? Can't you just fly in and grab Roberta with this nifty gadget?"

There was silence. *"Oh. I never considered that, Wayne. I guess I think of you as the tough guy. You can deal with Blick."*

Deal with him? he thought, filled instantly with bile. I'll tear the son of a bitch's balls off. He squeezed his eyes tight, tried to calm himself in the way that poor schmuck Nathan Pritchett had tried to teach him. "Is she still alive?" he asked, then. City lights were coming on ahead. New Braunfels, maybe?

"Barely," the kid's voice said in his ear. *"Paul's treatment isn't a miracle. They* want *to kill her!"* The kid's tone, Wayne observed, expressed the kind of profound and cynical shock of detachment that precedes a cool assessing awakening into adult maturity. Then he asked himself: Where did *that* come from? You bastard, Gibson, he thought with a rueful smile. You've changed me, you and your damned shots. He wriggled his new fingers. Maybe everyone will wake up, he thought, once this thing catches on. I hope so. He closed his eyes against the rush and cold tang of the dusk air. I hope so. It was almost a prayer.

169: WEDNESDAY, JULY 24

Maureen opened her wet eyes. Enya's voice floated from the sound system in a blue Celtic dream. Beside her, Drew lay on his back, breathing hard. She touched his dear face, felt sweat.

"You stink," she told him. "We both stink."

"I love making love in summer afternoons, love," he murmured, turning to kiss her fingers.

"That's a lot of love, love," she said teasingly.

He rolled on to his side, propped up on an elbow. He touched her belly, still only slightly swollen.

"Last of the old-style humans."

"He'll catch it from us," she said. "Won't he?"

"Might even pass through the placenta. Lord, I hope this thing we've unleashed really *isn't* a time bomb."

She traced his train of thought as if it were her own; they had spent hour upon hour agonizing over the ethics of what he and Paul had released into the wild, into the world. "*Silent Spring,*" she said softly. Her own hand reached down protectively to cover her womb. "No, I can't believe that. This is a *good* thing you've done."

He said nothing for a time. Celtic woodwinds moved in the air. He said then, "Silent world, perhaps. No warmth, no laughter."

"No," Maureen said fiercely, and sat up. "That's your mother speaking. That's Alyssa's superstitions. Don't give in to that silliness now, lover. The auxosome means *more* life, not less. You and Paul told me that a hundred times, and you're both right. Hey, know what else? Wonderful news from Mexico!"

Drew quirked his lips. He knew when he was beaten. "Tell me."

"Jill was scared the auxosomes had made her sterile. I mean, sheer phobia, the Terminator code hadn't even.... Anyway. See, she hasn't had a period for—"

He covered his face in mock alarm in the lacy-edged pillow. "Hey! Too *much* information."

"No, you idiot. I said this is *good* news. Jill's pregnant too!"

170: WEDNESDAY, JULY 24

The thing wrapping Wayne Elliot in its levitating embrace dropped him in a series of small jolts to the sidewalk outside some darkened university building. San Marcos was a small campus town, he'd heard, a place of college footballers and smiling, prancing cheer-leaders. Once or twice, passing through, he'd driven Fern's blue Impala into the pretty green park that cupped the clear water of Spring Lake. Cypress and pecan trees were dark against the darkening sky. He looked for street signs. Sessom and Comanche. To the...south?...a large building was marked as the Joann Cole Mitte Art Center. What the hell kind of name was that? A teenaged student hurried past, talking on his cell phone. "No, babe, I *am* happy. Really. It's just that...." His moved on, voice fading.

"Which way, partner?"

The tiny voice said, *"She's near you, that's all I know. I should have this thing set up for video but I didn't have time."* The boy sounded guilty and tremendously anxious.

"Hey, calm down. This is my end of the job, okay?" Inwardly he was starting to seethe again, as finally he closed in on his prey. This was the beast who smashed his mind, who sent him clawing through memories and delusions, who treated him as nothing more than a tool to be used foully and discarded. He found that he was panting in his rage. He tried to calm himself. He looked north, swinging his eyes along the curve of Sessom. There it was. Two stories of windowless black evil.

"I have it."

As he crossed the street, a car did its best to run him down. What the *fuck!* He gave the asshole the finger, didn't even get the satisfaction of an angry honk in reply..

"Roberta's in pain," the boy said. He seemed at the edge of exhaustion. *"Find a way in. Quick."*

"They're going to have surveillance six ways from Sunday, Alex."

"Nobody can see you. The shell is warping the light around you."

Wayne stopped stock still. He felt for a moment that he might just let the accumulating shock overwhelm him, drive him into a sobbing crouch on the sidewalk.

Instead he drew in a shuddering breath and stretched out his arms. Yes, something uncanny still surrounded him. It felt like... like waxy crayon, the kind he'd used in kindergarten as a child. A phantom smell filled his nostrils. Those had been happy days.

And later, when for the first time he'd been with Melody, and—

"Wayne! Wayne! What's up, partner?"

Shivering, he walked with a thick taste in his mouth toward the dark building. He found a small notice: CLINICAL SCIENCES SUPPLIES. Christ! Hidden in plain sight. But in a hick town like this, beautiful and inoffensive as it was, plain sight was not very visible. He pressed against the door, hard. Cold, unyielding as steel. He looked for the cameras, found three small lenses guarding the front approaches.

"Trying the rear," he whispered. "You hear me, boy?"

"Yes, but please hurry!"

A large black van was backed up to a loading apron, behind fencing that was surely electrified.

"Lift me up and over," he whispered. "Okay, now just drift me forward a tad. And down."

He ran quickly to the apron, slapped his hand hard on the van. Hooting burst out, the moronic yapping of a vehicle alarm system. Spot lights splashed instantly. Invisible but unable to believe it at the gut level, he held himself motionless like a trapped animal, all his instincts telling him he was a dead man. He swallowed a guffaw, bitter. A dead man was what he was in truth, and now alive again. You can kill me, he thought ferociously, but you can't hide.

The door opened and a lean man with a rifle stepped out, looking carefully and without panic from side to side. Wayne bitch-slapped him upside the head, saw him topple with an incredulous cry over the lip of the apron. The door was still closing. Invisible Wayne was through it in two steps, closed it tight.

He ran toward stairs, checking locked doors. No lights shone under them. Which way? How could he tell? All hell was about to break loose.

"Warmer," the tiny voice said. *"Your resonance and Roberta's, they're...merging. I think she's higher up than you."*

He tore up the stairs in two-step bounds. A nurse was entering a room, carrying a tray of medical instruments. He slammed her against the wall, realized as he did that this was the stupidest thing he could have done. *She couldn't see him!* Her shriek told everyone in the building that he was inside and on the attack. Idiot! Idiot! He burst through a second door into the room. Air pushed in after him. Puzzled eyes stared through him. A table. Naked woman with...dear Lord, they'd cut her abdomen open. Roberta. He thought of June beetles and shuddered. She was unconscious. A doctor in green, face masked in plastic sheeting. Nurses, running at the door. Blick. The man had stood behind Rutherford, in the darkness, at the edge of the light.

Dear sweet Jesus God. It *was* his tormentor, suit marked with drying blood, plastic mask covering his face. The man looked ill. He seemed to be having trouble breathing.

It was the blood, Wayne understood in a burning instant of insight. Blick was doused in blood teeming with auxosome. And not just from this vile torture he inflicted on Roberta Treadwell. The crusted stuff on his suit and shirt was dried. Wayne took this in like a photograph of a lightning flash, instantly and terribly. Blick was infected with deathlessness.

§

Payback woke. He hurled aside the crayon-stench magic shell that held him from his persecutor's gaze. With one out-flung arm he struck a brown-skinned nurse into unconsciousness. The other he felled with a vicious upward blow of his knee, driven into the man's crotch. The doctor was cowering away from his onslaught, hiding behind the surgical table. Only Blick held his ground. He reached into his pocket and held his gun at Payback, who did not pause for an instant. They crashed together, and the weapon hissed. Not a gun, a tranquilizer. The needle jet entered the fleshy pad of his outstretched hand, rushed into his blood stream, coursed quickly to his heart and flung him to the floor in a hopeless daze.

Green light buzzed in his eyes.

"Wake up! Wake up! Wake up!"

Blick looked down upon him, eyes bloodshot, wheezing with the healing illness of the auxosome. His hand shook, and light shattered from it. The scalpel was edged with blood.

"You creature," Bruce Blick said. "You unspeakable *thing*. How dare you enter in here and disturb me?"

Robbie was drowning. Roberta lay dying again on the bloody sheets. Blick cut him, deeply, and again. There was no pain, just the pressure of the blade. He lay on the tiles and his own blood pulsed out. He took in one long, suffering breath and lunged his face at Blick. His teeth closed on the man's cheek, locked into the aging sour flesh, pulled him close. Blick screeched, a pain in Payback's ear that echoed to his soul. It was the sound of joy. It was the trumpet blare of vengeance. His right arm, heavy as molten iron, rose from the floor and his hand found the back of Blick's bald head. His left hand found the jaw, lightly bristled. His fingers closed tight. He took his teeth out of the man's flesh and twisted once, then once more, the way Rutherford had taught him. Blick's body fell against him in spasm.

Payback, too, fell like a stone from a high place, into Wayne. He lay face down against cold tile and tried to laugh despite the locking paralysis of the tranquilizer.

Dead, finally, you evil son of a bitch.

But not necessarily for long, god damn it.

EPILOGUE

171: MONDAY, MAY 2,
THREE YEARS LATER

"Morbius," the little girl said. Tongue stuck out the side of her mouth, she tried to coordinate her chubby fingers and seal closed the strip of heavy paper she had daubed with glue at each end.

Alex laughed out loud, delighted. The two-year-old sent him a hurt glance, then looked back in concentration to her task. One end of the strip whipped free, straightened.

"Oh no!" she cried.

"Never mind, sweetheart. Try again. It's going to be beautiful." Baby-sitting is never an eleven year old boy's favorite task, especially on his birthday, but Alex was immensely fond of his brilliant half-sister. "That's it. Now twist the end...."

Estella frowned, rotated one end of the strip, held both ends parallel, pressed the glued tips together. They locked instantly. The match was not perfect, but both children gazed in satisfaction at the famous puzzling shape. One side of the heavy paper was luminously purple; the other dull old gold. The boundary where they met was abrupt, yet as Estella fed the closed circle through her fat little fingers, around the half twist, it was shockingly apparent that the strip had only one side.

"The road goes ever on," Alex sang in a melodious soprano. "Morbius strip!"

The night before, the Peters family had watched one of Paul's favorite science fiction classics, *Forbidden Planet,* an unintentionally funny space opera made half a century earlier. Dr. Morbius, the tragic mad scientist, had enthralled little Estella. She'd laughed at the antics of Robby the Robot, but the intense, deep-voiced Morbius held her silent.

"August Ferdinand Möbius," Alex said carefully. "Not Morbius and not Morpheus. This is a Möbius strip. MER-bee-us. Great German mathematician."

"Huh," the little girl said, winding the unending strip through her fingers. She gave a gasp of delight. "Only one edge!"

"You clever little darling!" Alex cried. He picked her up and tossed her giggling into the air. Green and pink globes of light swirled around them, guardians, gateways. "I was at least *ten* before I worked that out."

A man came out of the house, stood watching them at play on the bright grass. Estella noticed his presence first, ran up to him with her hands outstretched.

"Unca Bruce! Gi' me a ride on your back!"

Alex watched tensely. It was something he would come to terms with, he knew, in the fullness of time. Redemption and recovery, the acquisition of maturity in men and women cruelly damaged by history's poisons and limits. He walked across the grass, hands in his pockets. Roberta and the Changs, Drew and Maureen and little Carlos, Carol Glassman whom he still thought of fondly as an adopted auntie, the whole crew were flying down for his birthday party in the MJT jet and he wanted to be neatly dressed for them, within the limits of cool. Blick glanced directly at him across his sister's shoulder. Luminously prismatic tears stood in the corners of the man's eyes. He said nothing.

Alex nodded, expression neutral, and stepped into the cool shadows of the hacienda. His mother's voice floated to him from her study, playing her guitar, singing lightly in Spanish. He was not sure what he would do after today, but he would think of something.

172: MONDAY, MAY 2

Two young women approached and stood diffidently, waiting for King Wayne to notice them. "Eleanor! Gracie!" He was genuinely glad to see them willing to consult him in a dispute. Two years ago, they had been mentally retarded, abused or ignored by almost everyone, barely able to cope with life.

Gracie smiled and blushed, Eleanor frowned.

"We need an intervention," Gracie said shyly.

"No problem. Who'll speak first?"

Eleanor stepped forward. "Grace is always going off in the morning, leaving stuff strewn all over the place. She keeps food over there, and—"

"I do *not!*"

"One at a time. Eleanor?"

"Half the time she forgets she's got food stashed 'til it starts to stink. Lord knows what kind of bugs she got crawling around in her bed."

The other woman opened her mouth wide, indignant.

"Wait, Gracie, you'll get your turn. Eleanor, what would you like to do about this problem?"

"I just want you to tell her to move her stuff and sleep somewheres else if she gone be such a slob."

"Anything more?" In the fire flicker, King Wayne kept his expression neutral.

"No." Eleanor glared.

"Gracie, what's your take on the problem?

"True I'm not the neatest person, but I'm *not* dirty. I took food back to my place once, maybe twice, when I was sick. She just *lying* about it being rotten."

Eleanor shrieked denial, but Wayne held up a hand.

"She want me to move so her boyfriend have my space. He been sleeping with her every night, and half the time put his stuff in my space, and...." Tears rolled down Gracie's face, and she swiped a hand under her nose. "Last night he threaten me with a knife. Man, I swear he gonna cut me bad."

"Okay, Gracie. What would you like to do about the problem?"

"*Eleanor* be the one to move. I been here longer than her, and nobody ever complain before. Her *boyfriend* need to be thrown out."

"Anything else?"

Gracie shook her head.

"Okay. First Gracie—I have seen your stuff scattered around. Clean up your act. Understand?"

"Yes, Wayne, I will."

"Good. I'll be watching. Now, Eleanor. You know the rules. One person to a space. You want your friend to have Gracie's space, she has to agree to it first. You might want to offer to pay her something, make it worthwhile for her to move. Otherwise, you and your boyfriend find another spot with two spaces side by side." He looked at her keenly. "About the knife—"

"A tiny little pocket knife! He didn't threaten to cut her none."

King Wayne said calmly, "I'll need to talk to your boyfriend. What's his name?"

"Freddie."

"Okay, please have Freddie come by and talk to me sometime tonight."

"All right," said Eleanor sullenly.

"Thank you, Wayne," said Gracie, "I'll keep my place neater from now on, I promise." They were dismissed.

Wayne gazed into the flames. Soon he would move on from here, as Curt had done last year, enter into the extraordinary world that was forming amid violence and confusion and exultation beyond this refuge of Les Misérables. He sighed, gazing across his small kingdom. The healing illness had passed through the encampment in waves, unremarked. Few of the indigent had appreciated their freedom from colds and sores, the improvement in their minds, although their growing hunger had driven some back to theft and others to work.

It seemed to Wayne, now that he paid attention to it, that the endless thudding sound of wheels above his head was more muted of late. Far fewer people were driving to work, of course, but the first wild upset-ant nest swarming had exhausted itself. A plague of intelligence was unhinging long-established social patterns and habits, and so was the sterility plague. For sure it was a disturbing time to be alive, especially for a man who had once been dead, and before that a madman and a killer. An exhilarating time.

Wayne rose, stretched, felt life surge in his muscles. He smiled. Mirth grew within him, burst from his lips, shook his chest. King Wayne laughed out loud with joy, and a ripple of laughter spread like a contagion through the ragged men and women who at last would leave this wretched place and join in creating a new world without death.

One day, too, the children would return.

ABOUT THE AUTHORS

Damien Broderick, Ph.D., and Barbara Lamar, J.D., married in Melbourne, Australia, in 2002, and live in San Antonio, Texas. Broderick, a senior fellow in the School of Culture and Communication at the University of Melbourne, is an award-winning Australian SF writer, editor, and critical theorist. Lamar is a Texan tax lawyer, author of the bestselling *The Tax-Payer's Life Preserver*, and permaculture farmer: http://huerto-de-altamira.blogspot.com/

Broderick has published some fifty books, including *Reading by Starlight*, *The Spike* (the first full-length treatment of the technological Singularity), and *The Last Mortal Generation* (on radical life extension science), was a finalist for the 2010 and 2011 Theodore Sturgeon Award, and was named the 2010 recipient of the A. Bertram Chandler Award for contributions to science fiction.

His 1980 novel *The Dreaming Dragons* (updated as *The Dreaming*) is listed in David Pringle's *Science Fiction: The 100 Best Novels, 1949-1984*, and with Paul Di Filippo he has written a sequel to Pringle's book examining the 101 best SF novels from 1985-2010. His latest novels are *I'm Dying Here*, *Dark Gray* and *Human's Burden* (all with Rory Barnes). Recent SF collections are *Uncle Bones*, *Climbing Mount Implausible*, and *The Qualia Engine*. He edited *Chained to the Alien* and *Skiffy and Mimesis*, essays from the fabled *Australian Science Fiction Review*, and with Van Ikin co-edited *Warriors of the Tao,* essays from Dr. Ikin's *Science Fiction: A Review of Speculative Literature.*

www.ingramcontent.com/pod-product-compliance
Lightning Source LLC
Chambersburg PA
CBHW020834030726
47496CB00001B/233